A MAGNUS THE BLACK MYSTERY

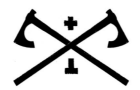

IMAGE COMICS, INC.
Robert Kirkman – Chief Operating Officer
Erik Larsen – Chief Financial Officer
Todd McFarlane – President
Marc Silvestri – Chief Executive Officer
Jim Valentino – Vice-President
Eric Stephenson – Publisher
Corey Murphy – Director of Sales
Jeff Boison – Director of Publishing Planning & Book Trade Sales
Jeremy Sullivan – Director of Digital Sales
Kat Salazar – Director of PR & Marketing
Branwyn Bigglestone – Controller
Sarah Mello – Accounts Manager
Drew Gill – Art Director
Jonathan Chan – Production Manager
Meredith Wallace – Print Manager
Briah Skelly – Publicist
Sasha Head – Sales & Marketing Production Designer
Randy Okamura – Digital Production Designer
David Brothers – Branding Manager
Olivia Ngai – Content Manager
Addison Duke – Production Artist
Vincent Kukua – Production Artist
Tricia Ramos – Production Artist
Jeff Stang – Direct Market Sales Representative
Emilio Bautista – Digital Sales Associate
Leanna Caunter – Accounting Assistant
Chloe Ramos-Peterson – Library Market Sales Representative
IMAGECOMICS.COM

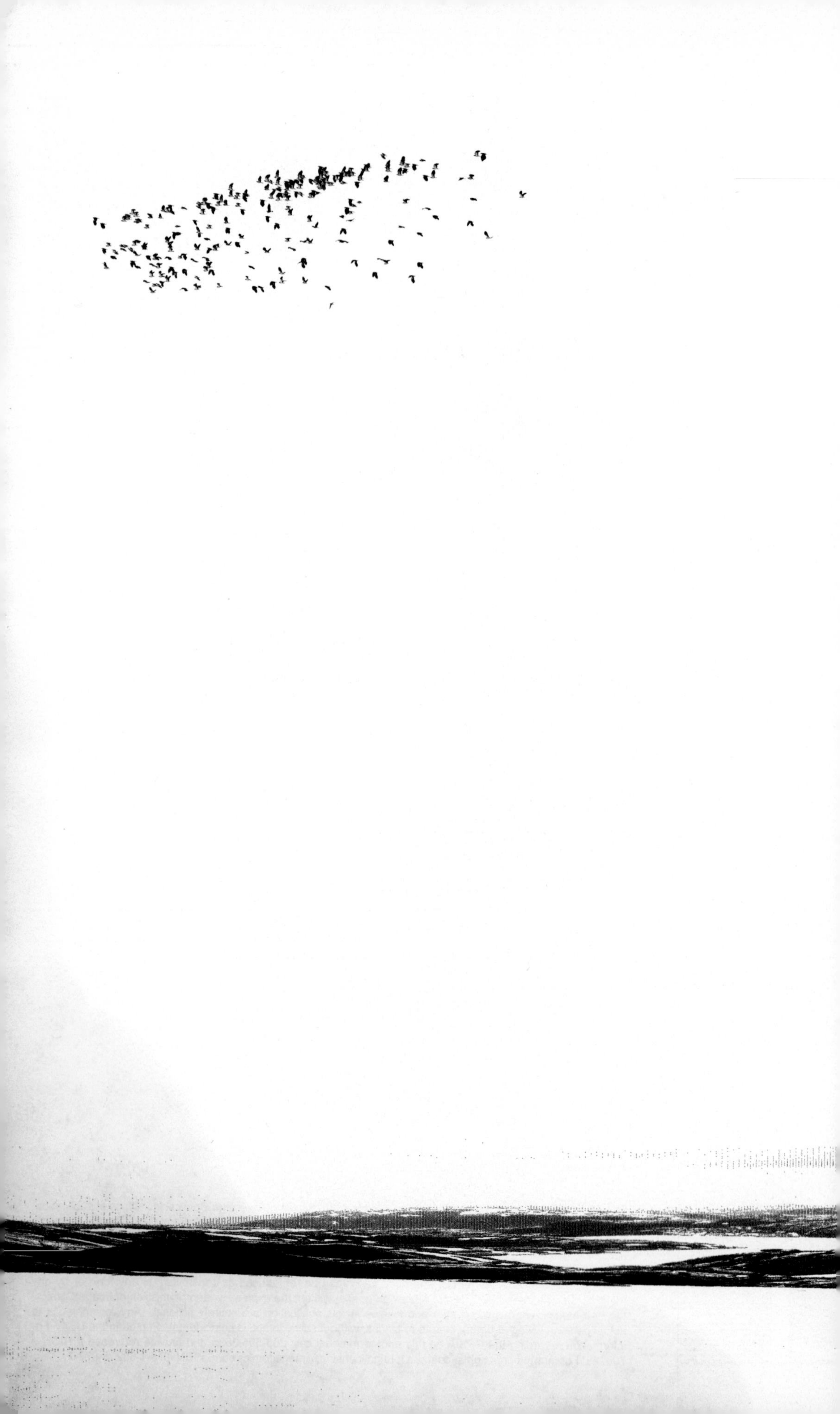

BLACK ROAD

VOL. I
"THE HOLY NORTH"

STORY: BRIAN WOOD
ART AND COVER: GARRY BROWN
COLORS: DAVE MCCAIG
LETTERING AND PRODUCTION: STEVE WANDS

BLACK ROAD IS CREATED BY BRIAN WOOD AND GARRY BROWN

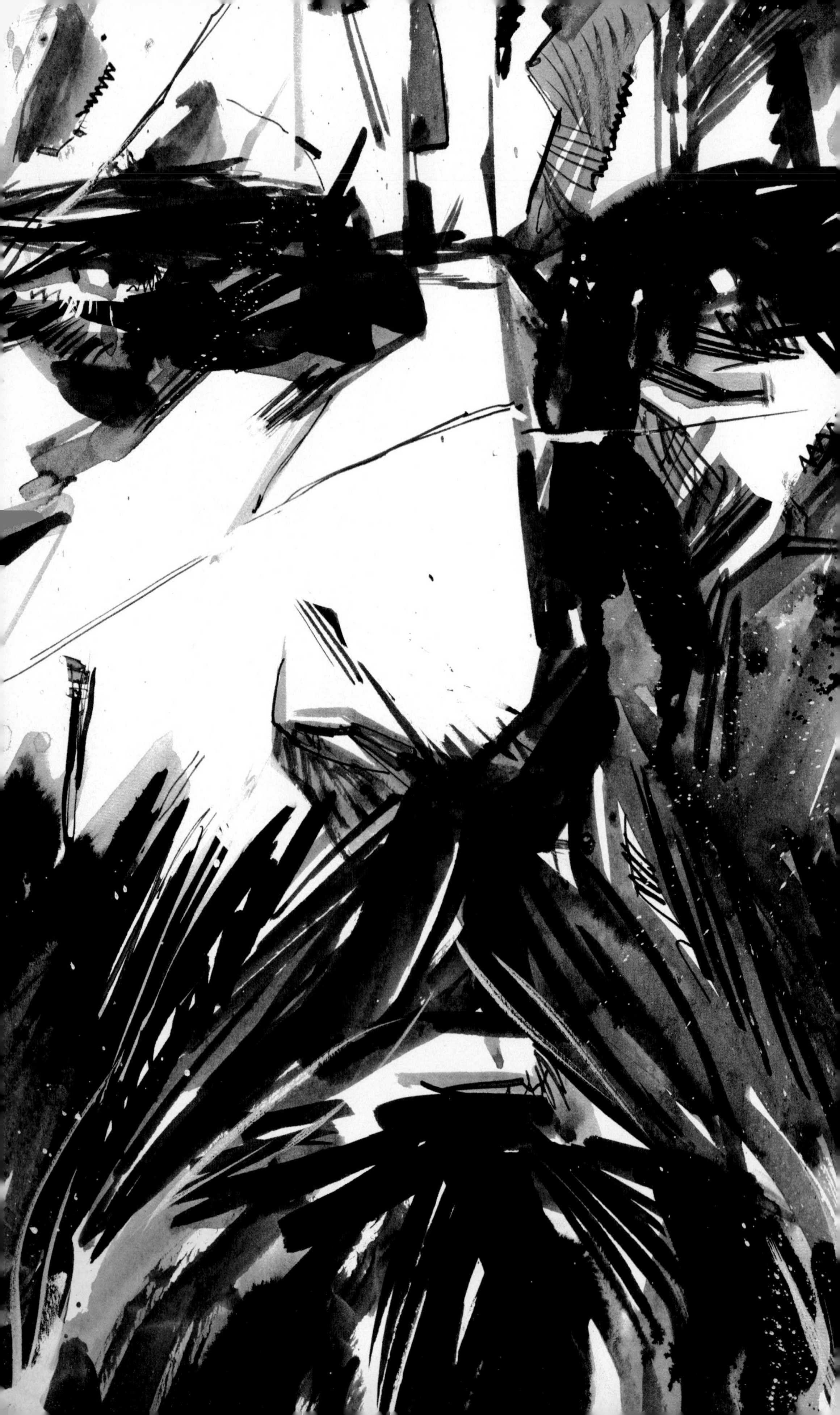

he ships rose and fell on huge ocean swells, vaulting skyward some forty feet and driving down into the bottom of the trough with sickening impact. The shallow bellied-hulls are better suited for coastal waters, not this frigid arctic bite.

ie lead ship skidded down the backside of the swell, its load of cargo shifting under the floorboards. captain cursed twice - once for the cargo, anonymously triple-bagged in greasy leather, and once for armed escorts that sat quietly aboard his ship. Bright red crosses covered their clothing, across their st, on their shoulders and back, their wrists, and often times incorporated into their weaponry. They were clearly pious men, but that didn't stop him from wondering if they had orders to kill him once offloading was complete.

nd was sighted the next morning, and with it Oakenfort's heresy. The massive compound practically t out at them, the raw pine boards bright in the dawn sun. It occupied high ground; its exterior walls built flush with the cliff face. From sea level the bastard was easily eighty feet tall.

:ut into the cliff face was a path, and the captain could already see more of the cross-heavy soldiers climbing down to meet them. This is it, he thought, steeling himself for a bloody death. But the soldiers disembarked with the cargo, and he was free of them.

ancing back over his shoulder as they reversed out of the harbor, he took in the mammoth structure. the ships turned east the church within its walls became visible - a wicked-looking thing, all angles l edges, and that stark, oversized cross at the top. The exterior wall was still incomplete on this side, l within the compound more buildings and barracks stood, alongside construction cranes, vast stacks of timber and stone, granaries and grow-houses. It was the labor of a thousand men at a minimum.

And it was right at this moment he noticed the siege equipment, emplaced and facing the sea, the ounterweights on the mighty stone-throwers already falling. He quickly averted his eyes, as if that would do any good, and then a sound like thunder cracked across the bay.

The first stone struck the water in front of his ship, creating a suction effect that spun it around broadside. The second hit two down the line, snapping its hull like a child's toy. The remaining ships, empty of cargo and light in the water, tangled in the whorls left by the missiles.

As his world splintered around him, the captain wondered why the fuck the Christians had come this far north.

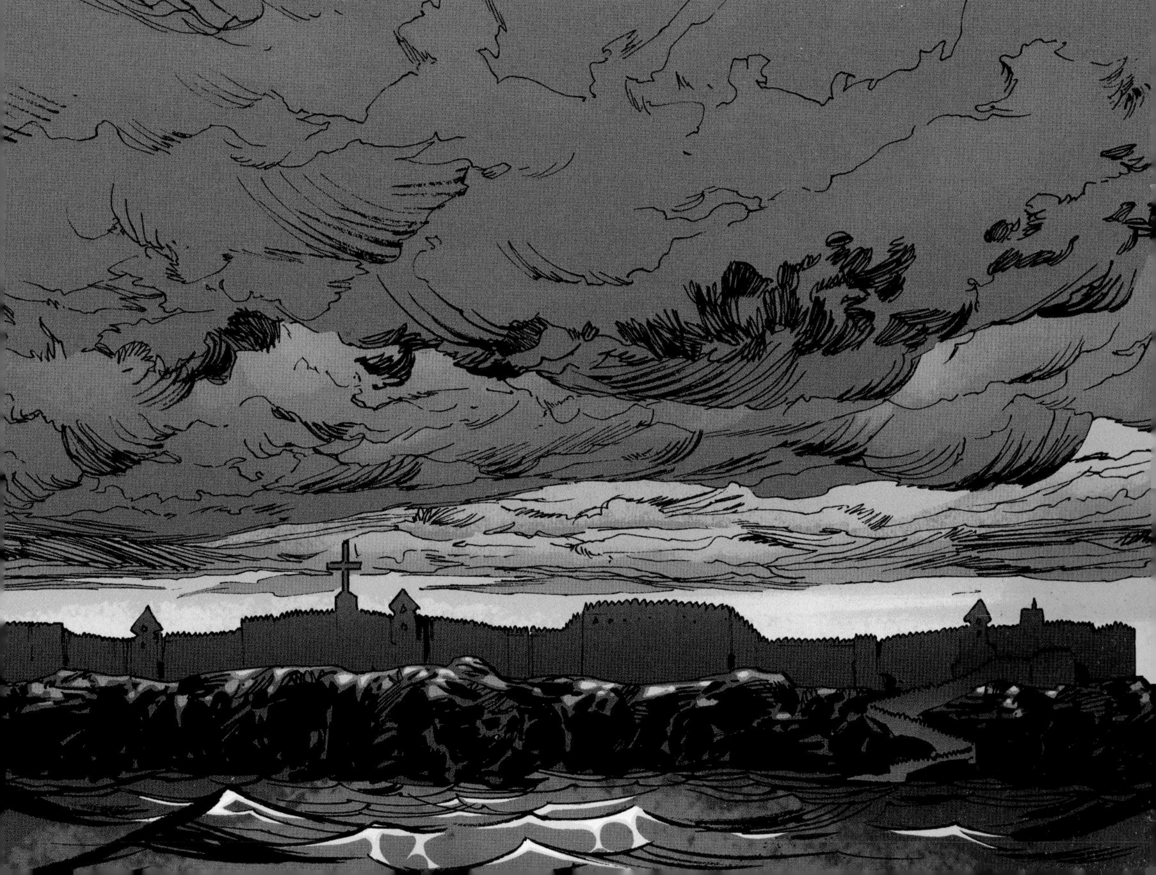

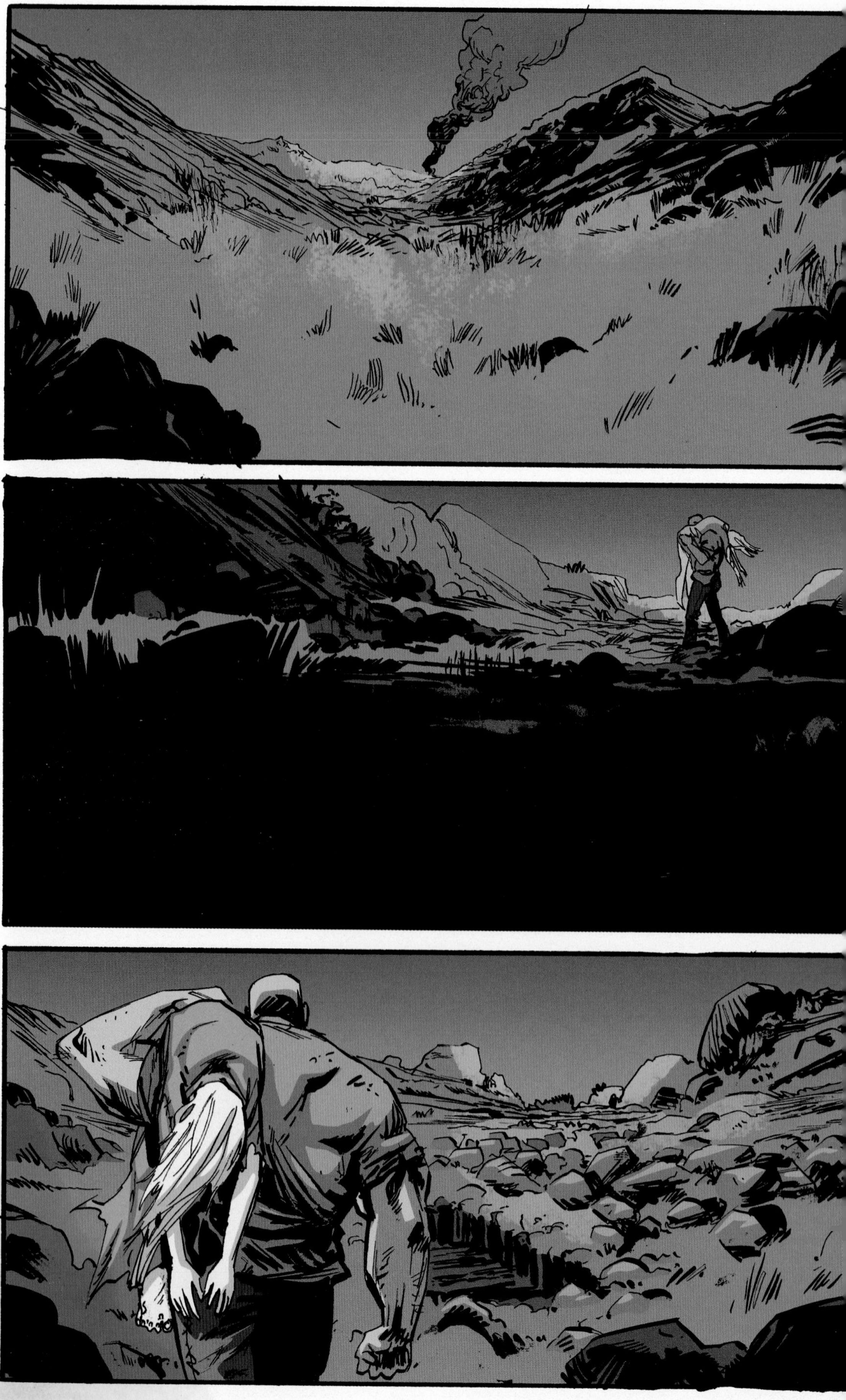

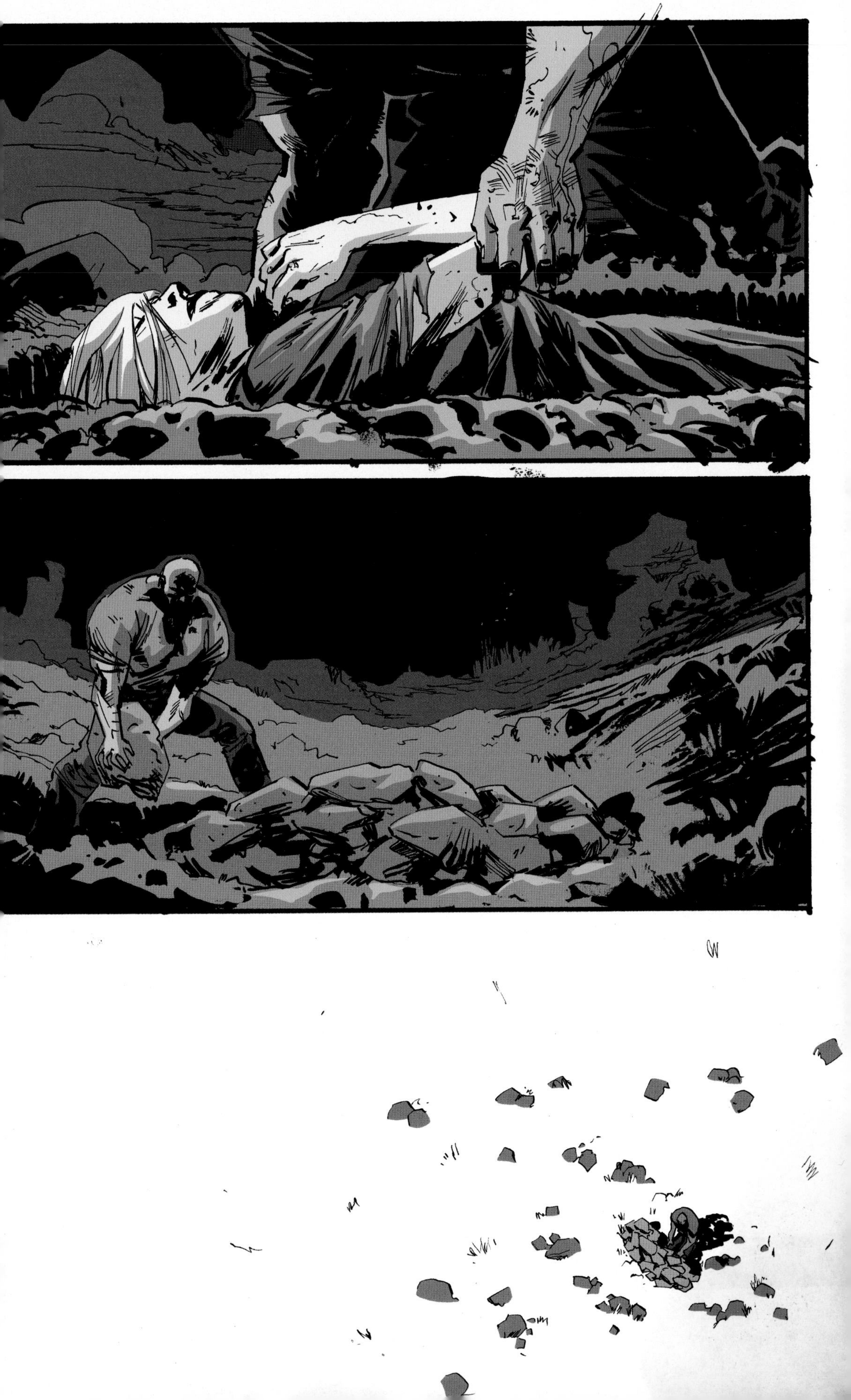

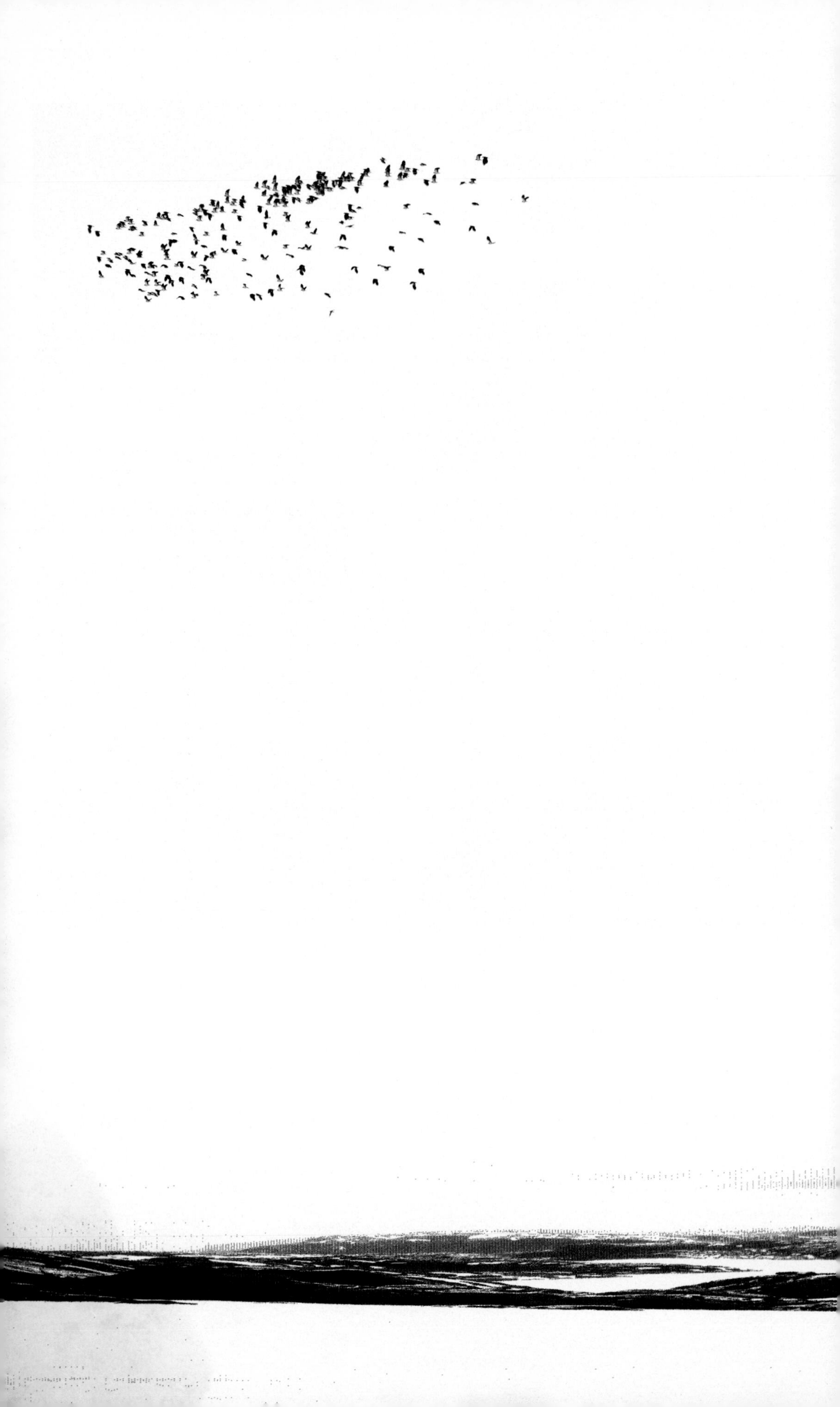

BRIAN WOOD / GARRY BROWN / DAVE McCAIG / STEVE WANDS

BLACK ROAD

#1 - "THE HOLY NORTH"

A MAGNUS THE BLACK MYSTERY

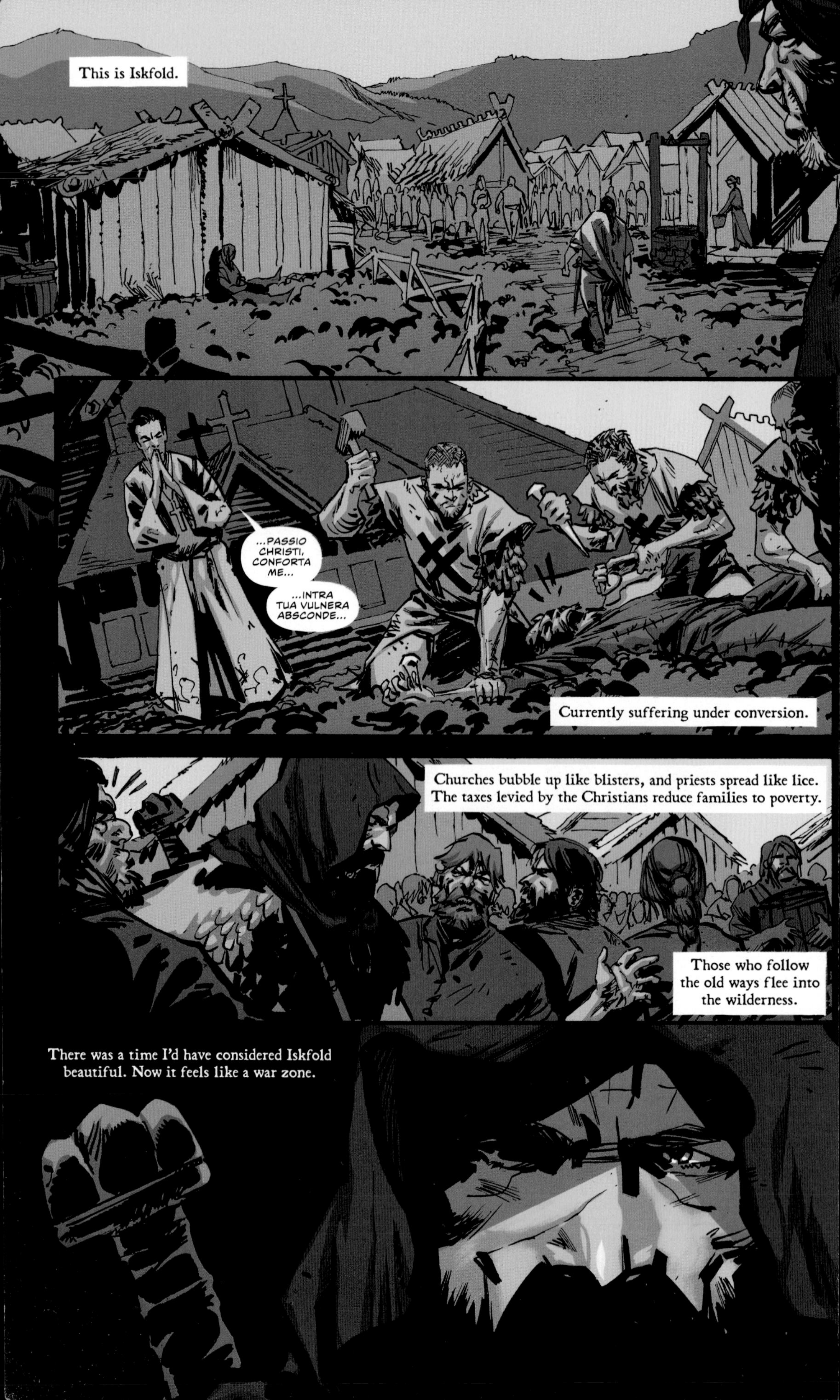
This is Iskfold.
...PASSIO CHRISTI, CONFORTA ME...
...INTRA TUA VULNERA ABSCONDE...
Currently suffering under conversion.
Churches bubble up like blisters, and priests spread like lice. The taxes levied by the Christians reduce families to poverty.
Those who follow the old ways flee into the wilderness.
There was a time I'd have considered Iskfold beautiful. Now it feels like a war zone.

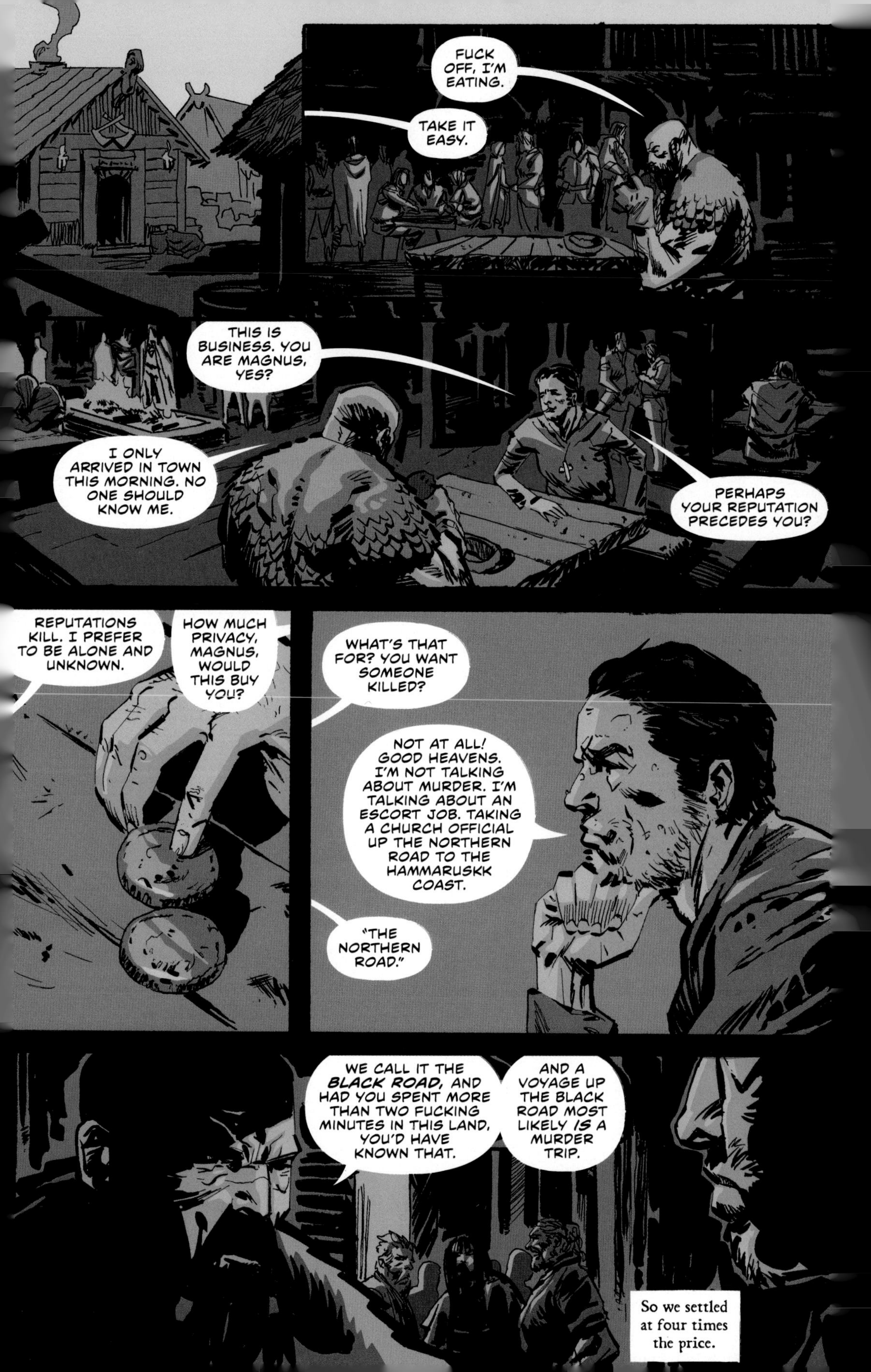

FUCK OFF, I'M EATING.
TAKE IT EASY.
THIS IS BUSINESS. YOU ARE MAGNUS, YES?
I ONLY ARRIVED IN TOWN THIS MORNING. NO ONE SHOULD KNOW ME.
PERHAPS YOUR REPUTATION PRECEDES YOU?
REPUTATIONS KILL. I PREFER TO BE ALONE AND UNKNOWN.
HOW MUCH PRIVACY, MAGNUS, WOULD THIS BUY YOU?
WHAT'S THAT FOR? YOU WANT SOMEONE KILLED?
NOT AT ALL! GOOD HEAVENS. I'M NOT TALKING ABOUT MURDER. I'M TALKING ABOUT AN ESCORT JOB. TAKING A CHURCH OFFICIAL UP THE NORTHERN ROAD TO THE HAMMARUSKK COAST.
"THE NORTHERN ROAD."
WE CALL IT THE *BLACK ROAD,* AND HAD YOU SPENT MORE THAN TWO FUCKING MINUTES IN THIS LAND, YOU'D HAVE KNOWN THAT.
AND A VOYAGE UP THE BLACK ROAD MOST LIKELY *IS* A MURDER TRIP.
So we settled at four times the price.

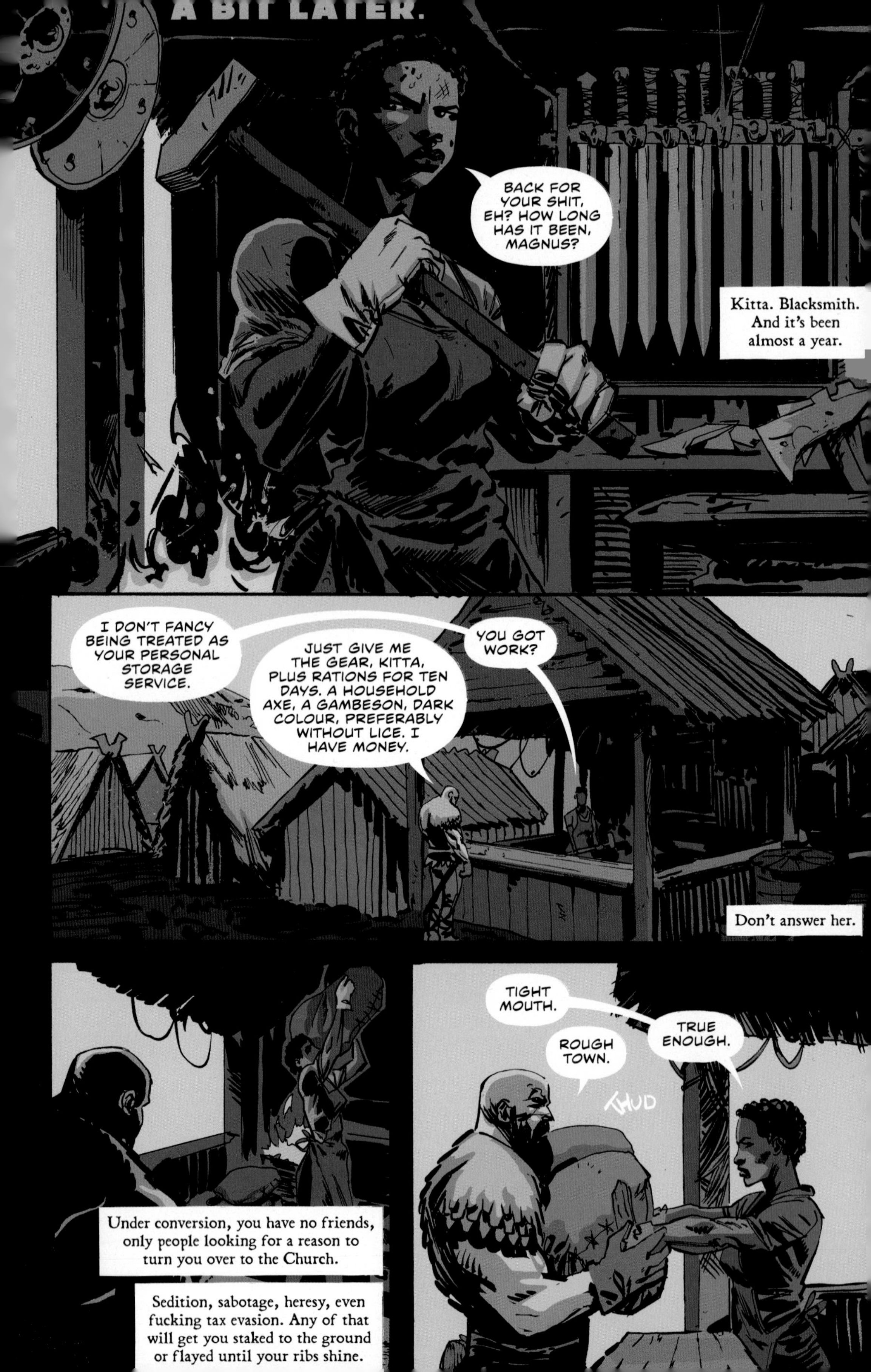
A BIT LATER.
BACK FOR YOUR SHIT, EH? HOW LONG HAS IT BEEN, MAGNUS?
Kitta. Blacksmith. And it's been almost a year.
I DON'T FANCY BEING TREATED AS YOUR PERSONAL STORAGE SERVICE.
YOU GOT WORK?
JUST GIVE ME THE GEAR, KITTA, PLUS RATIONS FOR TEN DAYS. A HOUSEHOLD AXE, A GAMBESON, DARK COLOUR, PREFERABLY WITHOUT LICE. I HAVE MONEY.
Don't answer her.
Under conversion, you have no friends, only people looking for a reason to turn you over to the Church.
Sedition, sabotage, heresy, even fucking tax evasion. Any of that will get you staked to the ground or flayed until your ribs shine.
TIGHT MOUTH.
TRUE ENOUGH.
ROUGH TOWN.
THUD

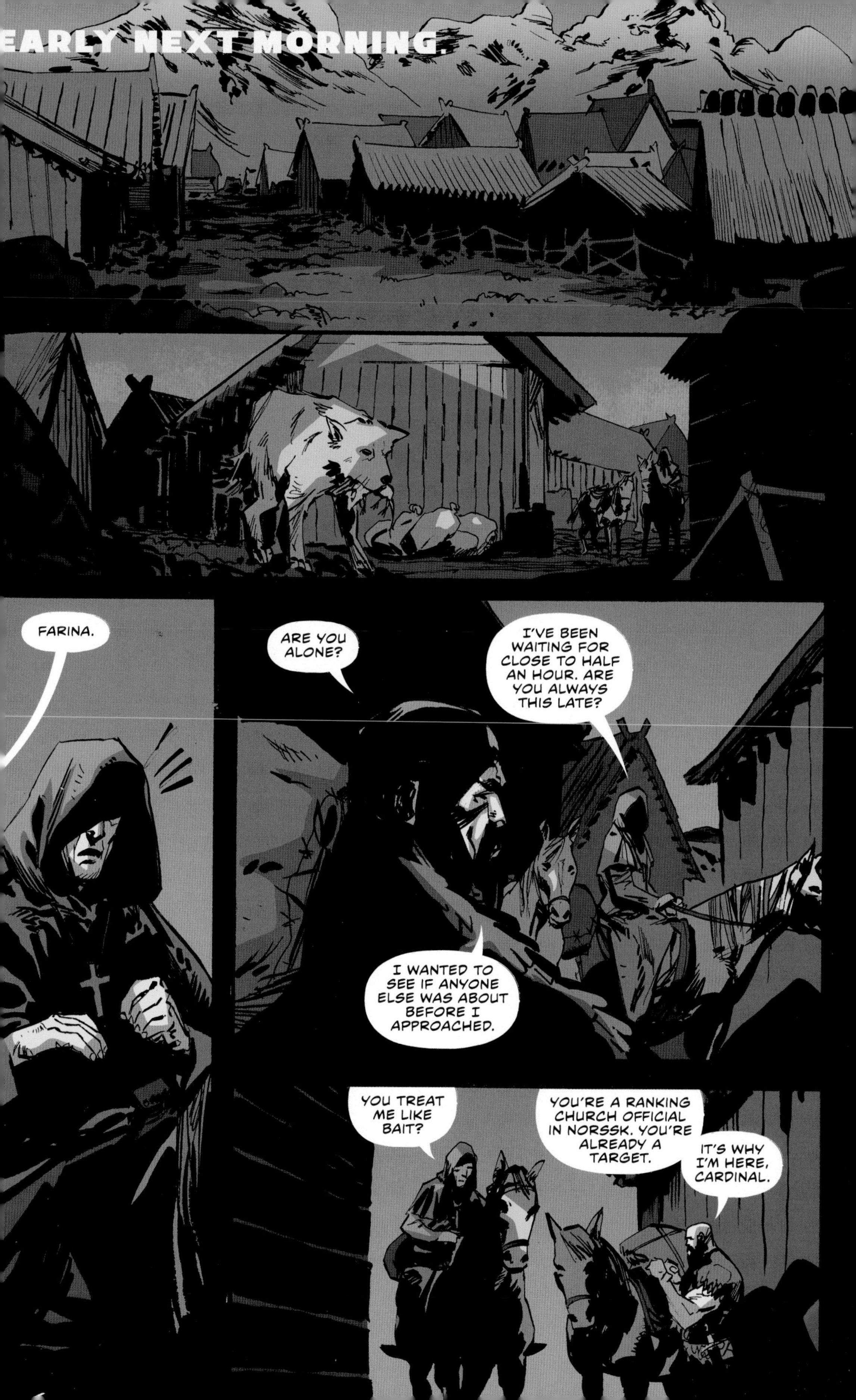
EARLY NEXT MORNING.
FARINA.
ARE YOU ALONE?
I'VE BEEN WAITING FOR CLOSE TO HALF AN HOUR. ARE YOU ALWAYS THIS LATE?
I WANTED TO SEE IF ANYONE ELSE WAS ABOUT BEFORE I APPROACHED.
YOU TREAT ME LIKE BAIT?
YOU'RE A RANKING CHURCH OFFICIAL IN NORSSK. YOU'RE ALREADY A TARGET.
IT'S WHY I'M HERE, CARDINAL.

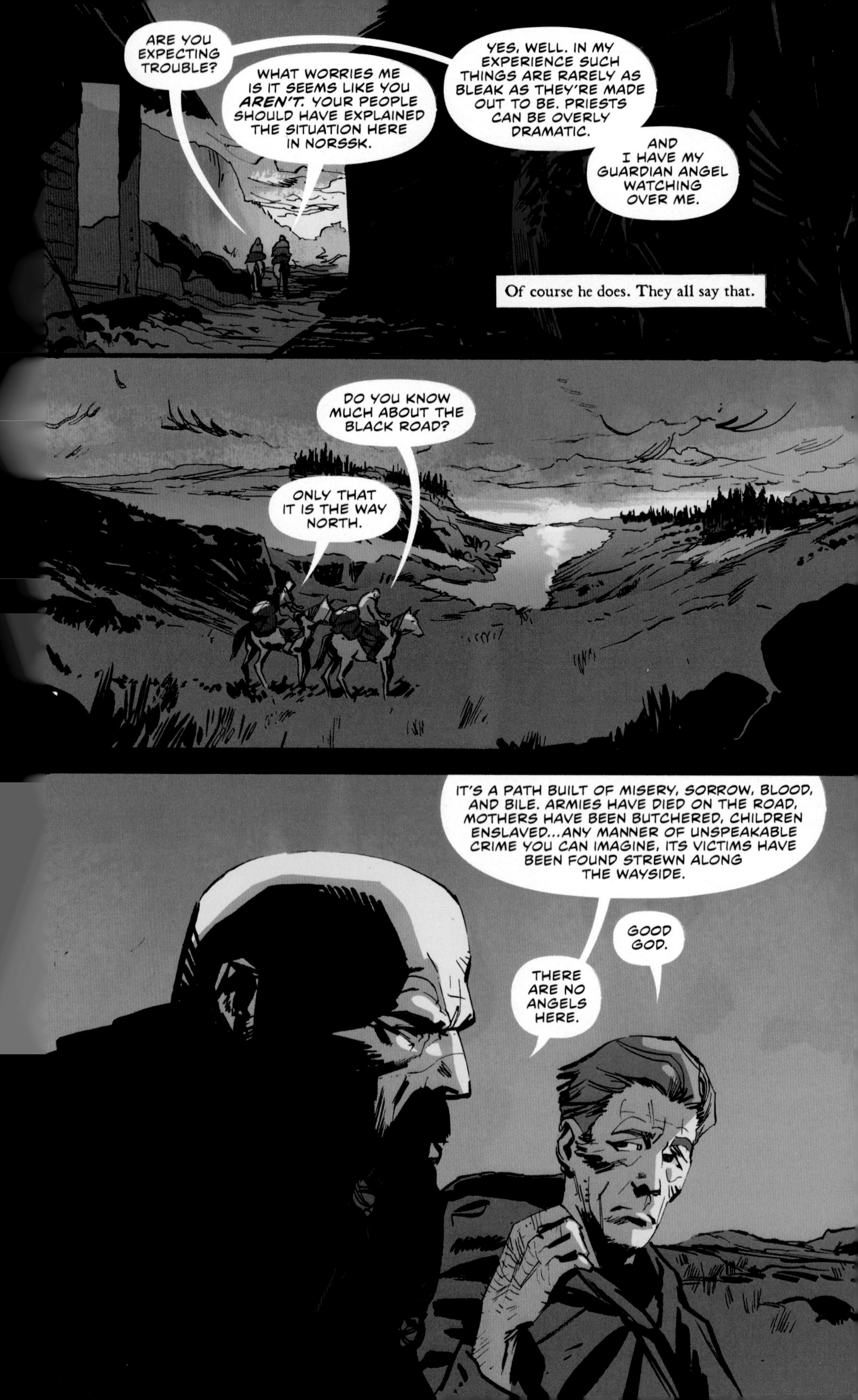
ARE YOU EXPECTING TROUBLE?
WHAT WORRIES ME IS IT SEEMS LIKE YOU *AREN'T*. YOUR PEOPLE SHOULD HAVE EXPLAINED THE SITUATION HERE IN NORSSK.
YES, WELL. IN MY EXPERIENCE SUCH THINGS ARE RARELY AS BLEAK AS THEY'RE MADE OUT TO BE. PRIESTS CAN BE OVERLY DRAMATIC.
AND I HAVE MY GUARDIAN ANGEL WATCHING OVER ME.
Of course he does. They all say that.
DO YOU KNOW MUCH ABOUT THE BLACK ROAD?
ONLY THAT IT IS THE WAY NORTH.
IT'S A PATH BUILT OF MISERY, SORROW, BLOOD, AND BILE. ARMIES HAVE DIED ON THE ROAD, MOTHERS HAVE BEEN BUTCHERED, CHILDREN ENSLAVED...ANY MANNER OF UNSPEAKABLE CRIME YOU CAN IMAGINE, ITS VICTIMS HAVE BEEN FOUND STREWN ALONG THE WAYSIDE.
GOOD GOD.
THERE ARE NO ANGELS HERE.

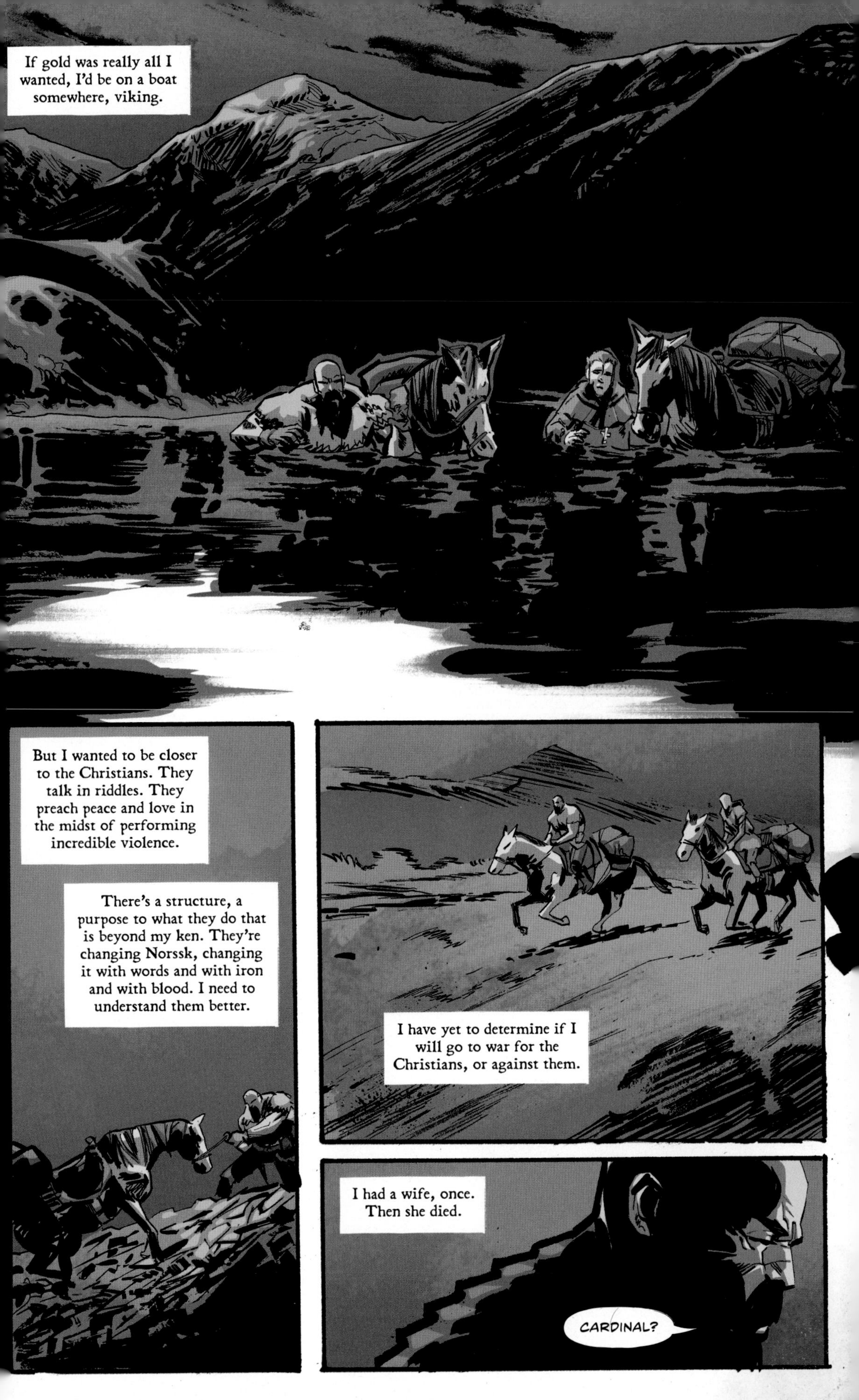
If gold was really all I wanted, I'd be on a boat somewhere, viking.
But I wanted to be closer to the Christians. They talk in riddles. They preach peace and love in the midst of performing incredible violence.
There's a structure, a purpose to what they do that is beyond my ken. They're changing Norssk, changing it with words and with iron and with blood. I need to understand them better.
I have yet to determine if I will go to war for the Christians, or against them.
I had a wife, once. Then she died.
CARDINAL?

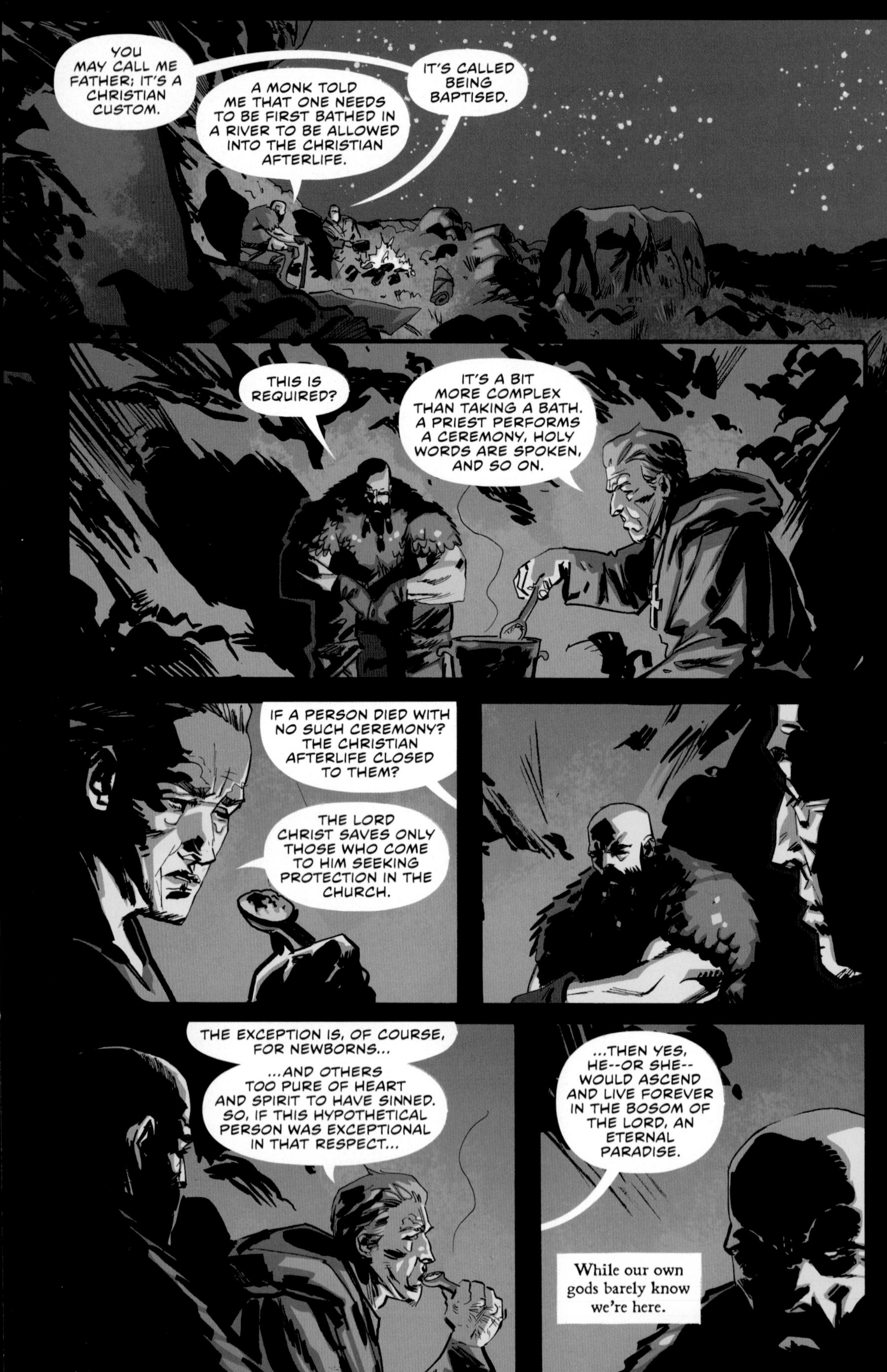
YOU MAY CALL ME FATHER; IT'S A CHRISTIAN CUSTOM.
A MONK TOLD ME THAT ONE NEEDS TO BE FIRST BATHED IN A RIVER TO BE ALLOWED INTO THE CHRISTIAN AFTERLIFE.
IT'S CALLED BEING BAPTISED.
THIS IS REQUIRED?
IT'S A BIT MORE COMPLEX THAN TAKING A BATH. A PRIEST PERFORMS A CEREMONY, HOLY WORDS ARE SPOKEN, AND SO ON.
IF A PERSON DIED WITH NO SUCH CEREMONY? THE CHRISTIAN AFTERLIFE CLOSED TO THEM?
THE LORD CHRIST SAVES ONLY THOSE WHO COME TO HIM SEEKING PROTECTION IN THE CHURCH.
THE EXCEPTION IS, OF COURSE, FOR NEWBORNS...
...AND OTHERS TOO PURE OF HEART AND SPIRIT TO HAVE SINNED. SO, IF THIS HYPOTHETICAL PERSON WAS EXCEPTIONAL IN THAT RESPECT...
...THEN YES, HE--OR SHE--WOULD ASCEND AND LIVE FOREVER IN THE BOSOM OF THE LORD, AN ETERNAL PARADISE.
While our own gods barely know we're here.

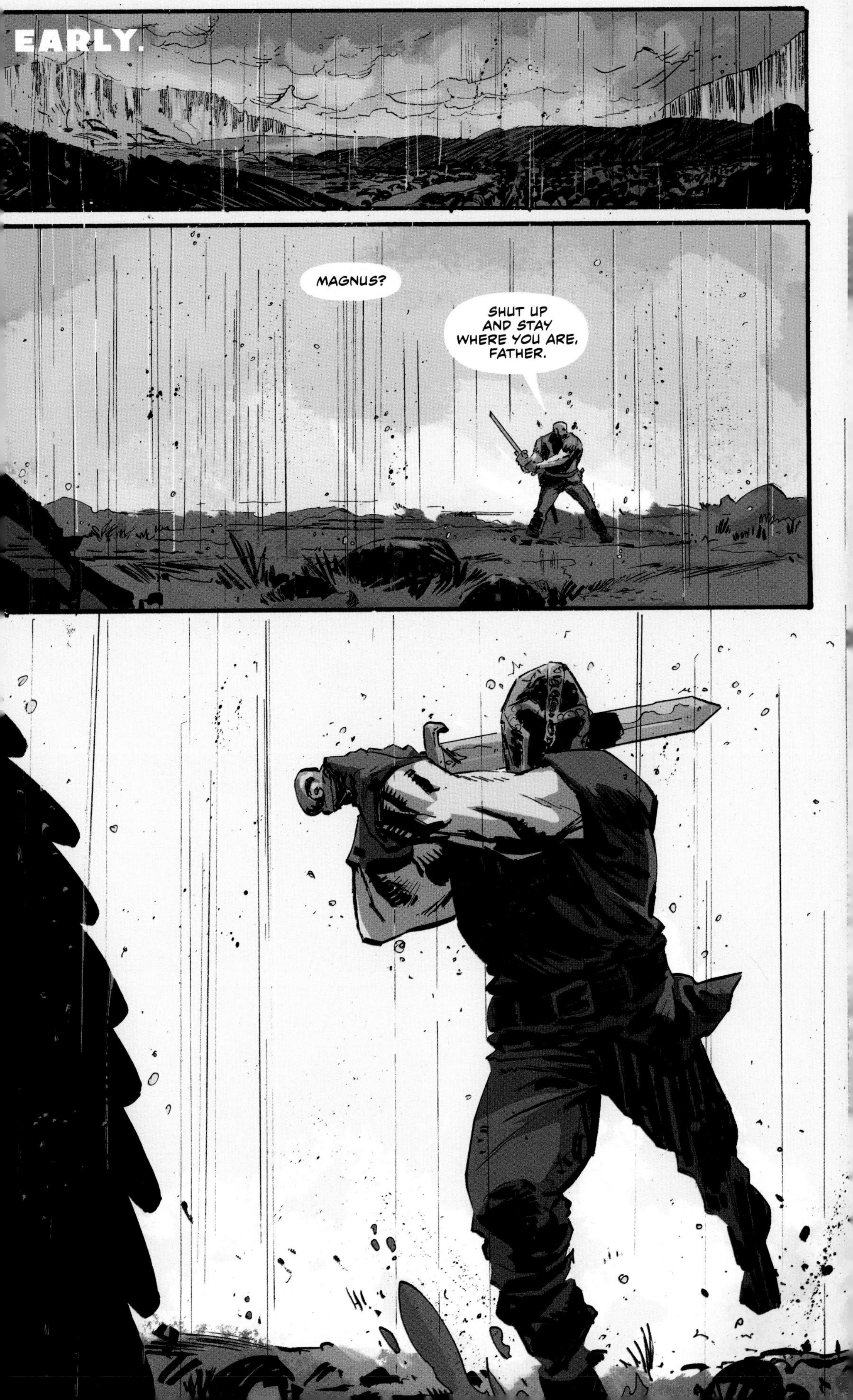
EARLY.
MAGNUS?
SHUT UP AND STAY WHERE YOU ARE, FATHER.

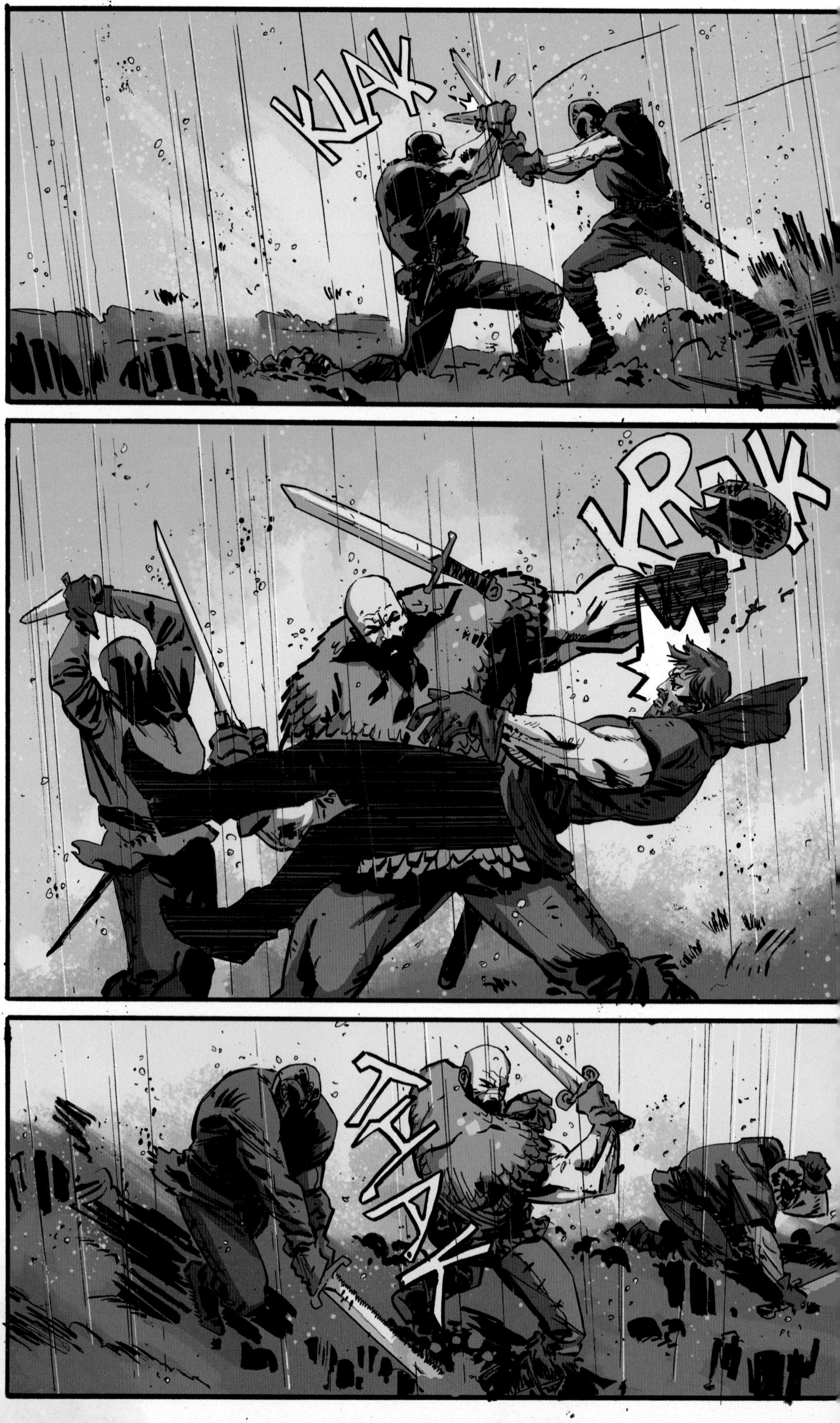
KLAK
VRAK
THAK

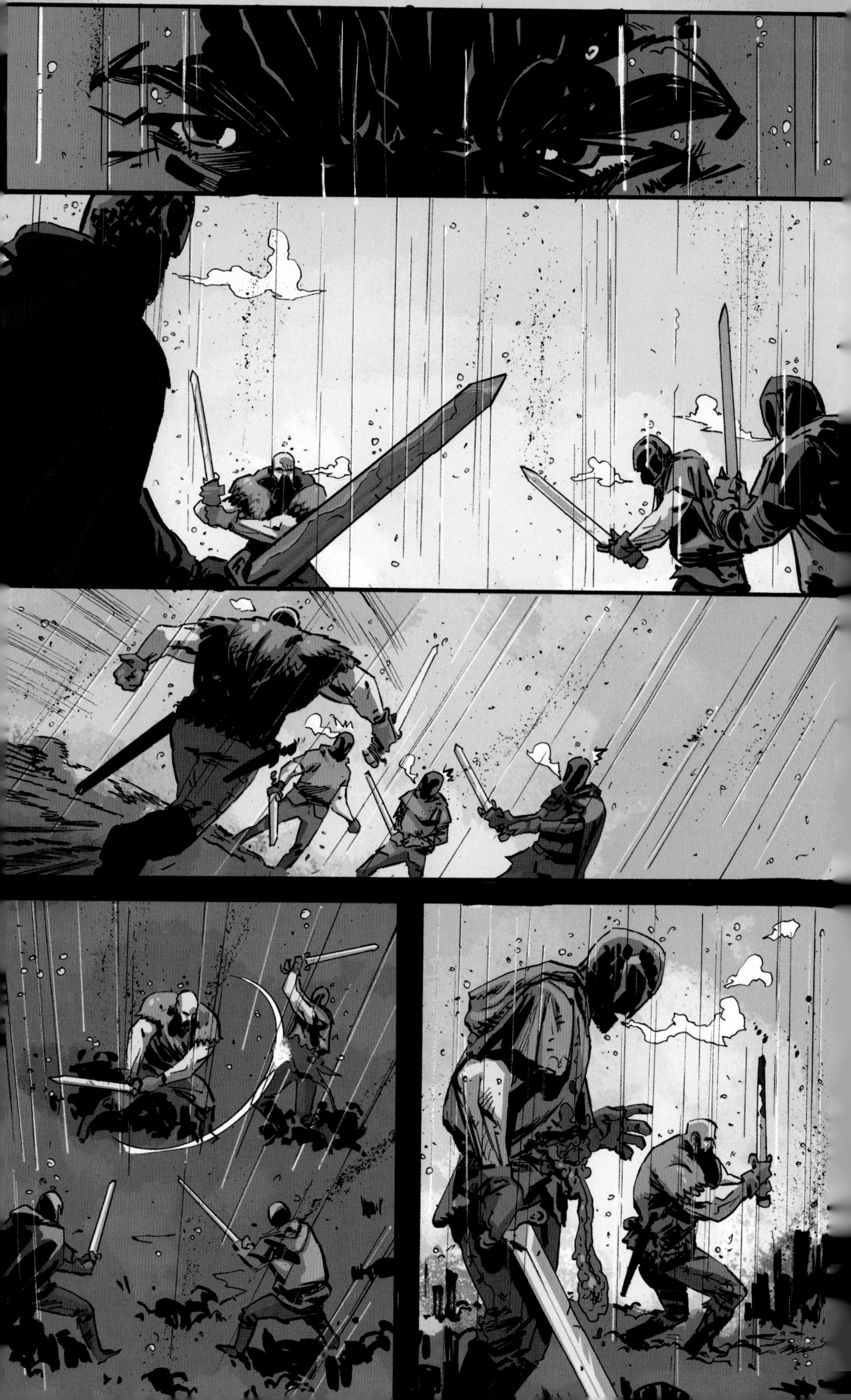

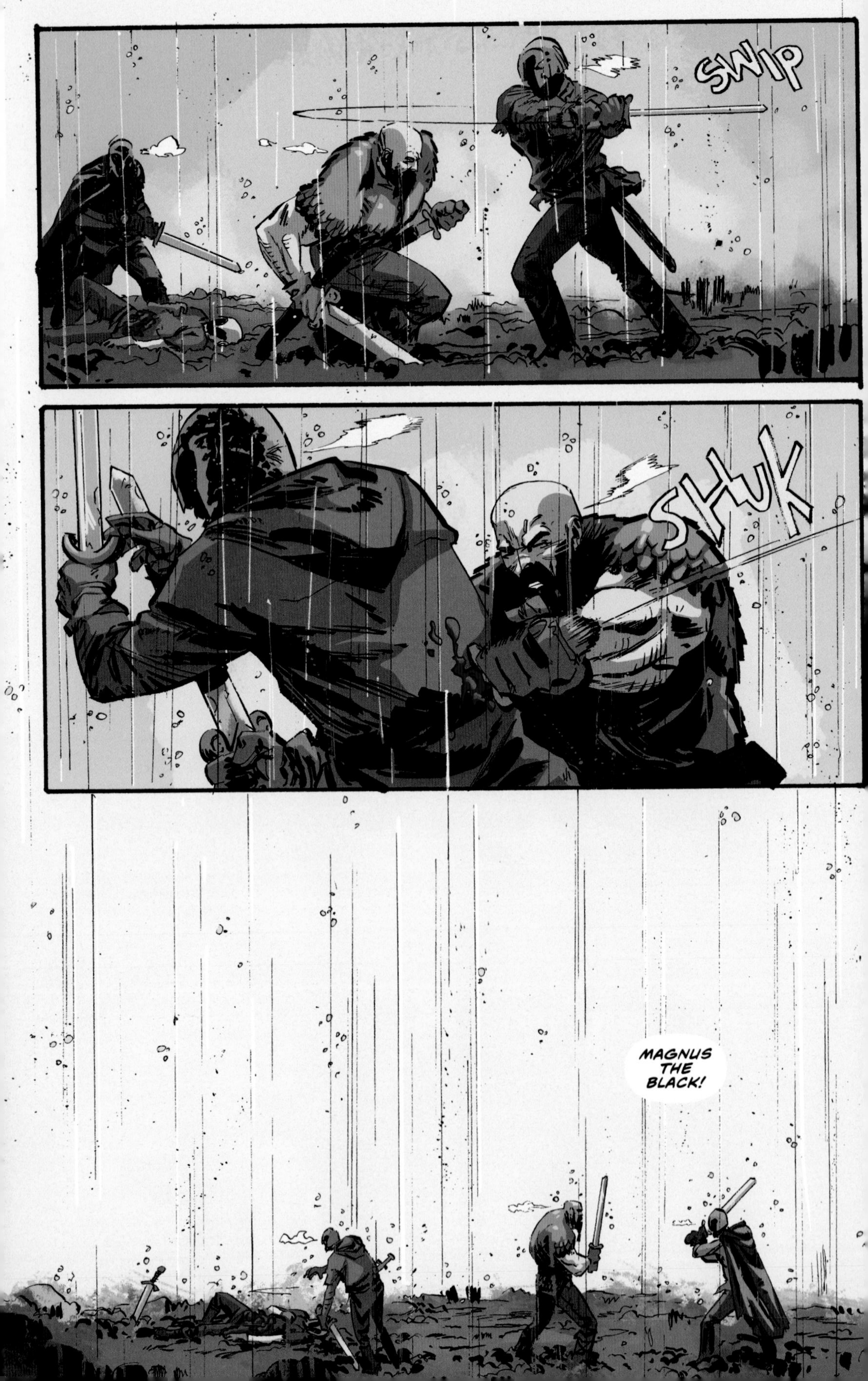
SWIP
SHUK
MAGNUS THE BLACK!

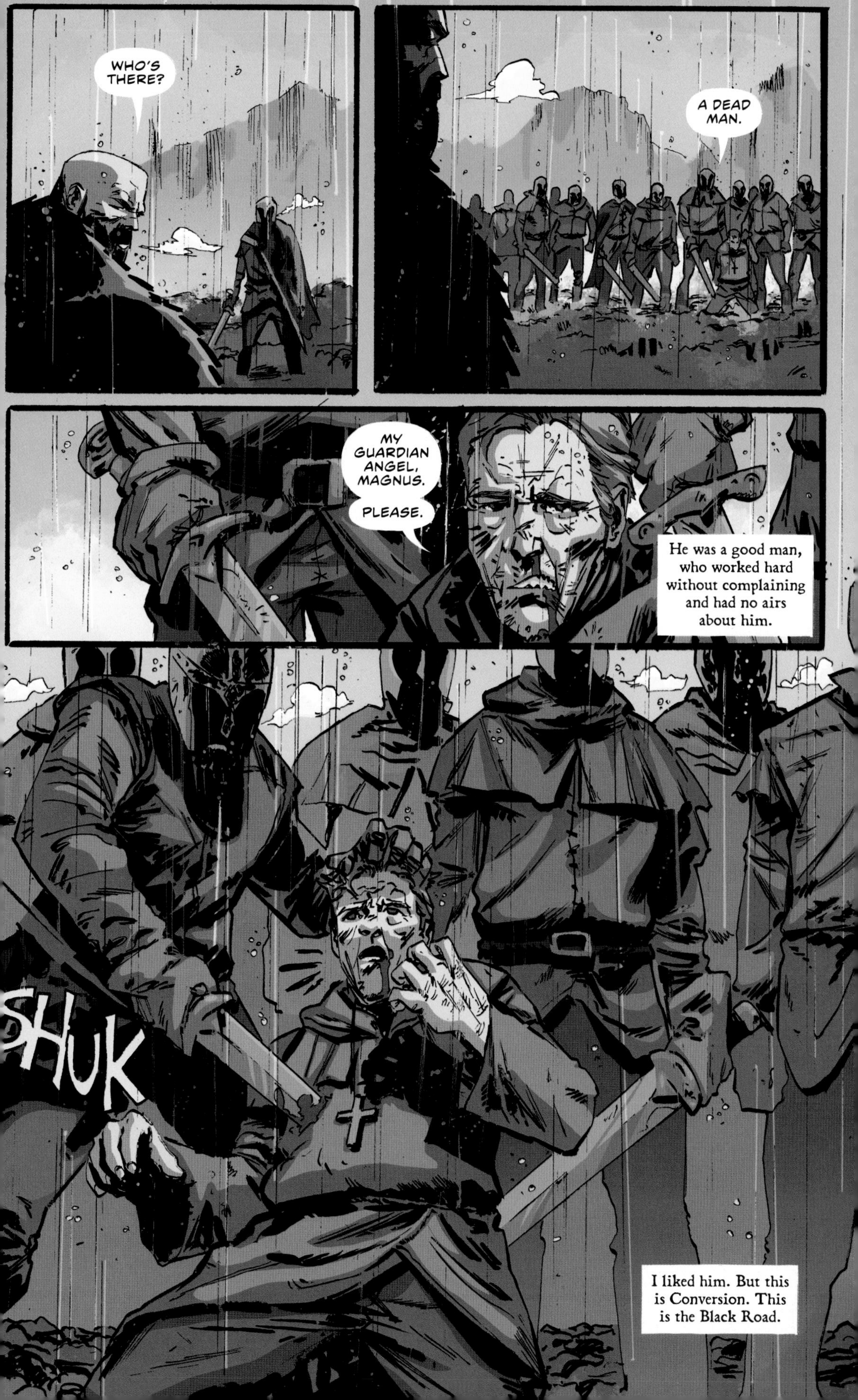
WHO'S THERE?
A DEAD MAN.
MY GUARDIAN ANGEL, MAGNUS.
PLEASE.
He was a good man, who worked hard without complaining and had no airs about him.
SHUK
I liked him. But this is Conversion. This is the Black Road.

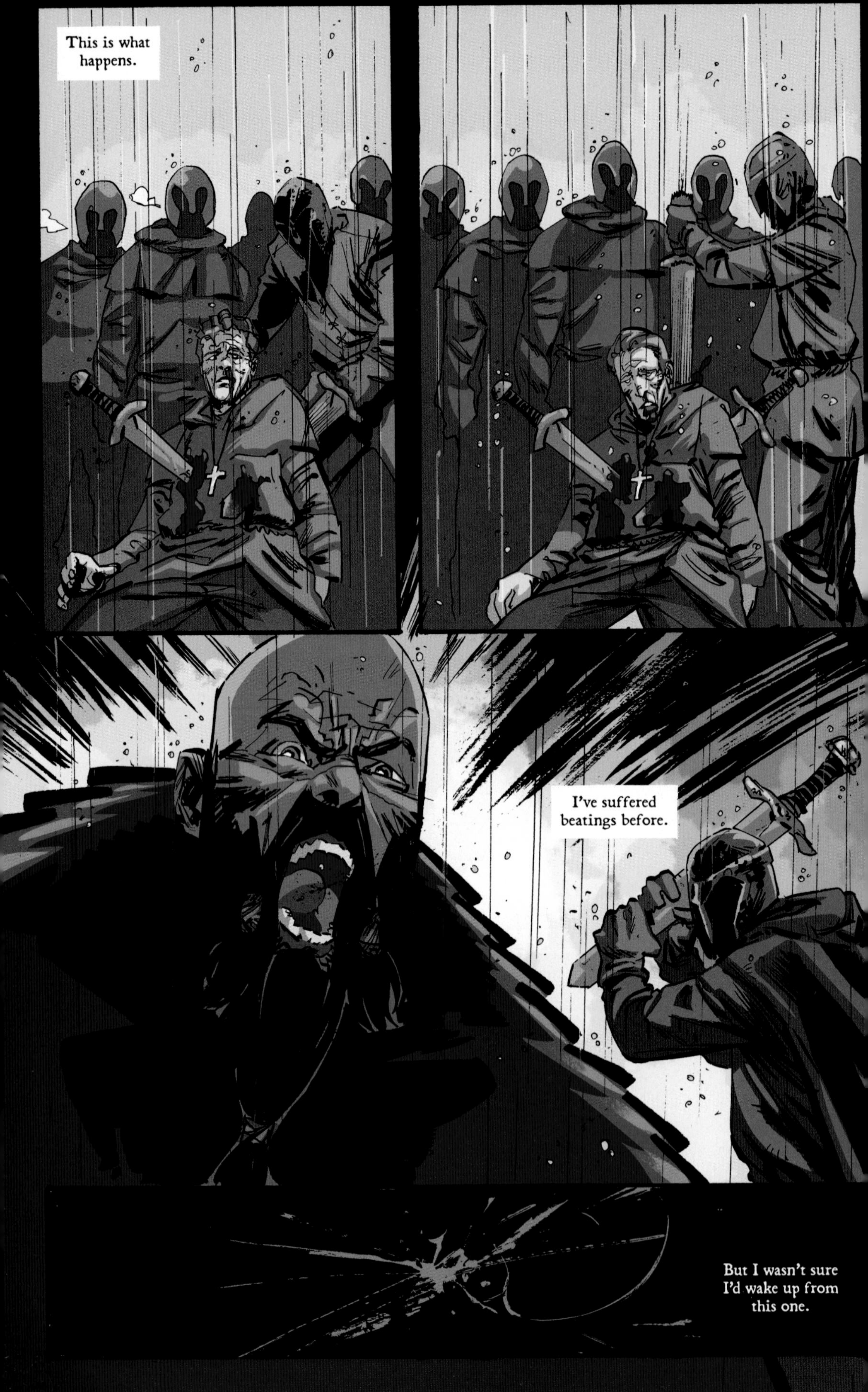
This is what happens.
I've suffered beatings before.
But I wasn't sure I'd wake up from this one.

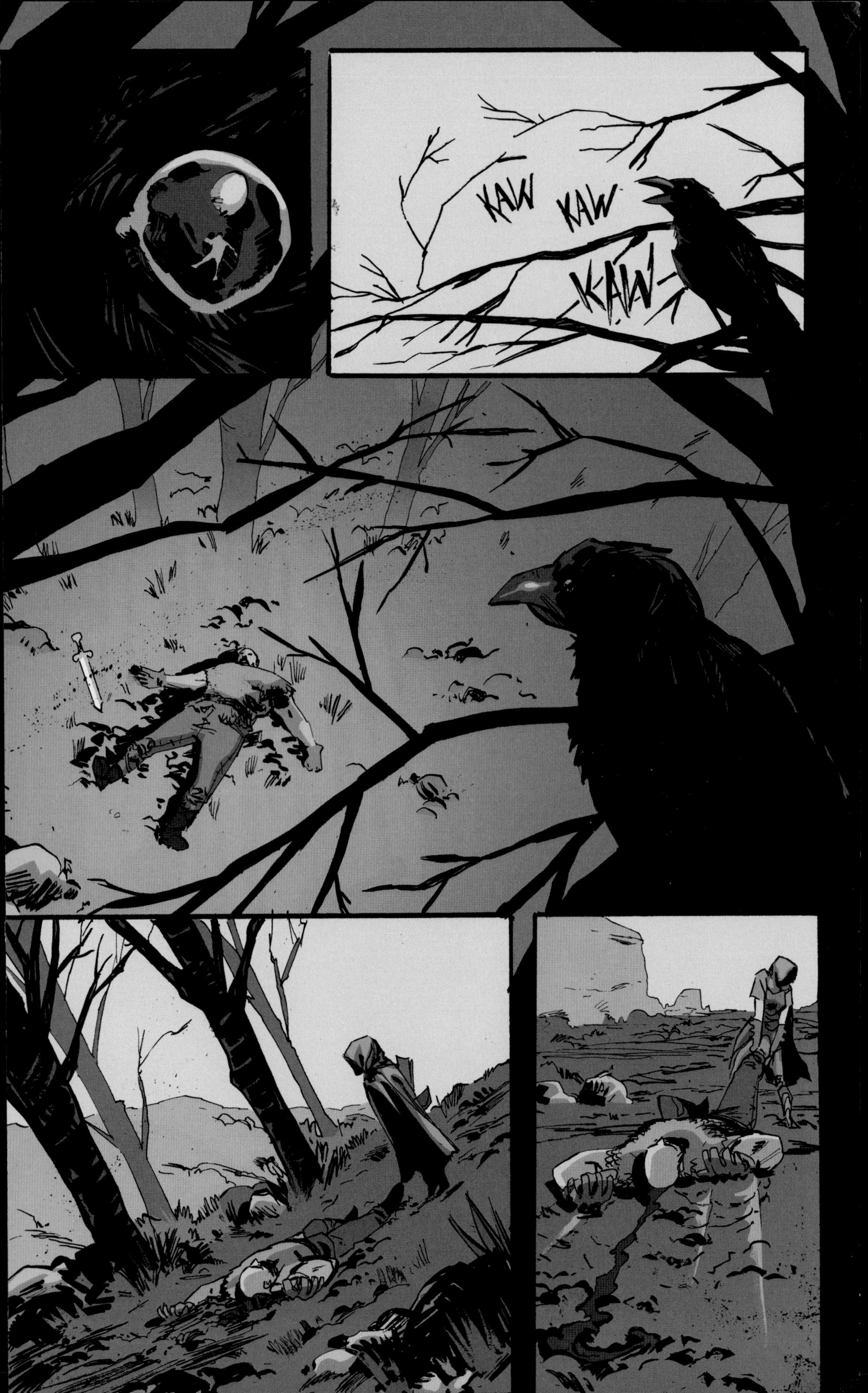
KAW
KAW
KAW

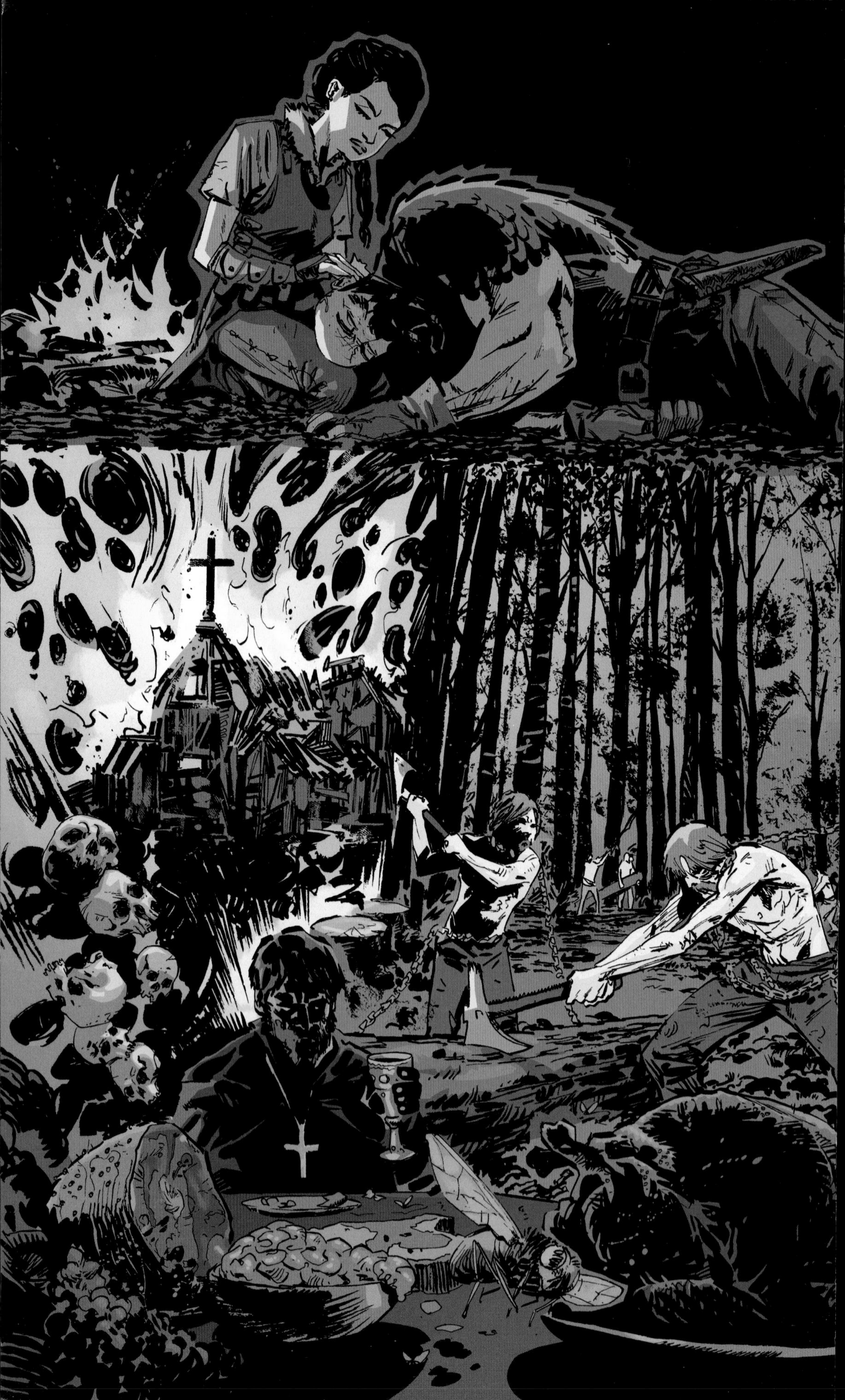

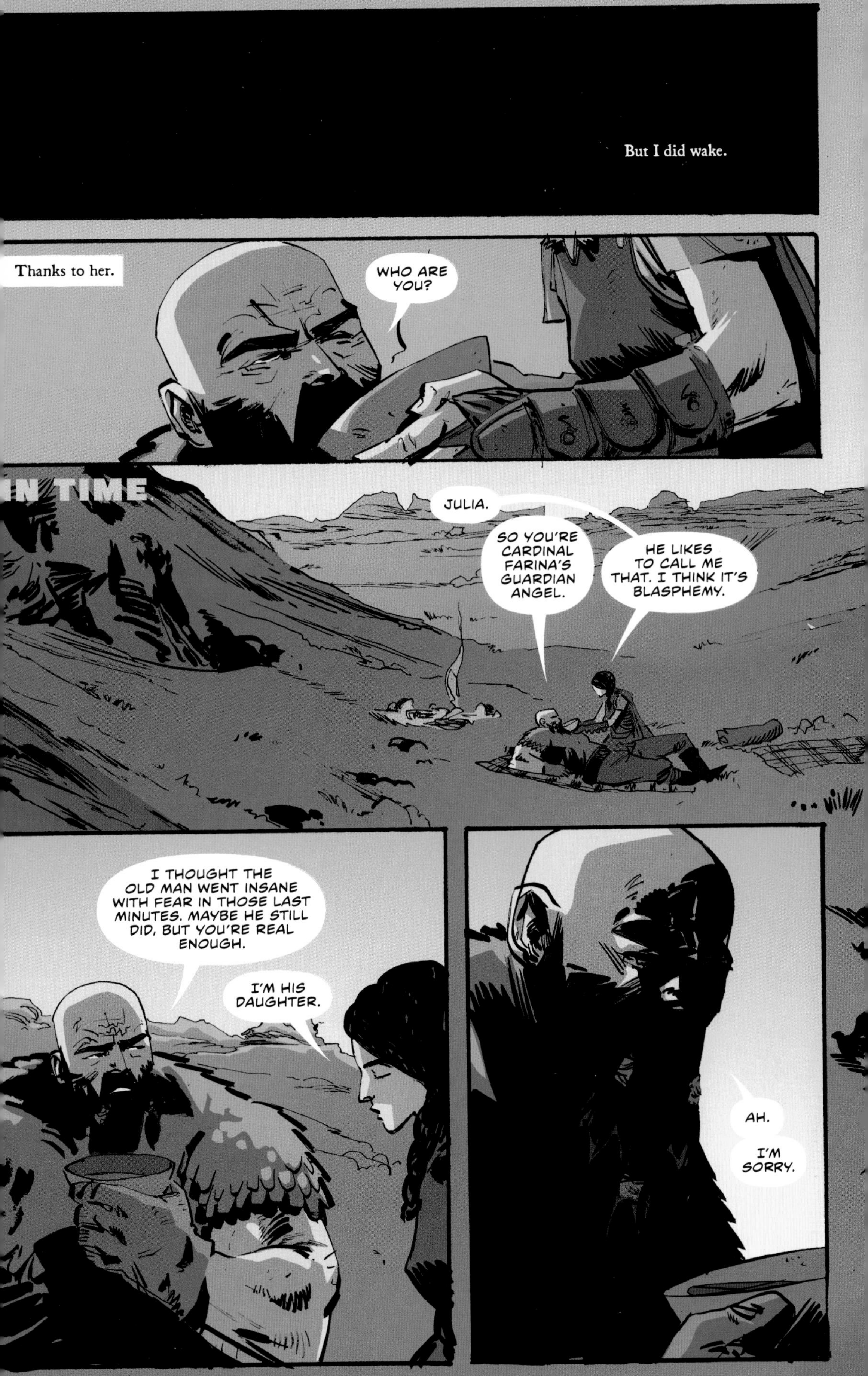
But I did wake.
Thanks to her.
WHO ARE YOU?
IN TIME
JULIA.
SO YOU'RE CARDINAL FARINA'S GUARDIAN ANGEL.
HE LIKES TO CALL ME THAT. I THINK IT'S BLASPHEMY.
I THOUGHT THE OLD MAN WENT INSANE WITH FEAR IN THOSE LAST MINUTES. MAYBE HE STILL DID, BUT YOU'RE REAL ENOUGH.
I'M HIS DAUGHTER.
AH.
I'M SORRY.

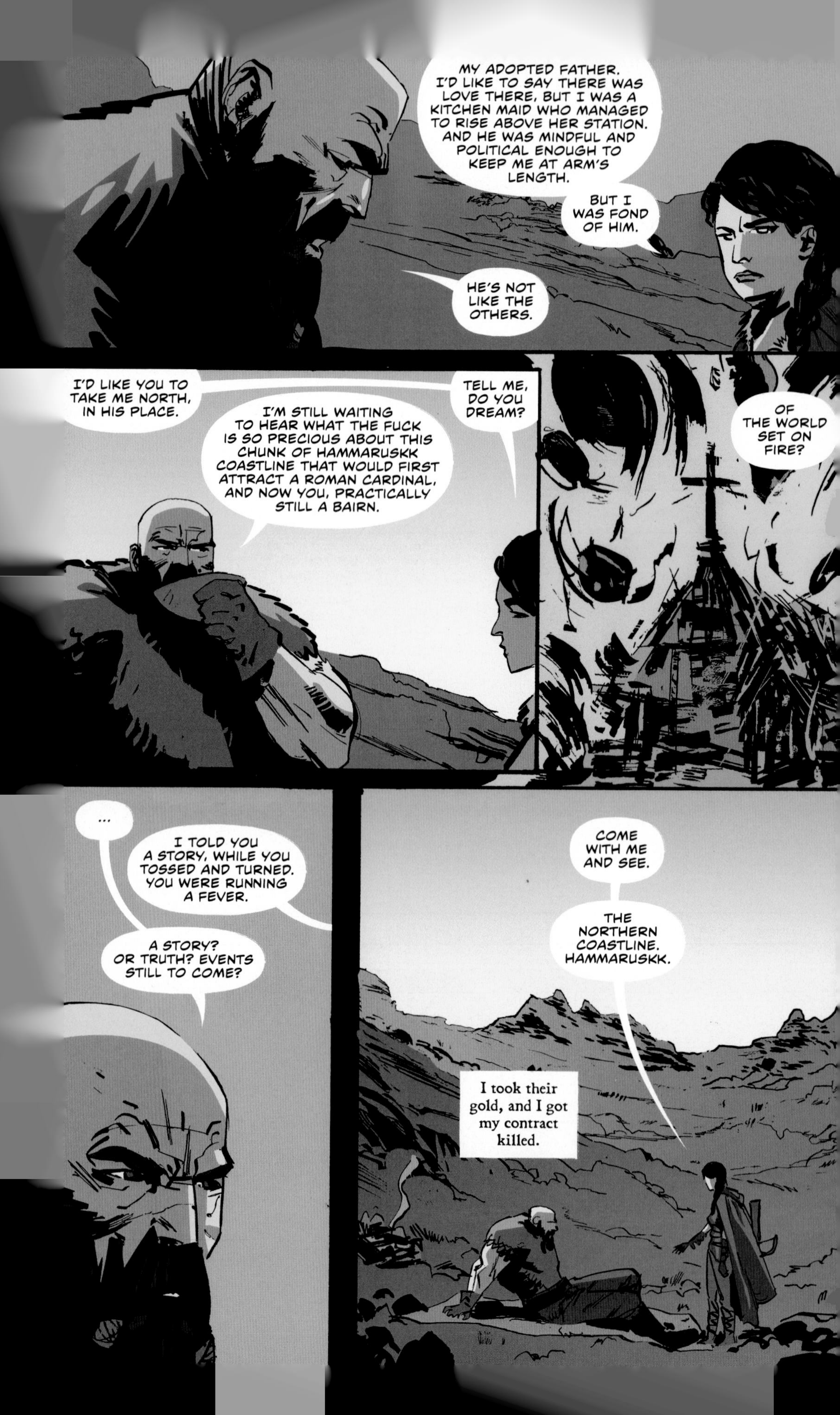
MY ADOPTED FATHER. I'D LIKE TO SAY THERE WAS LOVE THERE, BUT I WAS A KITCHEN MAID WHO MANAGED TO RISE ABOVE HER STATION. AND HE WAS MINDFUL AND POLITICAL ENOUGH TO KEEP ME AT ARM'S LENGTH.
BUT I WAS FOND OF HIM.
HE'S NOT LIKE THE OTHERS.
I'D LIKE YOU TO TAKE ME NORTH, IN HIS PLACE.
I'M STILL WAITING TO HEAR WHAT THE FUCK IS SO PRECIOUS ABOUT THIS CHUNK OF HAMMARUSKK COASTLINE THAT WOULD FIRST ATTRACT A ROMAN CARDINAL, AND NOW YOU, PRACTICALLY STILL A BAIRN.
TELL ME, DO YOU DREAM?
OF THE WORLD SET ON FIRE?
...
I TOLD YOU A STORY, WHILE YOU TOSSED AND TURNED. YOU WERE RUNNING A FEVER.
A STORY? OR TRUTH? EVENTS STILL TO COME?
COME WITH ME AND SEE.
THE NORTHERN COASTLINE. HAMMARUSKK.
I took their gold, and I got my contract killed.

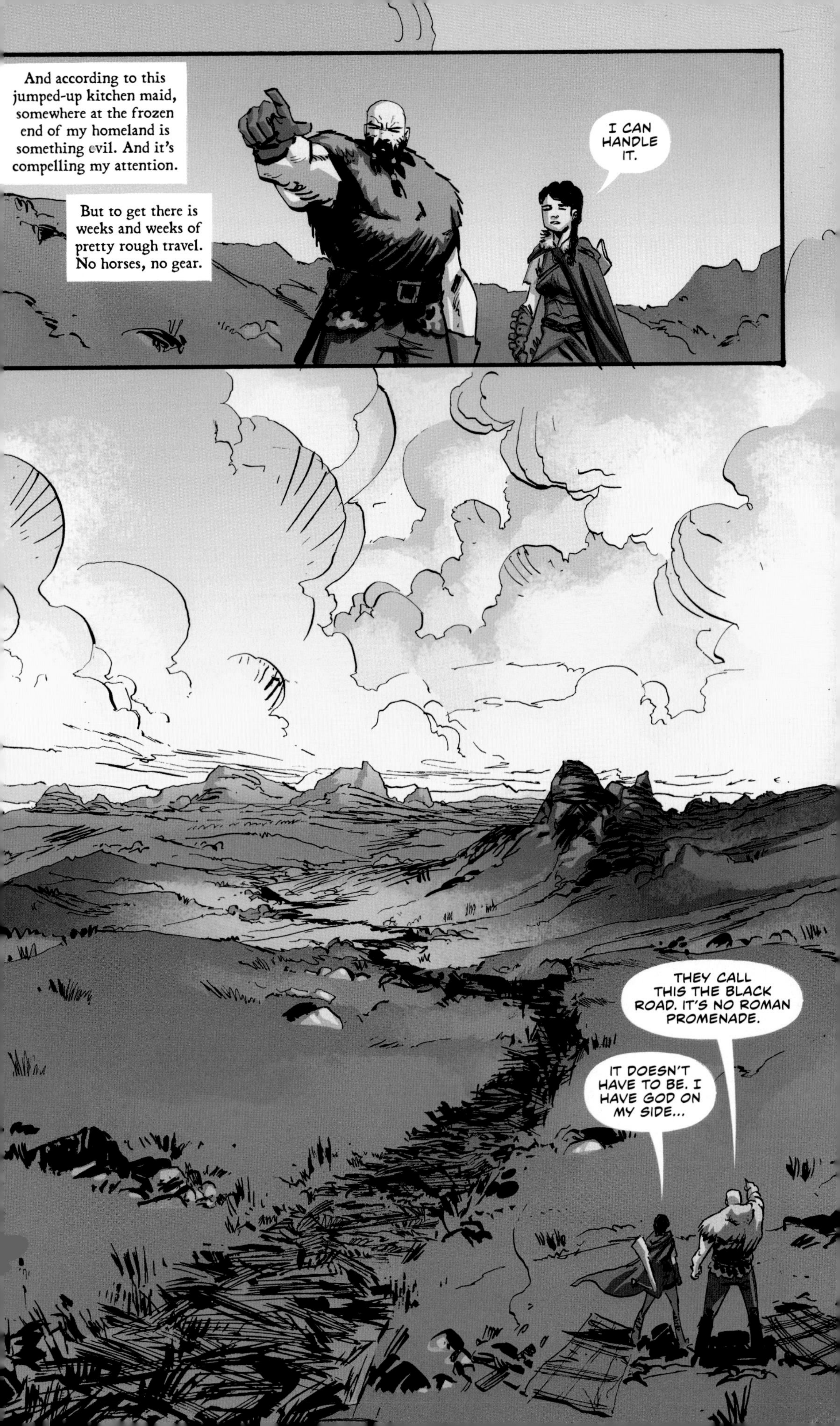
And according to this jumped-up kitchen maid, somewhere at the frozen end of my homeland is something evil. And it's compelling my attention.
But to get there is weeks and weeks of pretty rough travel. No horses, no gear.
I CAN HANDLE IT.
THEY CALL THIS THE BLACK ROAD. IT'S NO ROMAN PROMENADE.
IT DOESN'T HAVE TO BE. I HAVE GOD ON MY SIDE...

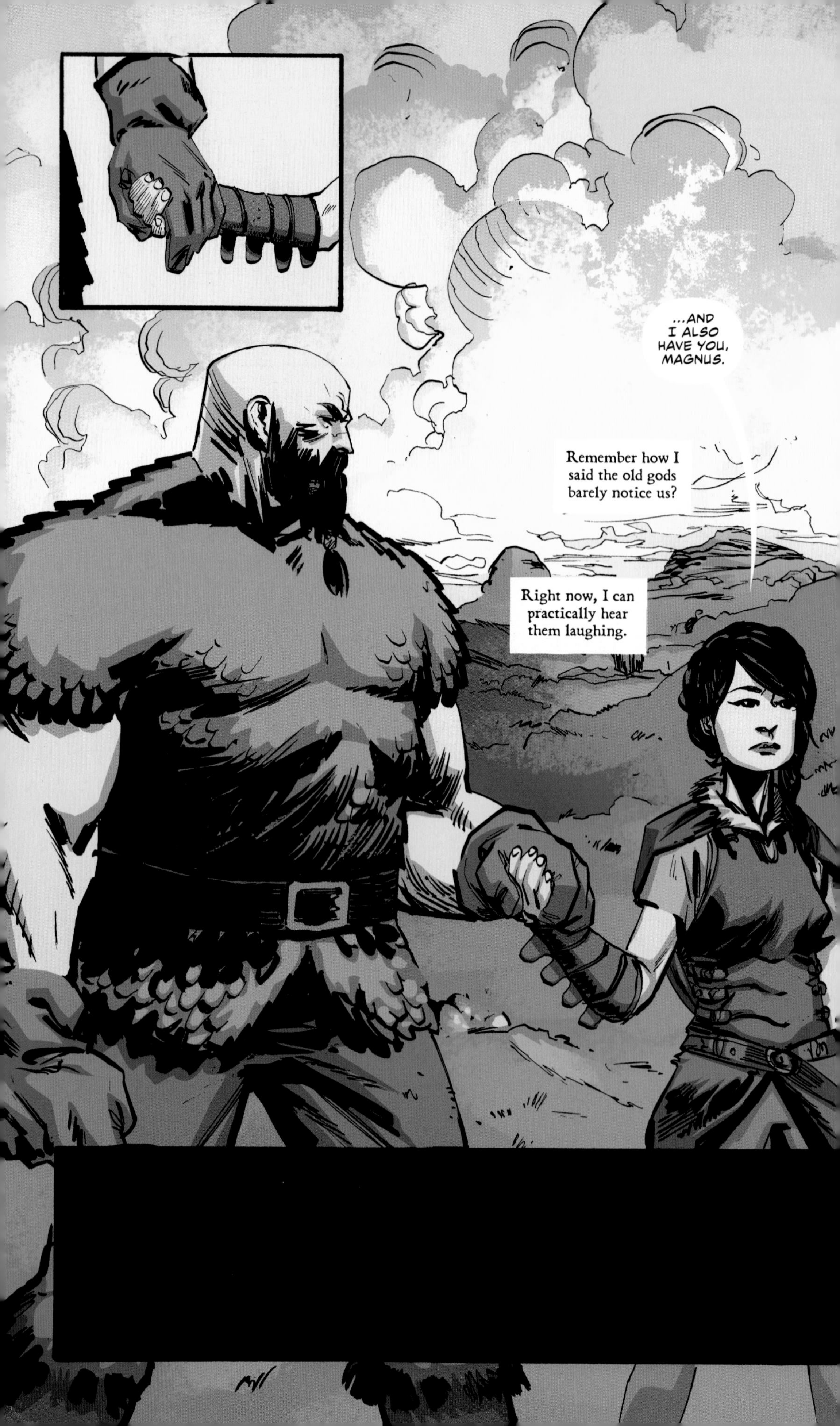
...AND I ALSO HAVE YOU, MAGNUS.
Remember how I said the old gods barely notice us?
Right now, I can practically hear them laughing.
[redacted]

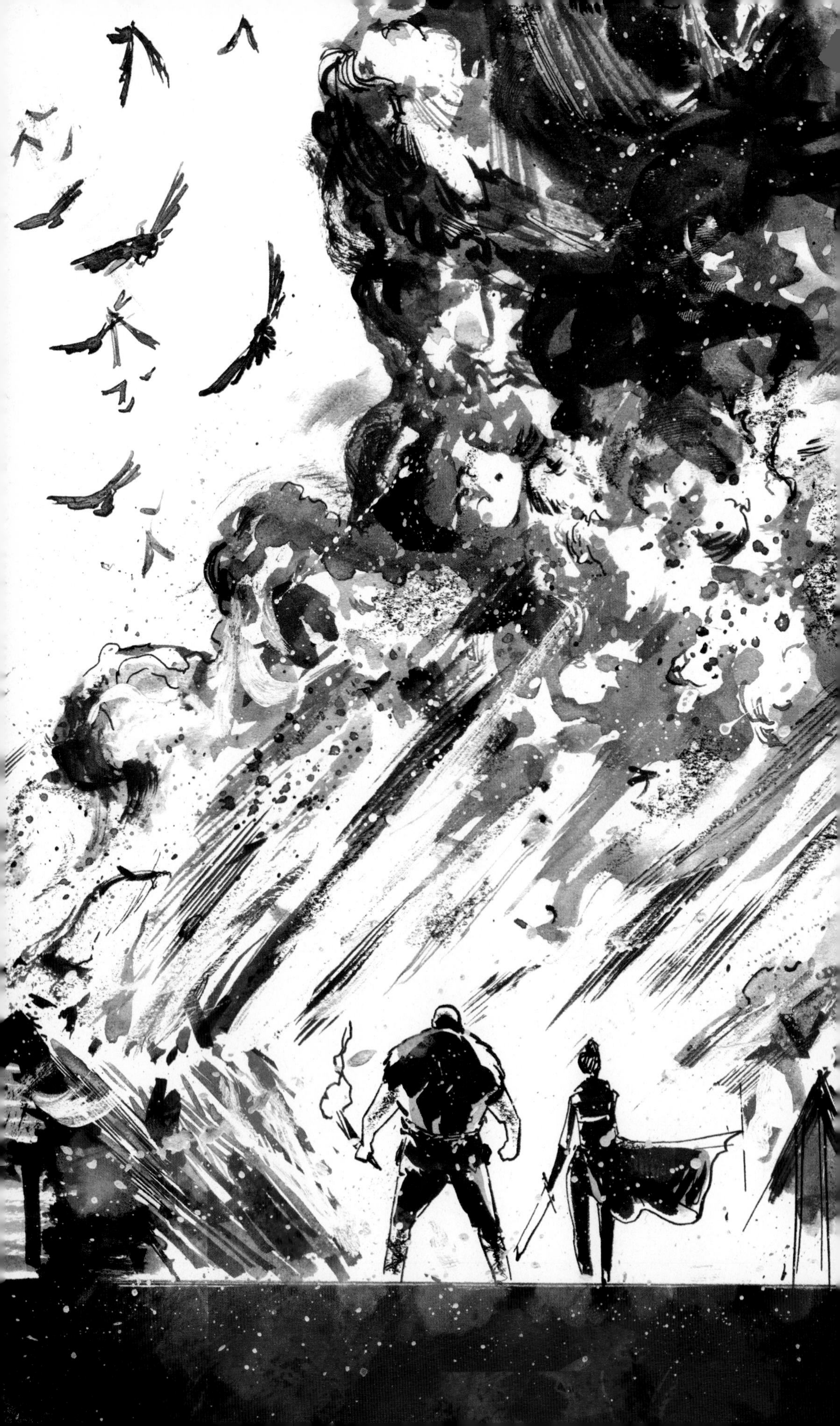

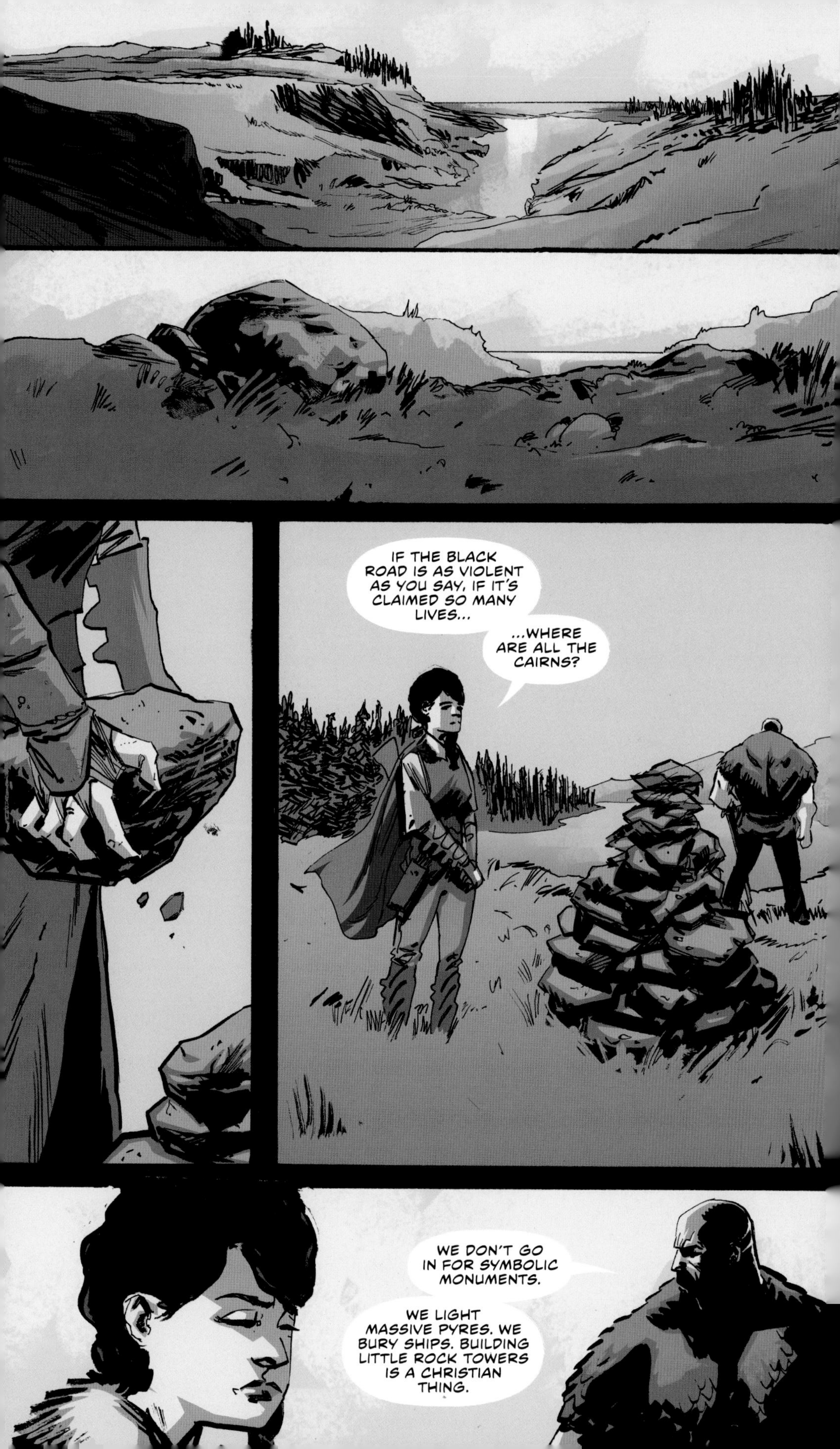
IF THE BLACK ROAD IS AS VIOLENT AS YOU SAY, IF IT'S CLAIMED SO MANY LIVES...
...WHERE ARE ALL THE CAIRNS?
WE DON'T GO IN FOR SYMBOLIC MONUMENTS.
WE LIGHT MASSIVE PYRES. WE BURY SHIPS. BUILDING LITTLE ROCK TOWERS IS A CHRISTIAN THING.

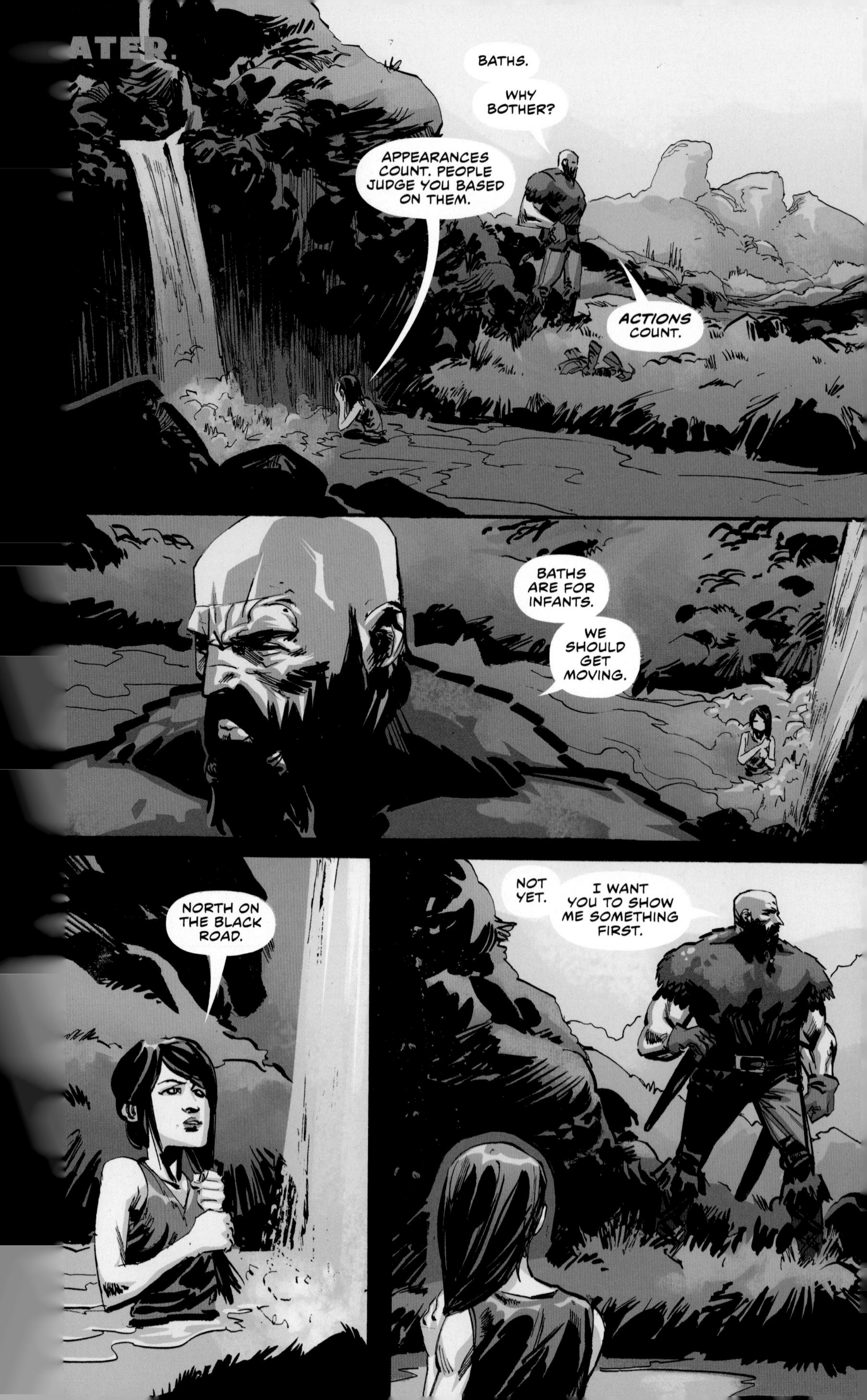
LATER.
BATHS.
WHY BOTHER?
APPEARANCES COUNT. PEOPLE JUDGE YOU BASED ON THEM.
ACTIONS COUNT.
BATHS ARE FOR INFANTS.
WE SHOULD GET MOVING.
NORTH ON THE BLACK ROAD.
NOT YET.
I WANT YOU TO SHOW ME SOMETHING FIRST.

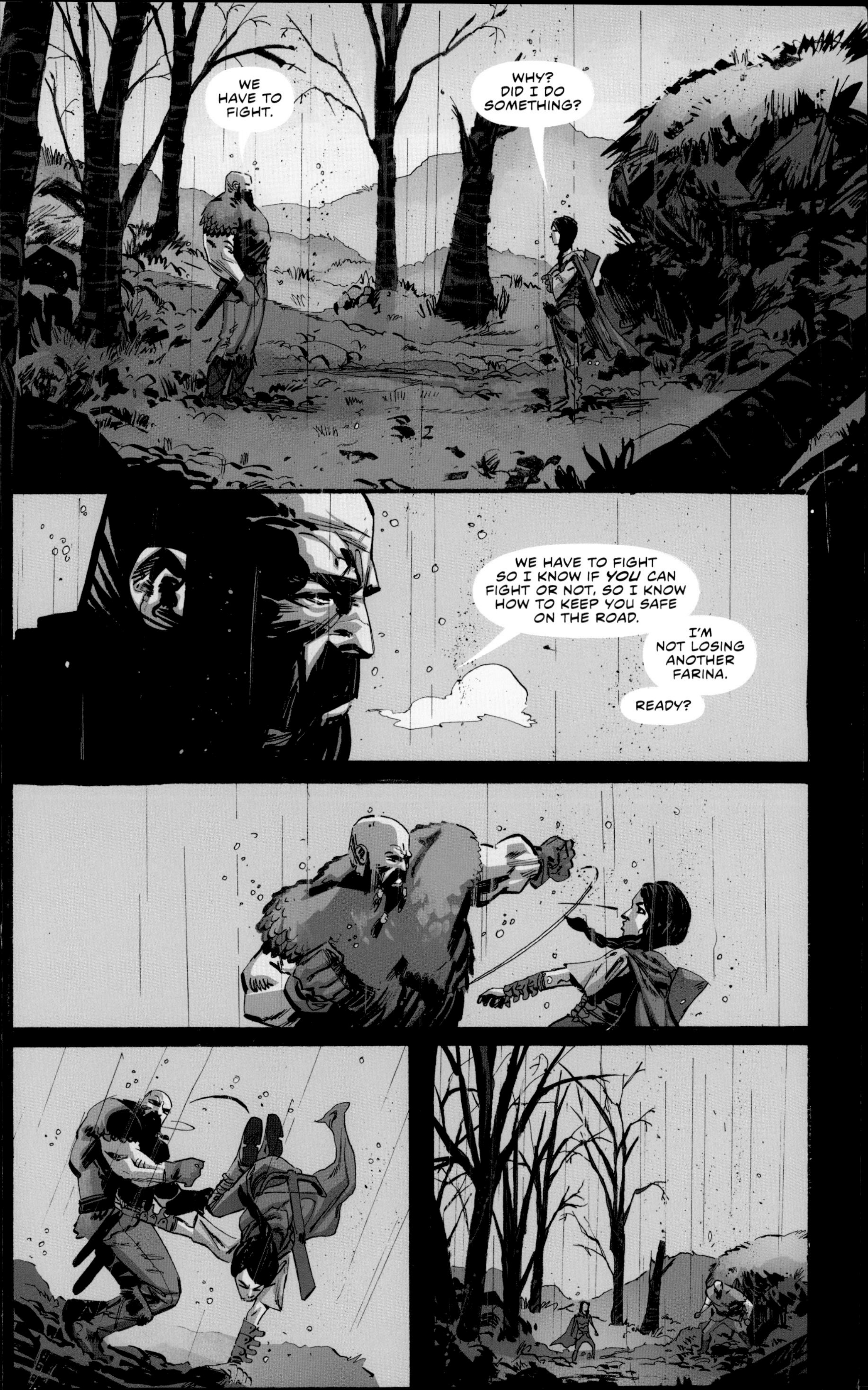

WE HAVE TO FIGHT.
WHY? DID I DO SOMETHING?
WE HAVE TO FIGHT SO I KNOW IF *YOU* CAN FIGHT OR NOT, SO I KNOW HOW TO KEEP YOU SAFE ON THE ROAD.
I'M NOT LOSING ANOTHER FARINA.
READY?

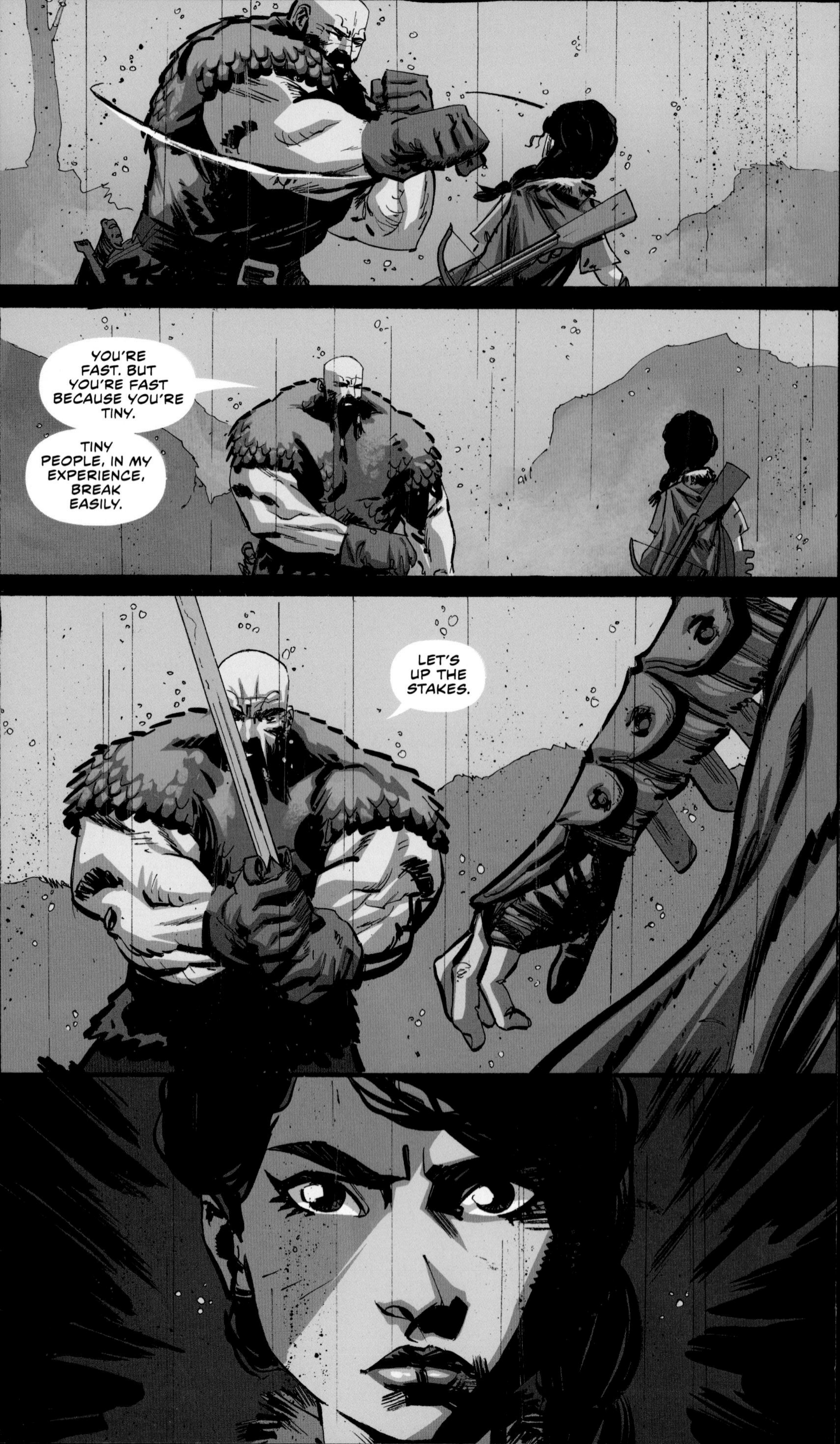
YOU'RE FAST. BUT YOU'RE FAST BECAUSE YOU'RE TINY.
TINY PEOPLE, IN MY EXPERIENCE, BREAK EASILY.
LET'S UP THE STAKES.

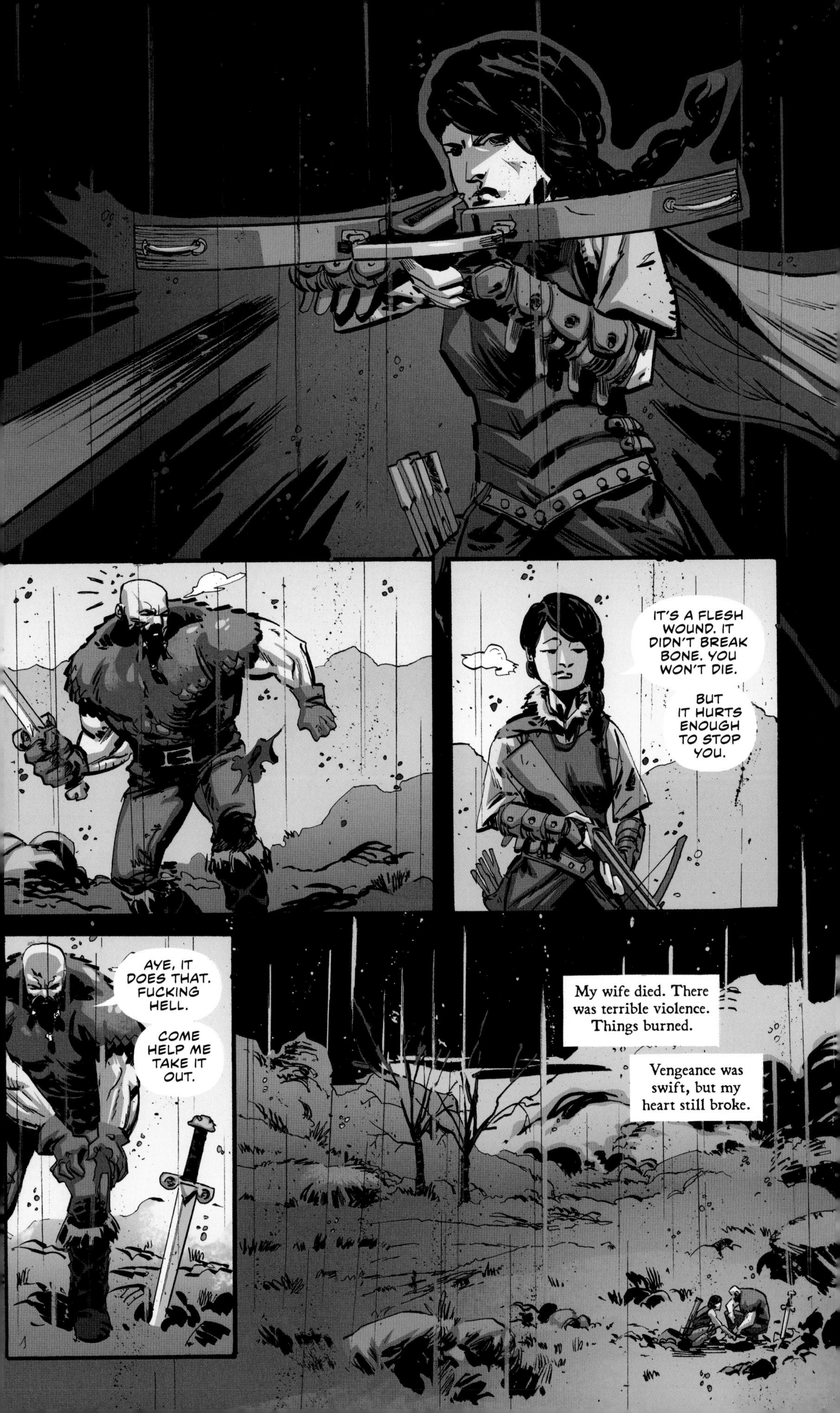
IT'S A FLESH WOUND. IT DIDN'T BREAK BONE. YOU WON'T DIE.
BUT IT HURTS ENOUGH TO STOP YOU.
AYE, IT DOES THAT. FUCKING HELL.
COME HELP ME TAKE IT OUT.
My wife died. There was terrible violence. Things burned.
Vengeance was swift, but my heart still broke.

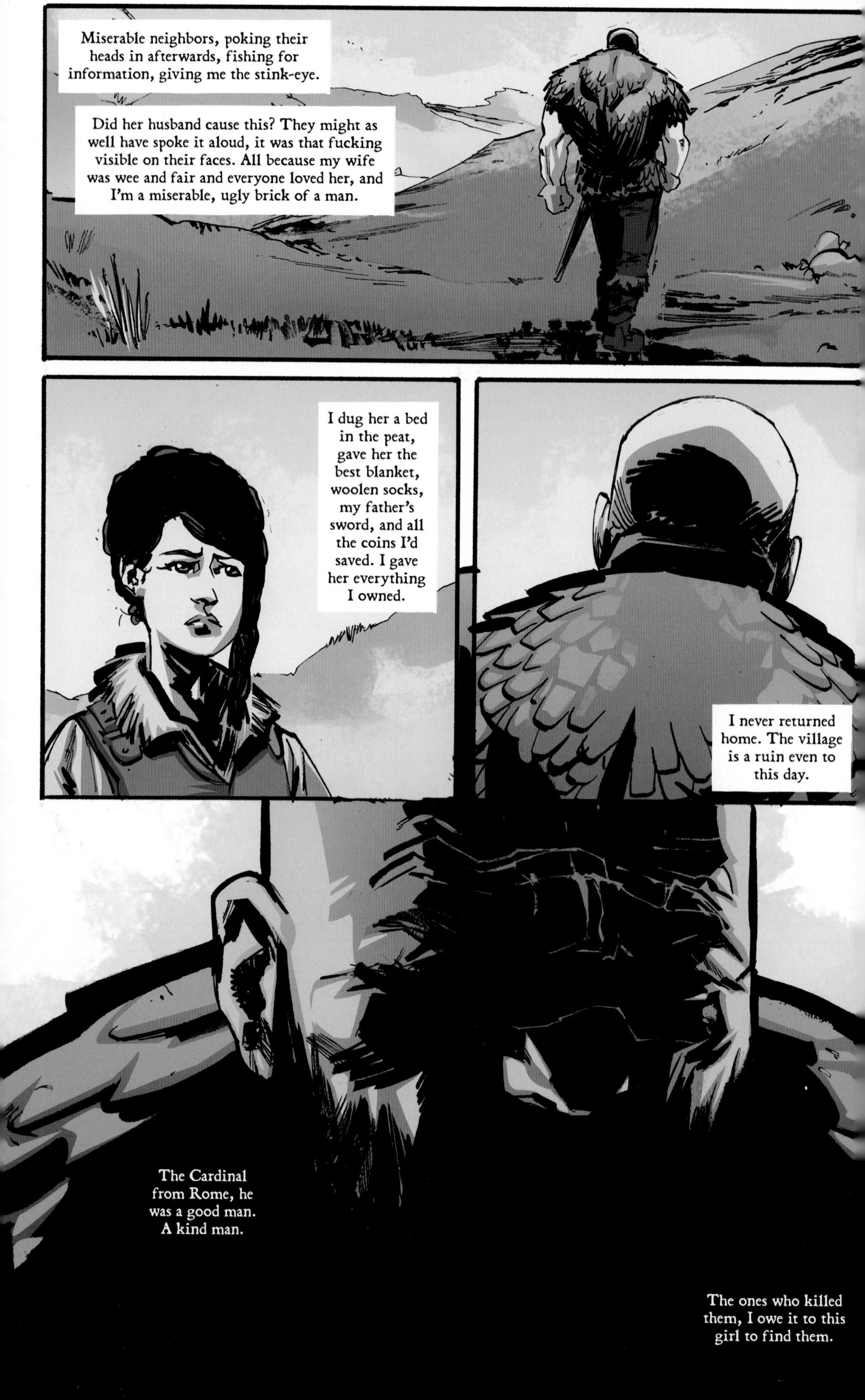

Miserable neighbors, poking their heads in afterwards, fishing for information, giving me the stink-eye.
Did her husband cause this? They might as well have spoke it aloud, it was that fucking visible on their faces. All because my wife was wee and fair and everyone loved her, and I'm a miserable, ugly brick of a man.
I dug her a bed in the peat, gave her the best blanket, woolen socks, my father's sword, and all the coins I'd saved. I gave her everything I owned.
I never returned home. The village is a ruin even to this day.
The Cardinal from Rome, he was a good man. A kind man.
The ones who killed them, I owe it to this girl to find them.

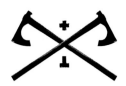

BRIAN WOOD / GARRY BROWN / DAVE McCAIG / STEVE WANDS

BLACK ROAD

#2 - "DAUGHTER OF ROME"

A MAGNUS THE BLACK MYSTERY

SOON.

We tracked the survivor, the man I wounded in the Farina execution, to some shit settlement in the bogs.

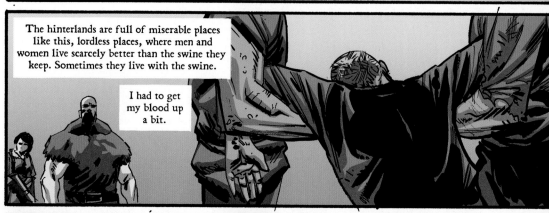

The hinterlands are full of miserable places like this, lordless places, where men and women live scarcely better than the swine they keep. Sometimes they live with the swine.

I had to get my blood up a bit.

But they soon saw reason and produced the Christian.

REMEMBER ME?

SPEAK UP.

YES. YES!

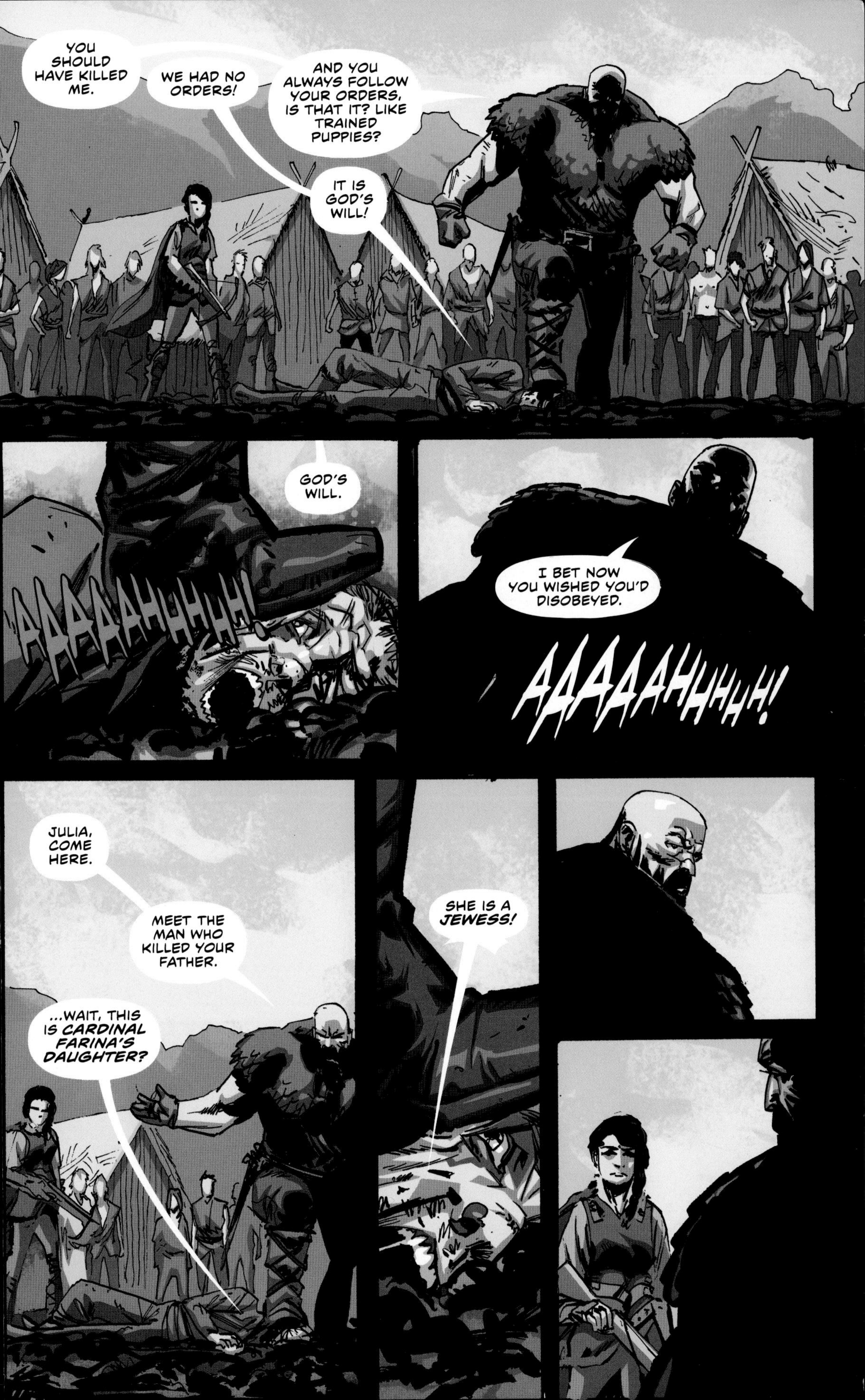
YOU SHOULD HAVE KILLED ME.
WE HAD NO ORDERS!
AND YOU ALWAYS FOLLOW YOUR ORDERS, IS THAT IT? LIKE TRAINED PUPPIES?
IT IS GOD'S WILL!
GOD'S WILL.
AAAAAHHHHH!
I BET NOW YOU WISHED YOU'D DISOBEYED.
AAAAAHHHHH!
JULIA, COME HERE.
MEET THE MAN WHO KILLED YOUR FATHER.
...WAIT, THIS IS CARDINAL FARINA'S DAUGHTER?
SHE IS A JEWESS!

I'M NOT SURE YOU'RE IN A POSITION TO JUDGE.

LISTEN! WHERE IS THIS MAN'S GEAR?

WE TOOK IT! WE'VE BEEN FEEDING THE PRICK! IT'S COMPENSATION!

TELL ME, WHAT DO YOU WANT WITH THE CARDINAL? WHY EXECUTE HIM ON THE BLACK ROAD?

HE IS AN APOSTATE!

IS THAT ALL? AND HERE I THOUGHT IT HAD SOMETHING TO DO WITH THE CHRISTIAN PROJECT UP NORTH.

HOW DO YOU KNOW-- AAAAAAHHH!

KRNNNCH

YOU'LL BURN IN HELL, PAGAN!

PROBABLY.

BUT AS LONG AS I WALK THIS WORLD, I TAKE MY JOB SERIOUSLY. AND YOU KILLED A CLIENT OF MINE.

WHO WAS ALSO SOMEONE'S FATHER.

I'M GOING TO ASK YOU SOME QUESTIONS. AND YOU SHOULD TALK TO ME, YOU KNOW. BECAUSE THE PEOPLE HOLDING YOU CAPTIVE?

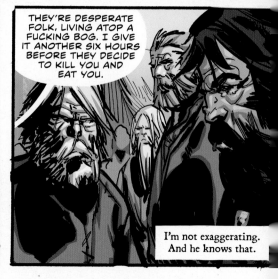

THEY'RE DESPERATE FOLK, LIVING ATOP A FUCKING BOG. I GIVE IT ANOTHER SIX HOURS BEFORE THEY DECIDE TO KILL YOU AND EAT YOU.

I'm not exaggerating. And he knows that.

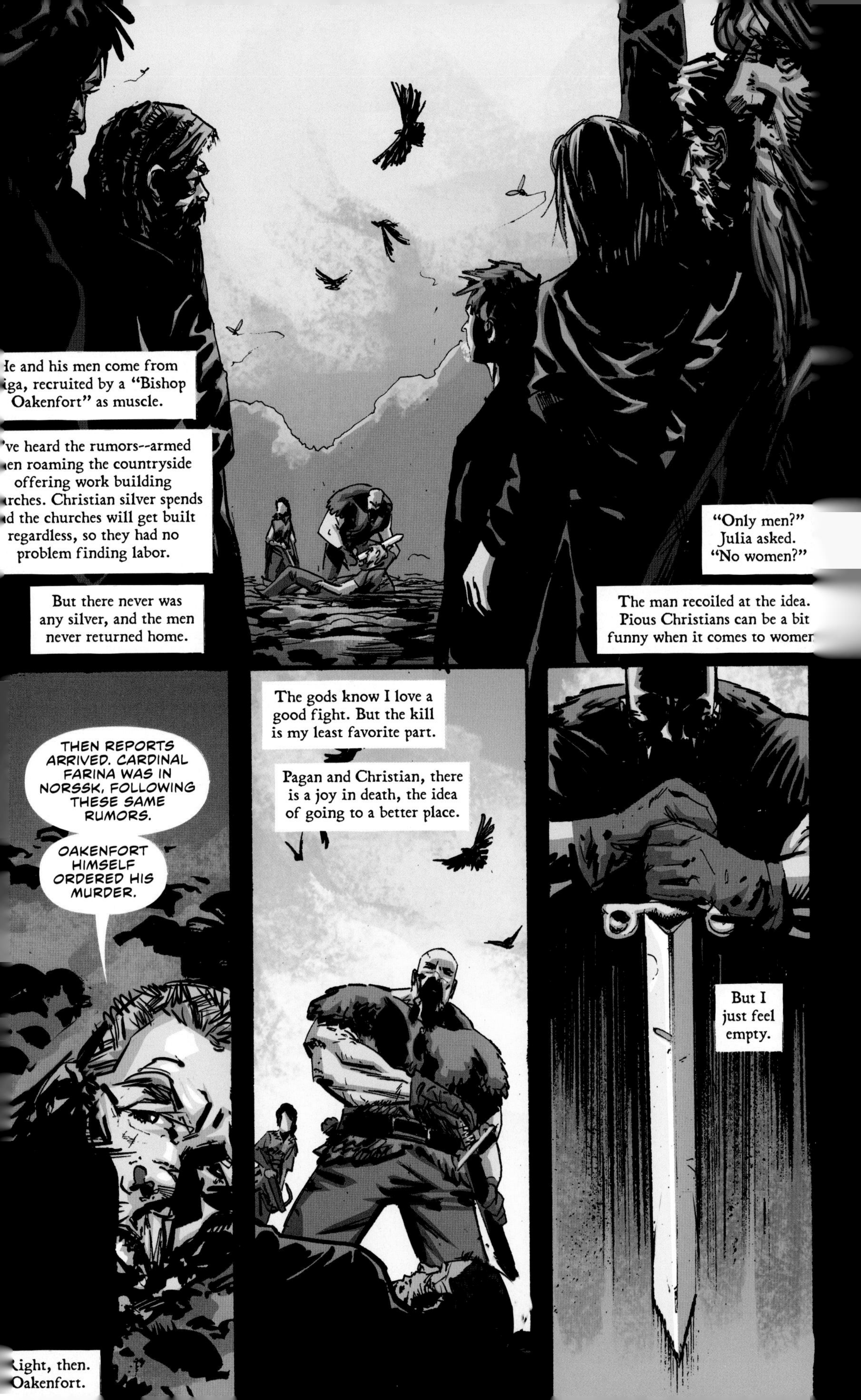

e and his men come from iga, recruited by a "Bishop Oakenfort" as muscle.
've heard the rumors--armed en roaming the countryside offering work building rches. Christian silver spends d the churches will get built regardless, so they had no problem finding labor.
But there never was any silver, and the men never returned home.
"Only men?" Julia asked. "No women?"
The man recoiled at the idea. Pious Christians can be a bit funny when it comes to women
THEN REPORTS ARRIVED. CARDINAL FARINA WAS IN NORSSK, FOLLOWING THESE SAME RUMORS.
OAKENFORT HIMSELF ORDERED HIS MURDER.
ight, then. Oakenfort.
The gods know I love a good fight. But the kill is my least favorite part.
Pagan and Christian, there is a joy in death, the idea of going to a better place.
But I just feel empty.

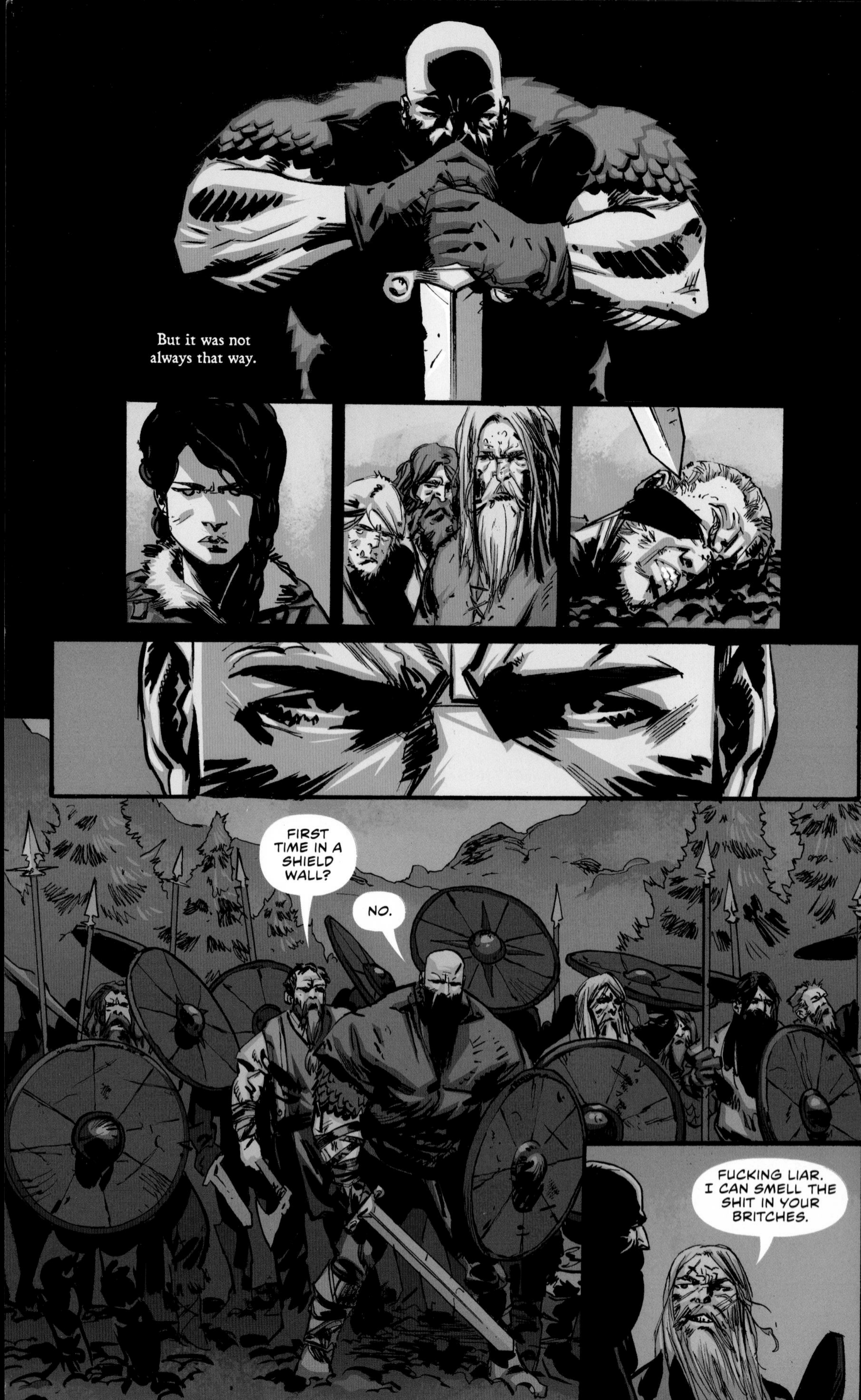
But it was not always that way.
FIRST TIME IN A SHIELD WALL?
NO.
FUCKING LIAR. I CAN SMELL THE SHIT IN YOUR BRITCHES.

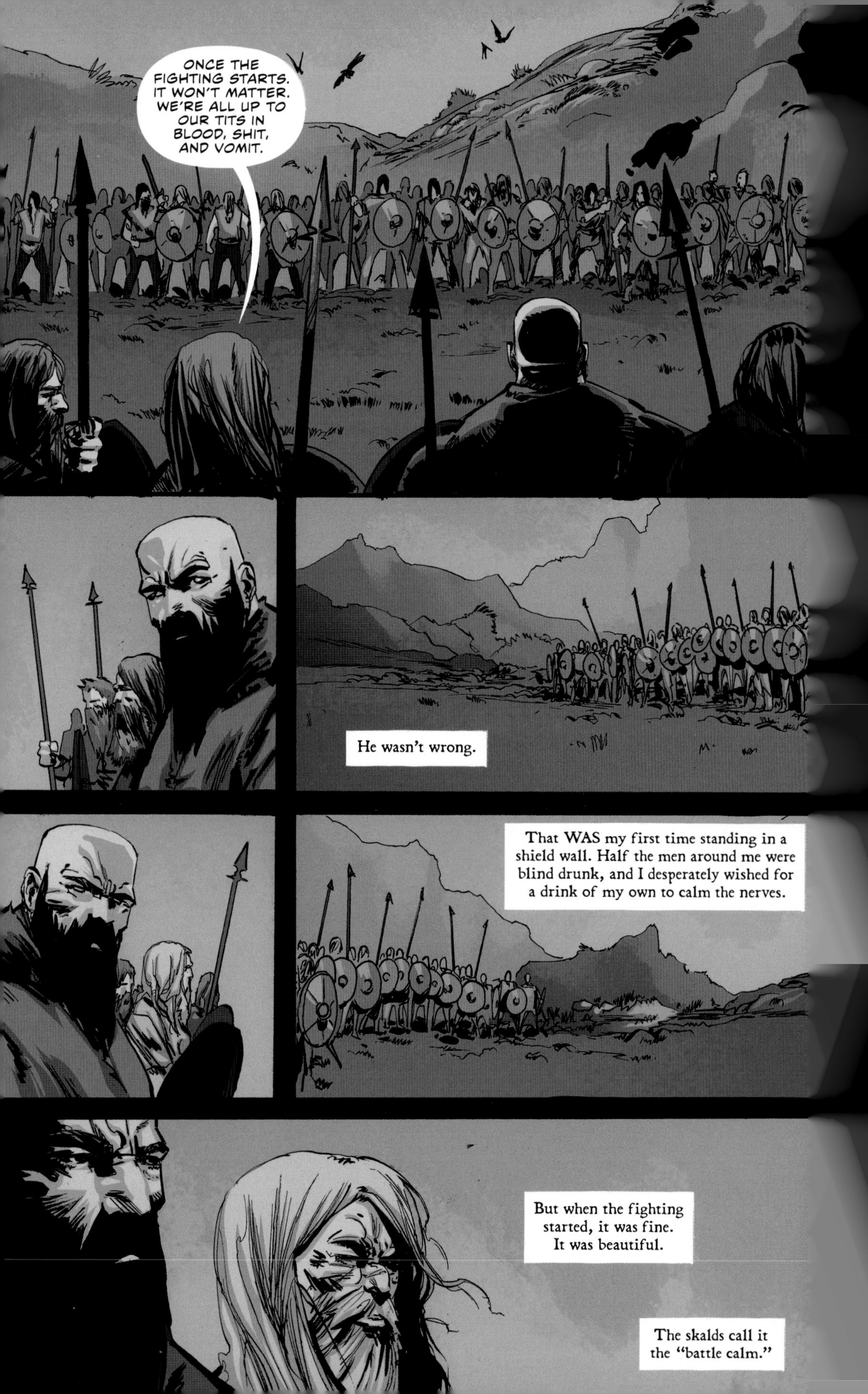
ONCE THE FIGHTING STARTS. IT WON'T MATTER. WE'RE ALL UP TO OUR TITS IN BLOOD, SHIT, AND VOMIT.
He wasn't wrong.
That WAS my first time standing in a shield wall. Half the men around me were blind drunk, and I desperately wished for a drink of my own to calm the nerves.
But when the fighting started, it was fine. It was beautiful.
The skalds call it the "battle calm."

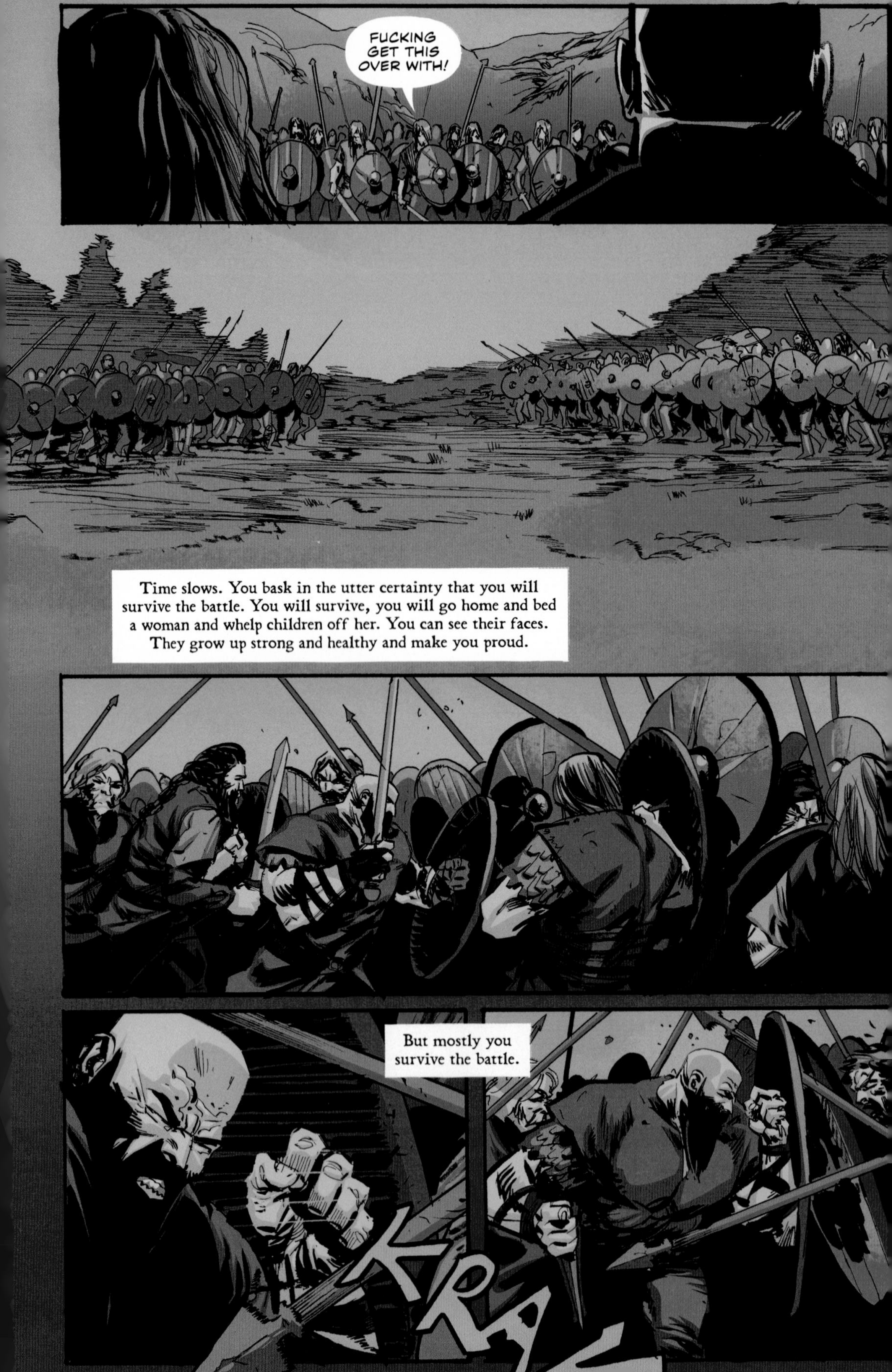
FUCKING GET THIS OVER WITH!
Time slows. You bask in the utter certainty that you will survive the battle. You will survive, you will go home and bed a woman and whelp children off her. You can see their faces. They grow up strong and healthy and make you proud.
But mostly you survive the battle.

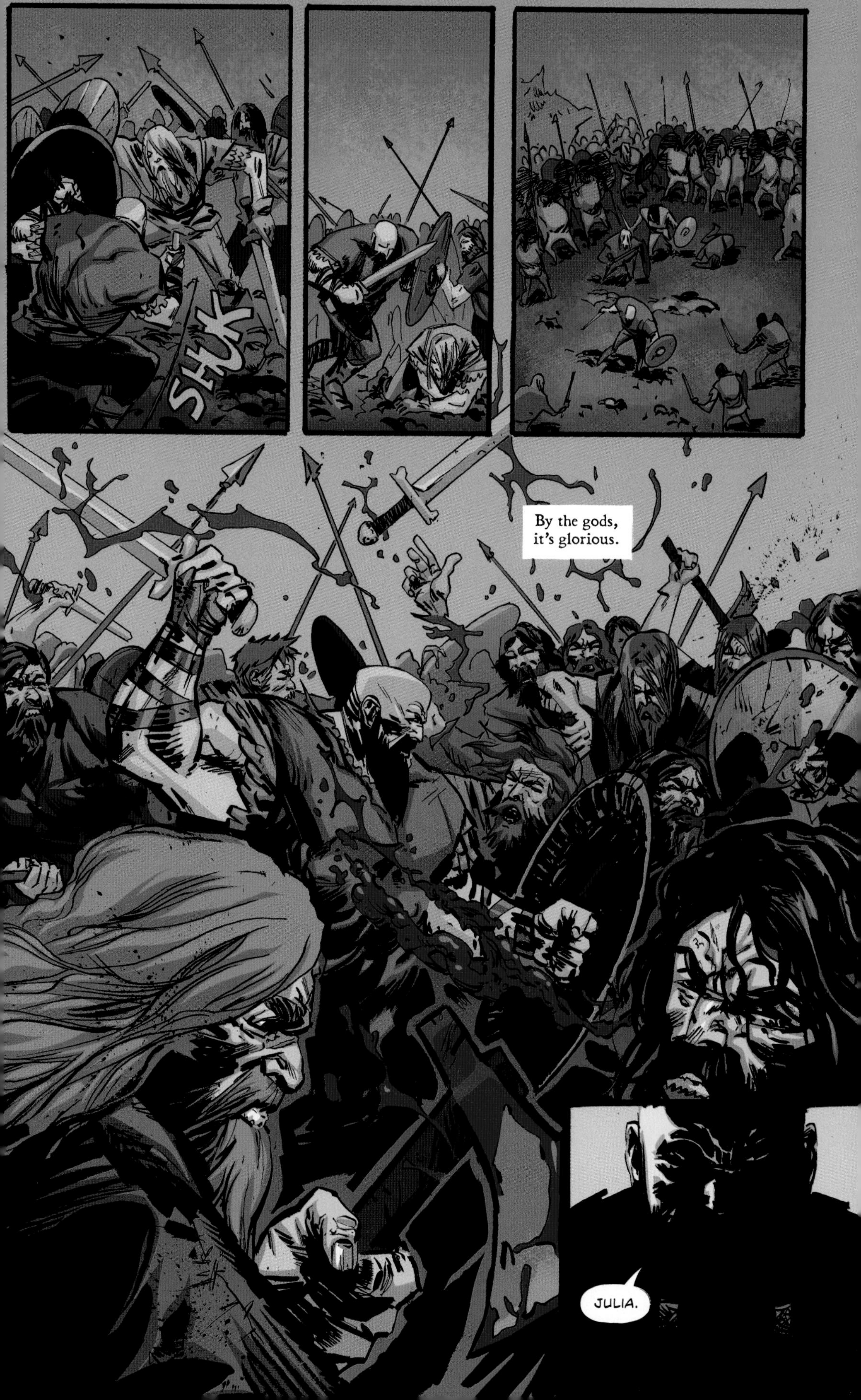
SHUK
By the gods,
it's glorious.
JULIA.

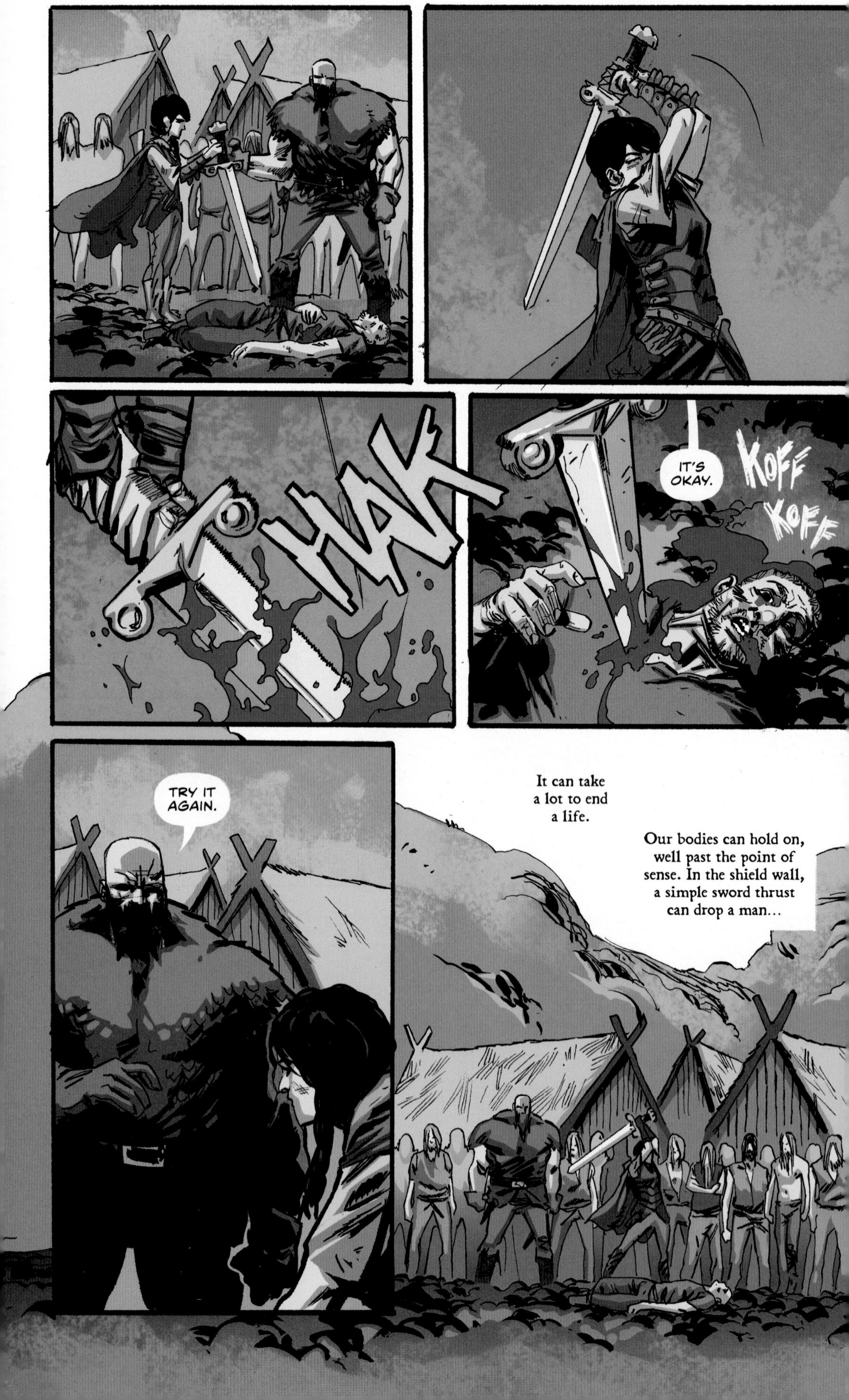
THAK
IT'S OKAY.
KOFF
KOFF
TRY IT AGAIN.
It can take a lot to end a life.
Our bodies can hold on, well past the point of sense. In the shield wall, a simple sword thrust can drop a man...

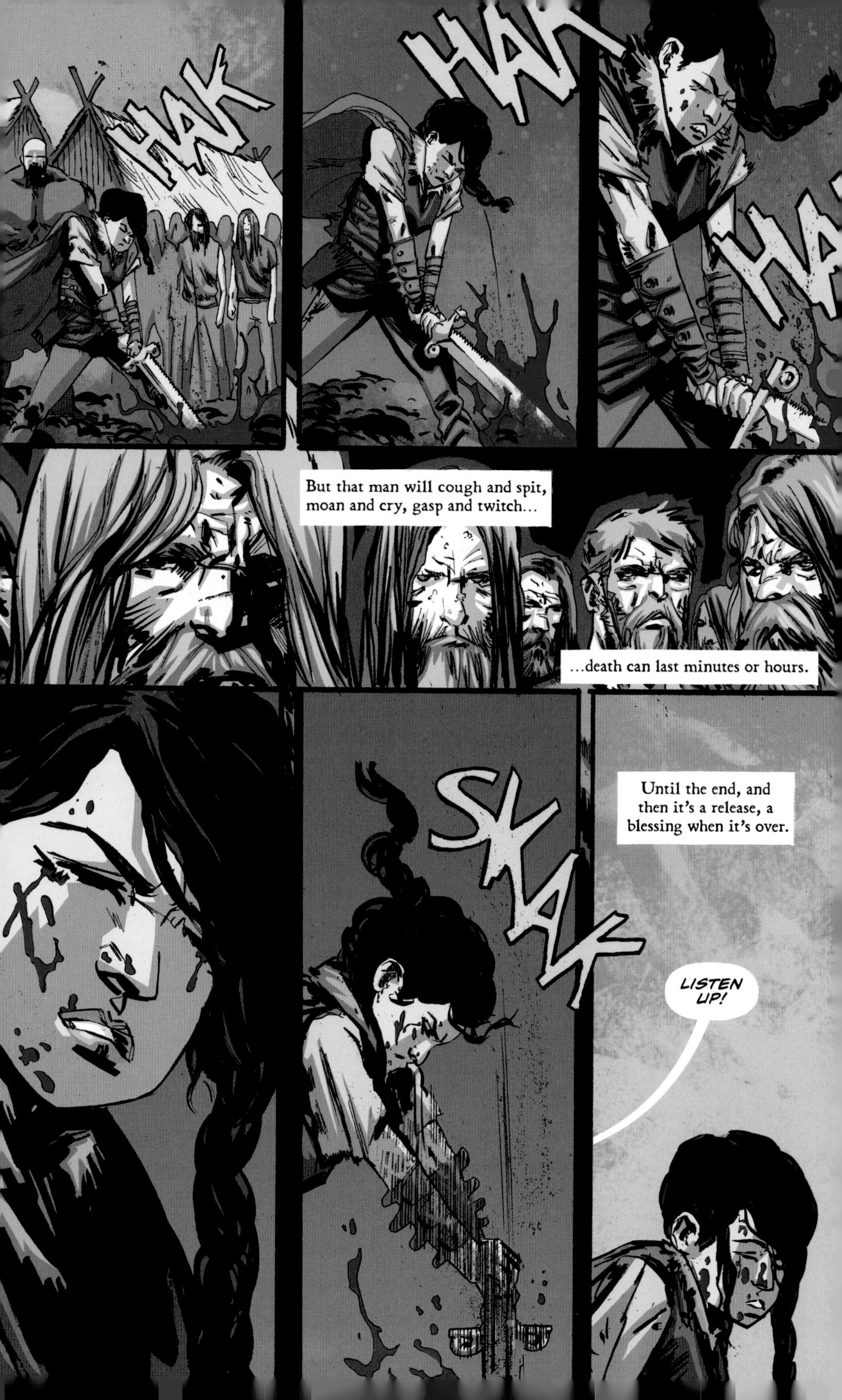
HAK
HAK
HA
But that man will cough and spit, moan and cry, gasp and twitch...
...death can last minutes or hours.
SKAK
Until the end, and then it's a release, a blessing when it's over.
LISTEN UP!

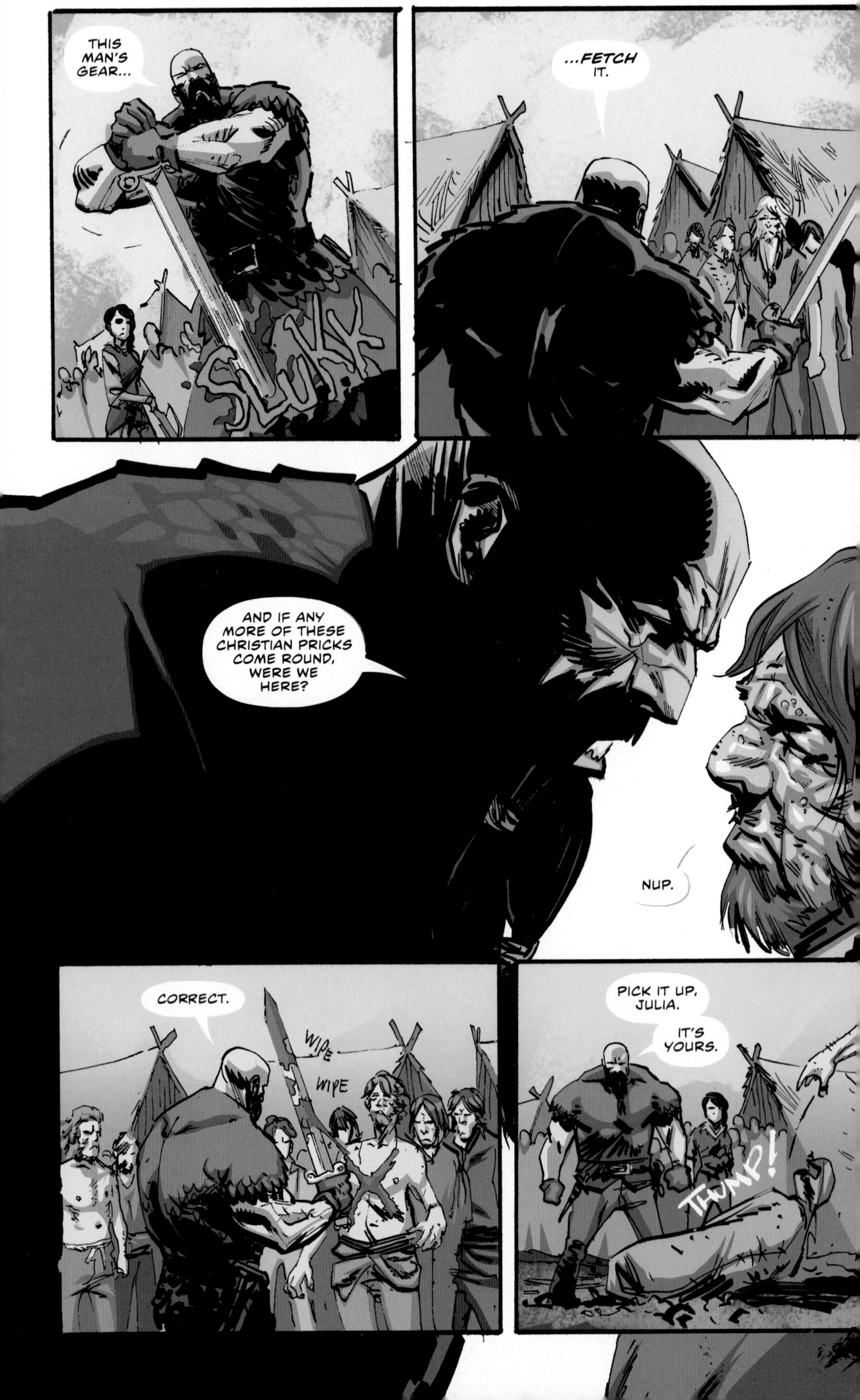
THIS MAN'S GEAR...
SLUKK
...FETCH IT.
AND IF ANY MORE OF THESE CHRISTIAN PRICKS COME ROUND, WERE WE HERE?
NUP.
CORRECT.
WIPE
WIPE
PICK IT UP, JULIA.
IT'S YOURS.
THUMP!

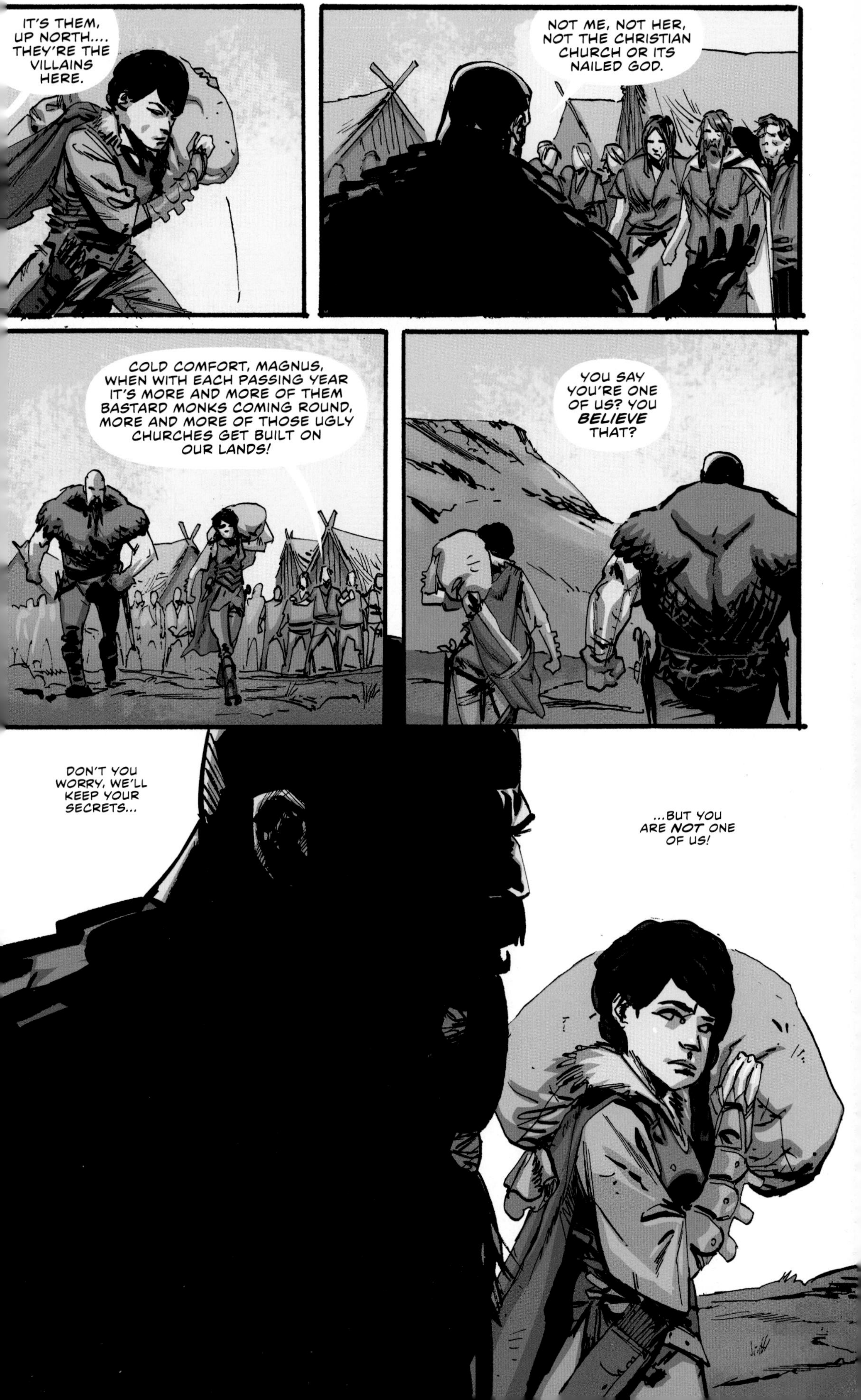
IT'S THEM, UP NORTH.... THEY'RE THE VILLAINS HERE.
NOT ME, NOT HER, NOT THE CHRISTIAN CHURCH OR ITS NAILED GOD.
COLD COMFORT, MAGNUS, WHEN WITH EACH PASSING YEAR IT'S MORE AND MORE OF THEM BASTARD MONKS COMING ROUND, MORE AND MORE OF THOSE UGLY CHURCHES GET BUILT ON OUR LANDS!
YOU SAY YOU'RE ONE OF US? YOU BELIEVE THAT?
DON'T YOU WORRY, WE'LL KEEP YOUR SECRETS...
...BUT YOU ARE NOT ONE OF US!

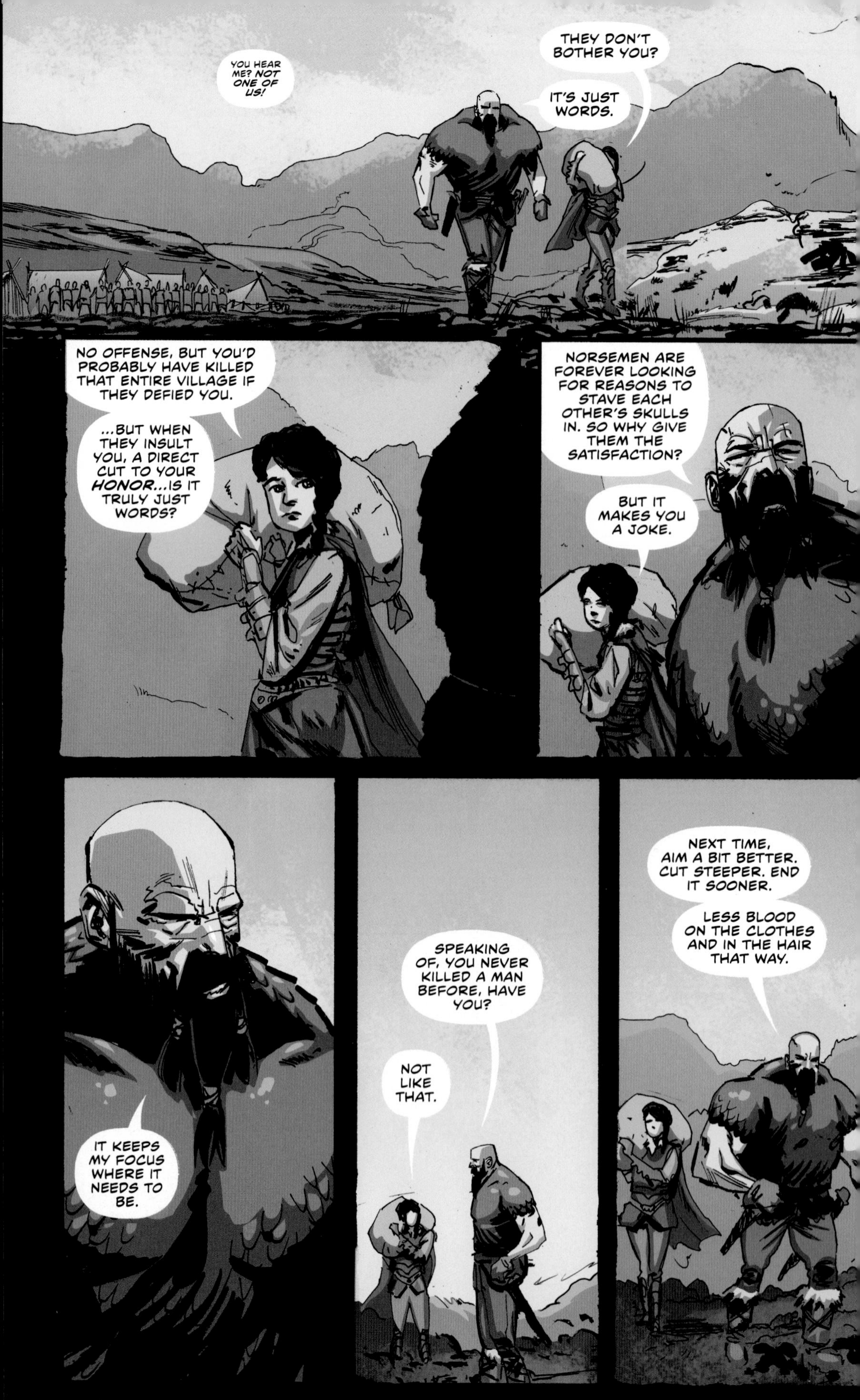
YOU HEAR ME? NOT ONE OF US!
THEY DON'T BOTHER YOU?
IT'S JUST WORDS.
NO OFFENSE, BUT YOU'D PROBABLY HAVE KILLED THAT ENTIRE VILLAGE IF THEY DEFIED YOU.
...BUT WHEN THEY INSULT YOU, A DIRECT CUT TO YOUR HONOR...IS IT TRULY JUST WORDS?
NORSEMEN ARE FOREVER LOOKING FOR REASONS TO STAVE EACH OTHER'S SKULLS IN. SO WHY GIVE THEM THE SATISFACTION?
BUT IT MAKES YOU A JOKE.
IT KEEPS MY FOCUS WHERE IT NEEDS TO BE.
SPEAKING OF, YOU NEVER KILLED A MAN BEFORE, HAVE YOU?
NOT LIKE THAT.
NEXT TIME, AIM A BIT BETTER. CUT STEEPER. END IT SOONER.
LESS BLOOD ON THE CLOTHES AND IN THE HAIR THAT WAY.

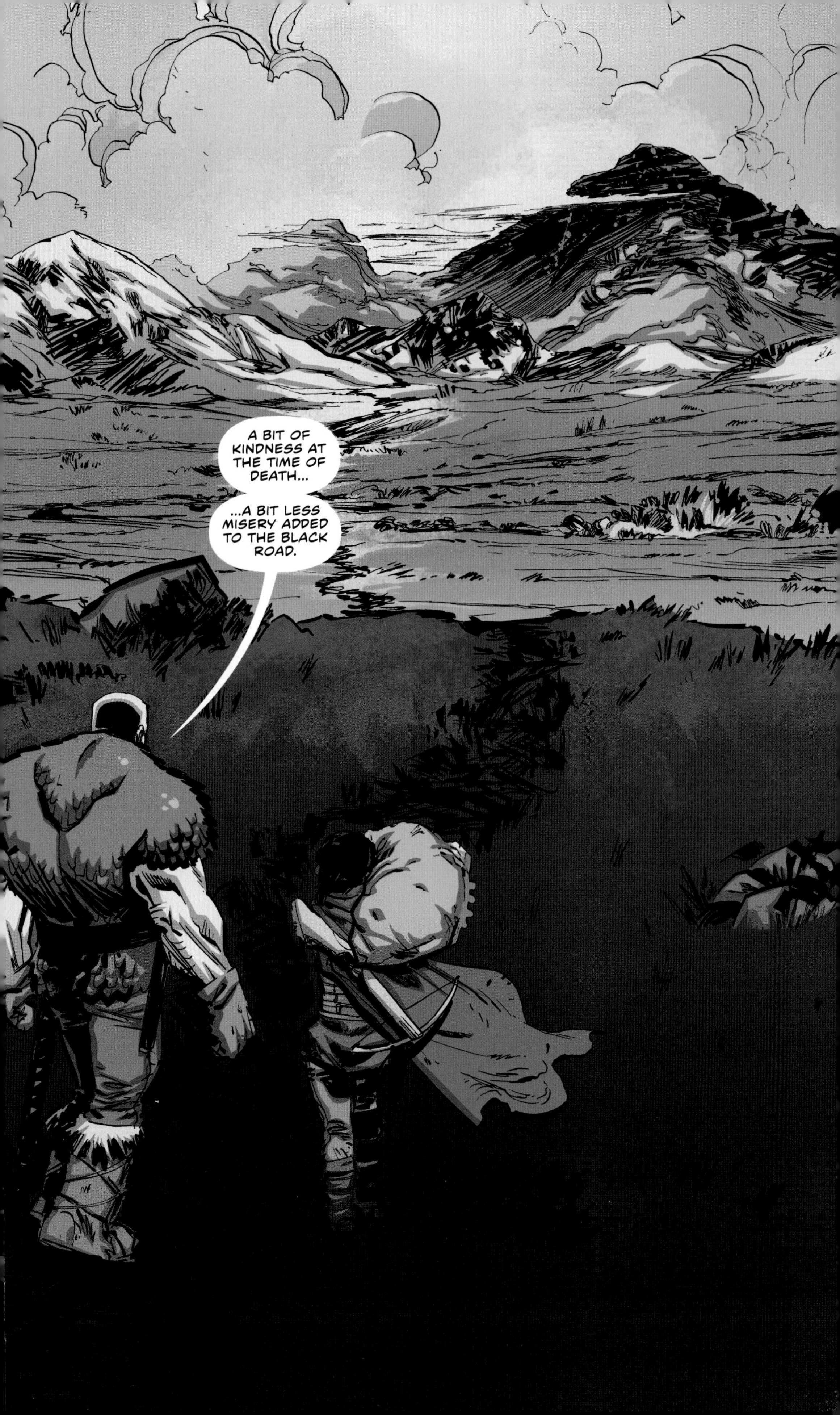
A BIT OF KINDNESS AT THE TIME OF DEATH...
...A BIT LESS MISERY ADDED TO THE BLACK ROAD.

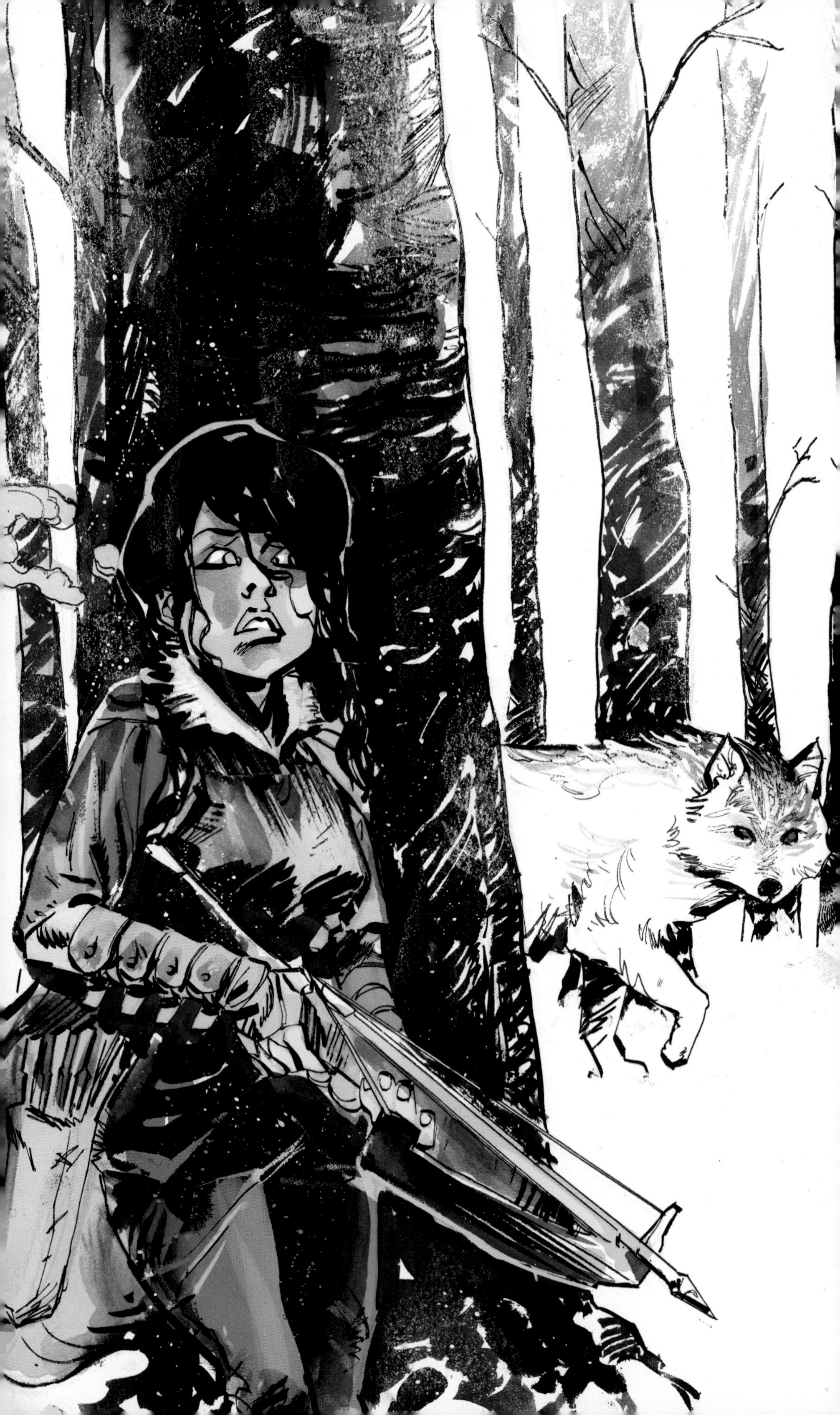

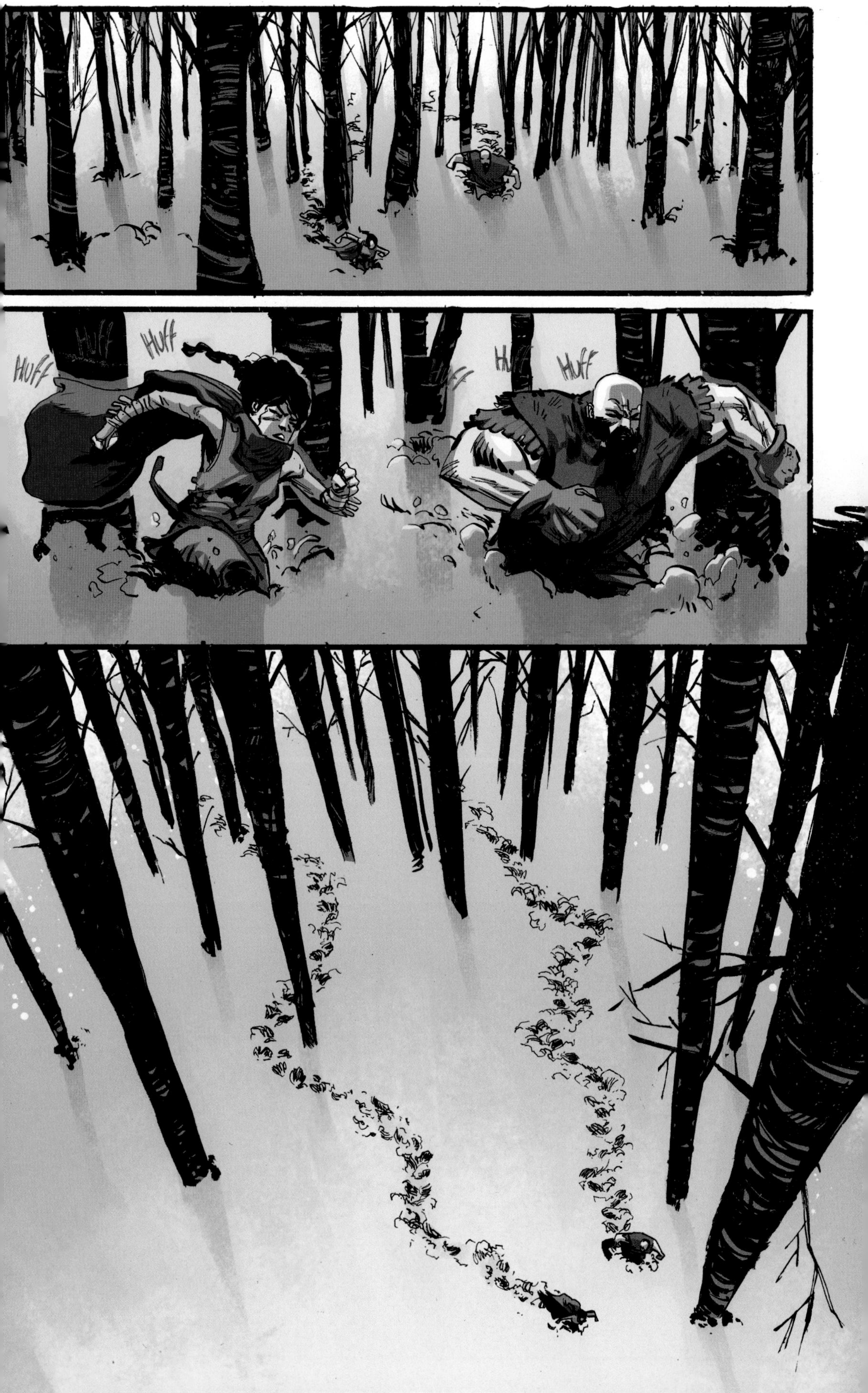

HUFF
HUFF
HUFF
HUFF
HUFF
HUFF

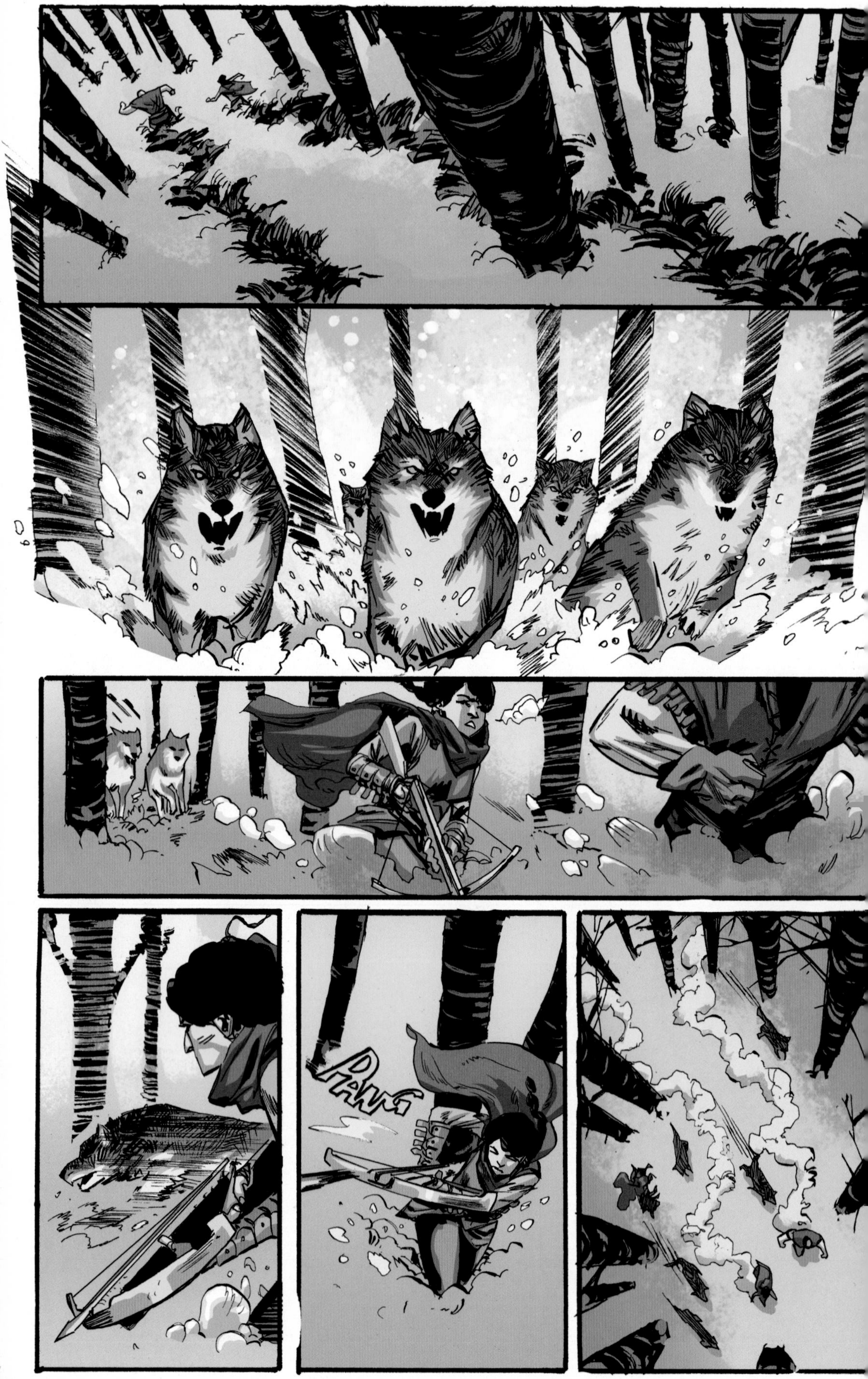
PTANG

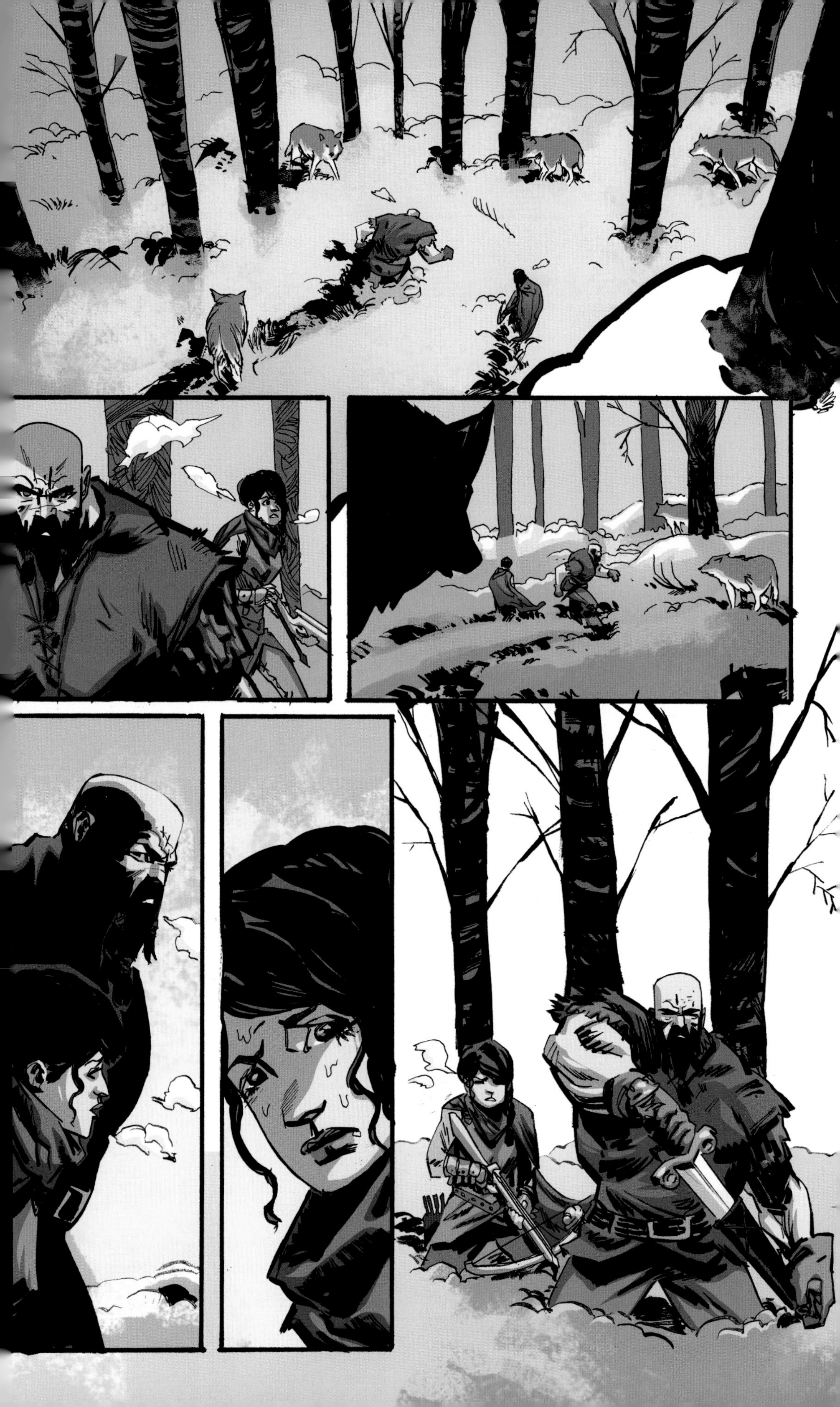

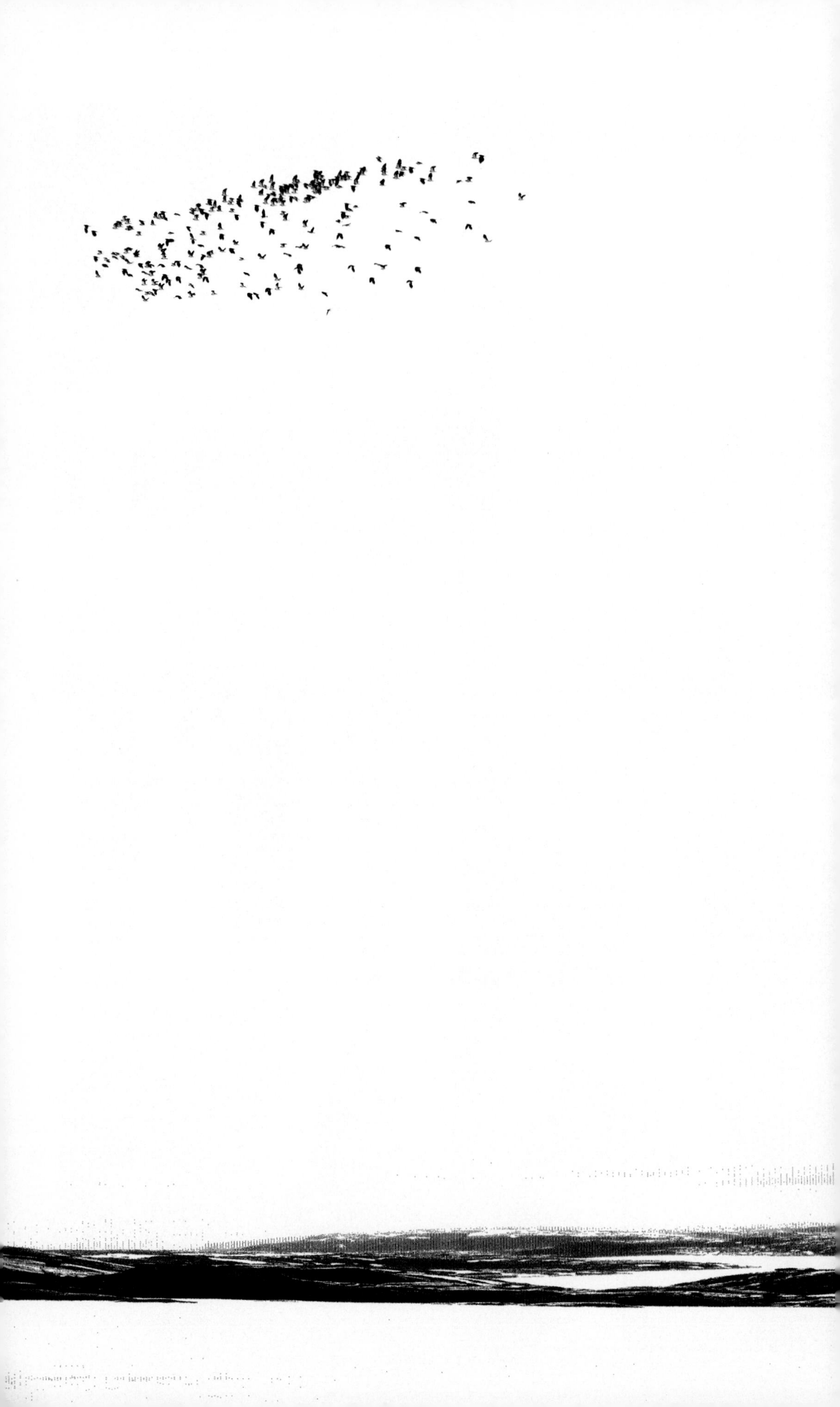

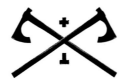

BRIAN WOOD / GARRY BROWN / DAVE McCAIG / STEVE WANDS

BLACK ROAD

#3 - OUT COME THE WOLVES

A MAGNUS THE BLACK MYSTERY

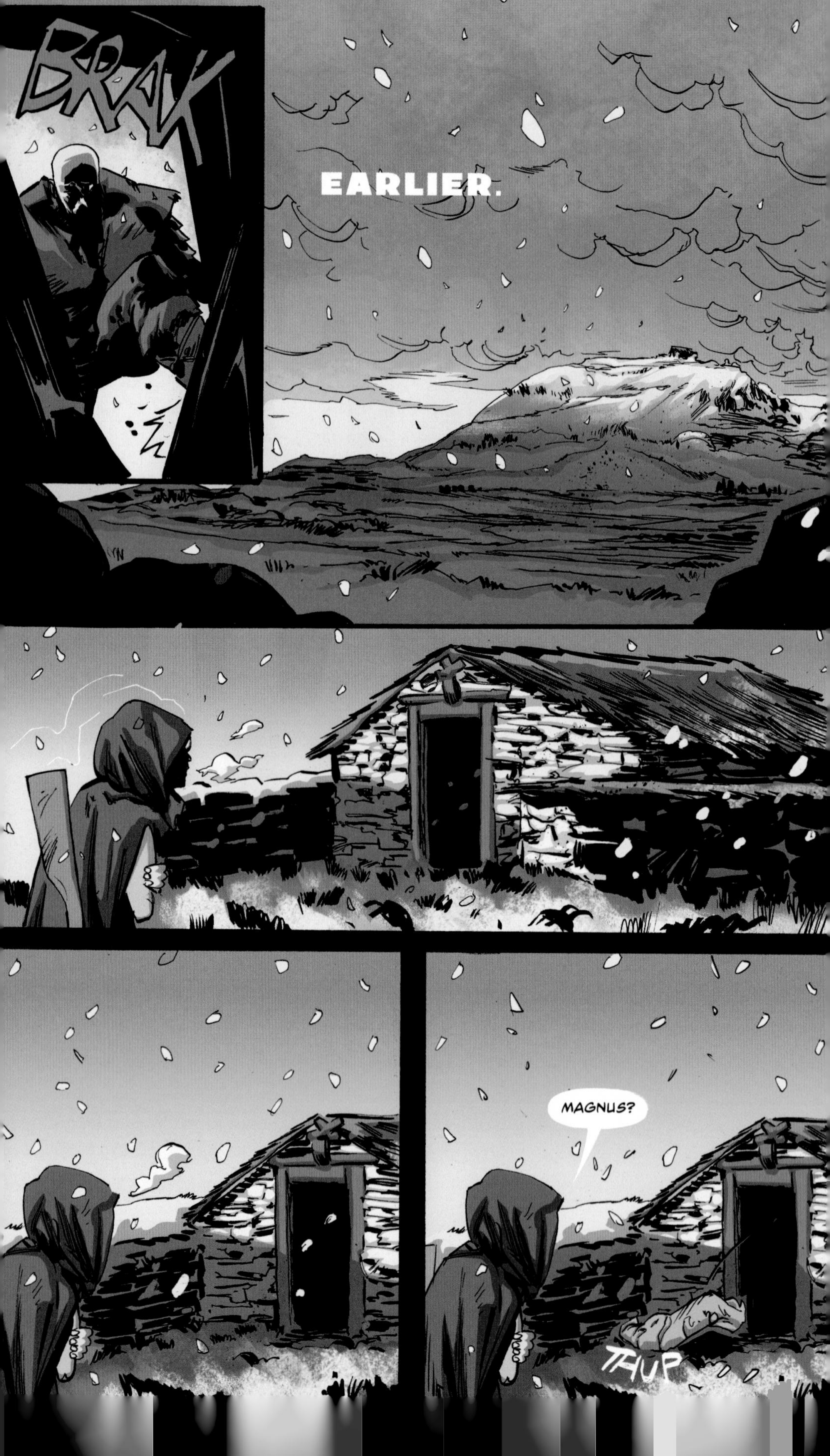
BRAK
EARLIER.
MAGNUS?
THUP

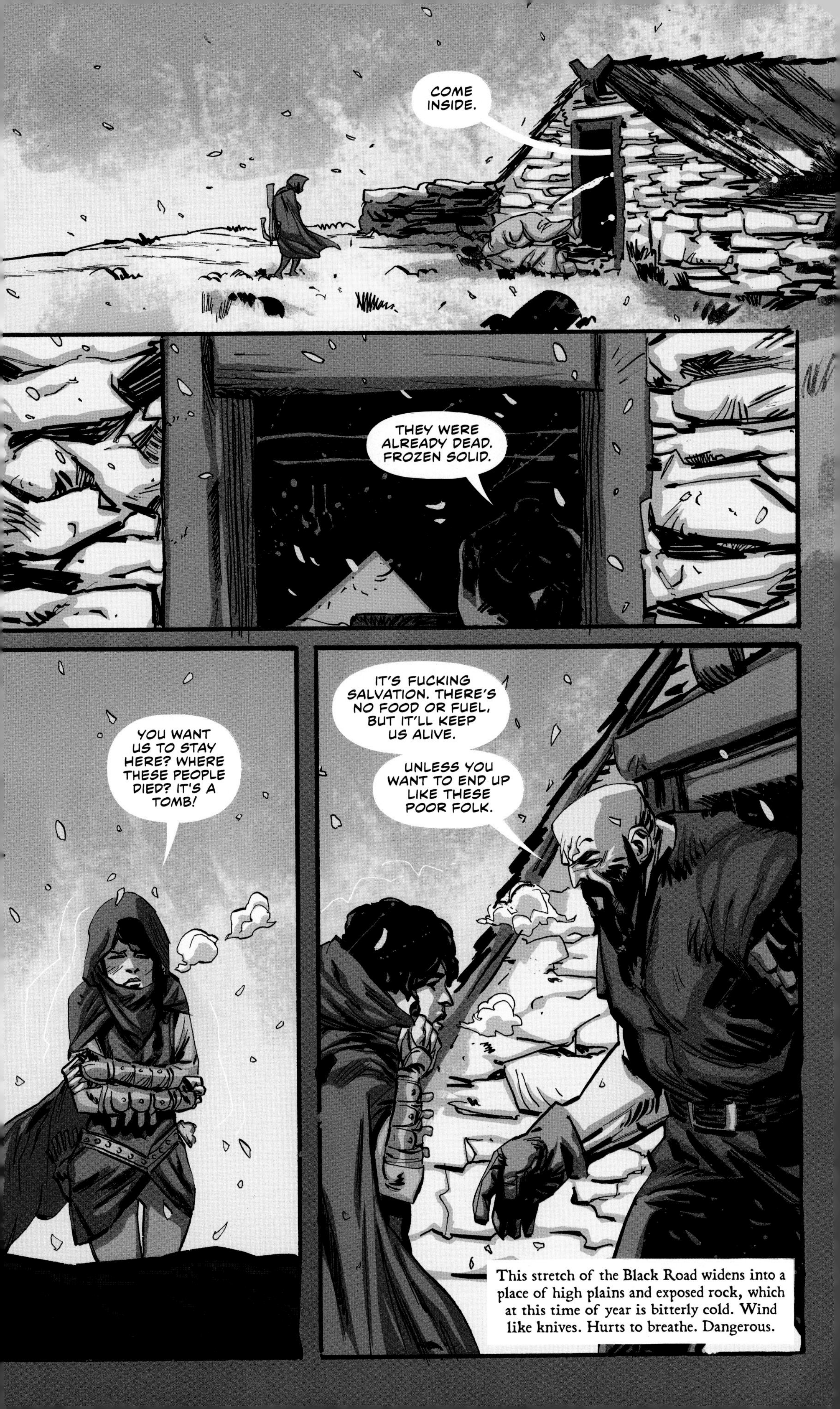
COME INSIDE.
THEY WERE ALREADY DEAD. FROZEN SOLID.
YOU WANT US TO STAY HERE? WHERE THESE PEOPLE DIED? IT'S A TOMB!
IT'S FUCKING SALVATION. THERE'S NO FOOD OR FUEL, BUT IT'LL KEEP US ALIVE.
UNLESS YOU WANT TO END UP LIKE THESE POOR FOLK.
This stretch of the Black Road widens into a place of high plains and exposed rock, which at this time of year is bitterly cold. Wind like knives. Hurts to breathe. Dangerous.

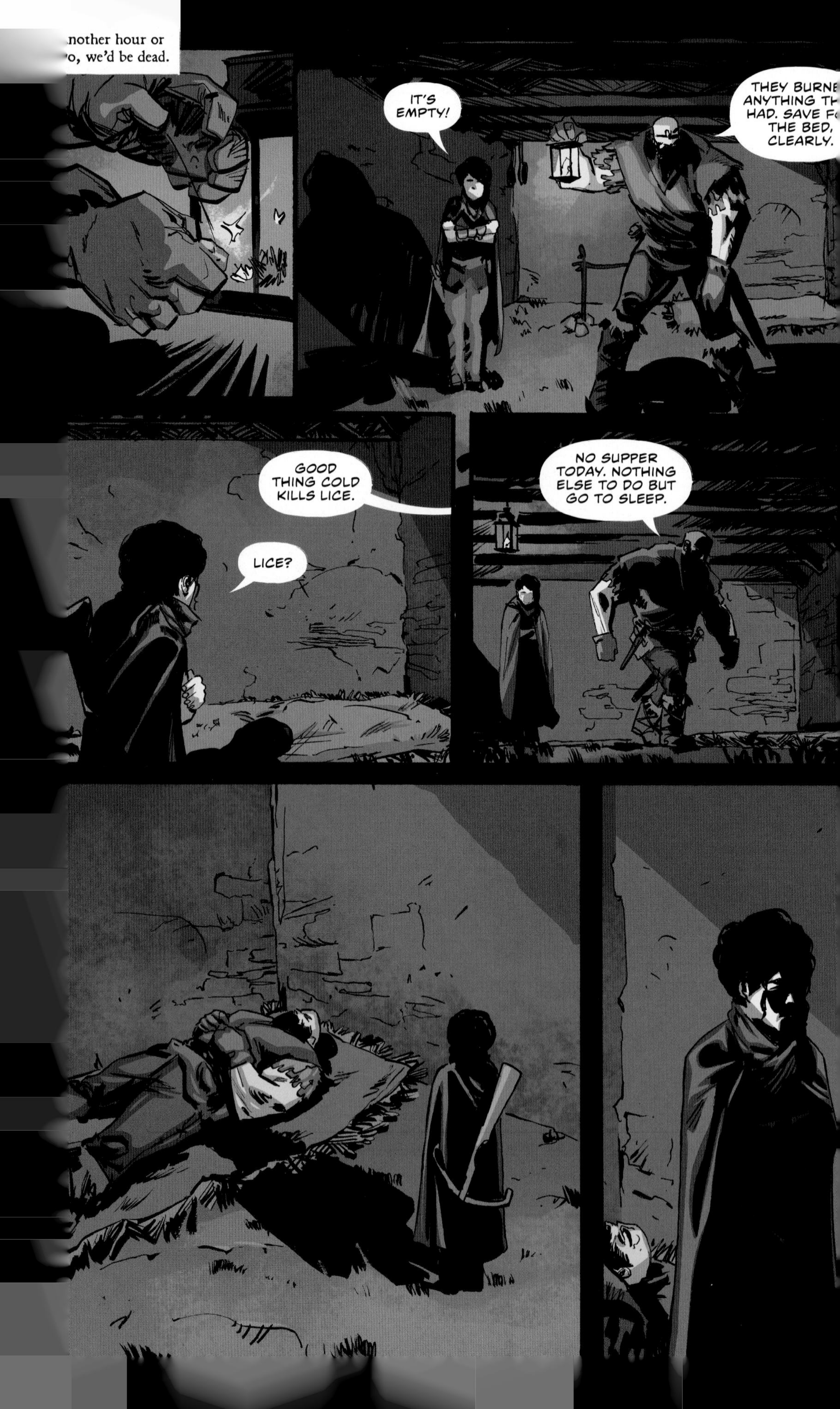
nother hour or
o, we'd be dead.
IT'S EMPTY!
THEY BURNE
ANYTHING T
HAD. SAVE F
THE BED,
CLEARLY.
GOOD THING COLD KILLS LICE.
LICE?
NO SUPPER TODAY. NOTHING ELSE TO DO BUT GO TO SLEEP.

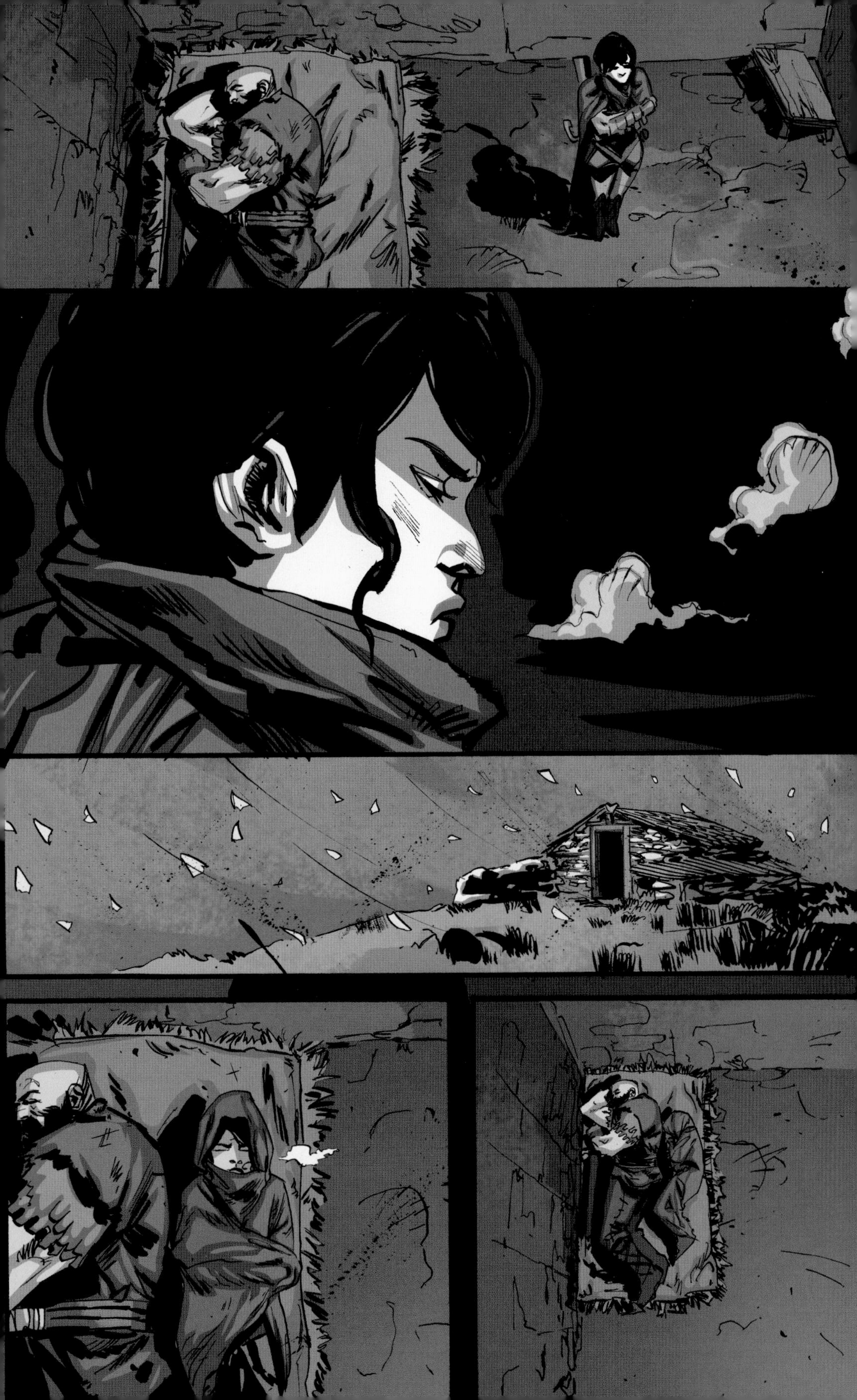

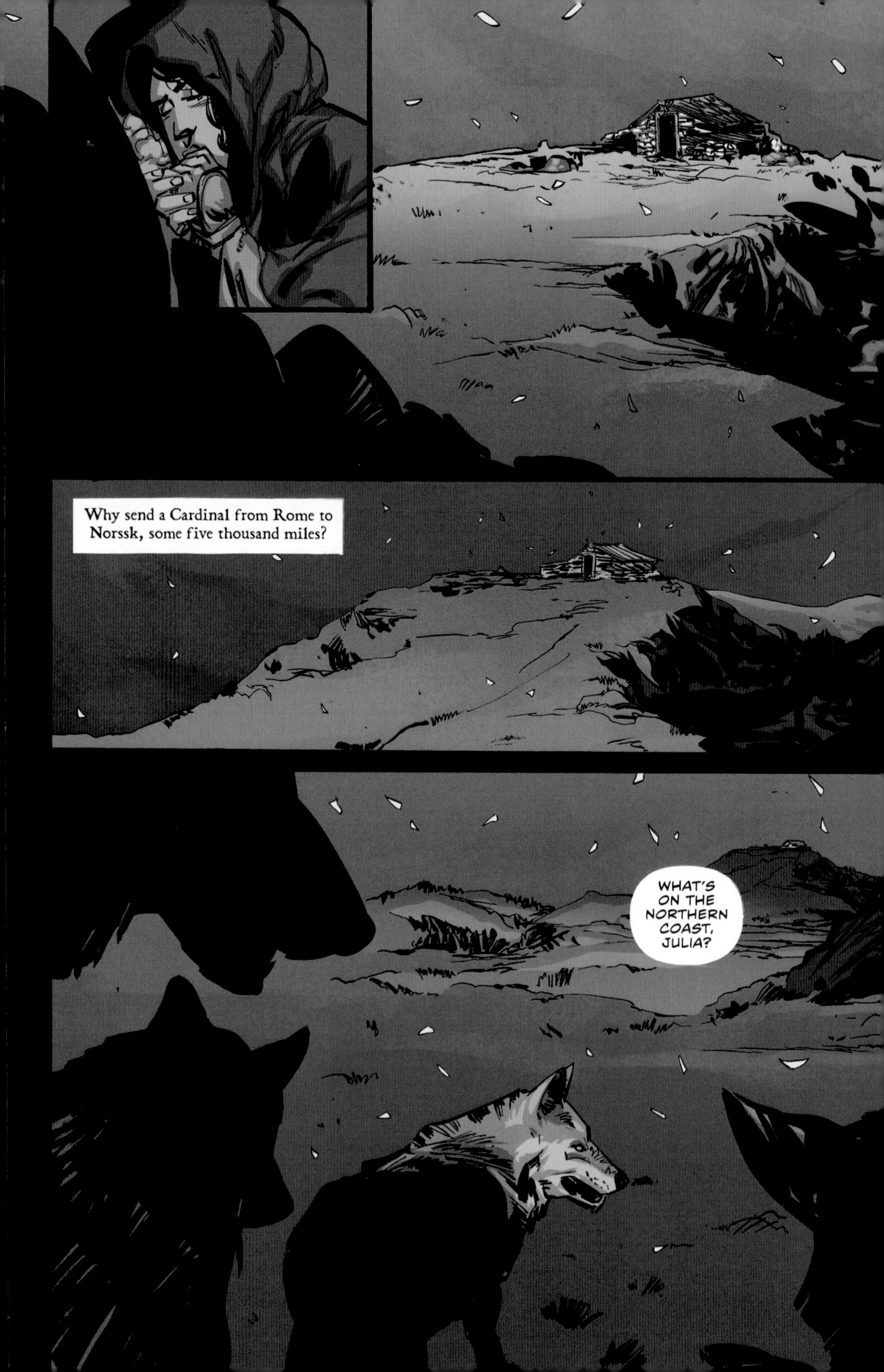
Why send a Cardinal from Rome to Norssk, some five thousand miles?
WHAT'S ON THE NORTHERN COAST, JULIA?

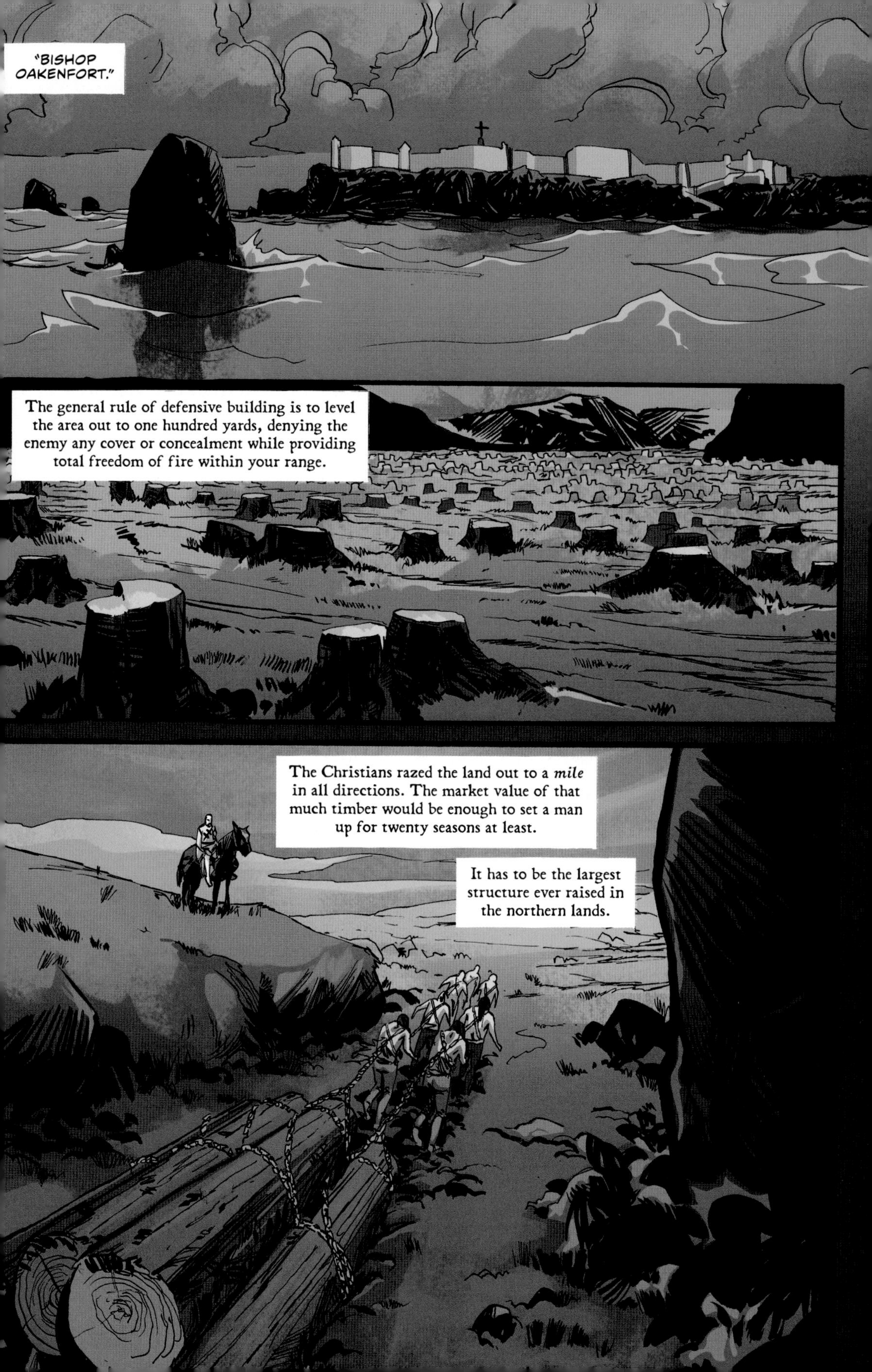
"BISHOP OAKENFORT."
The general rule of defensive building is to level the area out to one hundred yards, denying the enemy any cover or concealment while providing total freedom of fire within your range.
The Christians razed the land out to a *mile* in all directions. The market value of that much timber would be enough to set a man up for twenty seasons at least.
It has to be the largest structure ever raised in the northern lands.

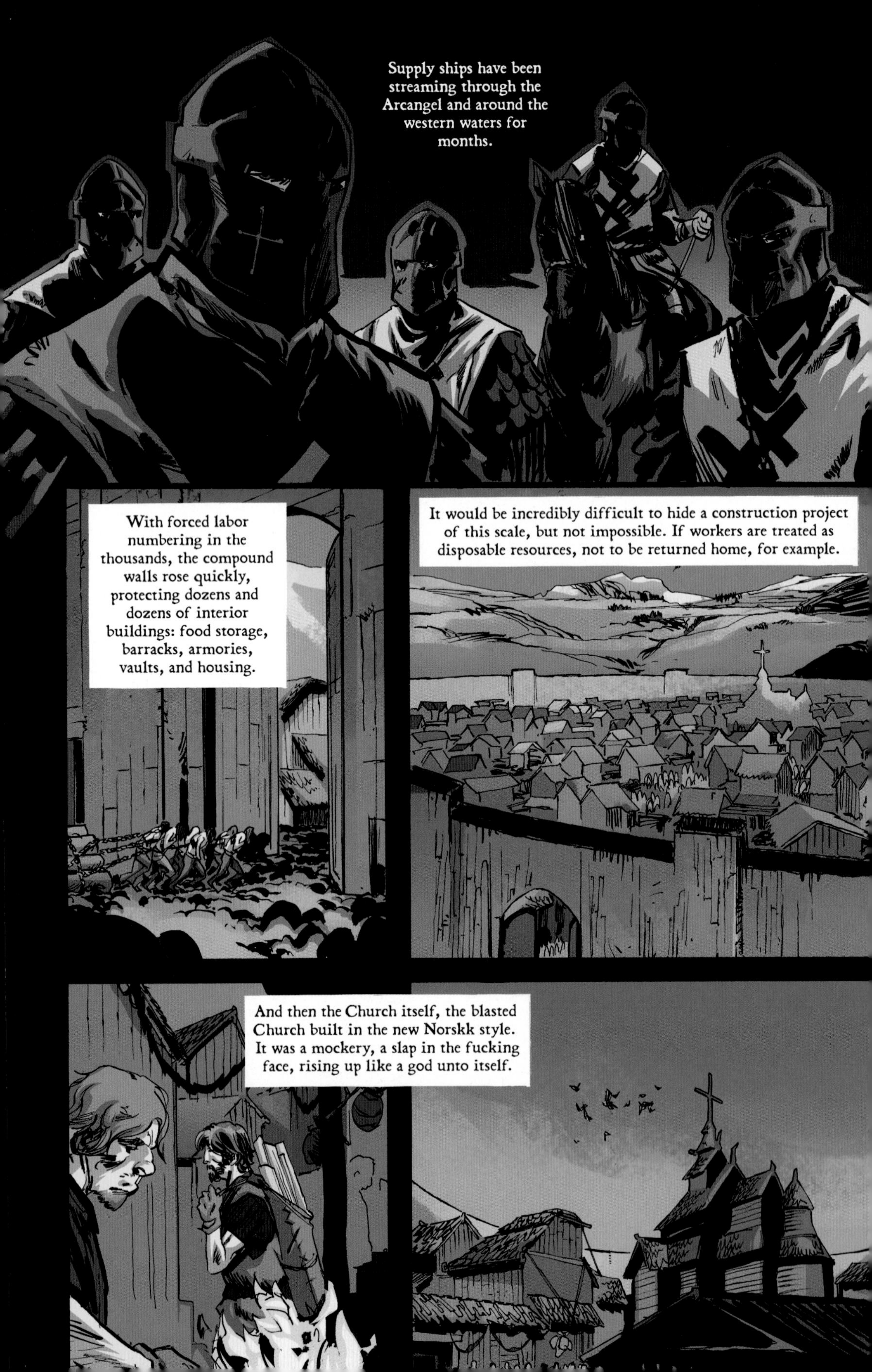
Supply ships have been streaming through the Arcangel and around the western waters for months.
With forced labor numbering in the thousands, the compound walls rose quickly, protecting dozens and dozens of interior buildings: food storage, barracks, armories, vaults, and housing.
It would be incredibly difficult to hide a construction project of this scale, but not impossible. If workers are treated as disposable resources, not to be returned home, for example.
And then the Church itself, the blasted Church built in the new Norskk style. It was a mockery, a slap in the fucking face, rising up like a god unto itself.

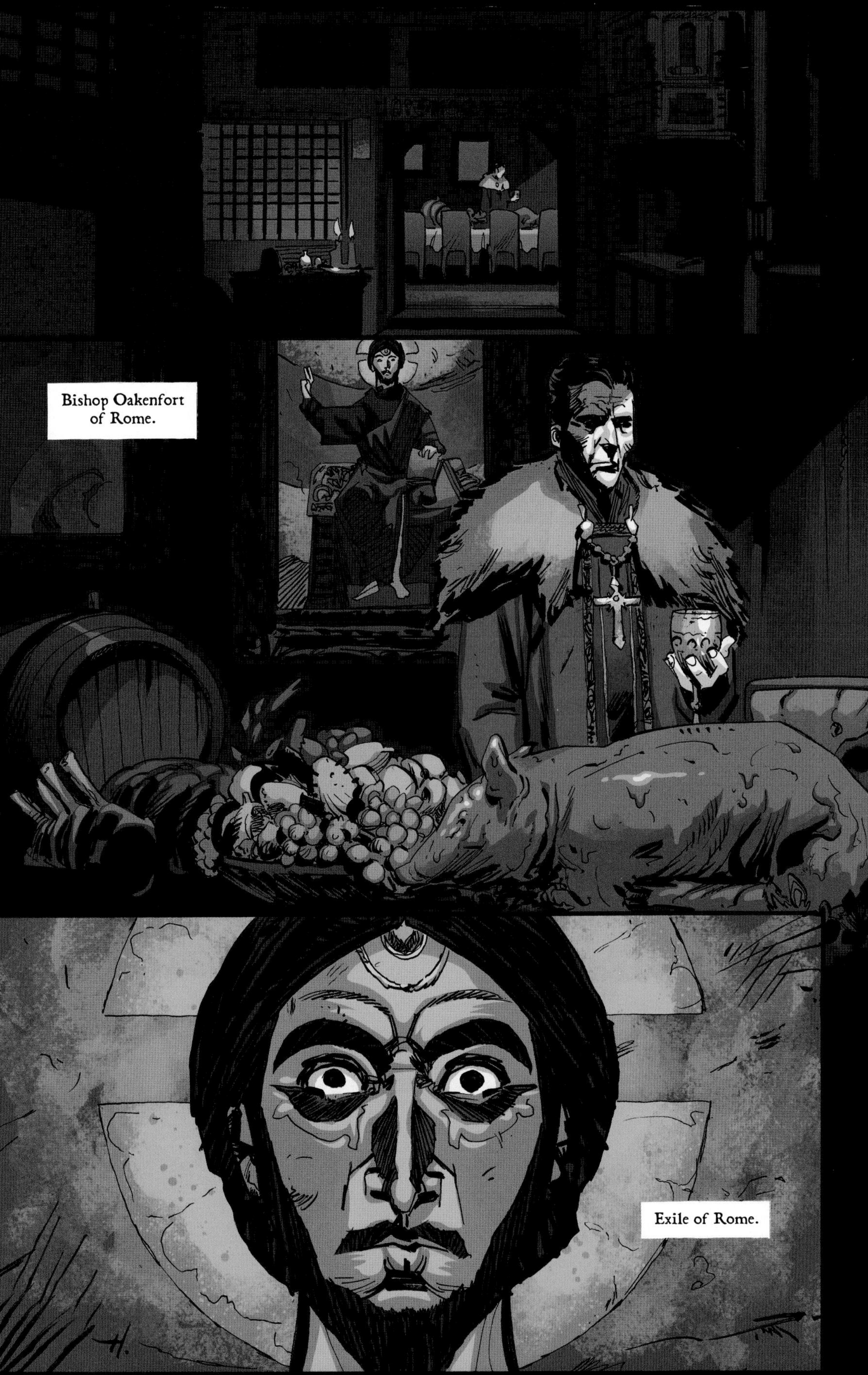
Bishop Oakenfort of Rome.
Exile of Rome.

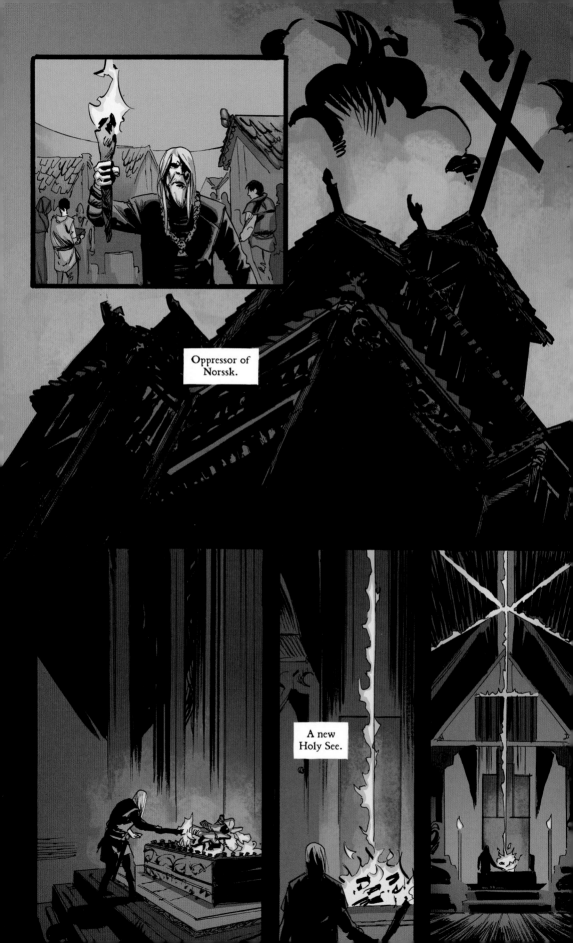

Oppressor of Norssk.

A new Holy See.

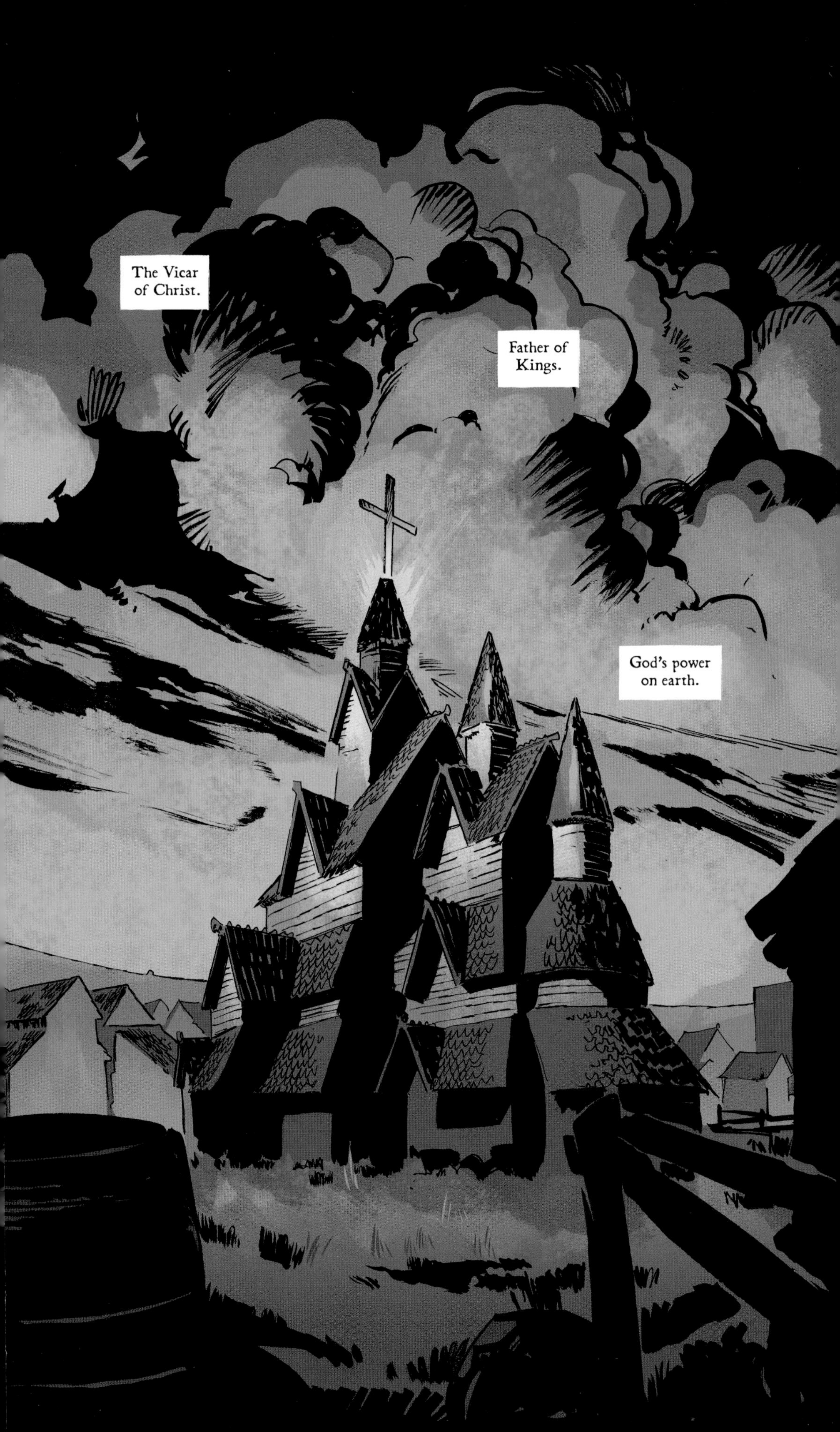
The Vicar
of Christ.
Father of
Kings.
God's power
on earth.

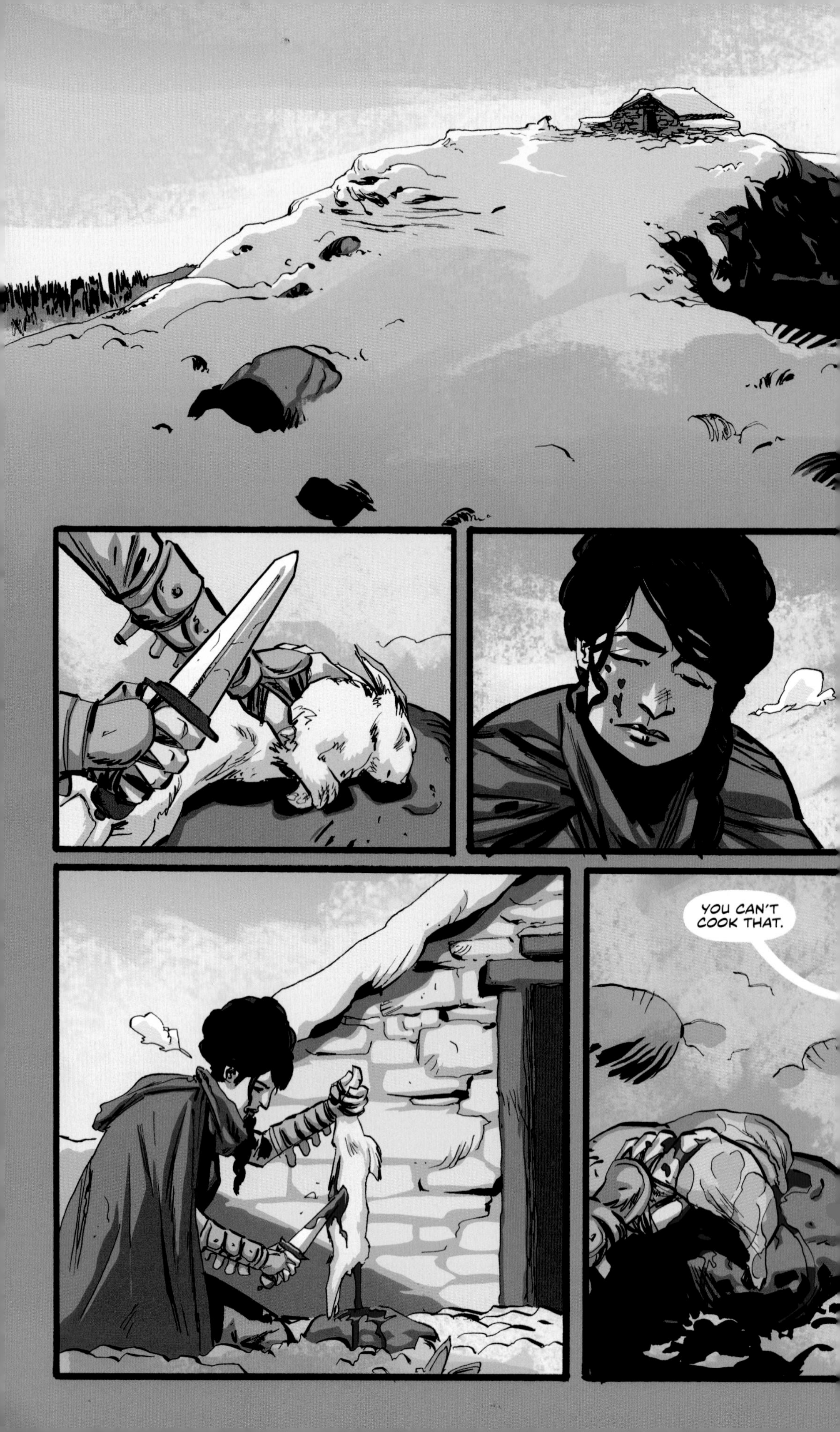
YOU CAN'T
COOK THAT.

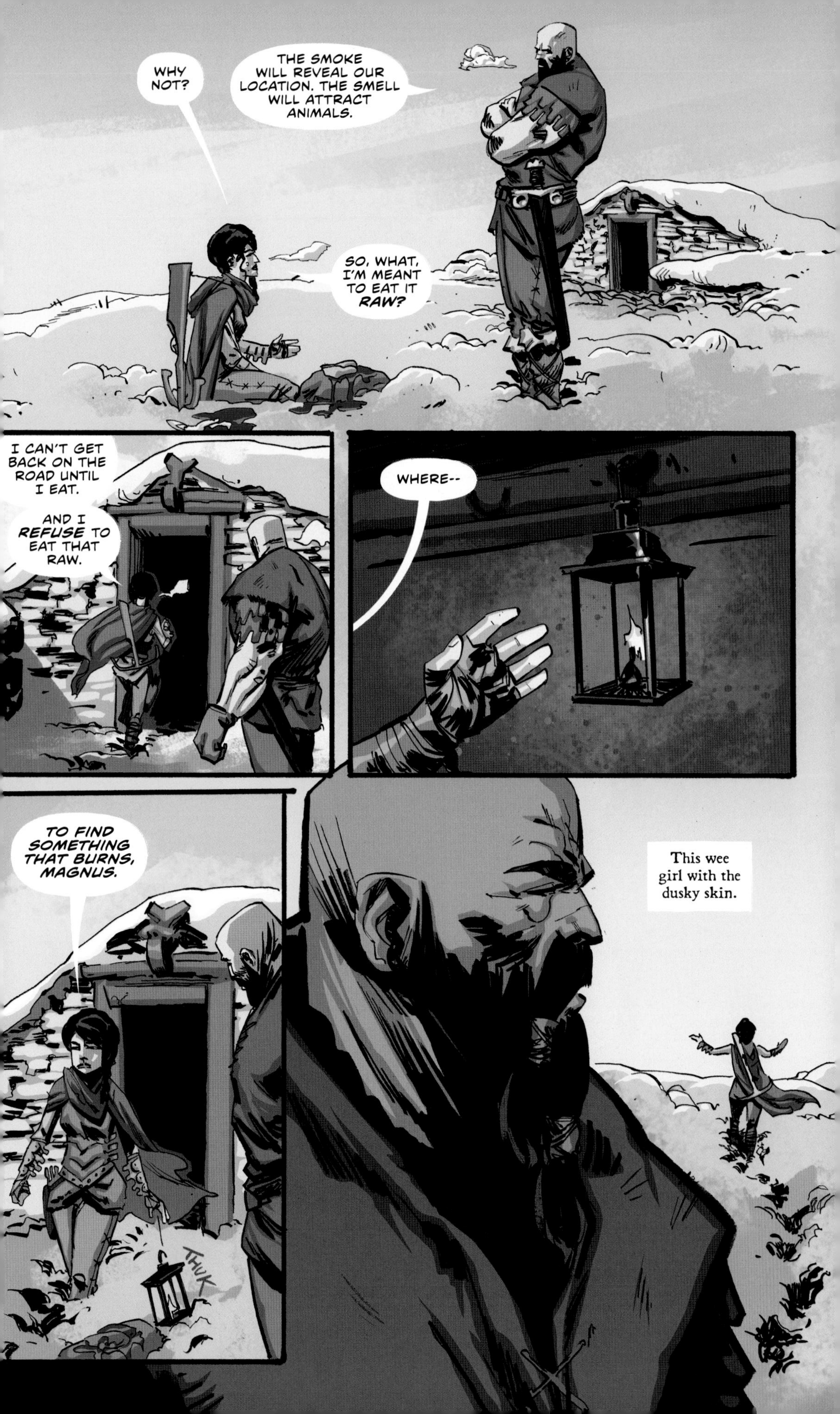

WHY NOT?
THE SMOKE WILL REVEAL OUR LOCATION. THE SMELL WILL ATTRACT ANIMALS.
SO, WHAT, I'M MEANT TO EAT IT *RAW?*
I CAN'T GET BACK ON THE ROAD UNTIL I EAT.
AND I *REFUSE* TO EAT THAT RAW.
WHERE--
TO FIND SOMETHING THAT BURNS, MAGNUS.
THUK
This wee girl with the dusky skin.

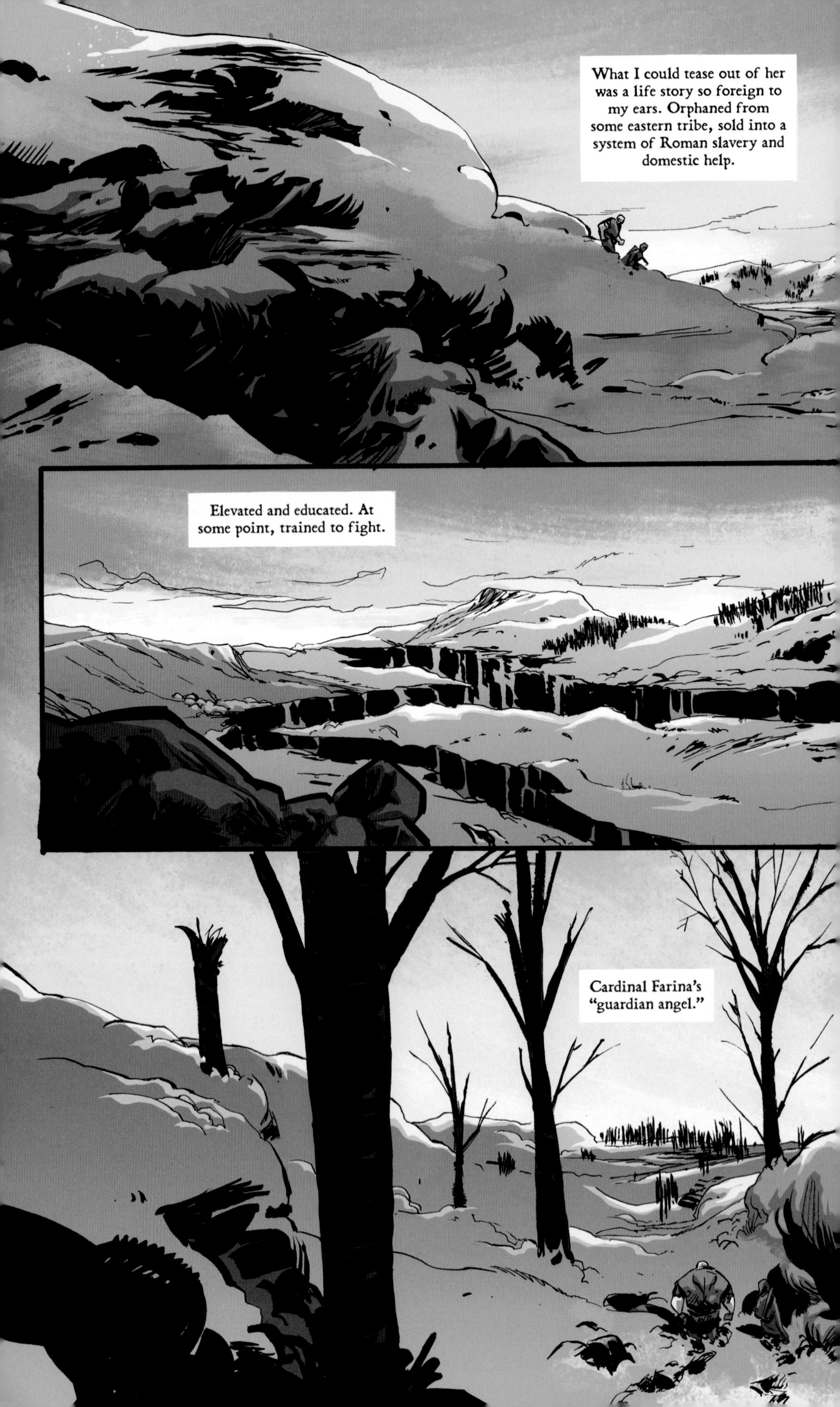
What I could tease out of her was a life story so foreign to my ears. Orphaned from some eastern tribe, sold into a system of Roman slavery and domestic help.
Elevated and educated. At some point, trained to fight.
Cardinal Farina's "guardian angel."

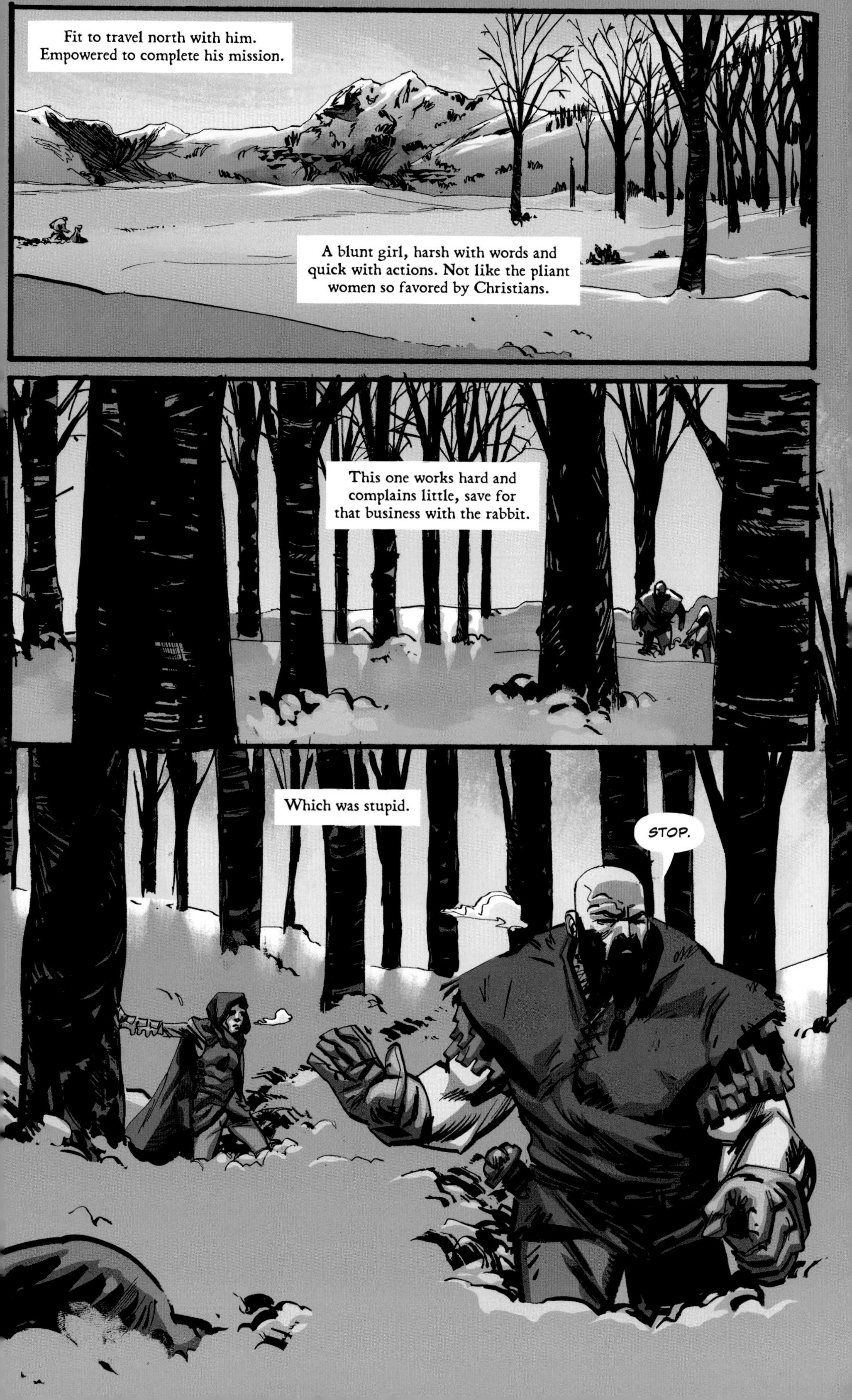
Fit to travel north with him. Empowered to complete his mission.
A blunt girl, harsh with words and quick with actions. Not like the pliant women so favored by Christians.
This one works hard and complains little, save for that business with the rabbit.
Which was stupid.
STOP.

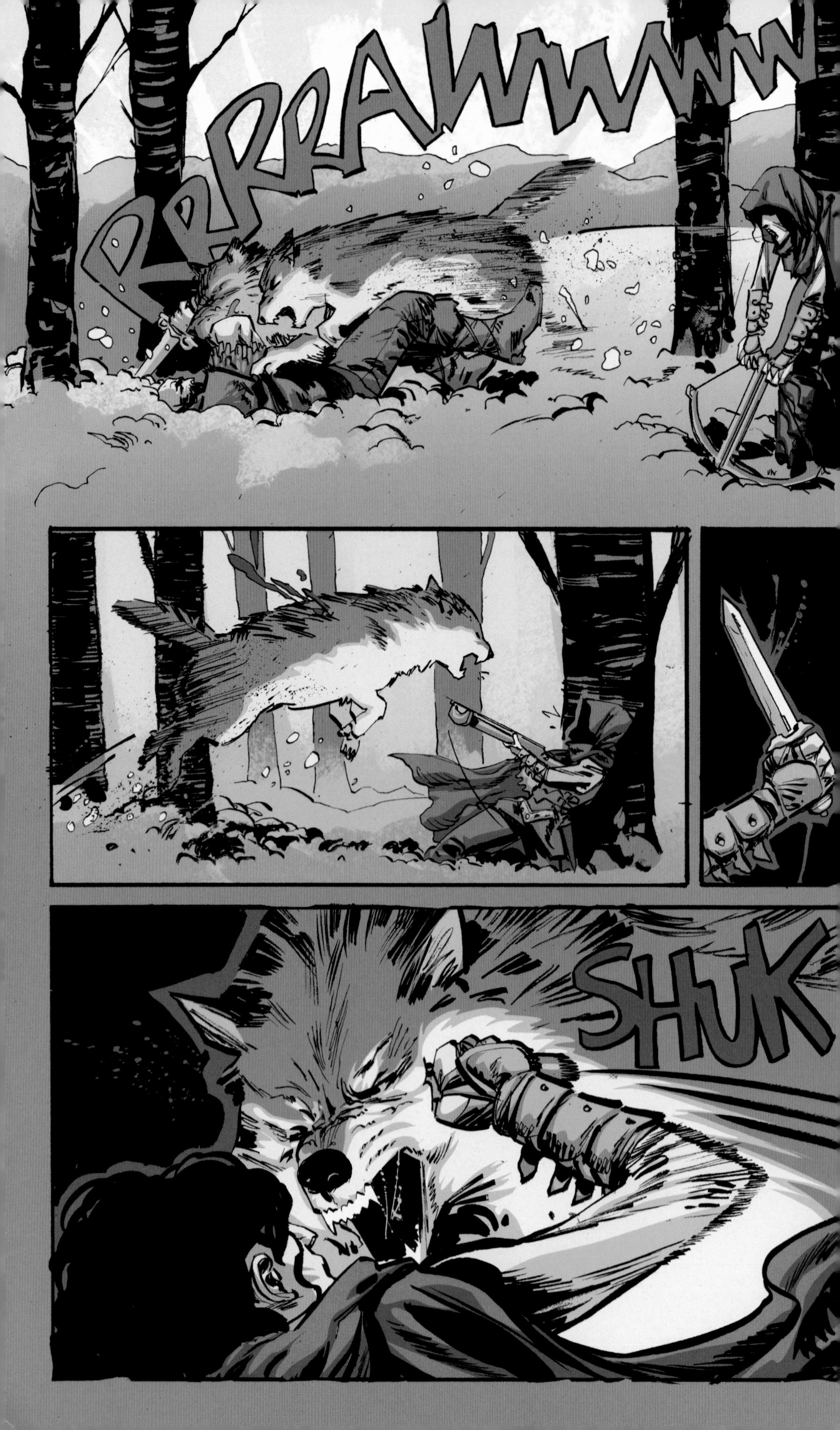
RRRRAWWWWWW
SHUK

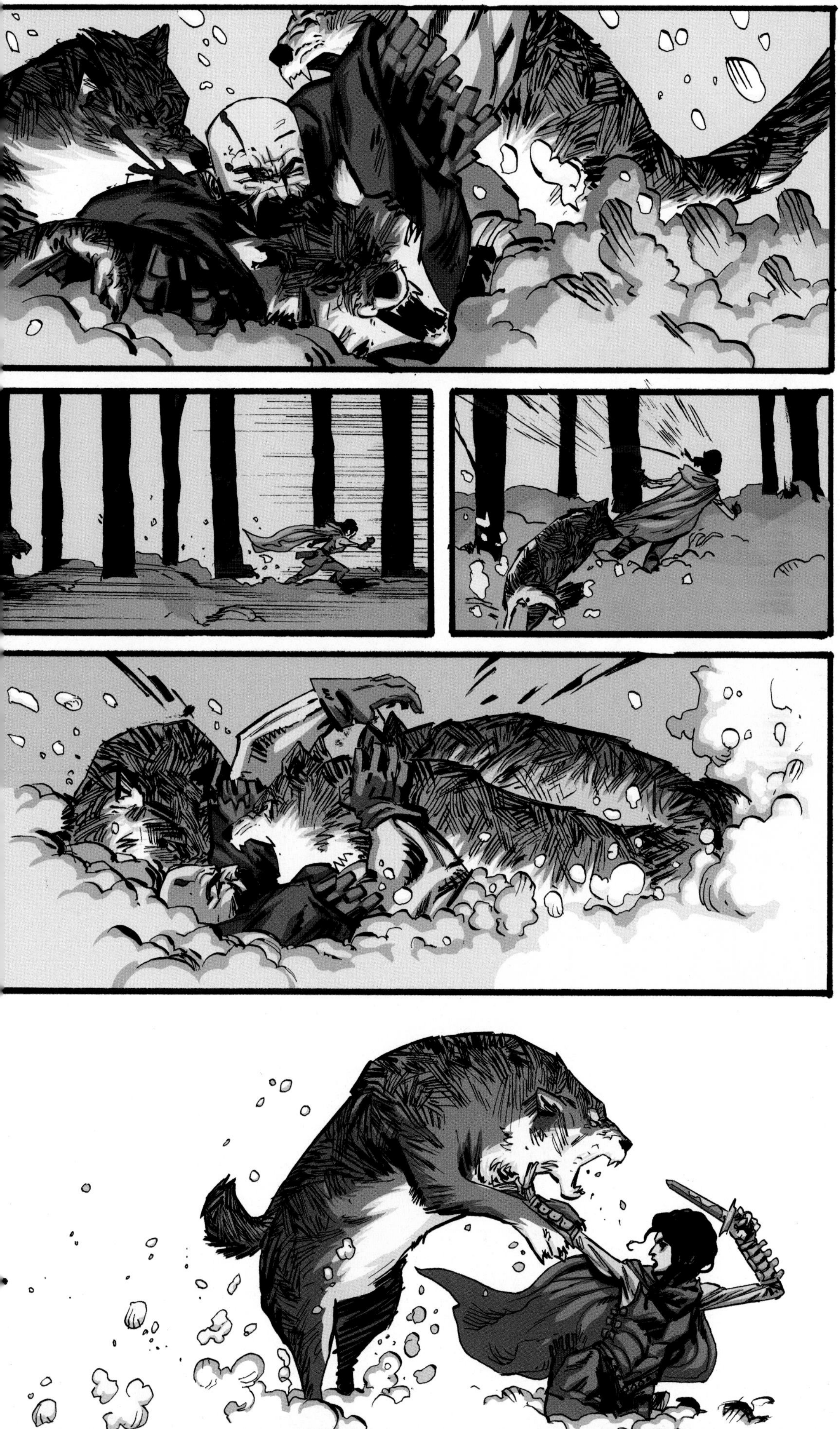

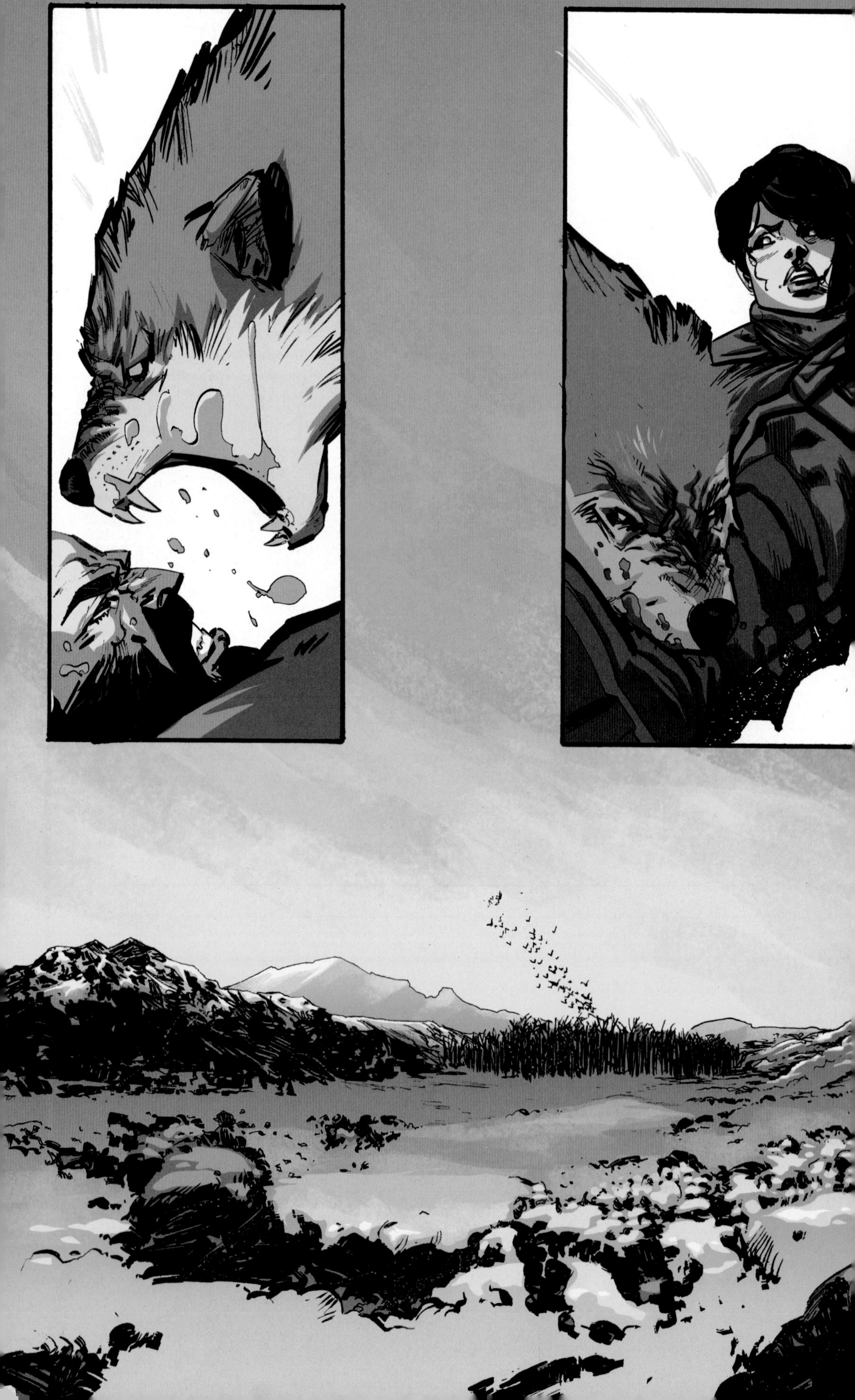

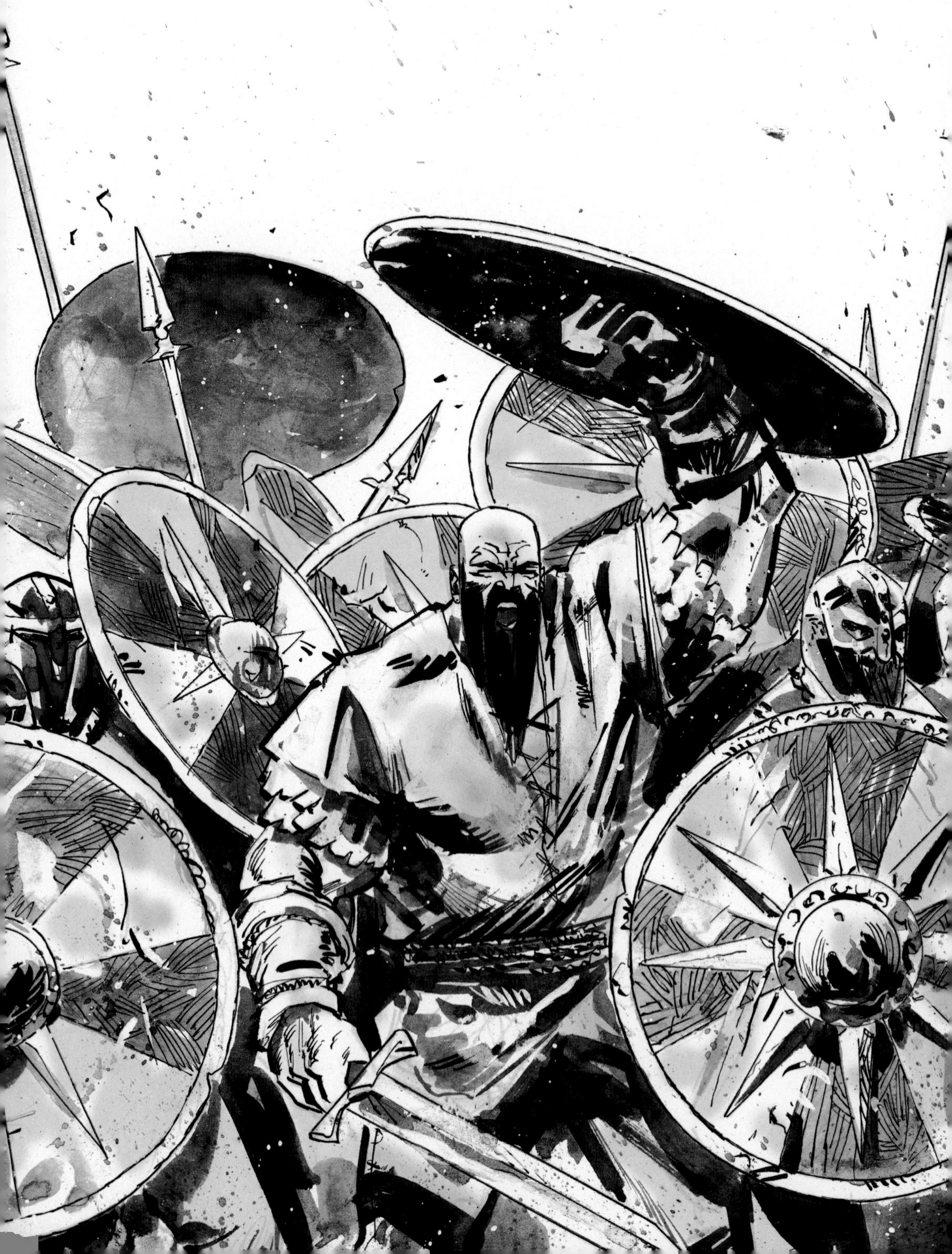

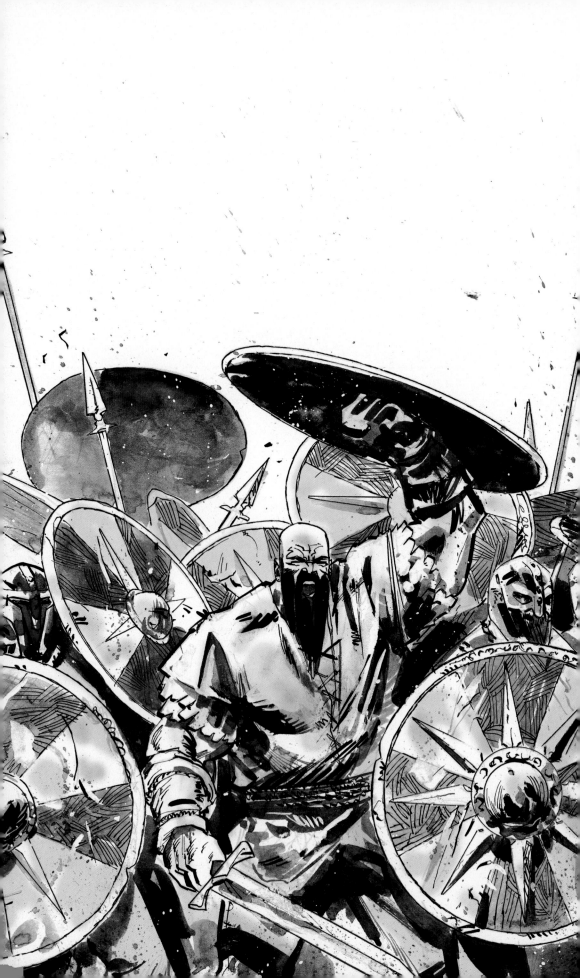

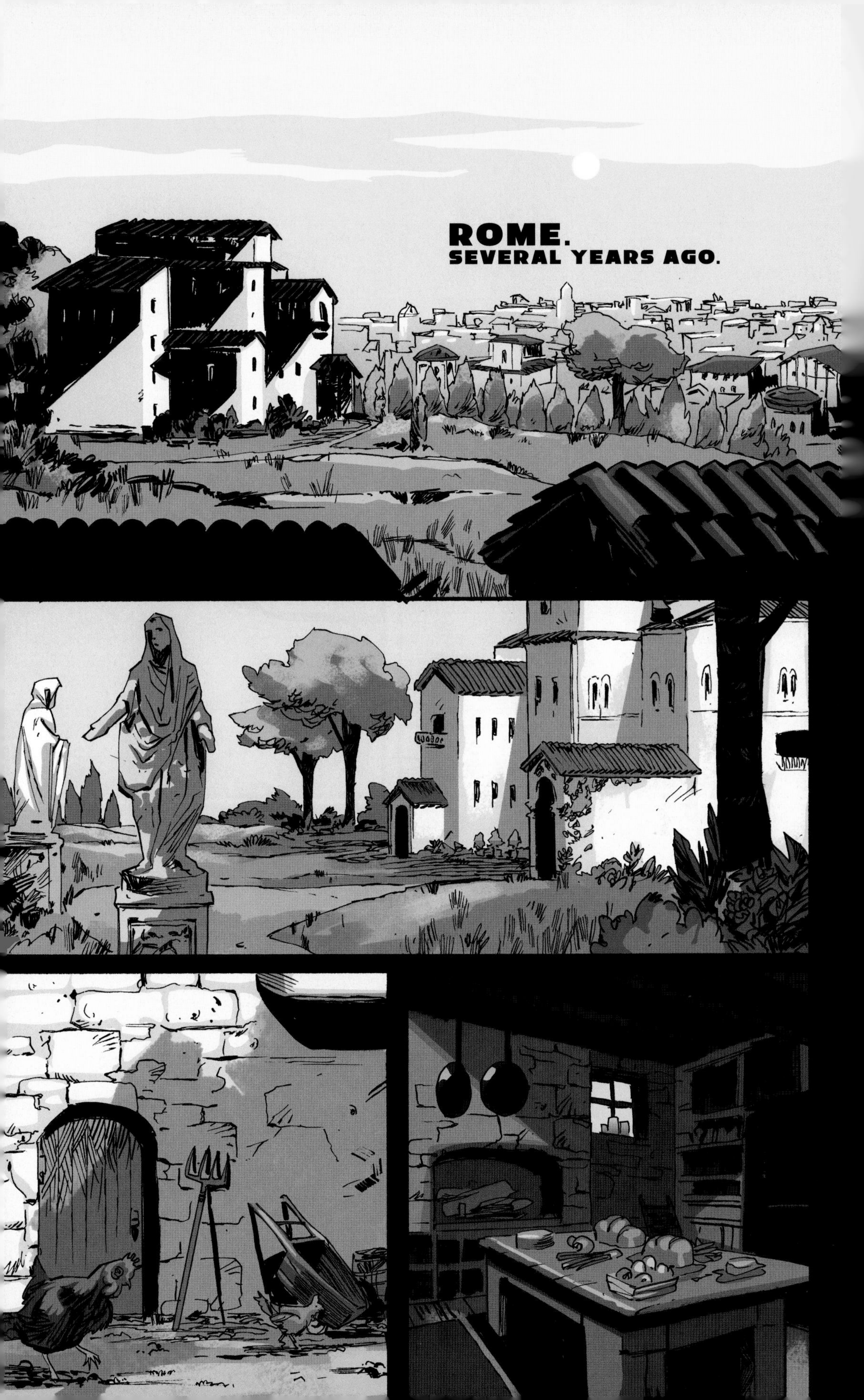
ROME.
SEVERAL YEARS AGO.

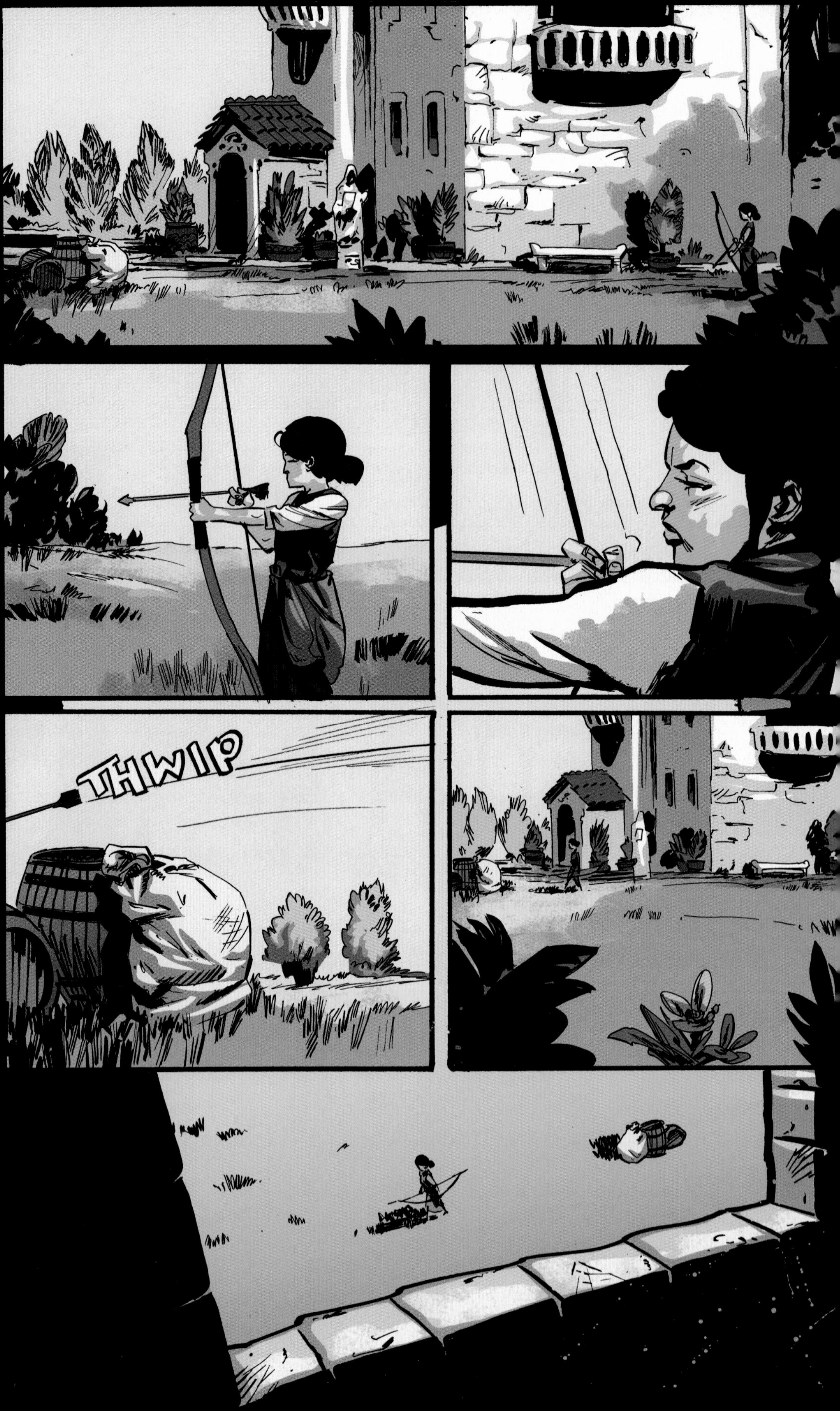
THWIP

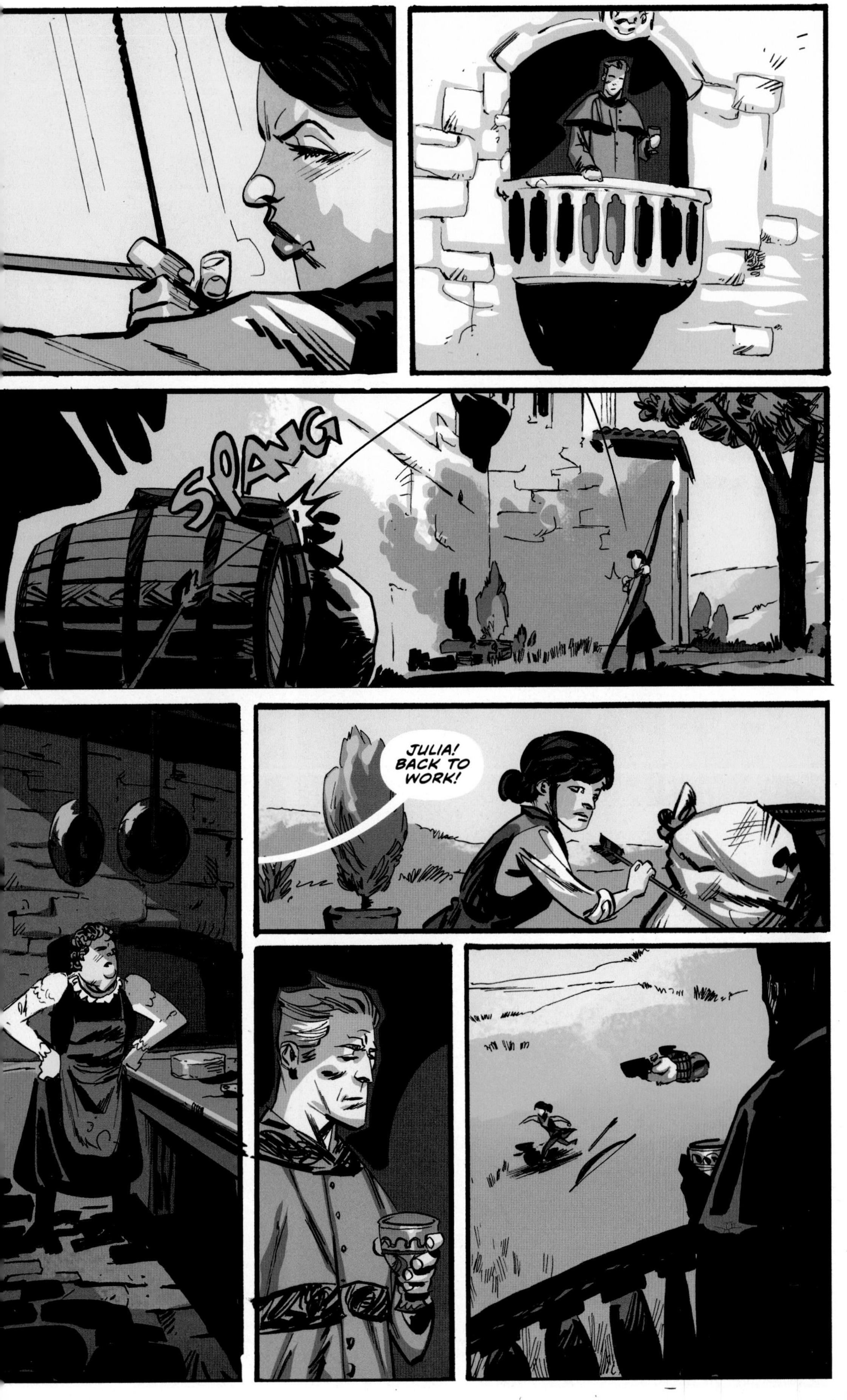

SPANG
JULIA! BACK TO WORK!

LATER

JULIA, IS IT?

I ACQUIRED YOU FROM THE HAIFA MARKET, YES?

YES, CARDINAL.

I WATCHED YOU EARLIER FROM MY WINDOW.

...

THAT BOW IS TOO BIG FOR YOU. IT PROBABLY ALWAYS WILL BE.

I WANT YOU TO GO SEE OSO, THE BIG FELLOW WHO WORKS IN THE ARMORY. I'LL WARN HIM YOU'RE COMING.

OSO WILL SHOW YOU THE CROSSBOW.

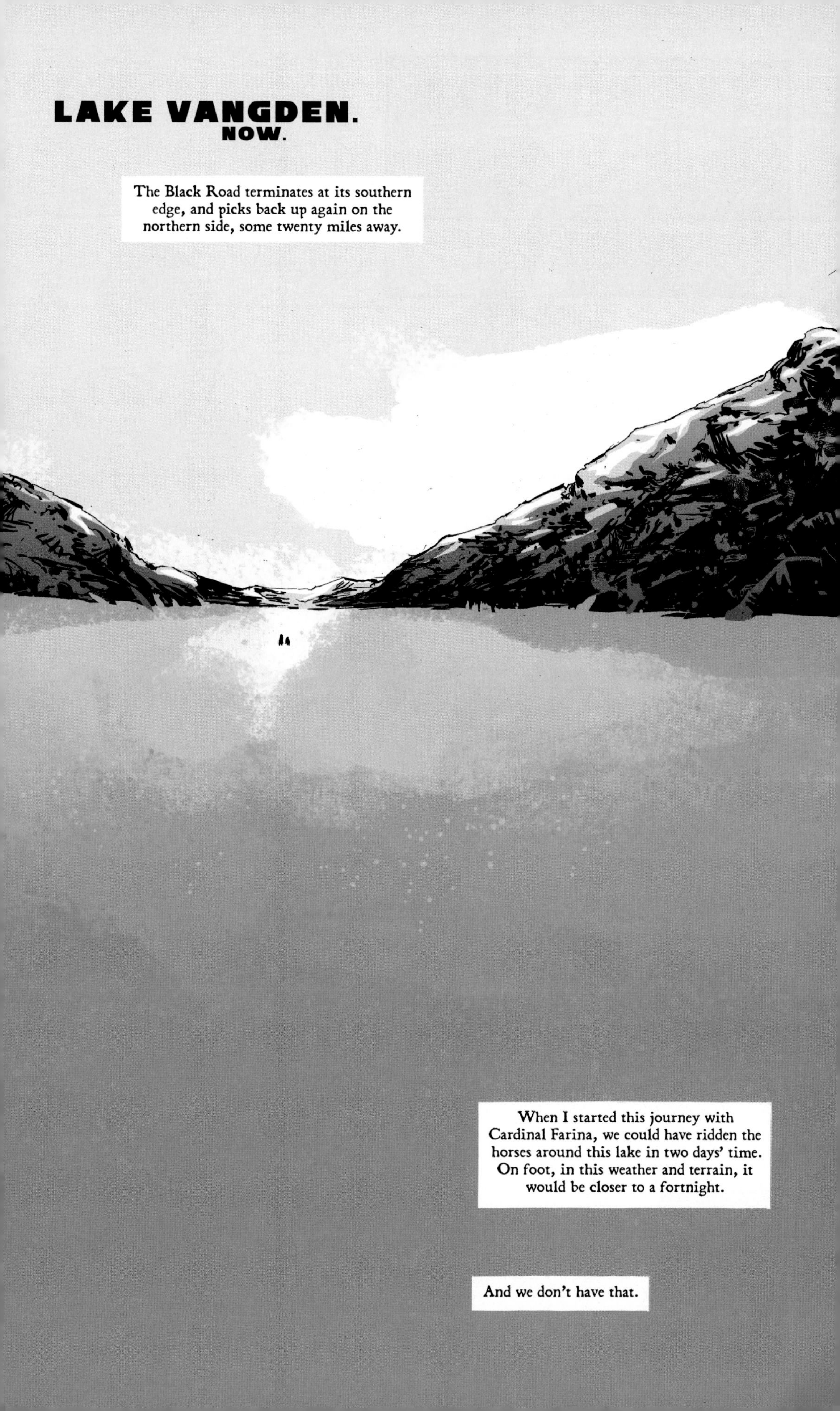
LAKE VANGDEN.
NOW.
The Black Road terminates at its southern edge, and picks back up again on the northern side, some twenty miles away.
When I started this journey with Cardinal Farina, we could have ridden the horses around this lake in two days' time. On foot, in this weather and terrain, it would be closer to a fortnight.
And we don't have that.

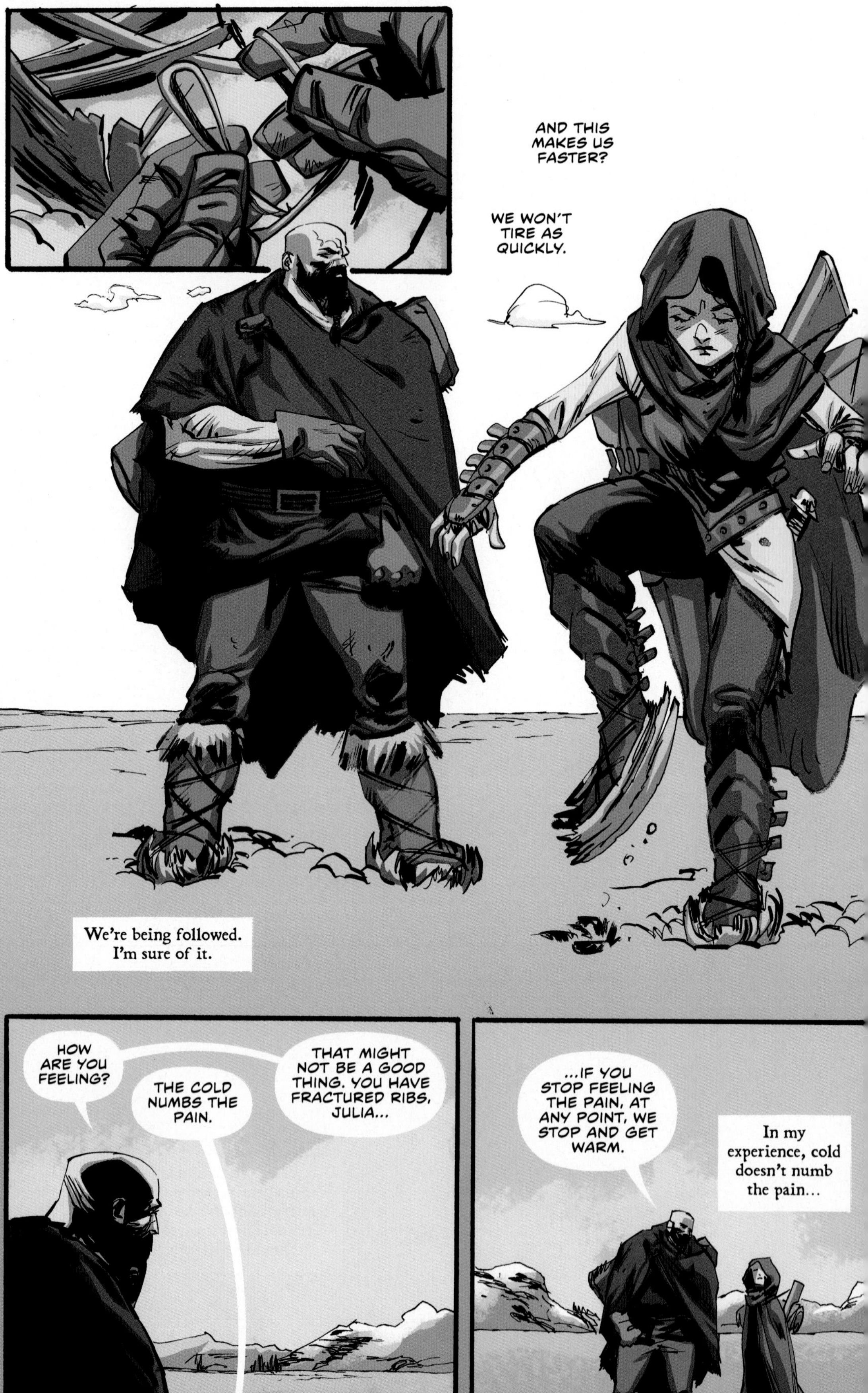
AND THIS MAKES US FASTER?
WE WON'T TIRE AS QUICKLY.
We're being followed. I'm sure of it.
HOW ARE YOU FEELING?
THE COLD NUMBS THE PAIN.
THAT MIGHT NOT BE A GOOD THING. YOU HAVE FRACTURED RIBS, JULIA...
...IF YOU STOP FEELING THE PAIN, AT ANY POINT, WE STOP AND GET WARM.
In my experience, cold doesn't numb the pain...

...it sharpens it.

I let Julia set the pace. This stage of the journey is not a race.

TELL ME THERE'S A NICE WARM INN ON THE NORTHERN SIDE, WITH HOT BROTH AND STRAW BEDS.

STERLET.

WHAT'S STERLET?

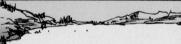

A FISH.

THEY CATCH STERLET AND FERMENT IT. THAT'S WHAT WE'LL FIND ON THE NORTHERN SIDE, A SMALL FISHING VILLAGE WHERE THEY DO THIS.

IN THE SUMMER MONTHS, THEY'LL PULL THOUSANDS OF THE FISH FROM THE LAKE, SALT, AND PACK IT IN THE GROUND UNTIL SPRING.

I'M FINE WITH BROTH.

IT'S A SUCCESSFUL VILLAGE.

On this lake, we trade speed for exposure. That may have been stupid of me. We're leaving a perfect trail for someone to follow.

I can practically feel his breath on the back of my neck.

We'll be lucky to make it across.

WE CAN RECOVER THERE.

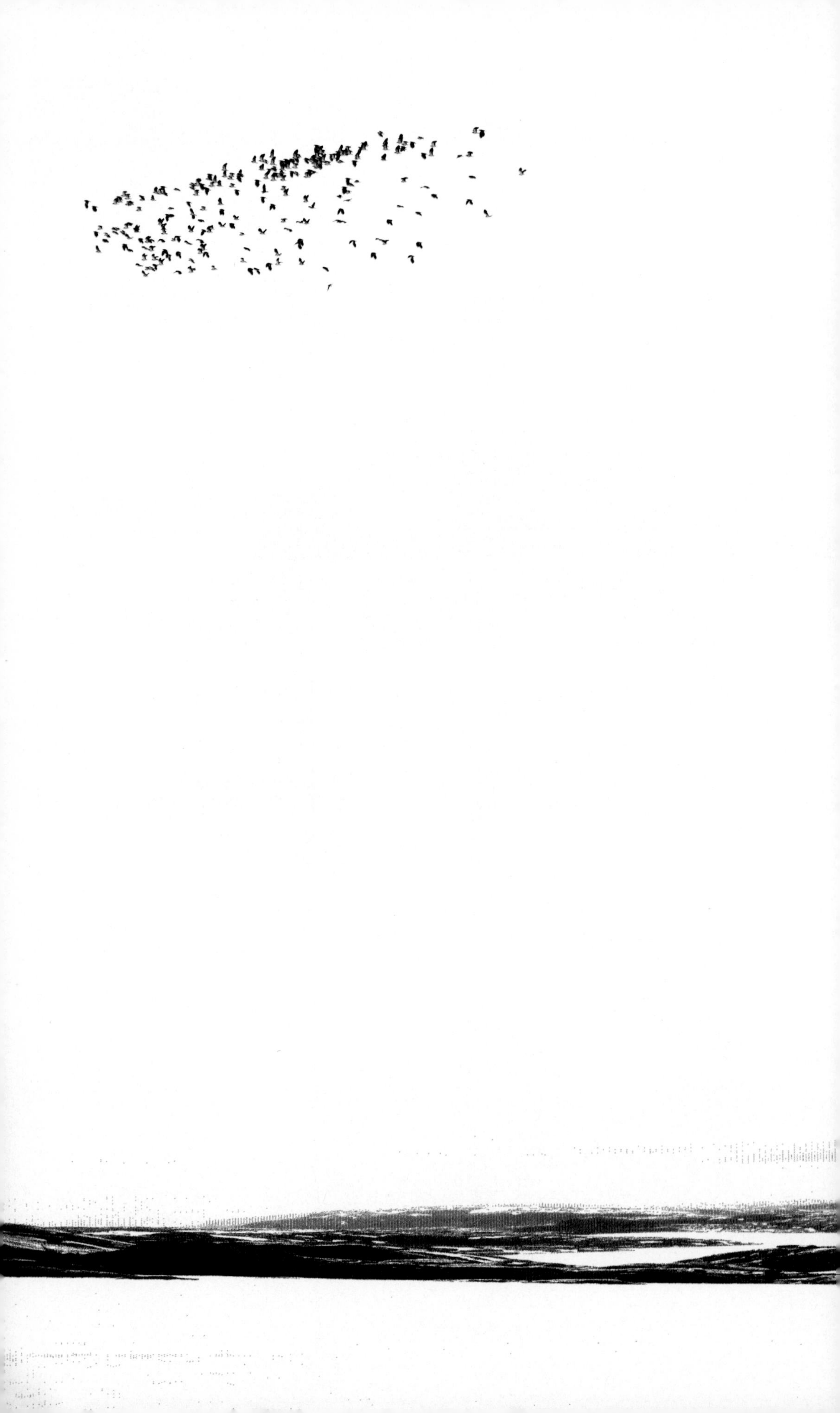

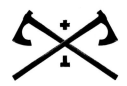

BRIAN WOOD / GARRY BROWN / DAVE McCAIG / STEVE WANDS

BLACK ROAD

#4 - SHIELD WALL

A MAGNUS THE BLACK MYSTERY

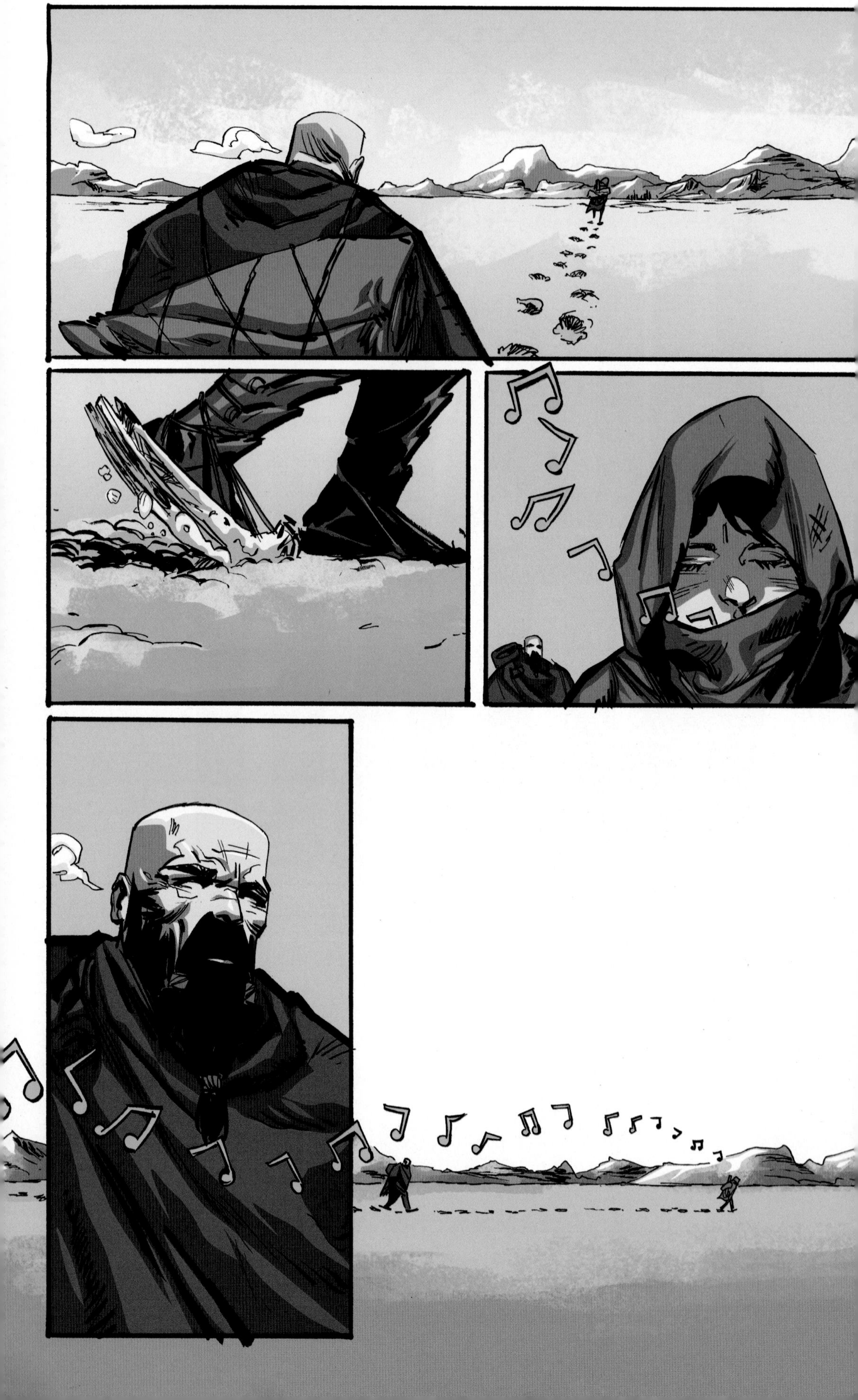

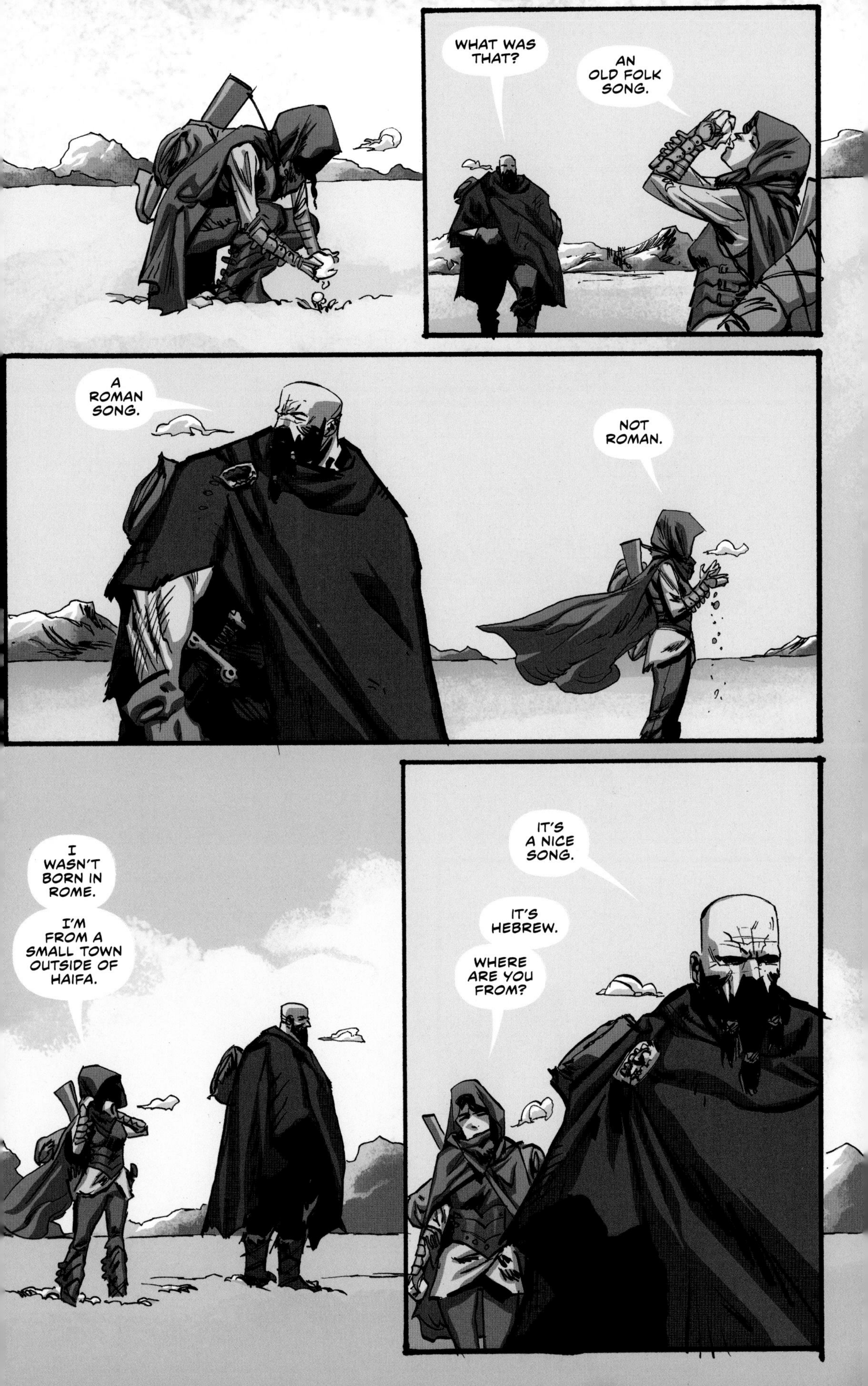
WHAT WAS THAT?
AN OLD FOLK SONG.
A ROMAN SONG.
NOT ROMAN.
I WASN'T BORN IN ROME.
I'M FROM A SMALL TOWN OUTSIDE OF HAIFA.
IT'S A NICE SONG.
IT'S HEBREW.
WHERE ARE YOU FROM?

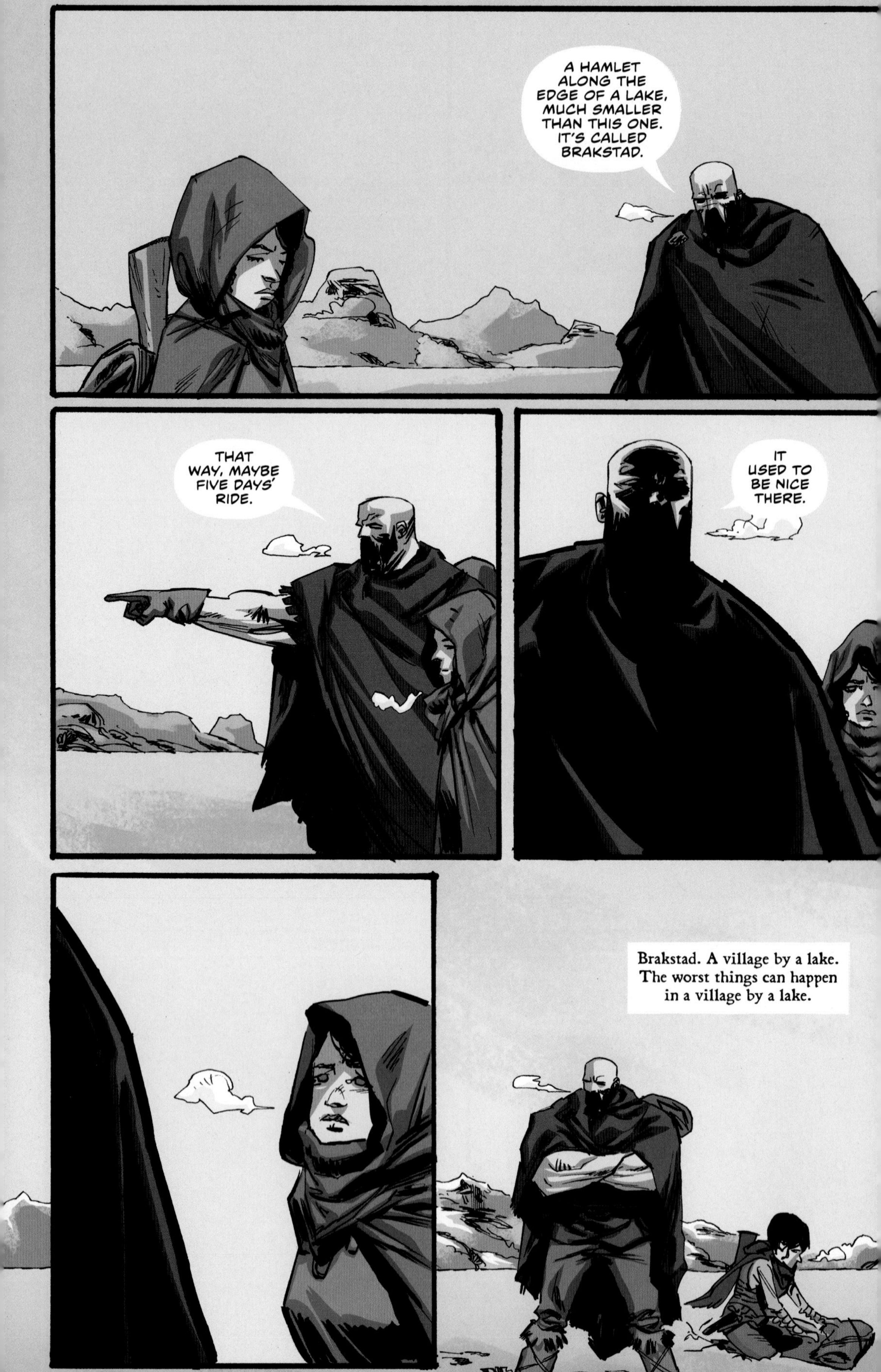
A HAMLET ALONG THE EDGE OF A LAKE, MUCH SMALLER THAN THIS ONE. IT'S CALLED BRAKSTAD.
THAT WAY, MAYBE FIVE DAYS' RIDE.
IT USED TO BE NICE THERE.
Brakstad. A village by a lake. The worst things can happen in a village by a lake.

I HAVE TO LEAVE.

PATIENCE.

YOU KNOW THAT'S NEVER BEEN A STRENGTH OF MINE.

THERE. ALL DONE.

I FEEL STRONGER, SOMEHOW.

A good thing, as we headed into battle.

As a household soldier of the local lord, I was duty-bound and oathsworn to lend my swords to whatever conflict rose up.

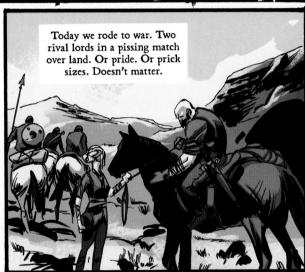

Today we rode to war. Two rival lords in a pissing match over land. Or pride. Or prick sizes. Doesn't matter.

SHAME TO COVER UP THAT MAGNIFICENT HEAD OF YOURS.

Fighting is what warriors do.

And we fought like demons.

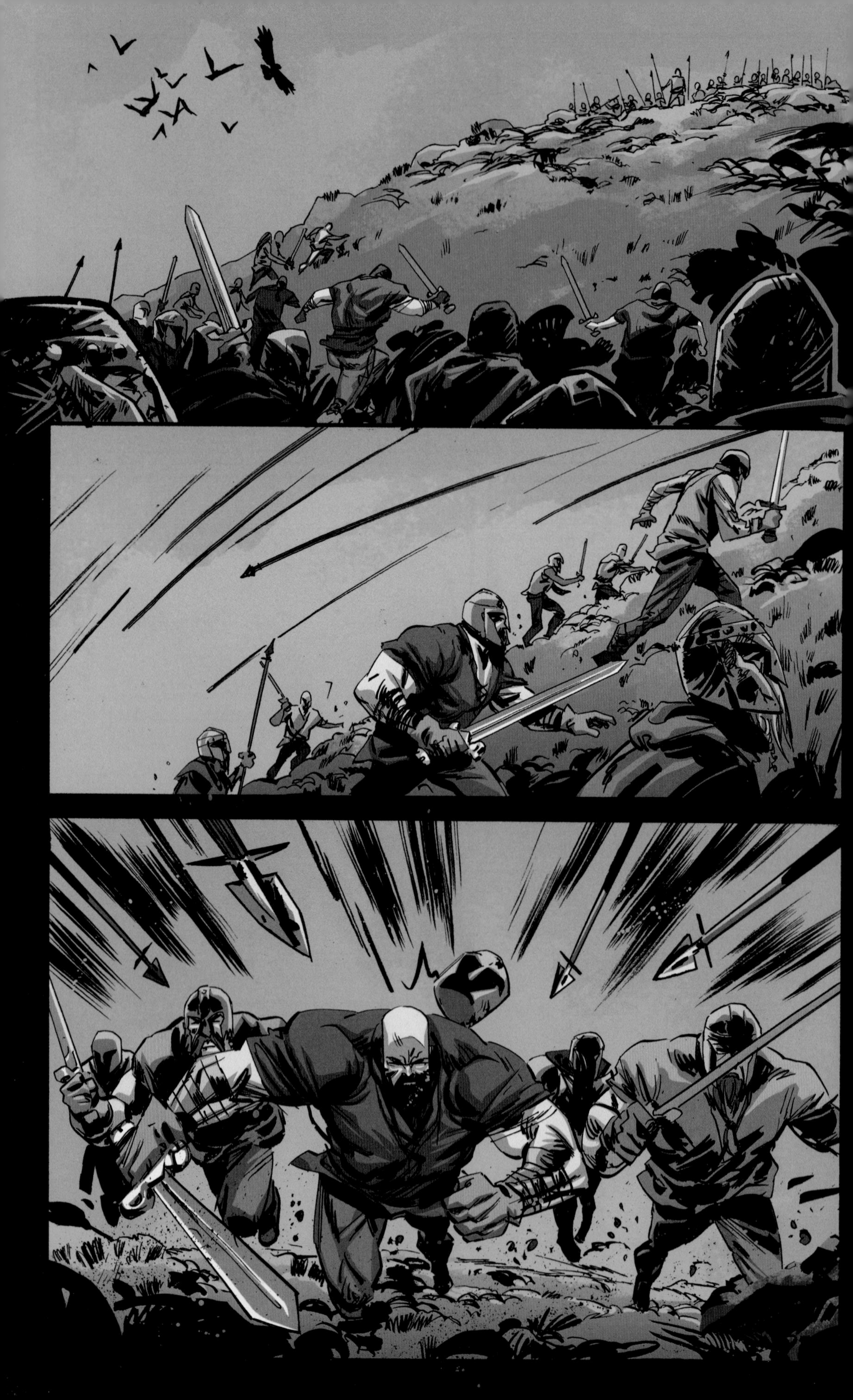

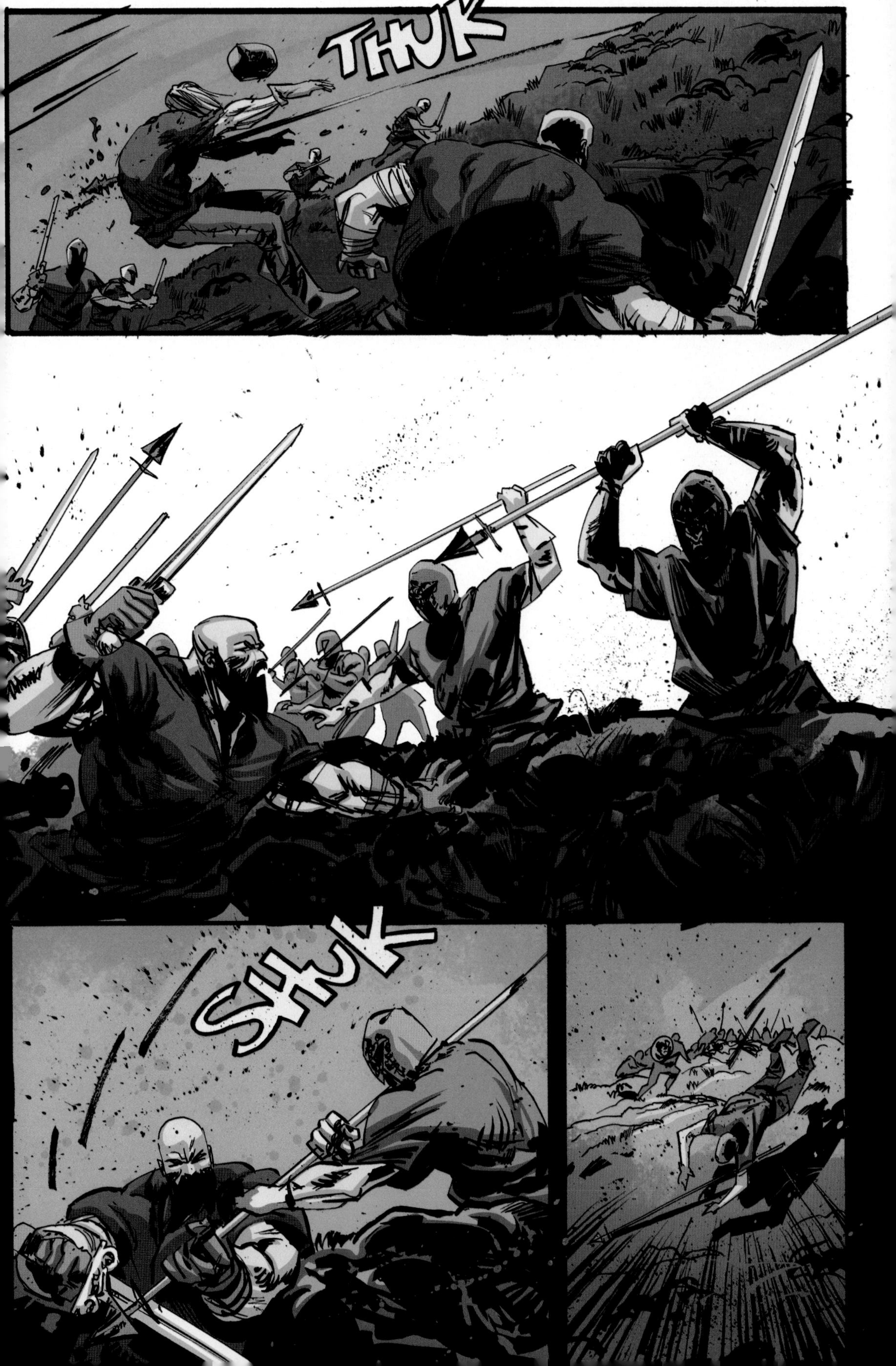
THUK
SHUK

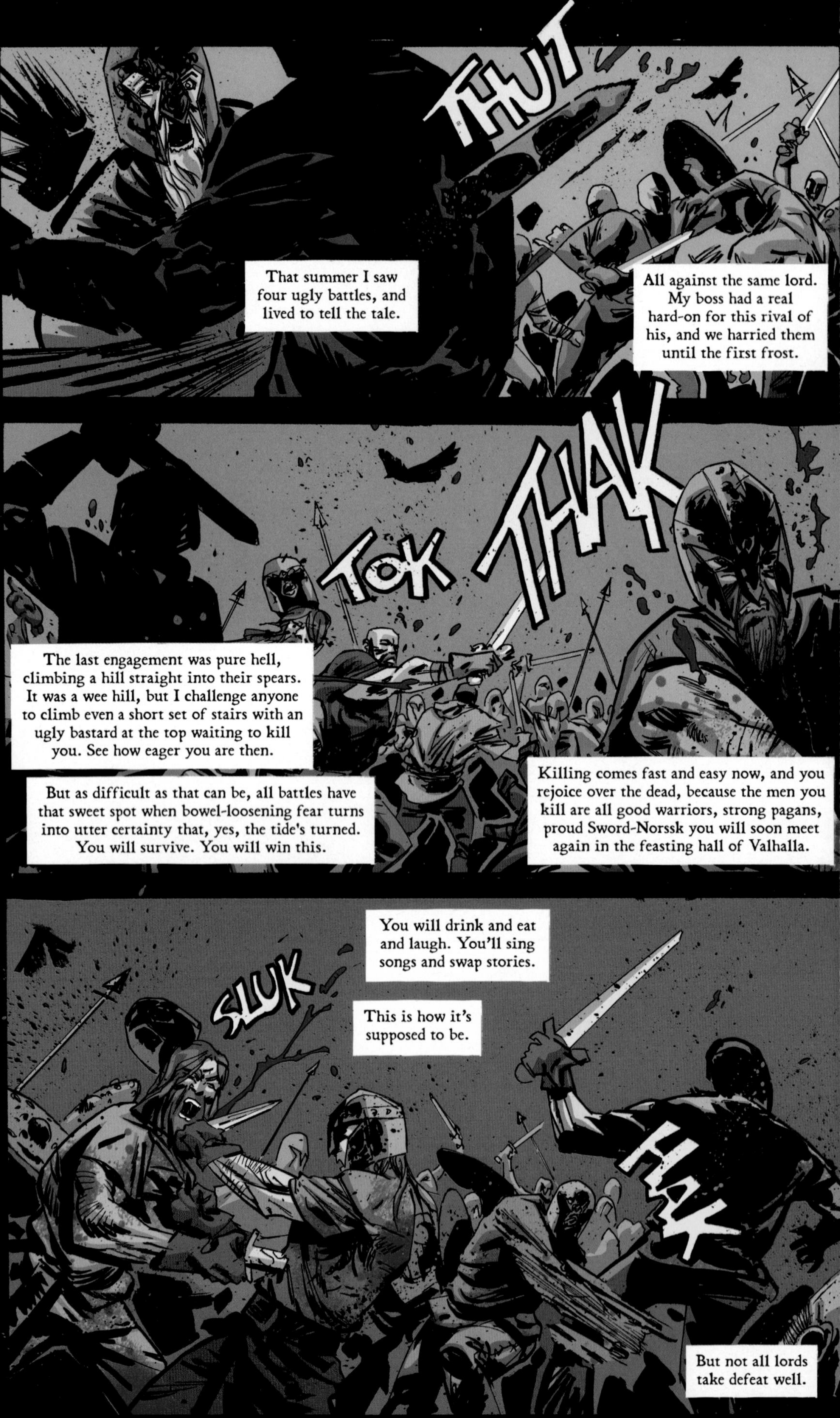
THUT
That summer I saw four ugly battles, and lived to tell the tale.
All against the same lord. My boss had a real hard-on for this rival of his, and we harried them until the first frost.
TOK
THAK
The last engagement was pure hell, climbing a hill straight into their spears. It was a wee hill, but I challenge anyone to climb even a short set of stairs with an ugly bastard at the top waiting to kill you. See how eager you are then.
But as difficult as that can be, all battles have that sweet spot when bowel-loosening fear turns into utter certainty that, yes, the tide's turned. You will survive. You will win this.
Killing comes fast and easy now, and you rejoice over the dead, because the men you kill are all good warriors, strong pagans, proud Sword-Norssk you will soon meet again in the feasting hall of Valhalla.
SLUK
You will drink and eat and laugh. You'll sing songs and swap stories.
This is how it's supposed to be.
HAK
But not all lords take defeat well.

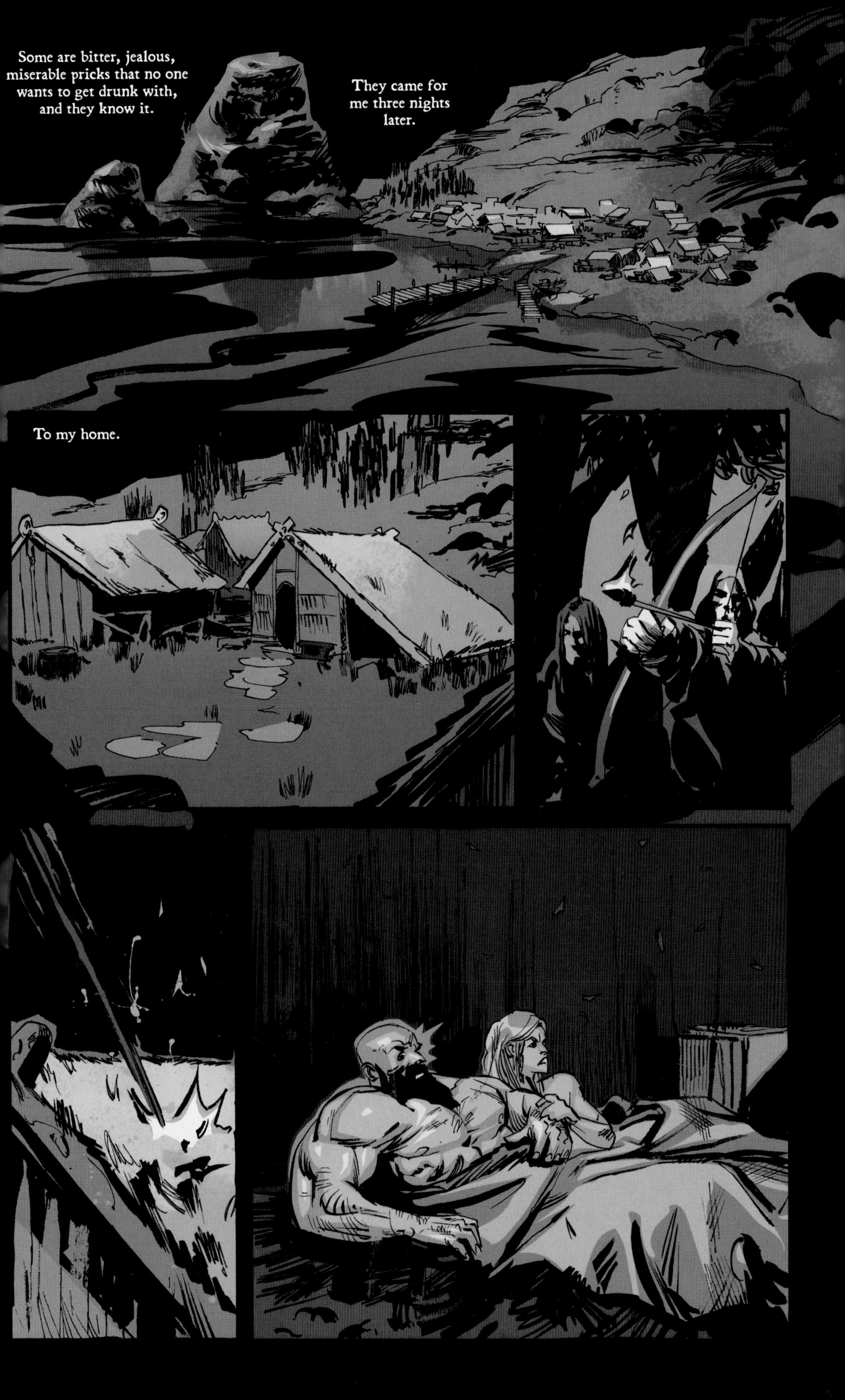
Some are bitter, jealous, miserable pricks that no one wants to get drunk with, and they know it.
They came for me three nights later.
To my home.

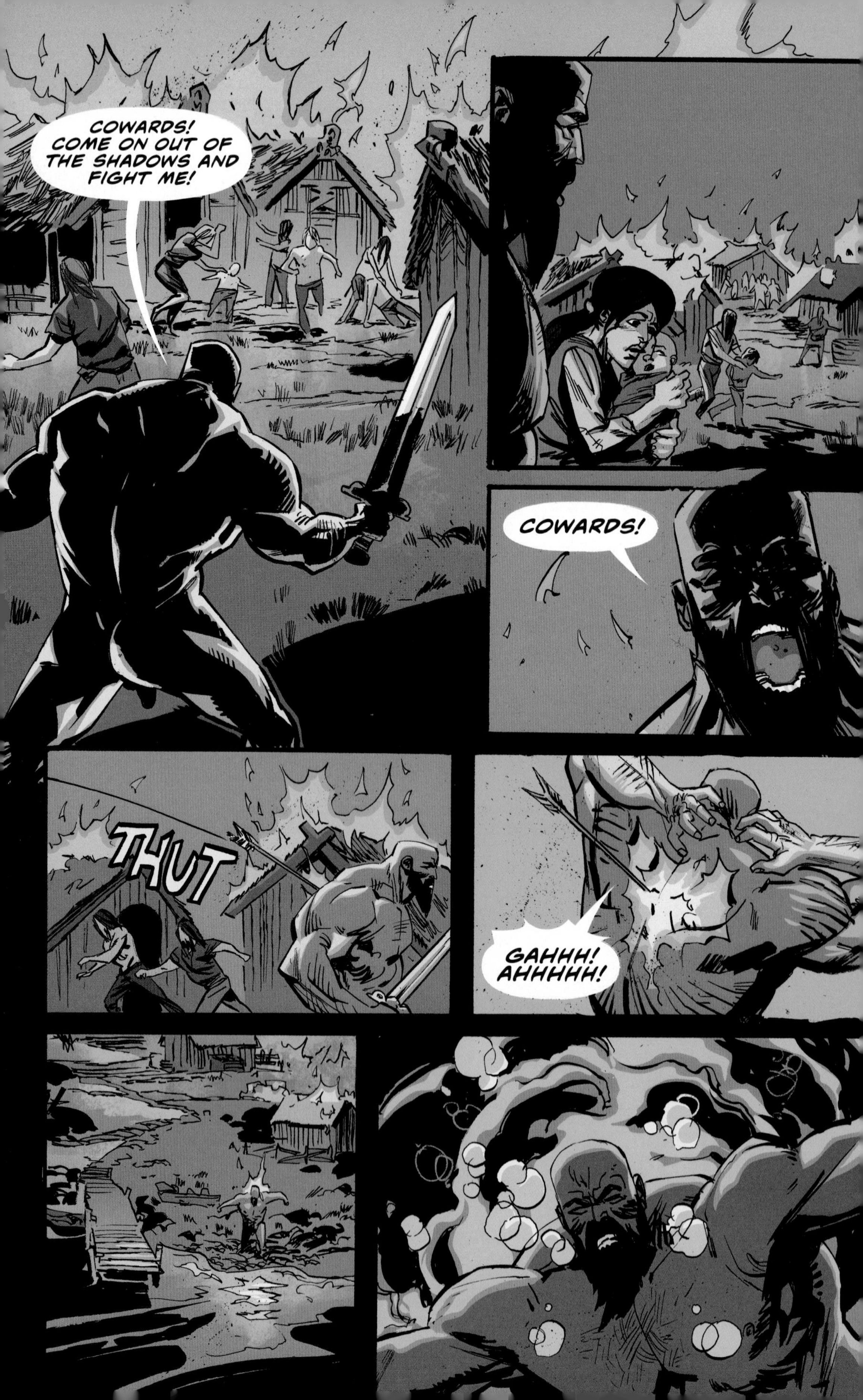
COWARDS! COME ON OUT OF THE SHADOWS AND FIGHT ME!
COWARDS!
THUT
GAHHH! AHHHHH!

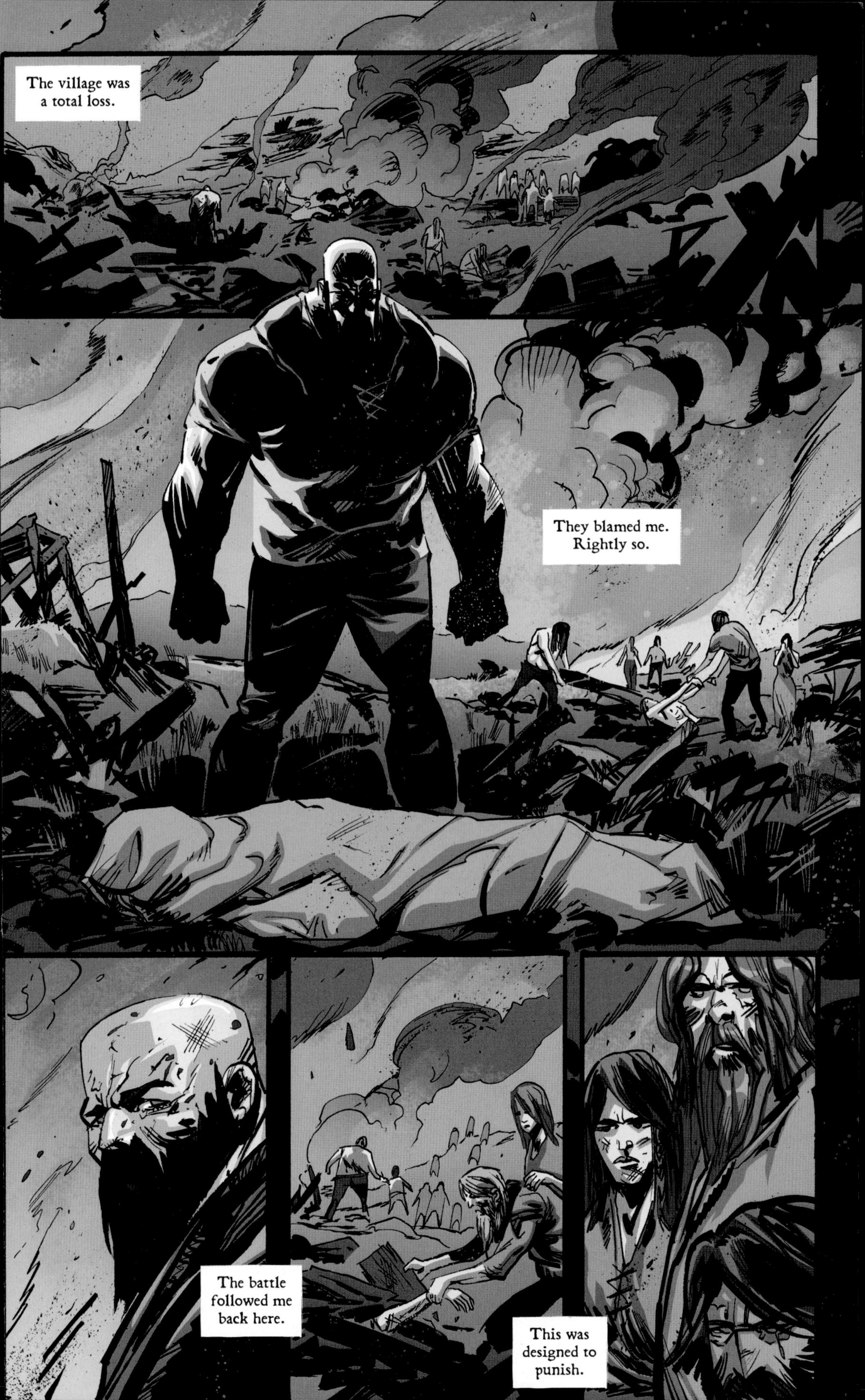
The village was a total loss.
They blamed me. Rightly so.
The battle followed me back here.
This was designed to punish.

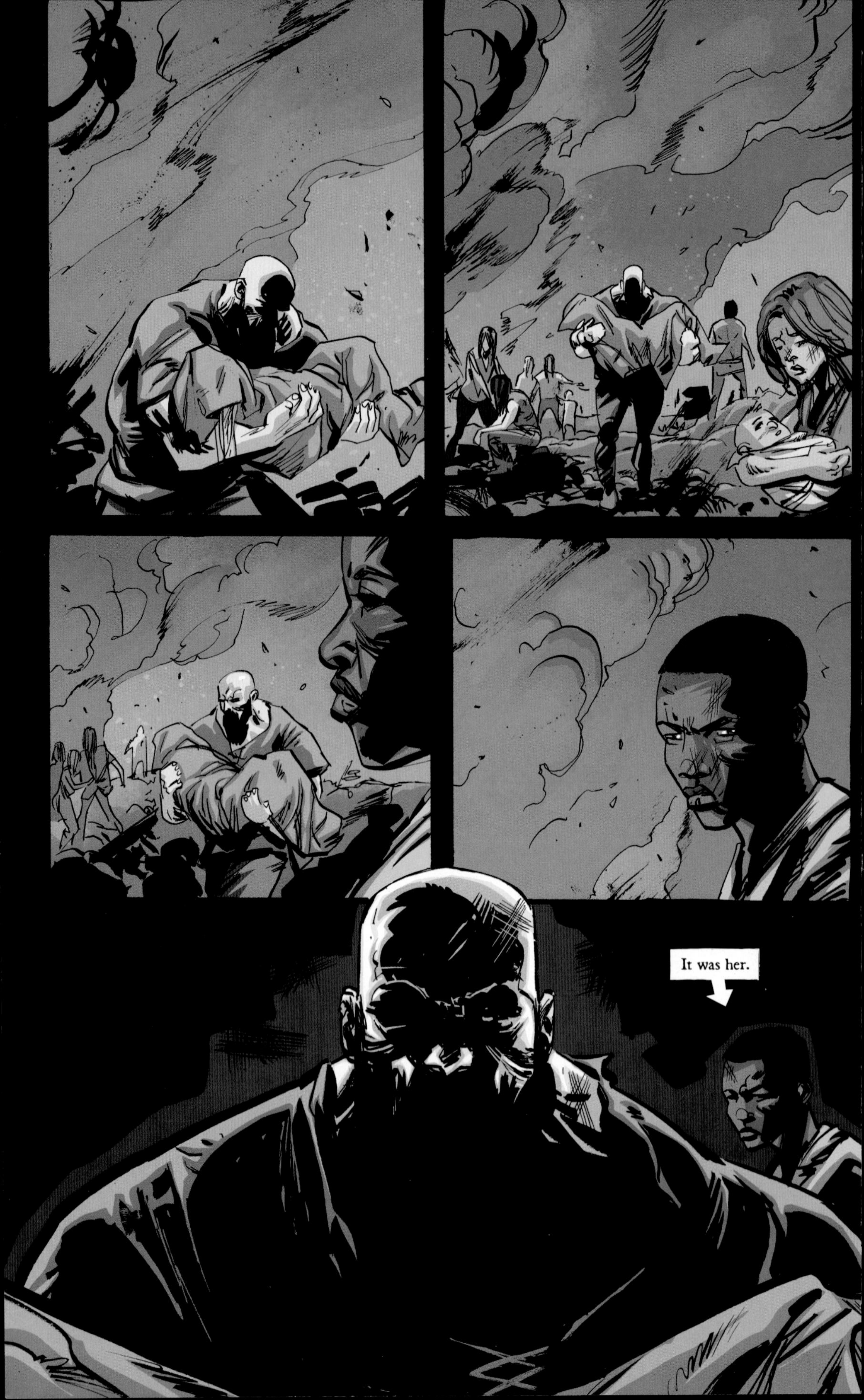
It was her.

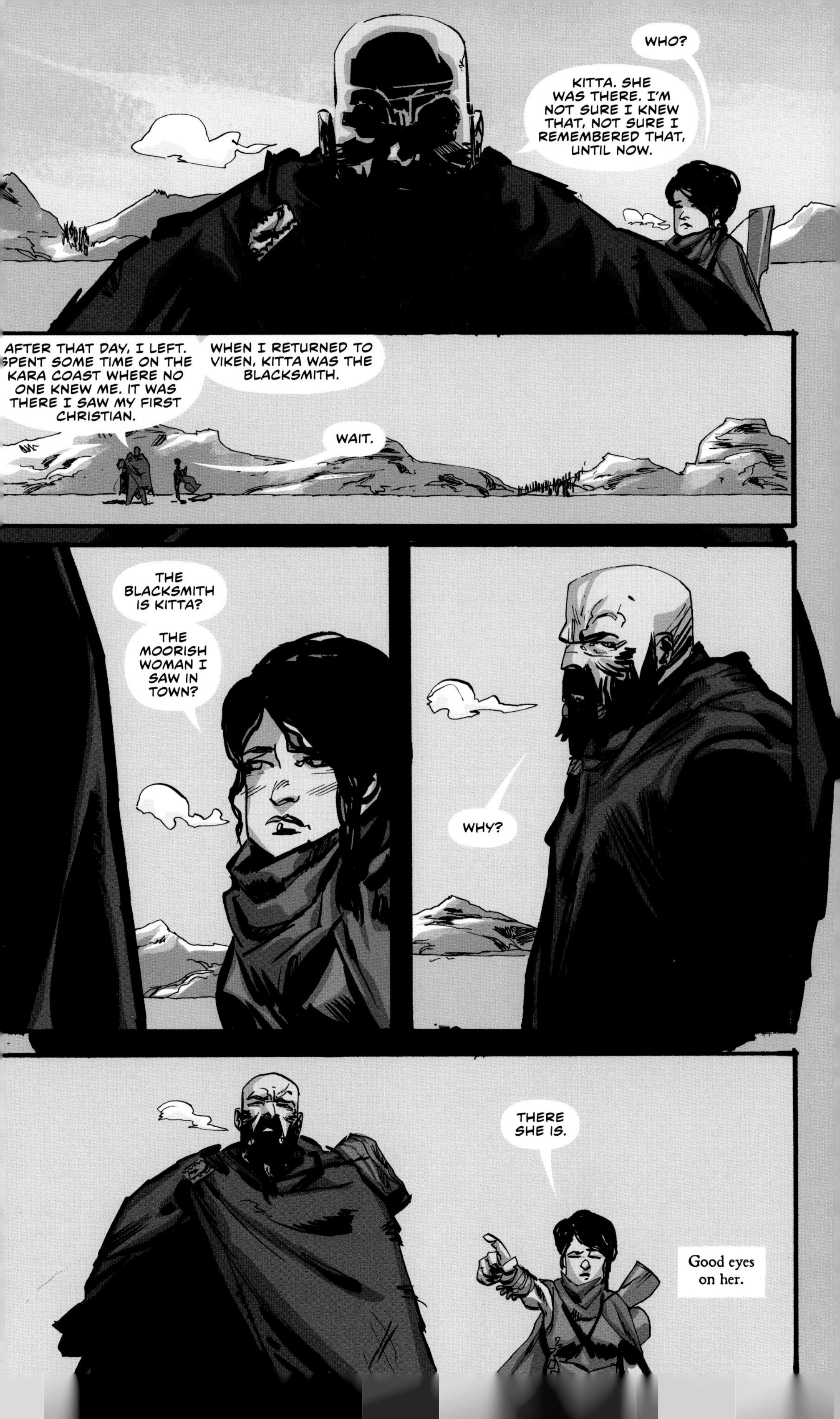
WHO?
KITTA. SHE WAS THERE. I'M NOT SURE I KNEW THAT, NOT SURE I REMEMBERED THAT, UNTIL NOW.
AFTER THAT DAY, I LEFT. SPENT SOME TIME ON THE KARA COAST WHERE NO ONE KNEW ME. IT WAS THERE I SAW MY FIRST CHRISTIAN.
WHEN I RETURNED TO VIKEN, KITTA WAS THE BLACKSMITH.
WAIT.
THE BLACKSMITH IS KITTA?
THE MOORISH WOMAN I SAW IN TOWN?
WHY?
THERE SHE IS.
Good eyes on her.

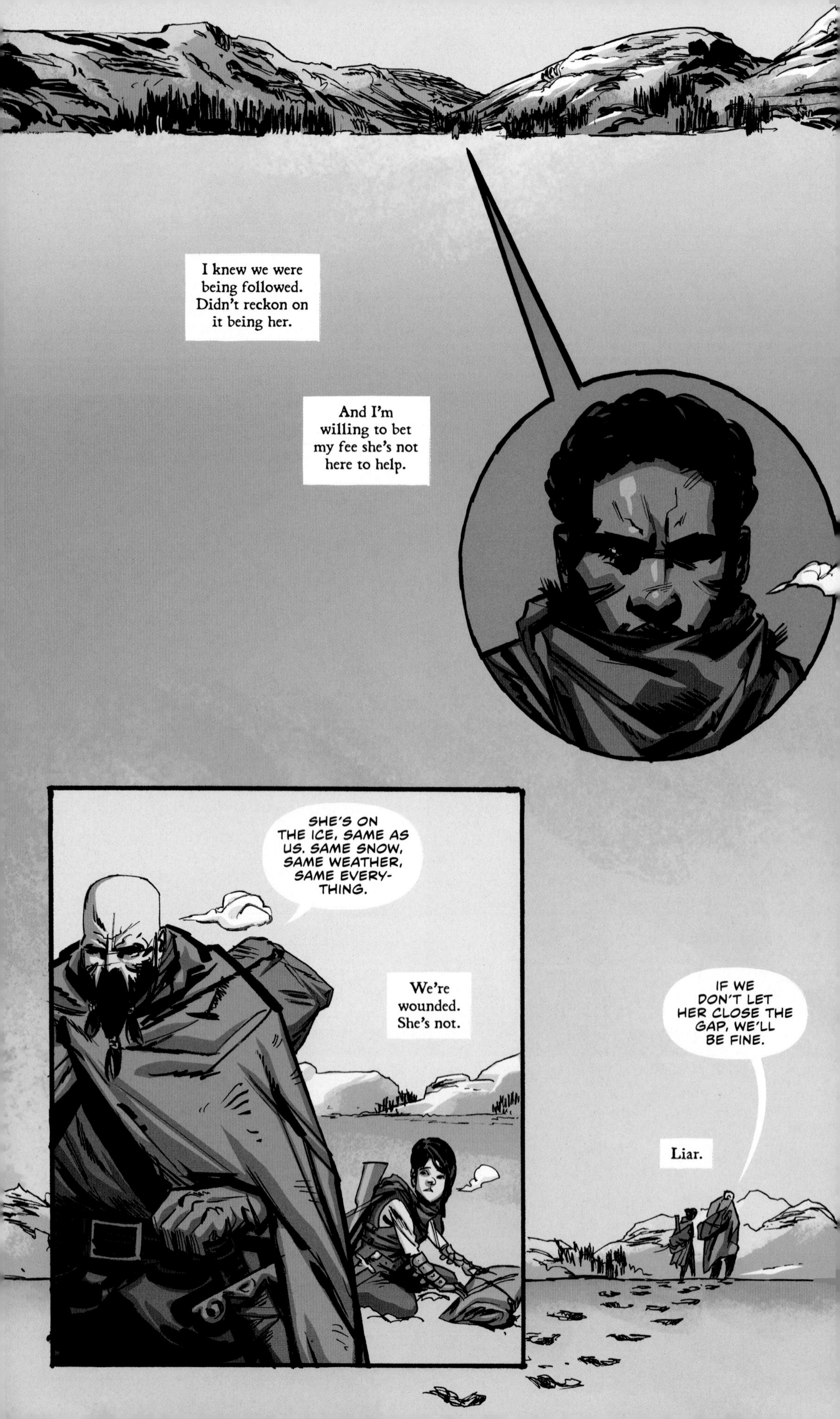
I knew we were being followed. Didn't reckon on it being her.
And I'm willing to bet my fee she's not here to help.
SHE'S ON THE ICE, SAME AS US. SAME SNOW, SAME WEATHER, SAME EVERY-THING.
We're wounded. She's not.
IF WE DON'T LET HER CLOSE THE GAP, WE'LL BE FINE.
Liar.

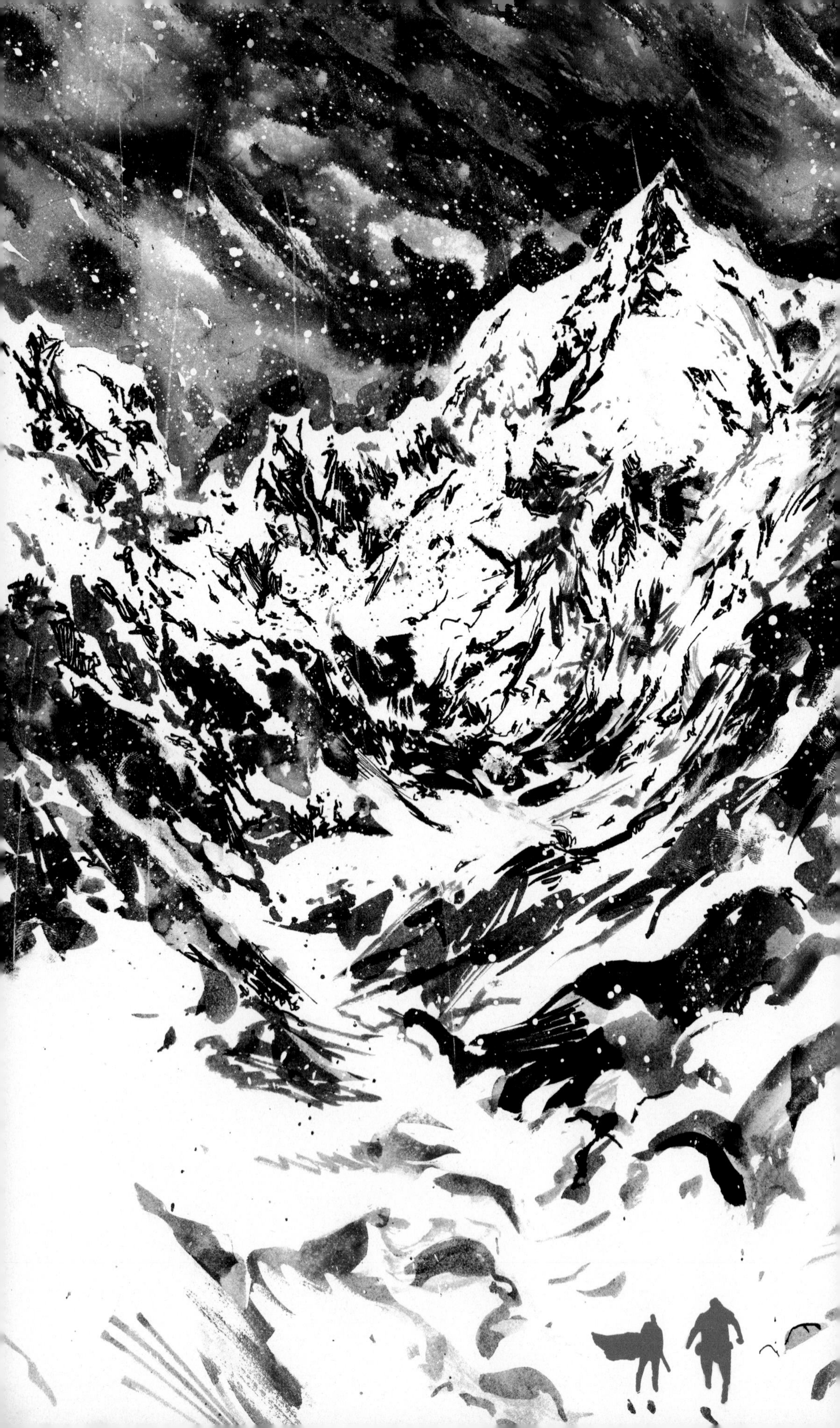

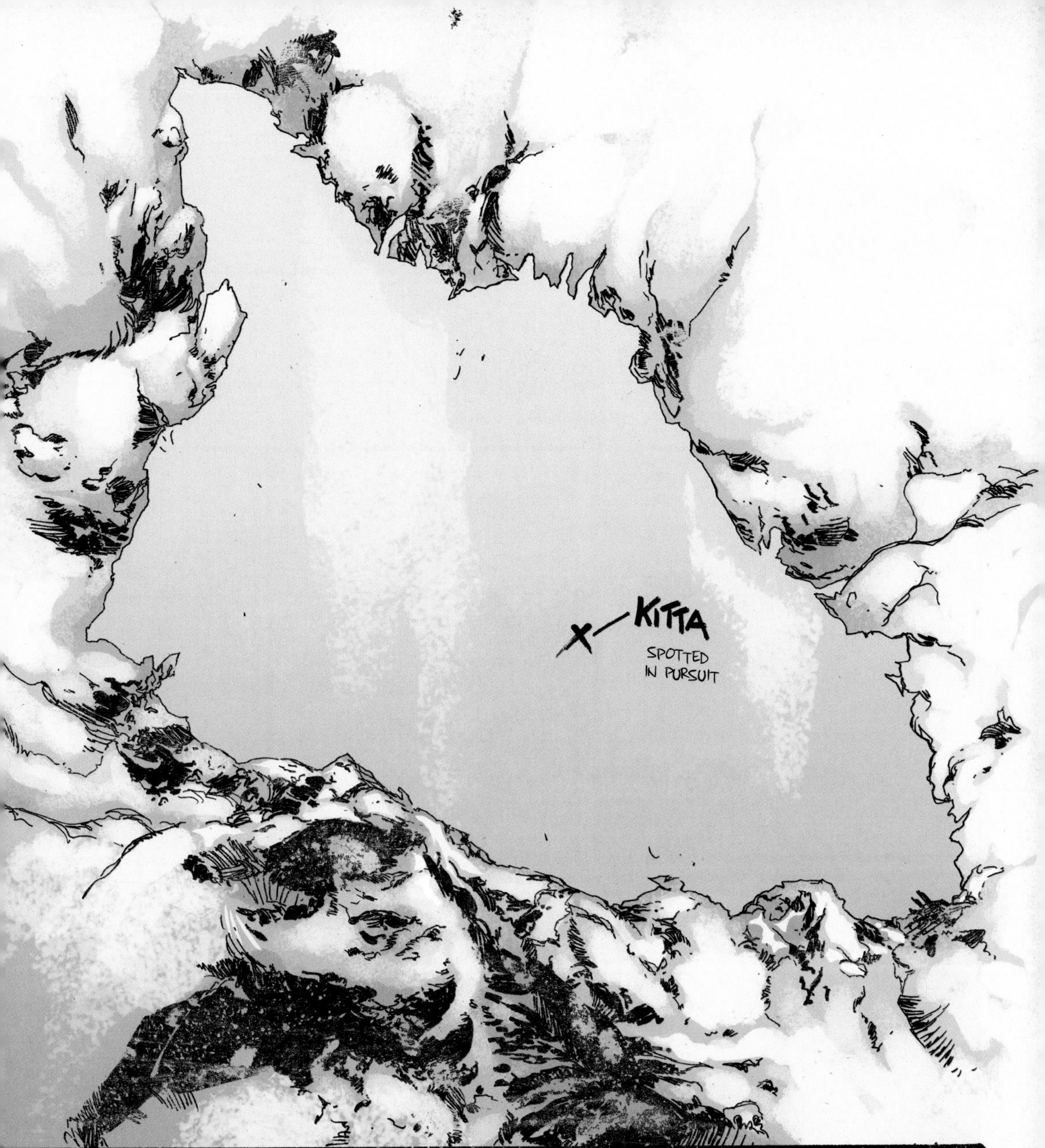
KITTA
SPOTTED
IN PURSUIT

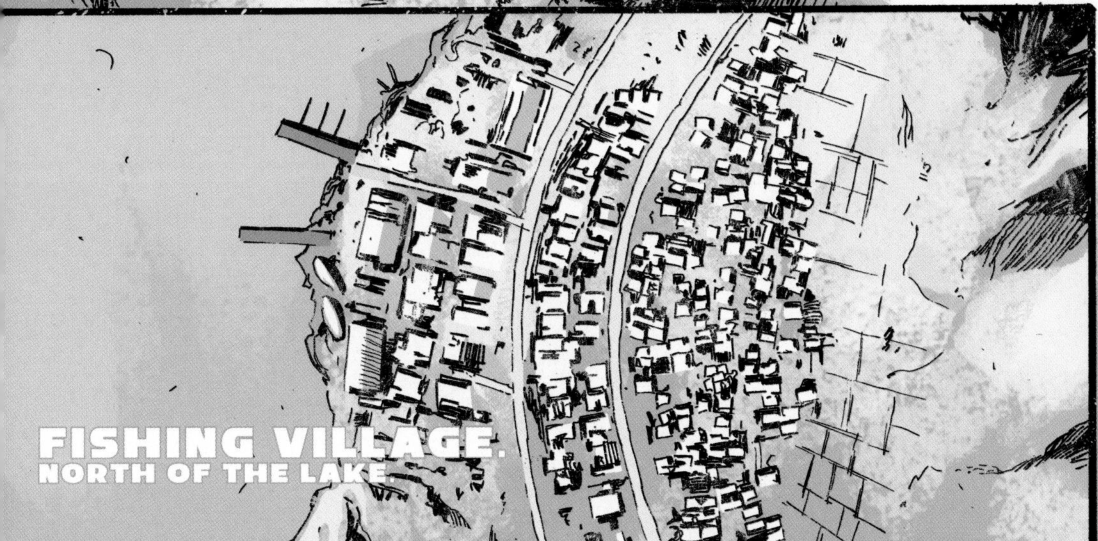
FISHING VILLAGE.
NORTH OF THE LAKE.

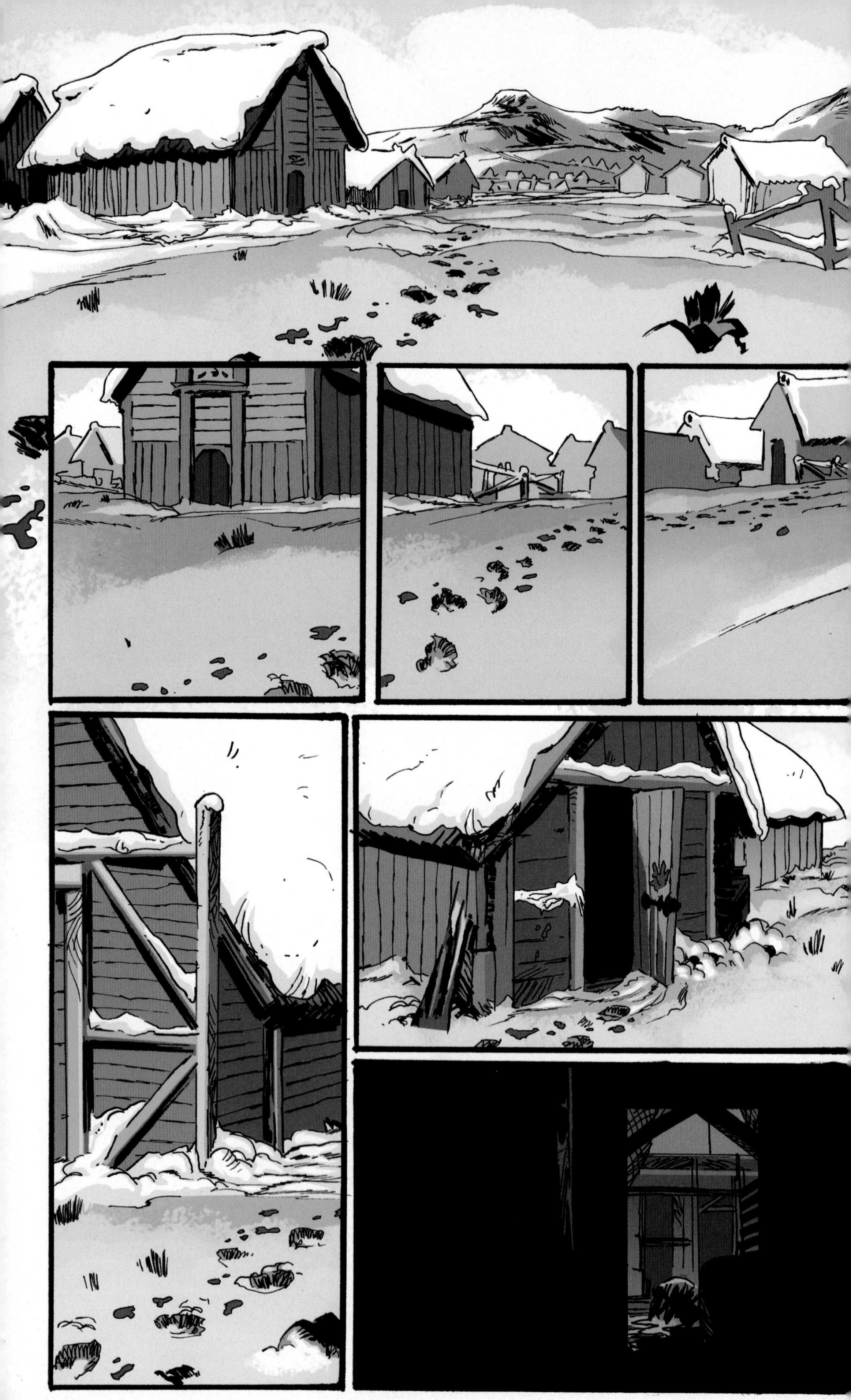

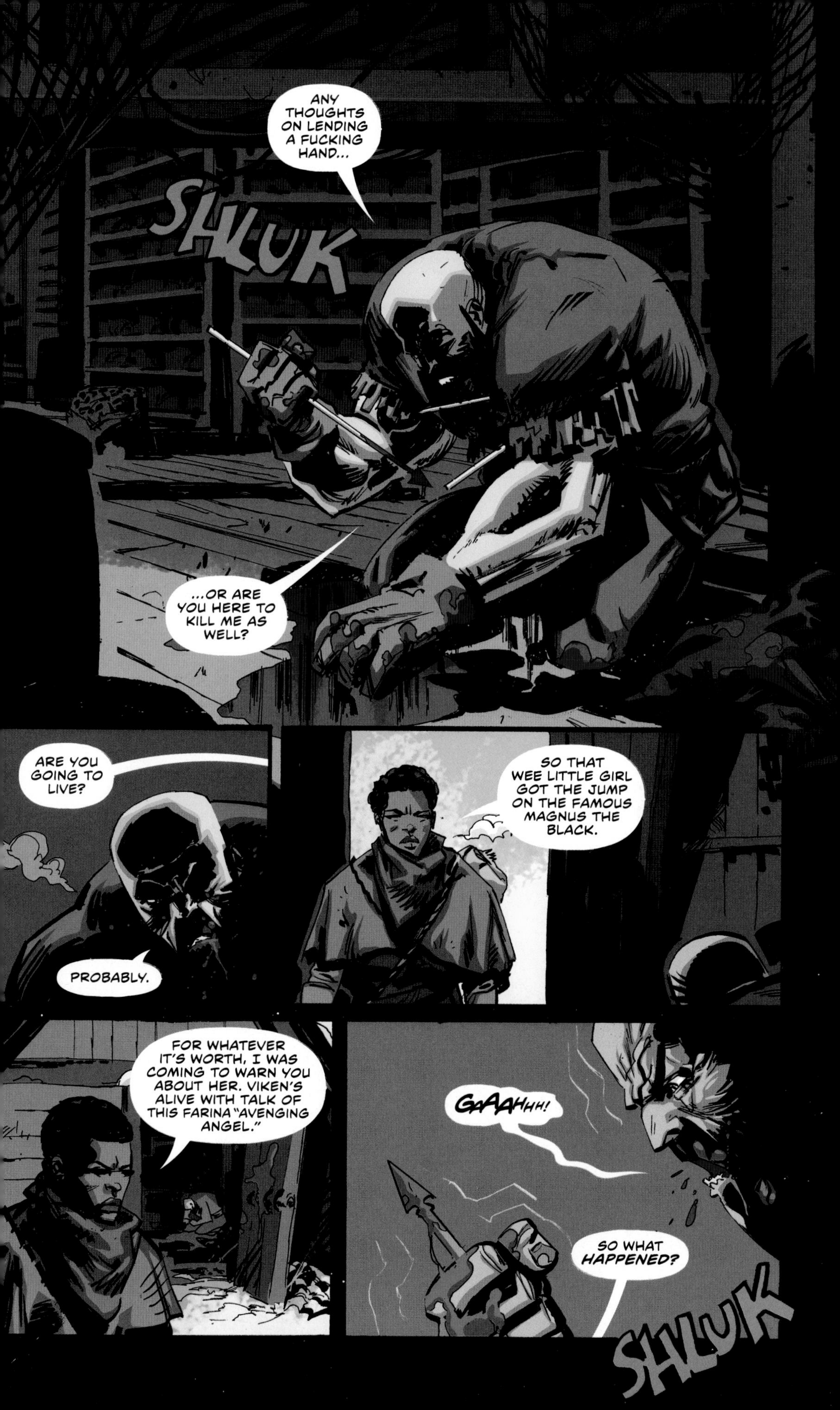
SHLUK
ANY THOUGHTS ON LENDING A FUCKING HAND...
...OR ARE YOU HERE TO KILL ME AS WELL?
ARE YOU GOING TO LIVE?
PROBABLY.
SO THAT WEE LITTLE GIRL GOT THE JUMP ON THE FAMOUS MAGNUS THE BLACK.
FOR WHATEVER IT'S WORTH, I WAS COMING TO WARN YOU ABOUT HER. VIKEN'S ALIVE WITH TALK OF THIS FARINA "AVENGING ANGEL."
GAAAHHH!
SO WHAT HAPPENED?
SHLUK

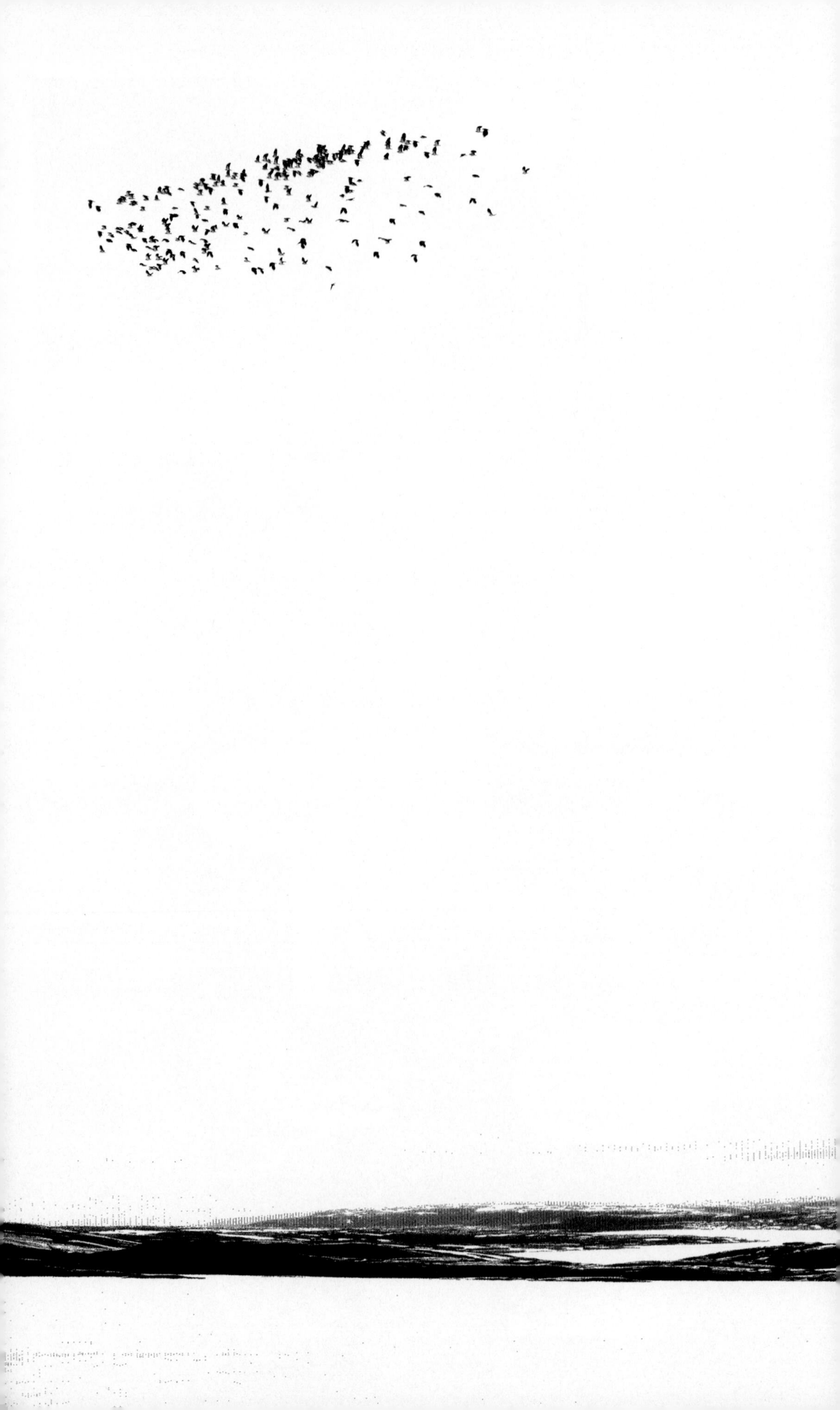

BRIAN WOOD / GARRY BROWN / DAVE McCAIG / STEVE WANDS

BLACK ROAD

#5 - THE VILLAGE NORTH OF THE LAKE

A MAGNUS THE BLACK MYSTERY

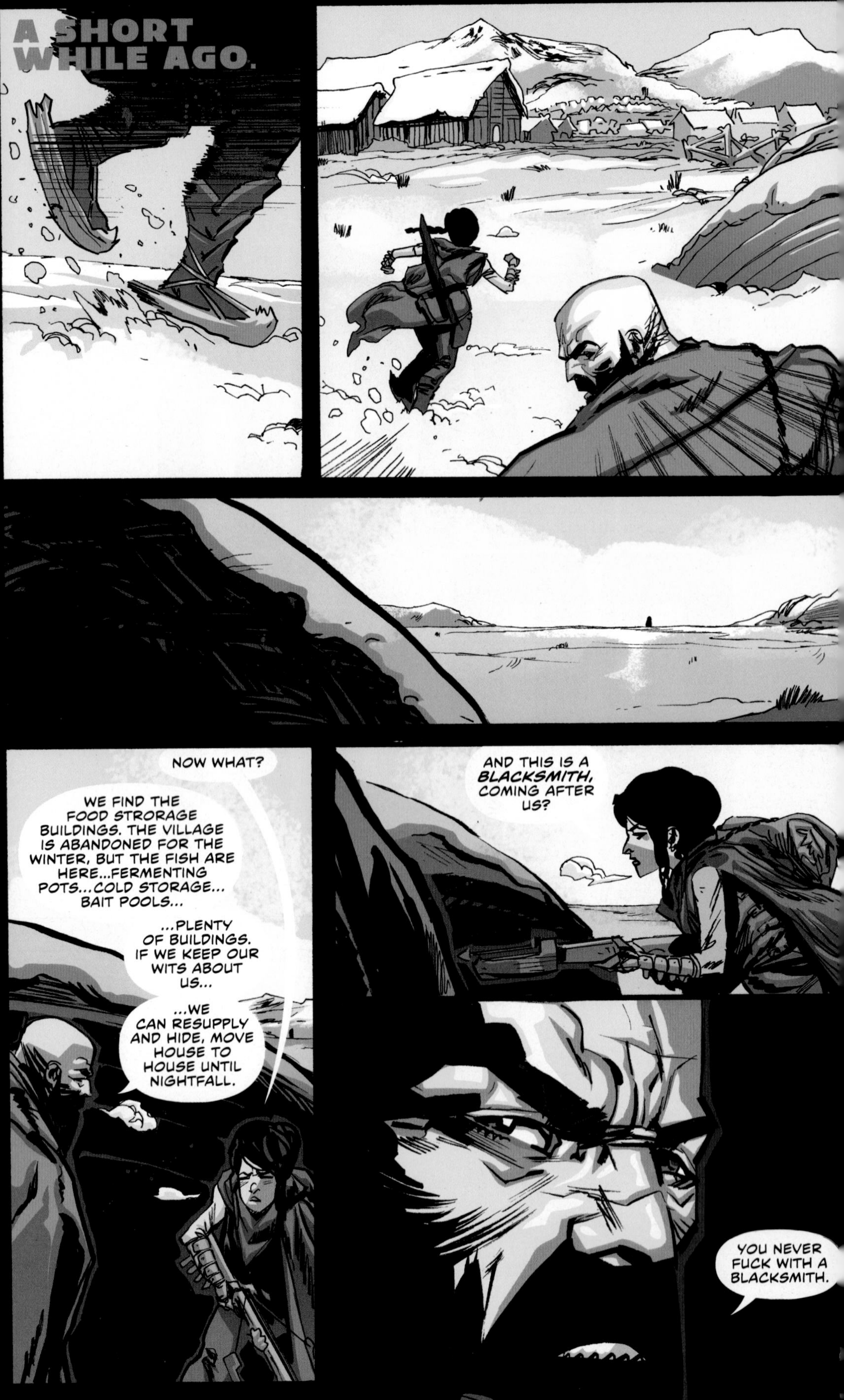
A SHORT WHILE AGO.
NOW WHAT?
WE FIND THE FOOD STRORAGE BUILDINGS. THE VILLAGE IS ABANDONED FOR THE WINTER, BUT THE FISH ARE HERE...FERMENTING POTS...COLD STORAGE... BAIT POOLS...
...PLENTY OF BUILDINGS. IF WE KEEP OUR WITS ABOUT US...
...WE CAN RESUPPLY AND HIDE, MOVE HOUSE TO HOUSE UNTIL NIGHTFALL.
AND THIS IS A BLACKSMITH, COMING AFTER US?
YOU NEVER FUCK WITH A BLACKSMITH.

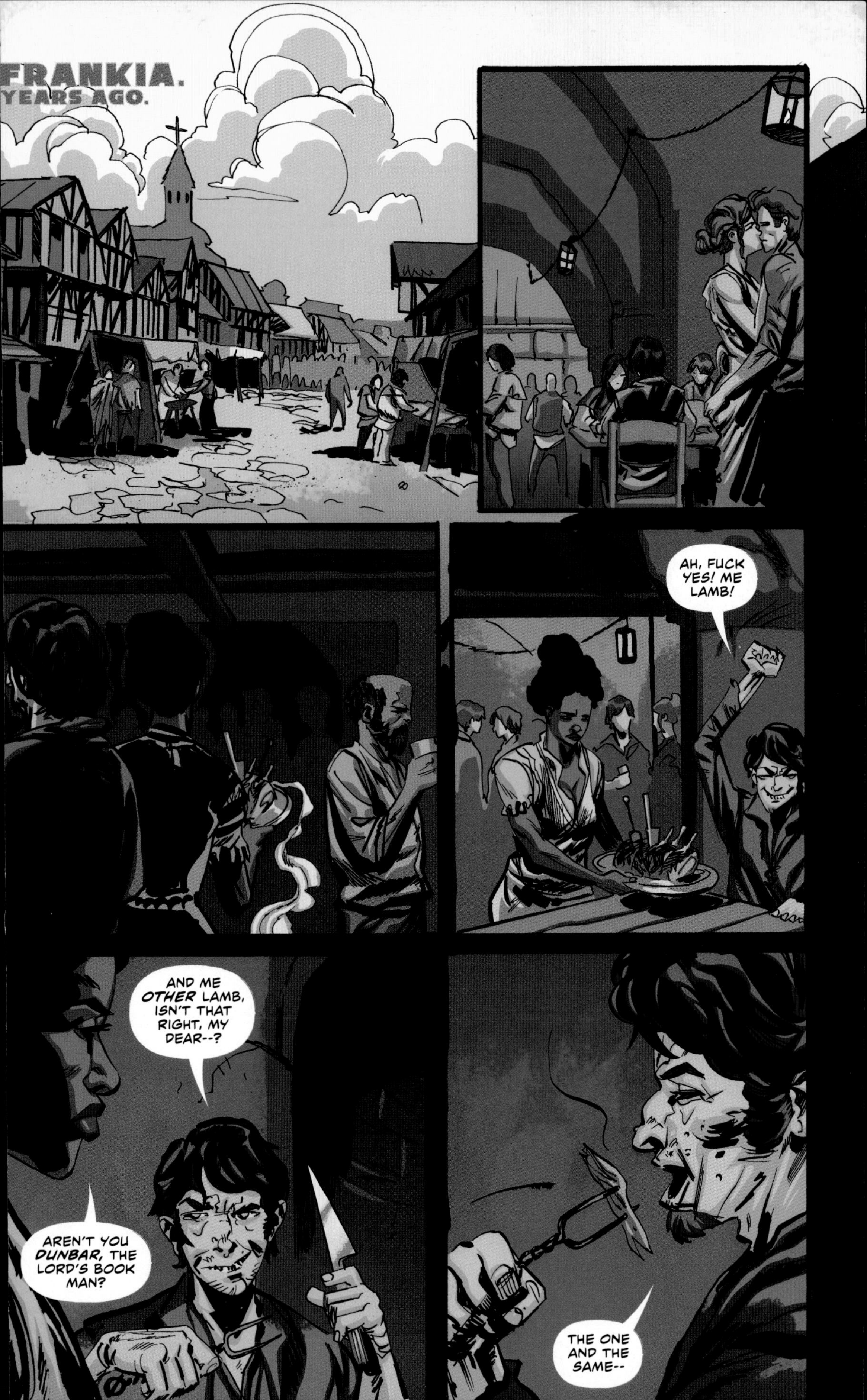
FRANKIA.
YEARS AGO.
AH, FUCK YES! ME LAMB!
AND ME *OTHER* LAMB, ISN'T THAT RIGHT, MY DEAR--?
AREN'T YOU *DUNBAR*, THE LORD'S BOOK MAN?
THE ONE AND THE SAME--

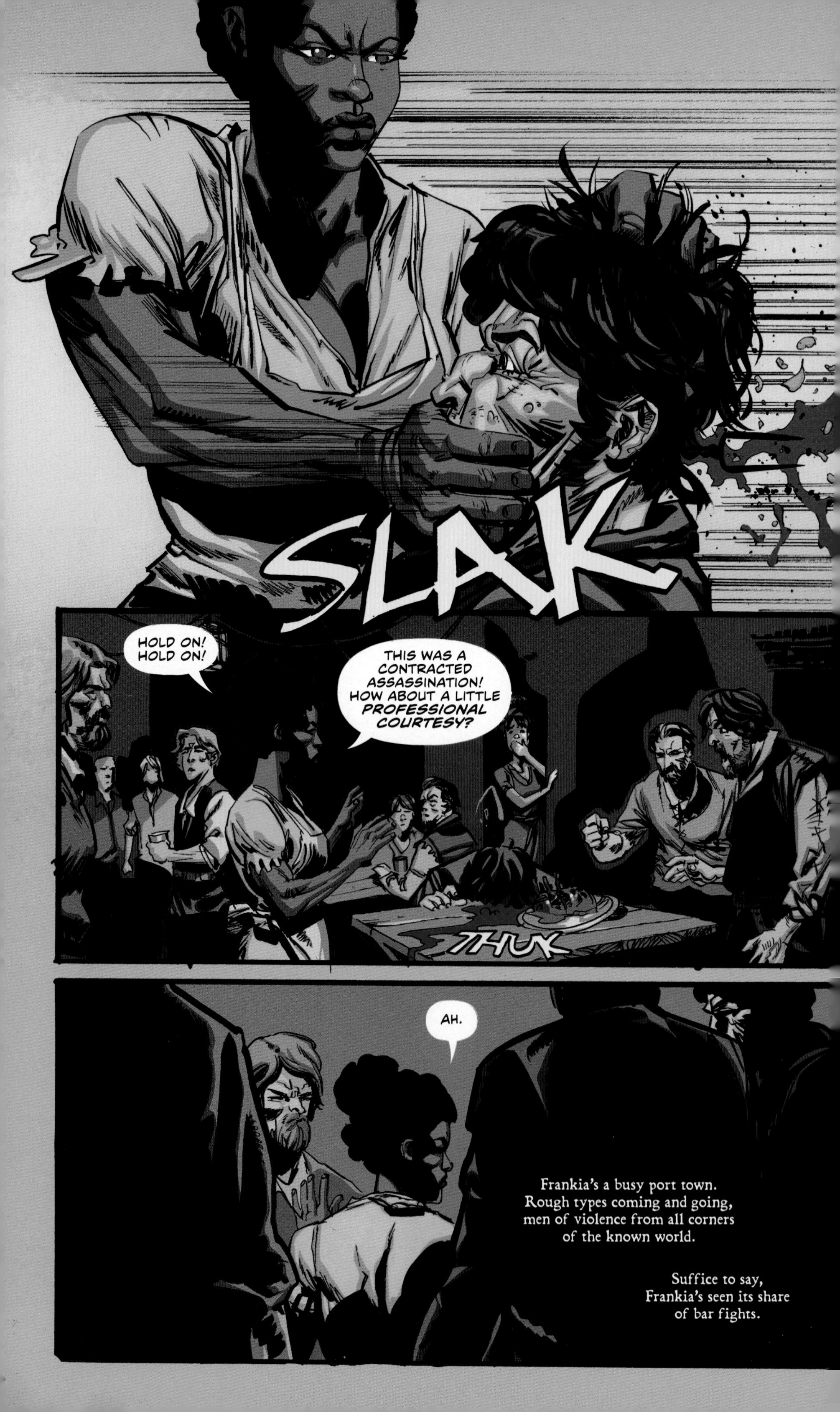
SLAK
HOLD ON! HOLD ON!
THIS WAS A CONTRACTED ASSASSINATION! HOW ABOUT A LITTLE PROFESSIONAL COURTESY?
THUK
AH.
Frankia's a busy port town. Rough types coming and going, men of violence from all corners of the known world.
Suffice to say, Frankia's seen its share of bar fights.

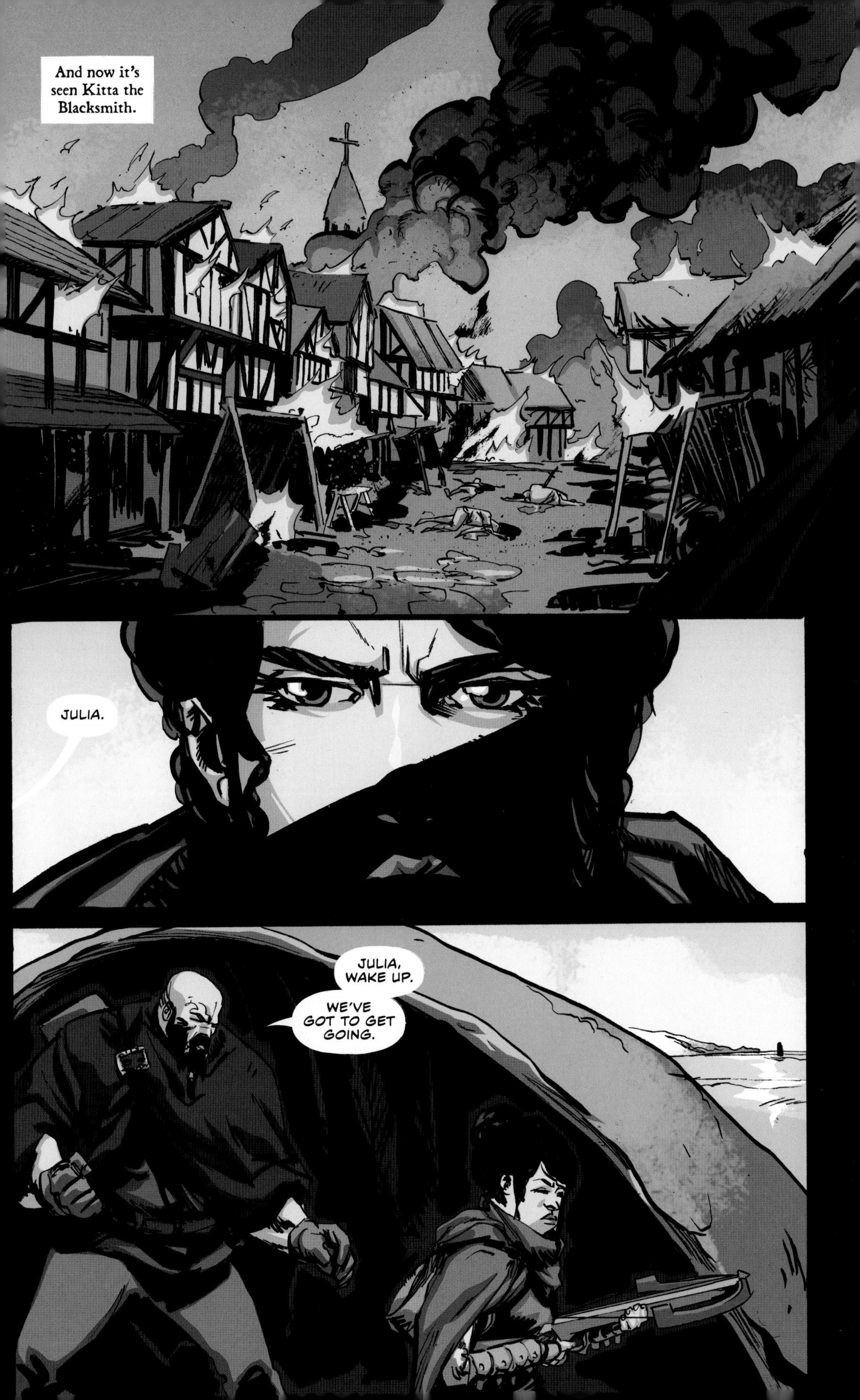
And now it's seen Kitta the Blacksmith.
JULIA.
JULIA, WAKE UP.
WE'VE GOT TO GET GOING.

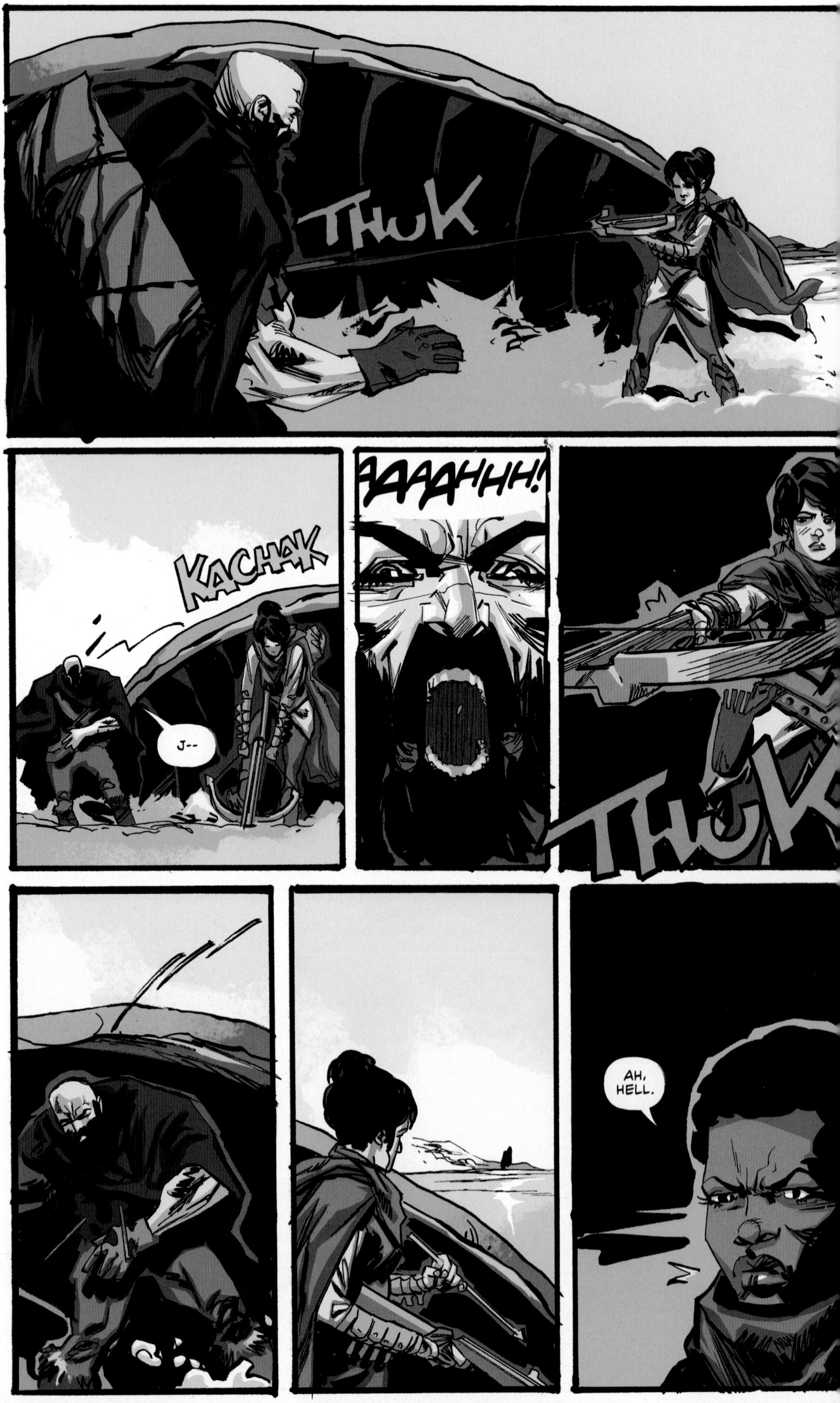
THUK
KACHAK
J--
AAAAHHH!
THUK
AH, HELL.

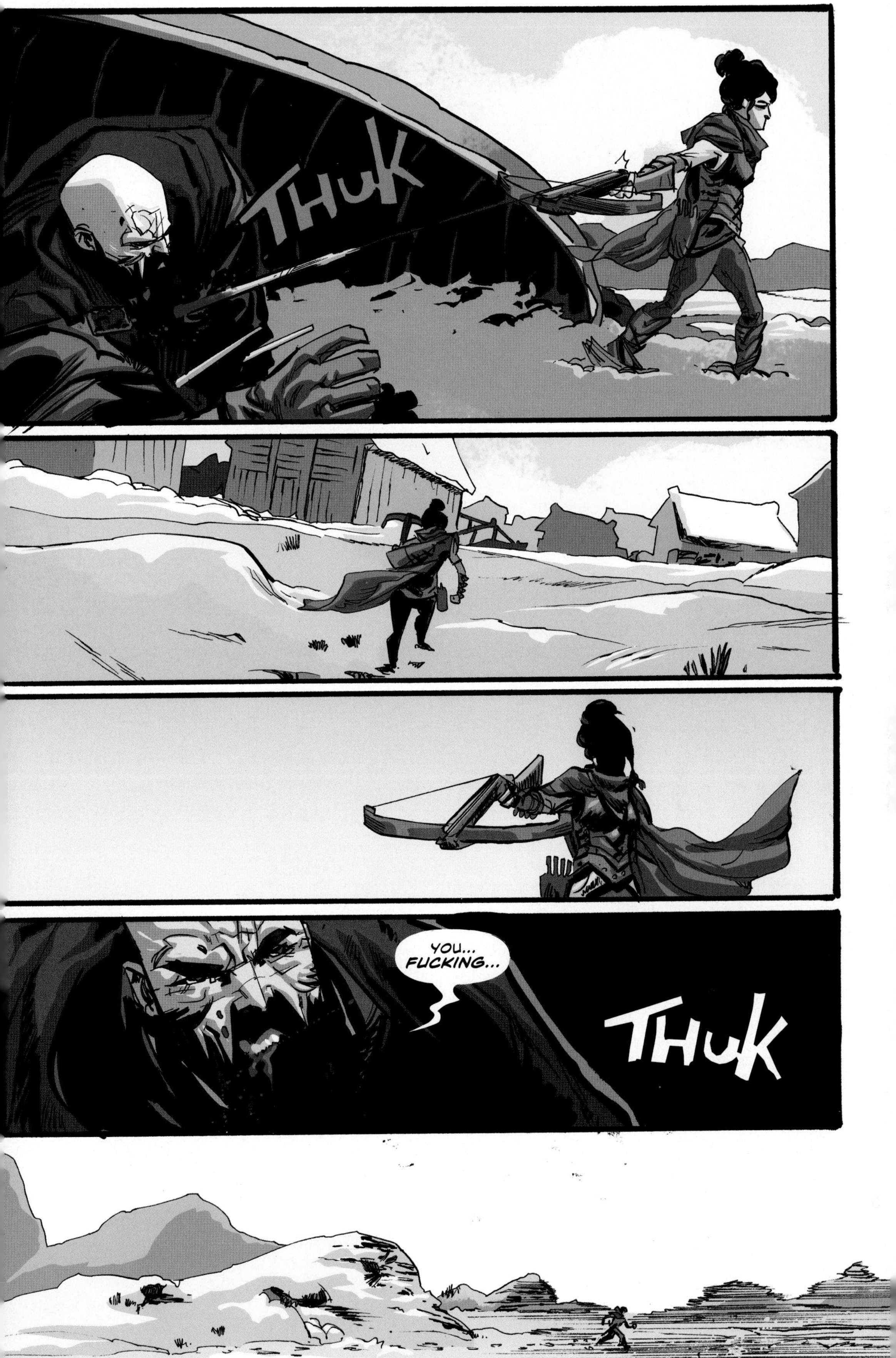
THUK
YOU... FUCKING...
THUK

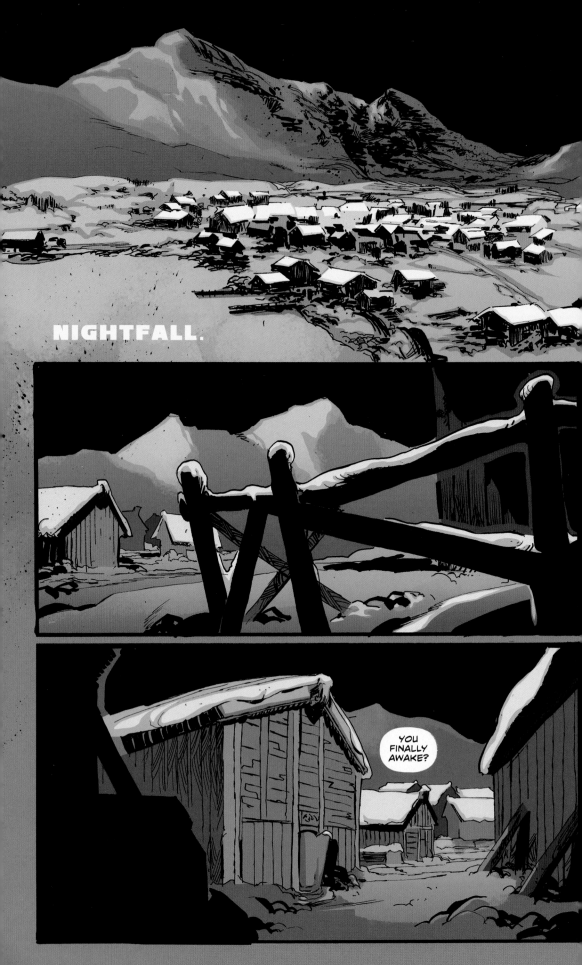

NIGHTFALL.

YOU FINALLY AWAKE?

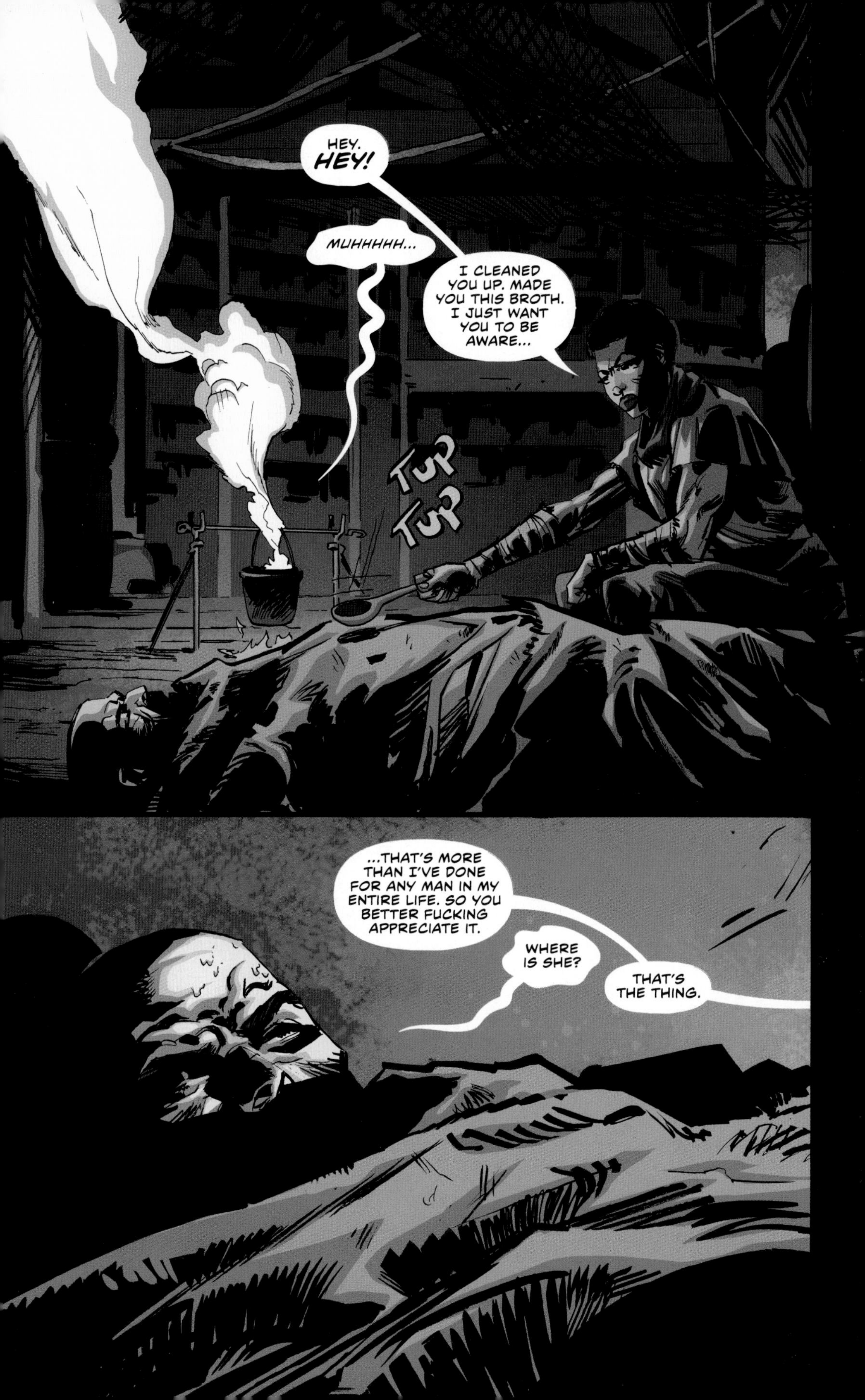
HEY. HEY!
MUHHHHH...
I CLEANED YOU UP. MADE YOU THIS BROTH. I JUST WANT YOU TO BE AWARE...
TUP TUP
...THAT'S MORE THAN I'VE DONE FOR ANY MAN IN MY ENTIRE LIFE. SO YOU BETTER FUCKING APPRECIATE IT.
WHERE IS SHE?
THAT'S THE THING.

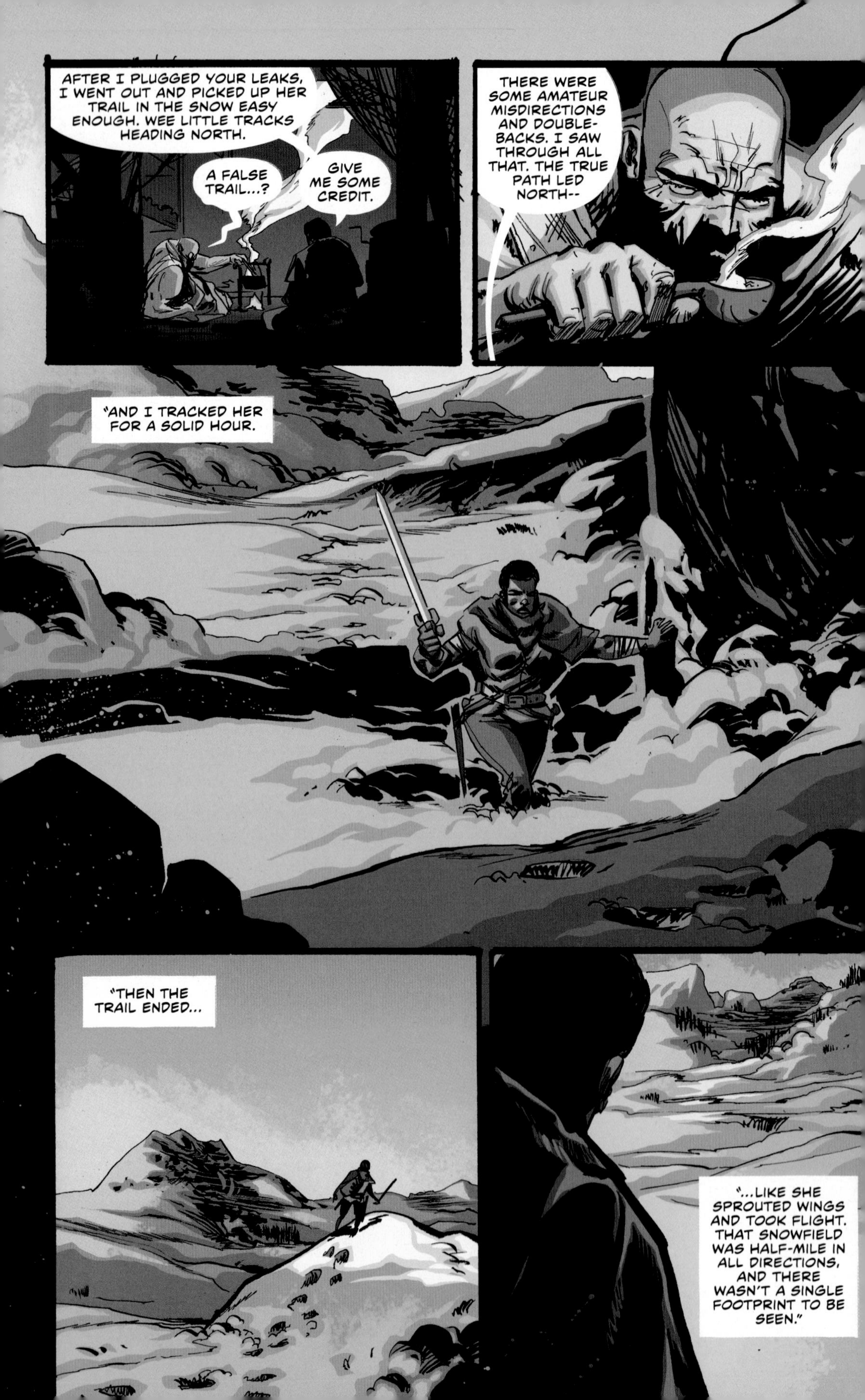
AFTER I PLUGGED YOUR LEAKS, I WENT OUT AND PICKED UP HER TRAIL IN THE SNOW EASY ENOUGH. WEE LITTLE TRACKS HEADING NORTH.
A FALSE TRAIL...?
GIVE ME SOME CREDIT.
THERE WERE SOME AMATEUR MISDIRECTIONS AND DOUBLE-BACKS. I SAW THROUGH ALL THAT. THE TRUE PATH LED NORTH--
"AND I TRACKED HER FOR A SOLID HOUR.
"THEN THE TRAIL ENDED...
"...LIKE SHE SPROUTED WINGS AND TOOK FLIGHT. THAT SNOWFIELD WAS HALF-MILE IN ALL DIRECTIONS, AND THERE WASN'T A SINGLE FOOTPRINT TO BE SEEN."

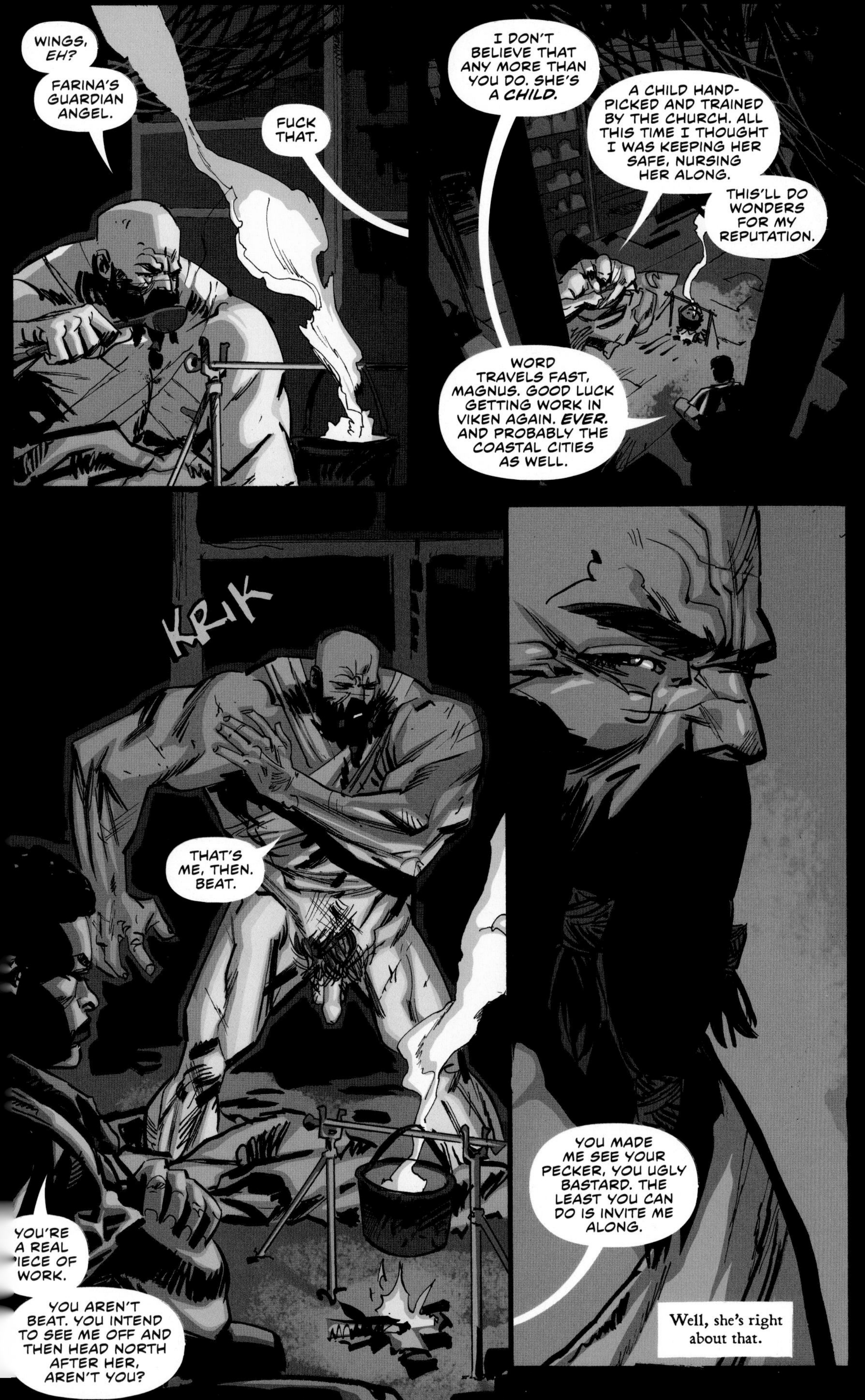
WINGS, EH?
FARINA'S GUARDIAN ANGEL.
FUCK THAT.
I DON'T BELIEVE THAT ANY MORE THAN YOU DO. SHE'S A *CHILD*.
A CHILD HAND-PICKED AND TRAINED BY THE CHURCH. ALL THIS TIME I THOUGHT I WAS KEEPING HER SAFE, NURSING HER ALONG.
THIS'LL DO WONDERS FOR MY REPUTATION.
WORD TRAVELS FAST, MAGNUS. GOOD LUCK GETTING WORK IN VIKEN AGAIN. *EVER.* AND PROBABLY THE COASTAL CITIES AS WELL.
KRIK
THAT'S ME, THEN. BEAT.
YOU'RE A REAL IECE OF WORK.
YOU AREN'T BEAT. YOU INTEND TO SEE ME OFF AND THEN HEAD NORTH AFTER HER, AREN'T YOU?
YOU MADE ME SEE YOUR PECKER, YOU UGLY BASTARD. THE LEAST YOU CAN DO IS INVITE ME ALONG.
Well, she's right about that.

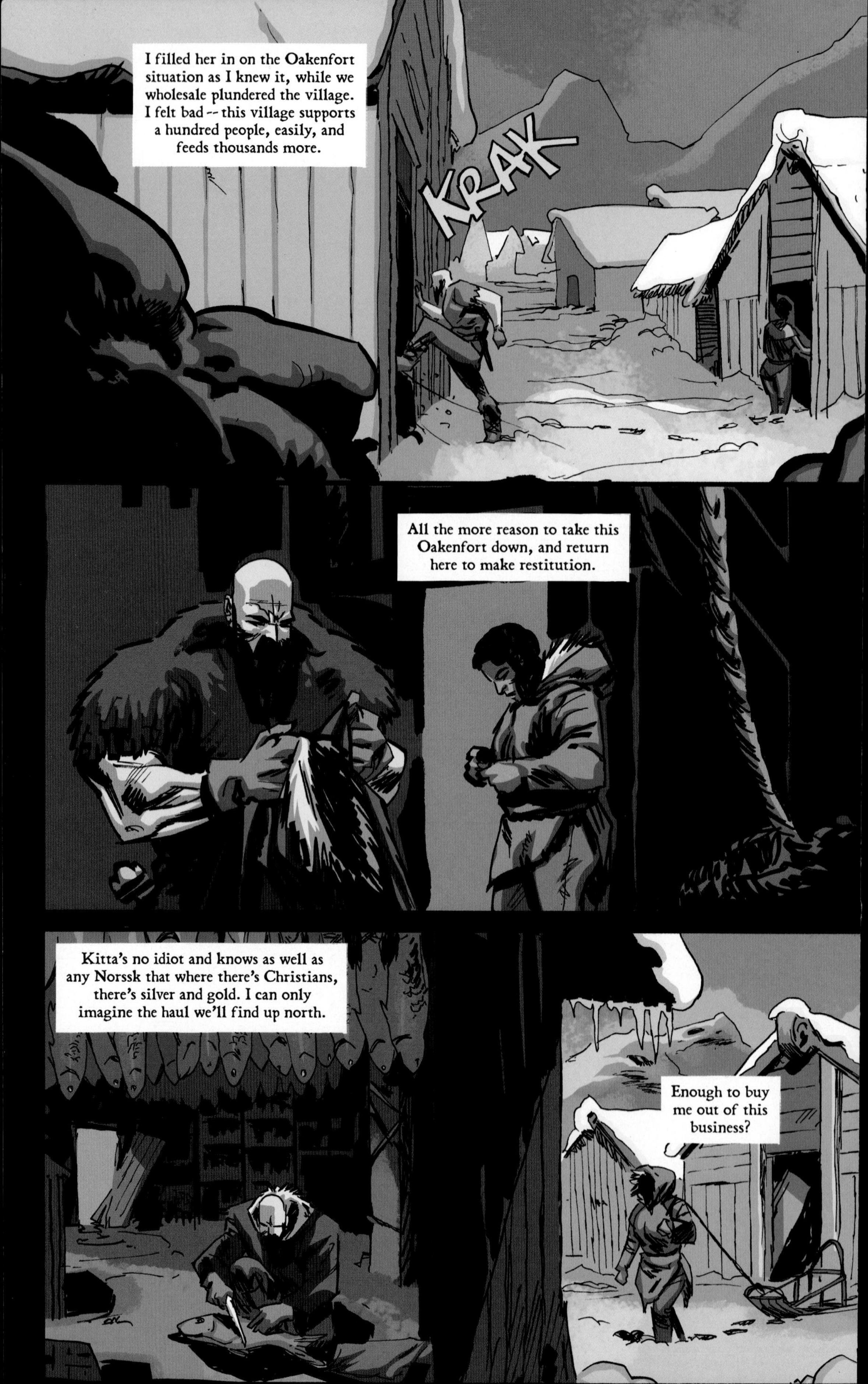
I filled her in on the Oakenfort situation as I knew it, while we wholesale plundered the village. I felt bad -- this village supports a hundred people, easily, and feeds thousands more.
KRAK
All the more reason to take this Oakenfort down, and return here to make restitution.
Kitta's no idiot and knows as well as any Norssk that where there's Christians, there's silver and gold. I can only imagine the haul we'll find up north.
Enough to buy me out of this business?

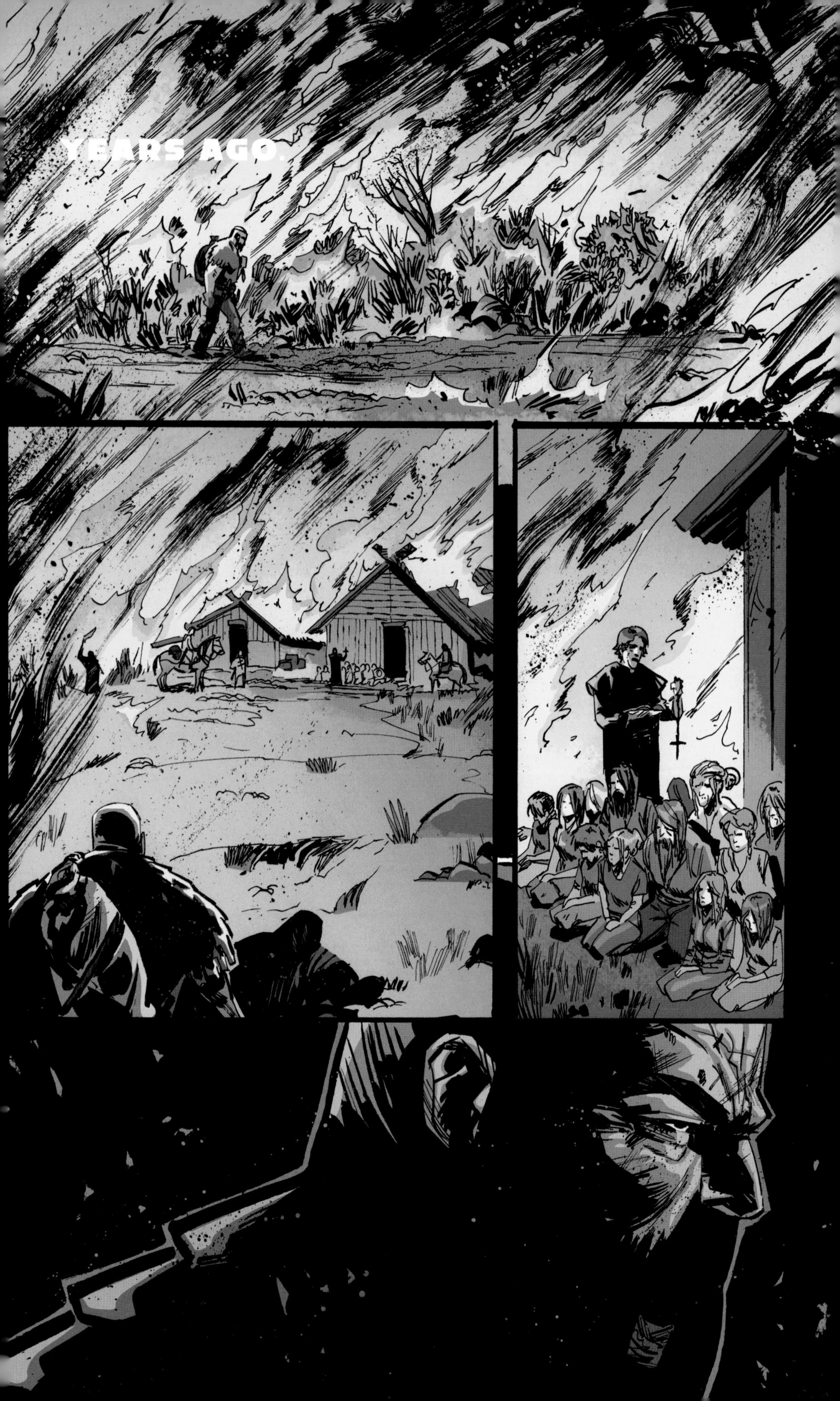
YEARS AGO.

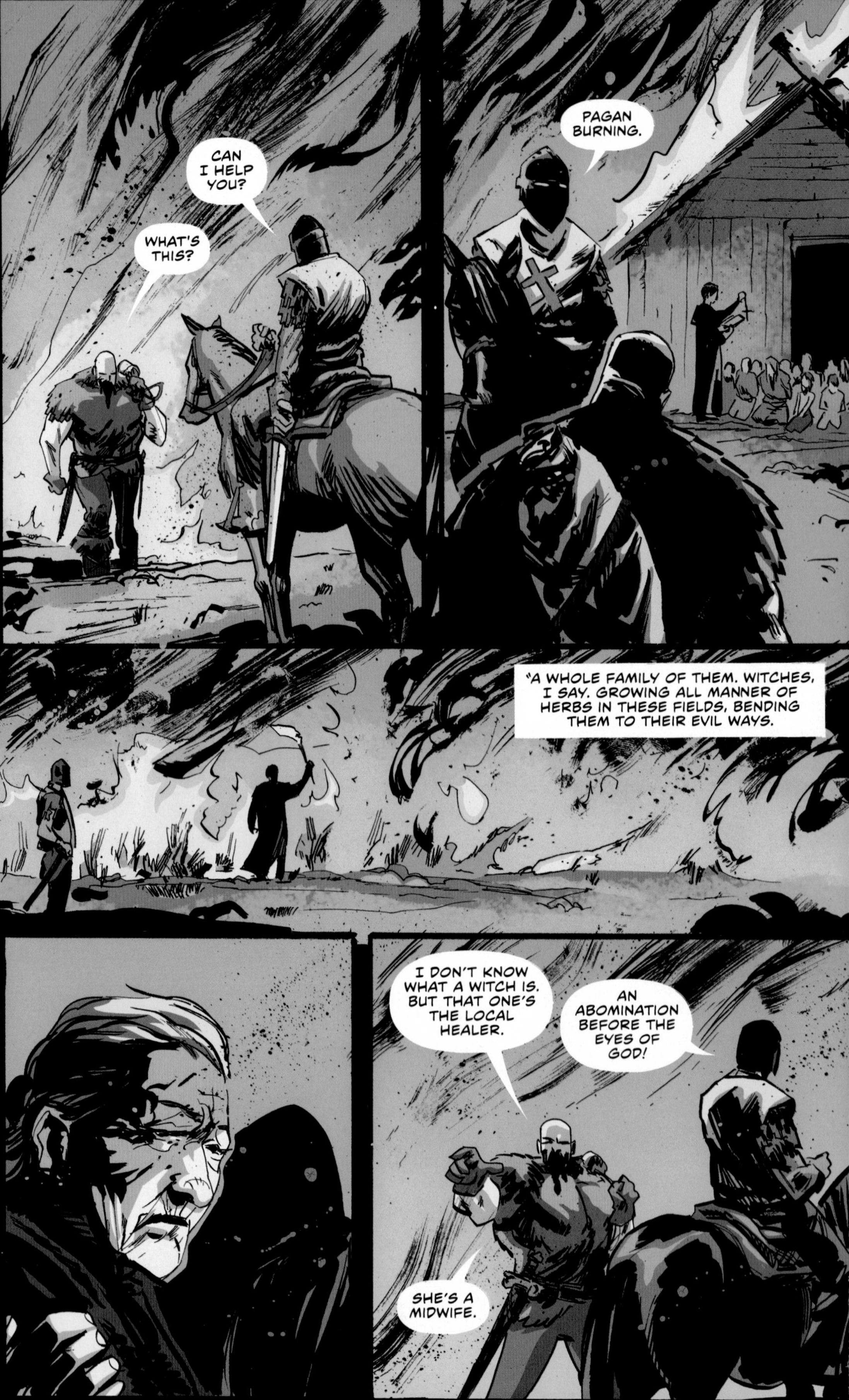

CAN I HELP YOU?
WHAT'S THIS?
PAGAN BURNING.
"A WHOLE FAMILY OF THEM. WITCHES, I SAY. GROWING ALL MANNER OF HERBS IN THESE FIELDS, BENDING THEM TO THEIR EVIL WAYS.
I DON'T KNOW WHAT A WITCH IS. BUT THAT ONE'S THE LOCAL HEALER.
AN ABOMINATION BEFORE THE EYES OF GOD!
SHE'S A MIDWIFE.

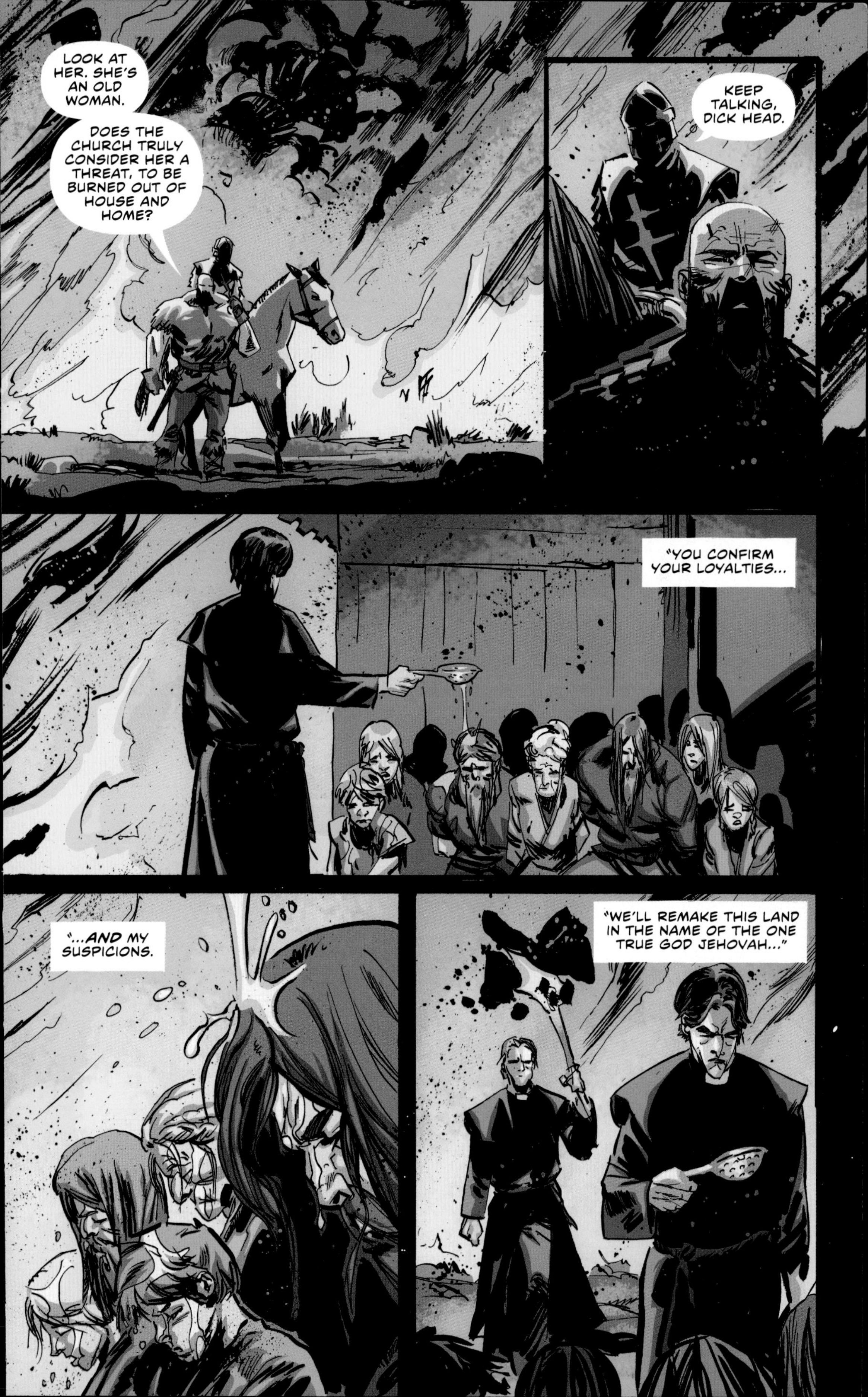
LOOK AT HER. SHE'S AN OLD WOMAN.
DOES THE CHURCH TRULY CONSIDER HER A THREAT, TO BE BURNED OUT OF HOUSE AND HOME?
KEEP TALKING, DICK HEAD.
"YOU CONFIRM YOUR LOYALTIES...
"...AND MY SUSPICIONS.
"WE'LL REMAKE THIS LAND IN THE NAME OF THE ONE TRUE GOD JEHOVAH..."

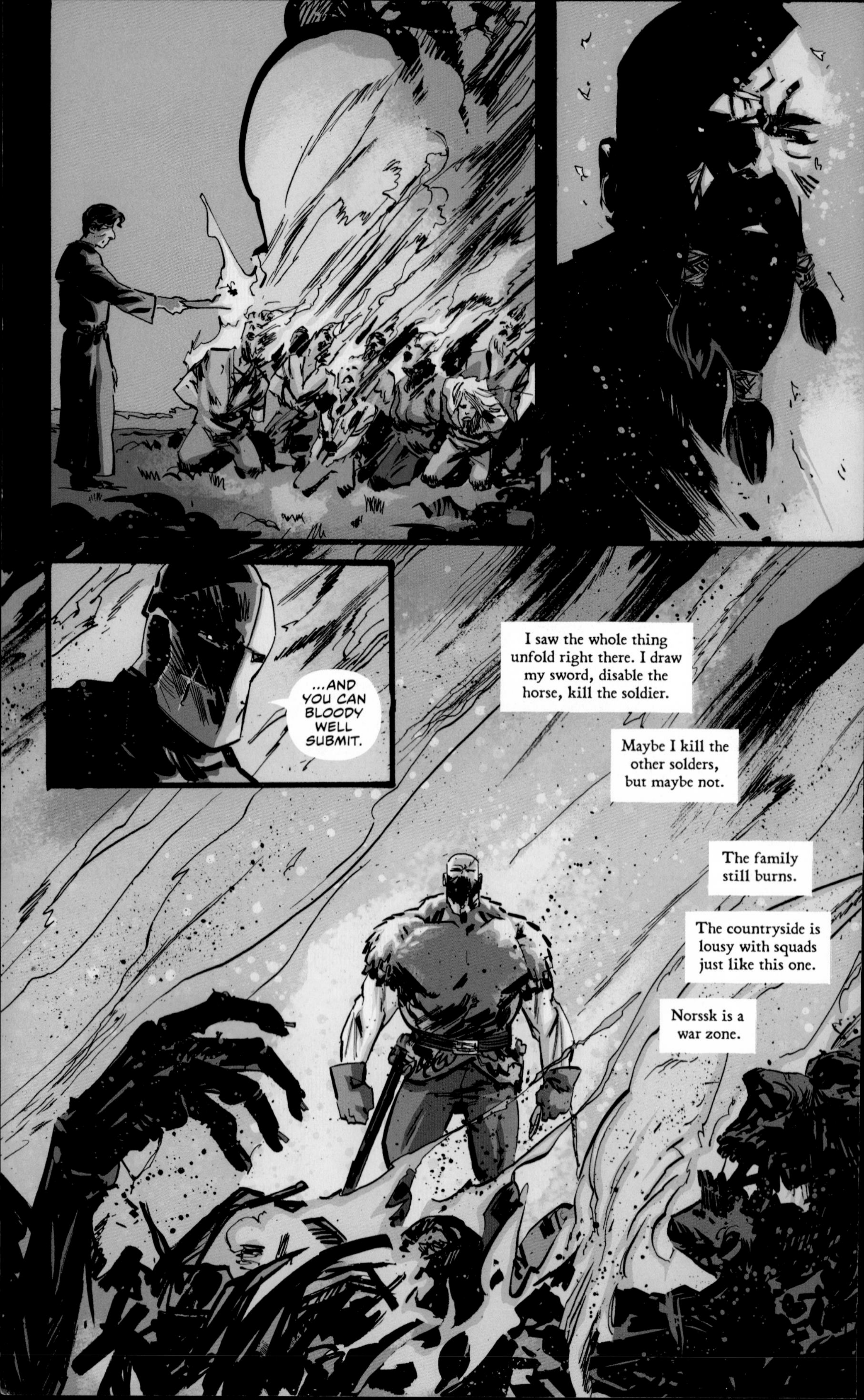

...AND YOU CAN BLOODY WELL SUBMIT.
I saw the whole thing unfold right there. I draw my sword, disable the horse, kill the soldier.
Maybe I kill the other solders, but maybe not.
The family still burns.
The countryside is lousy with squads just like this one.
Norssk is a war zone.

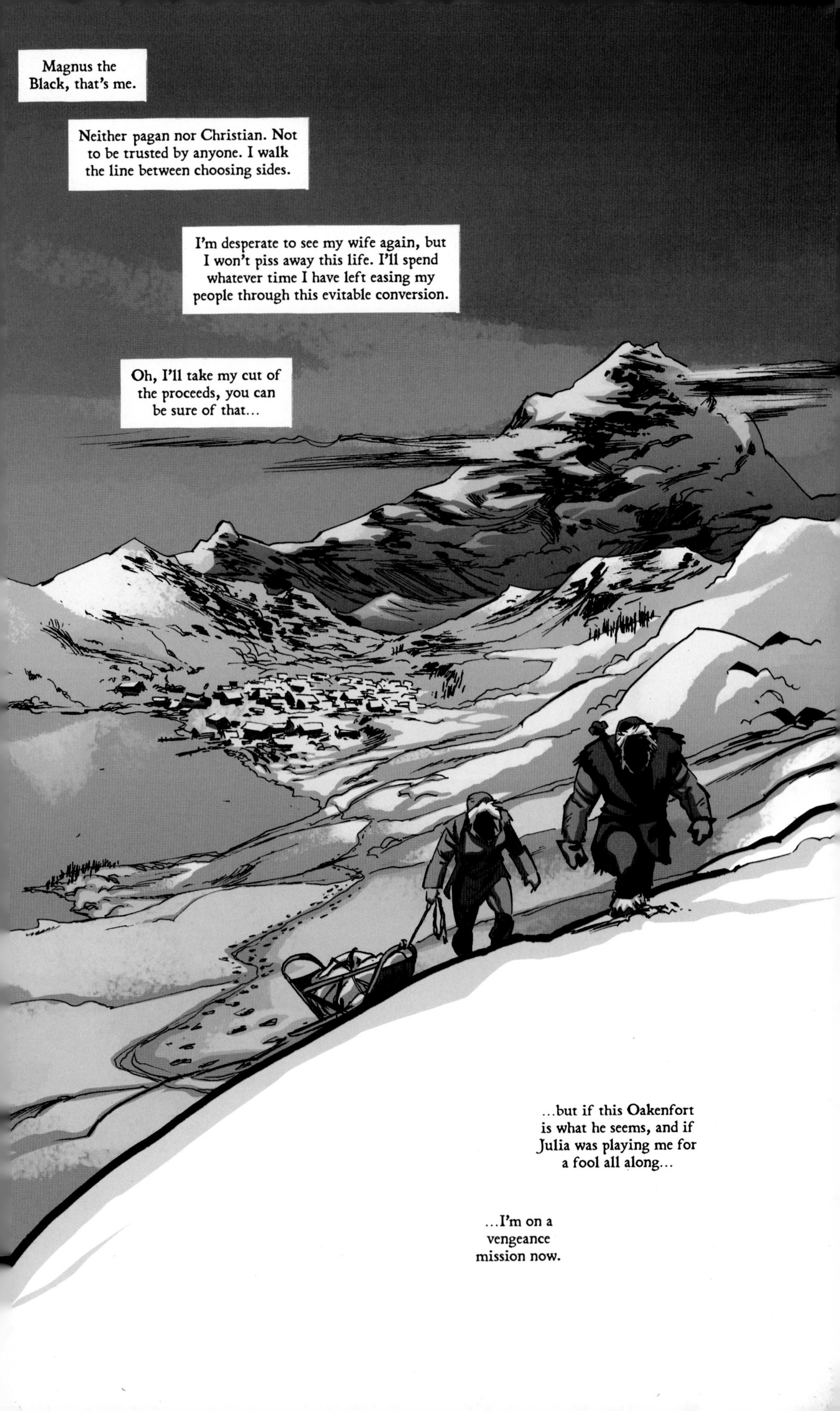

Magnus the Black, that's me.
Neither pagan nor Christian. Not to be trusted by anyone. I walk the line between choosing sides.
I'm desperate to see my wife again, but I won't piss away this life. I'll spend whatever time I have left easing my people through this evitable conversion.
Oh, I'll take my cut of the proceeds, you can be sure of that...
...but if this Oakenfort is what he seems, and if Julia was playing me for a fool all along...
...I'm on a vengeance mission now.

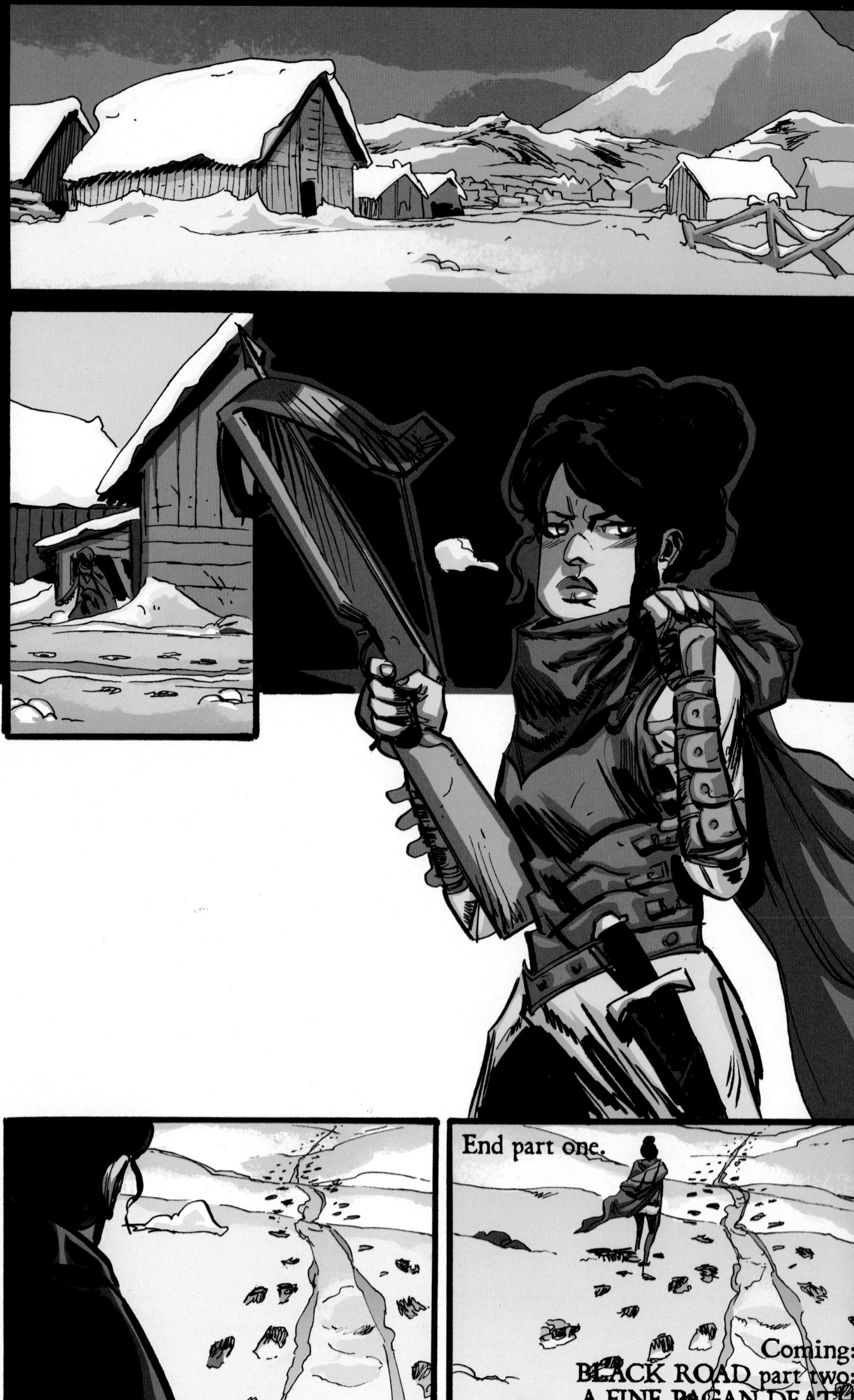
End part one.
Coming:
BLACK ROAD part two:
A FINE PAGAN DEATH

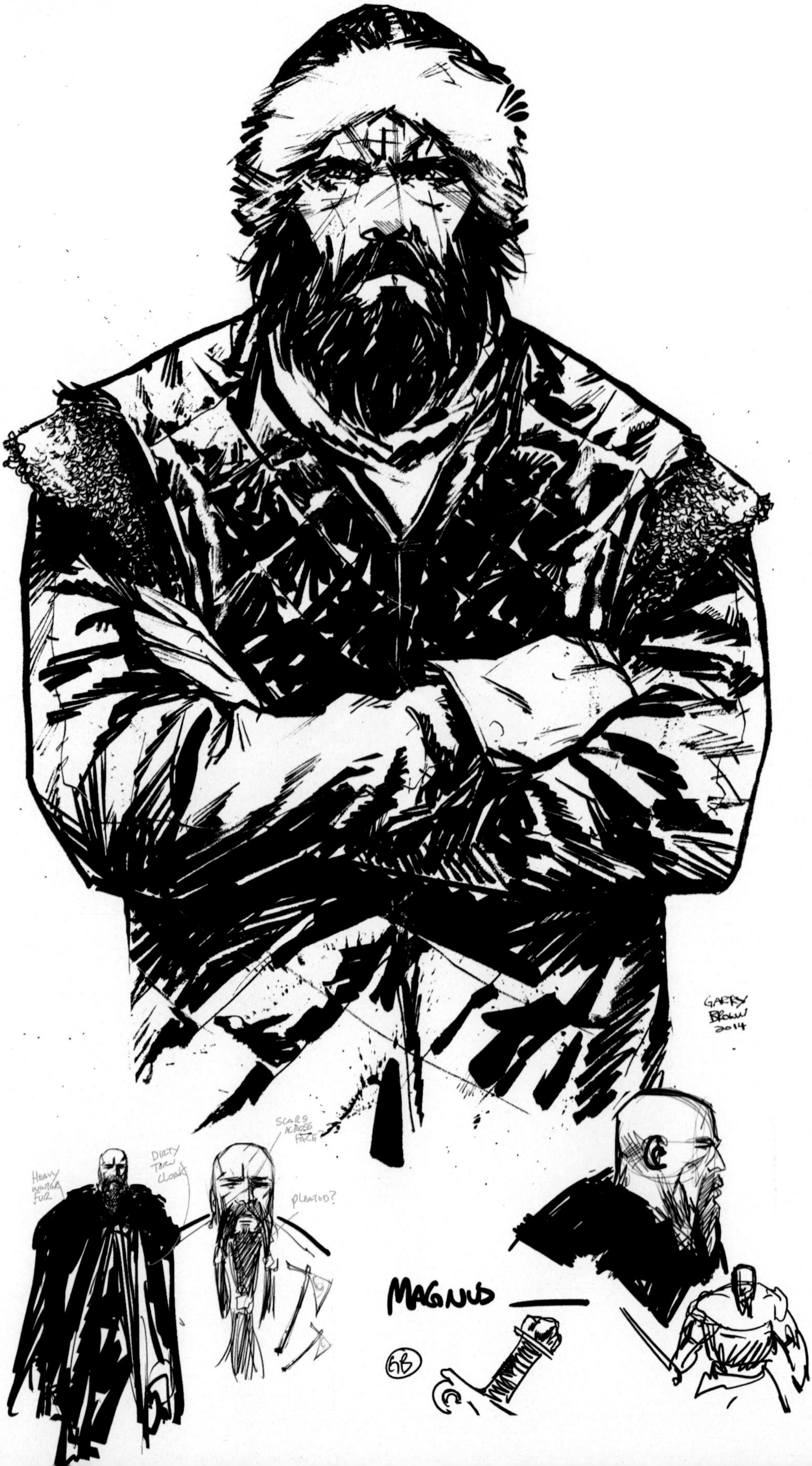
GARRY BROWN 2014
HEAVY WINTER FUR
DIRTY TORN CLOAK
SCARS ACROSS FACE?
PLEATED?
MAGNUS
GB

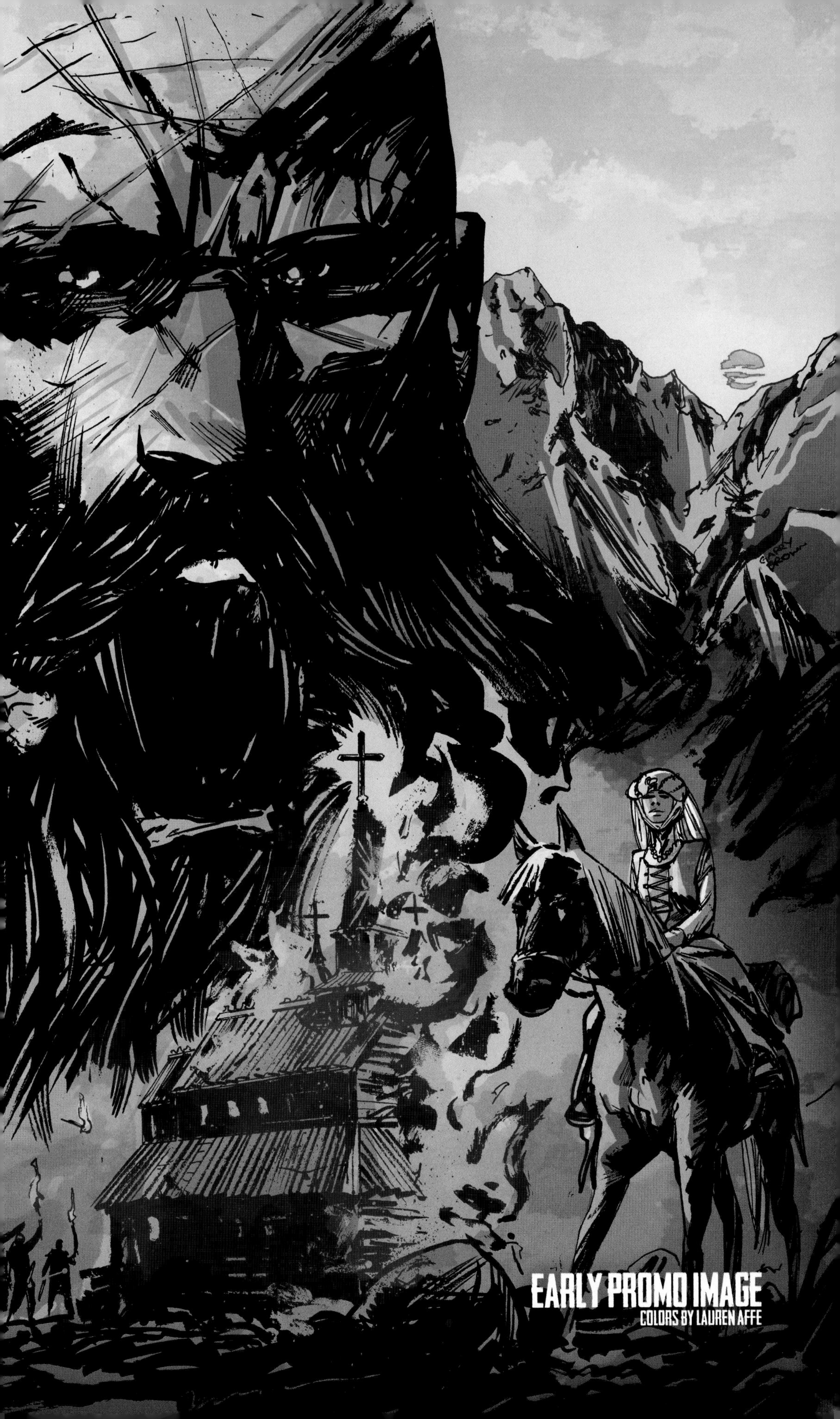

EARLY PROMO IMAGE
COLORS BY LAUREN AFFE

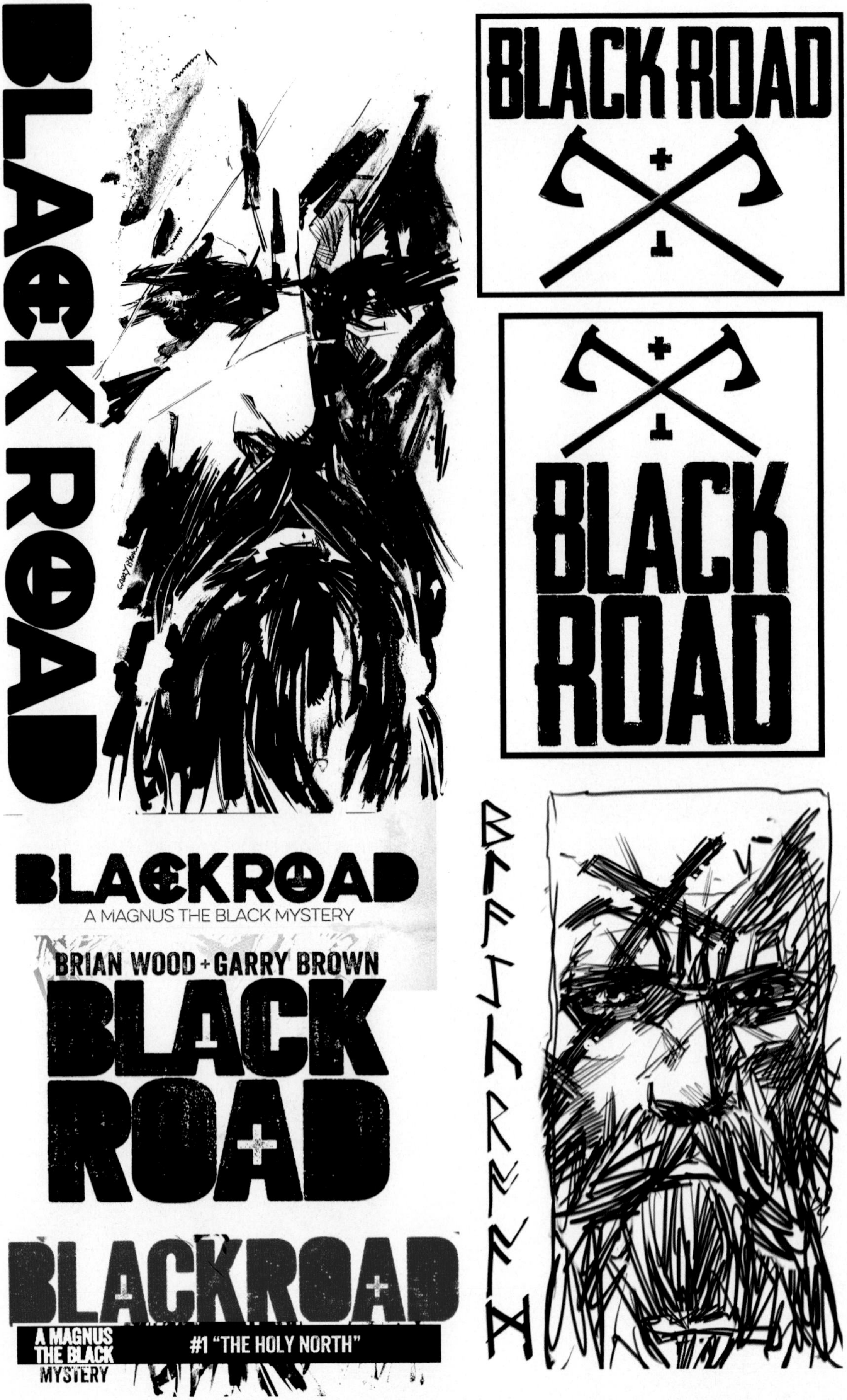

BLACK ROAD
BLACK ROAD
BLACK ROAD
BLACKROAD
A MAGNUS THE BLACK MYSTERY
BRIAN WOOD + GARRY BROWN
BLACK ROAD
BLACKROAD
A MAGNUS THE BLACK MYSTERY
#1 "THE HOLY NORTH"

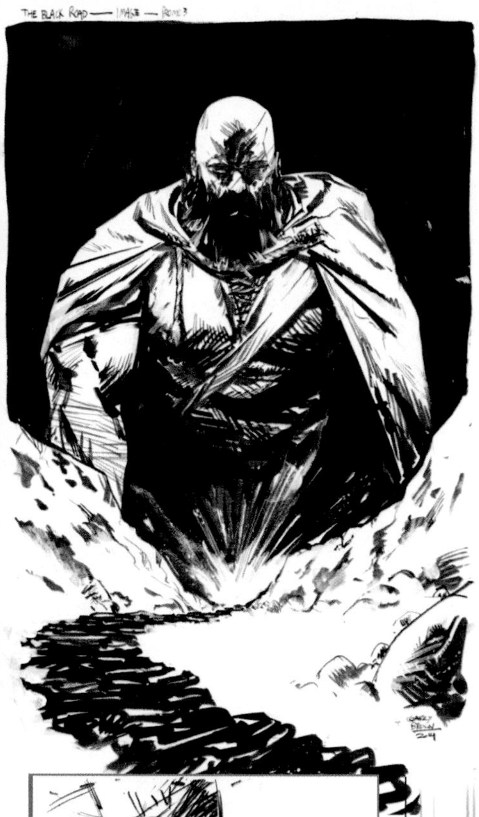
THE BLACK ROAD — IMAGE —

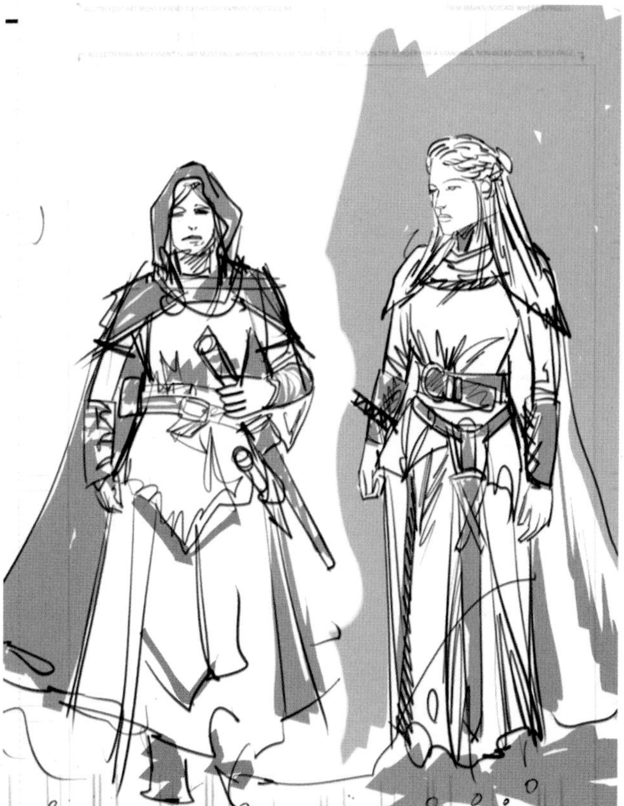

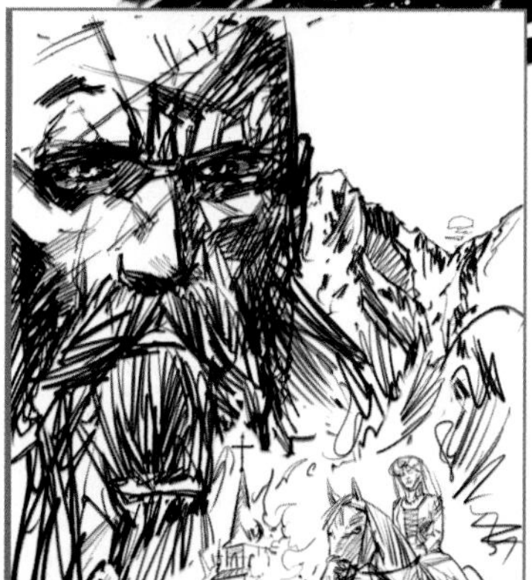

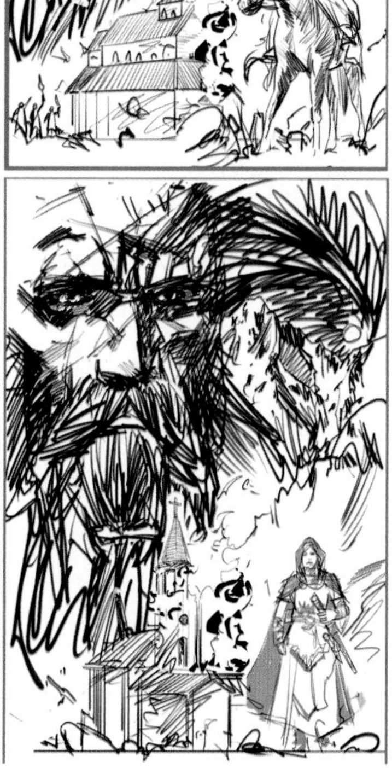

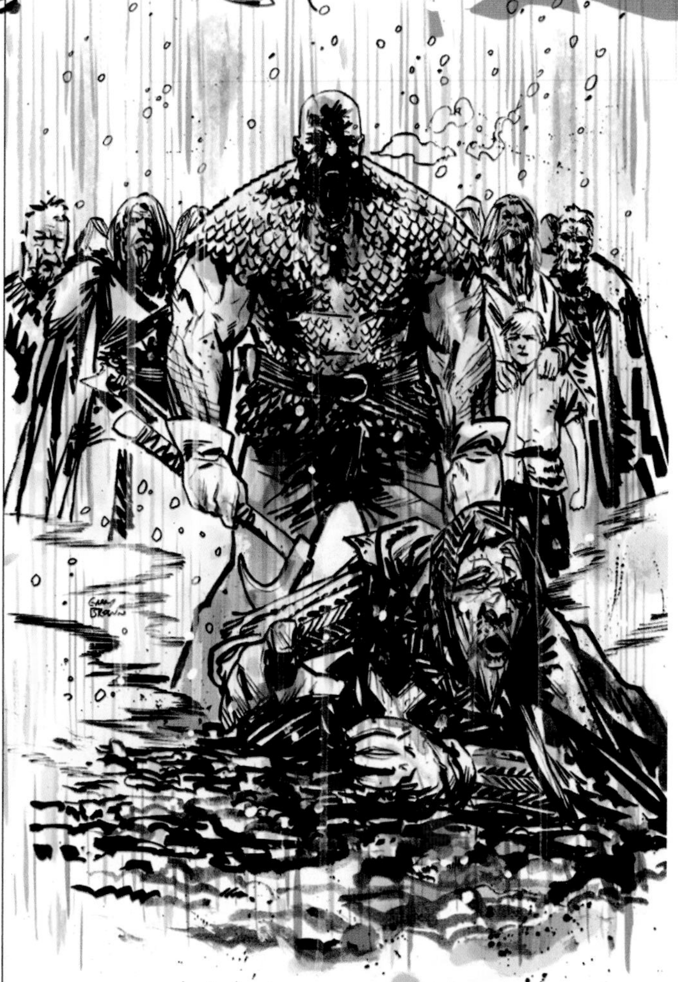

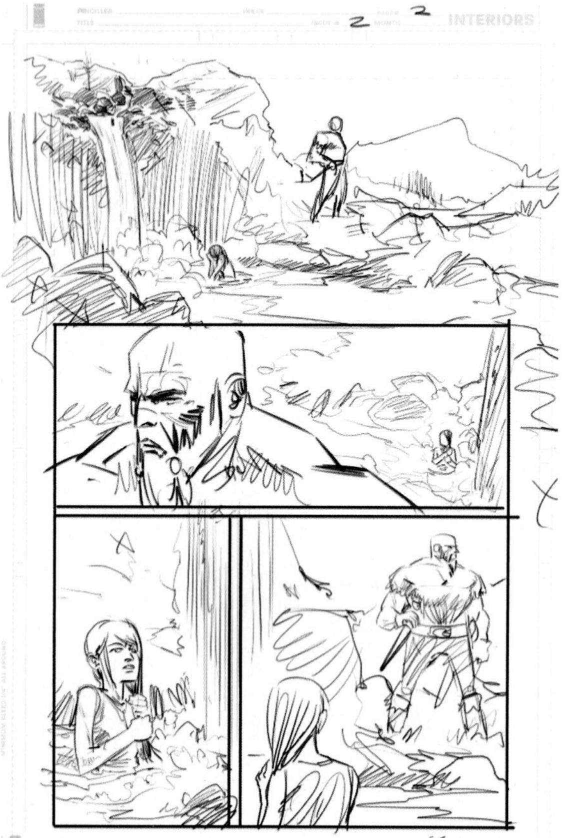
INTERIORS

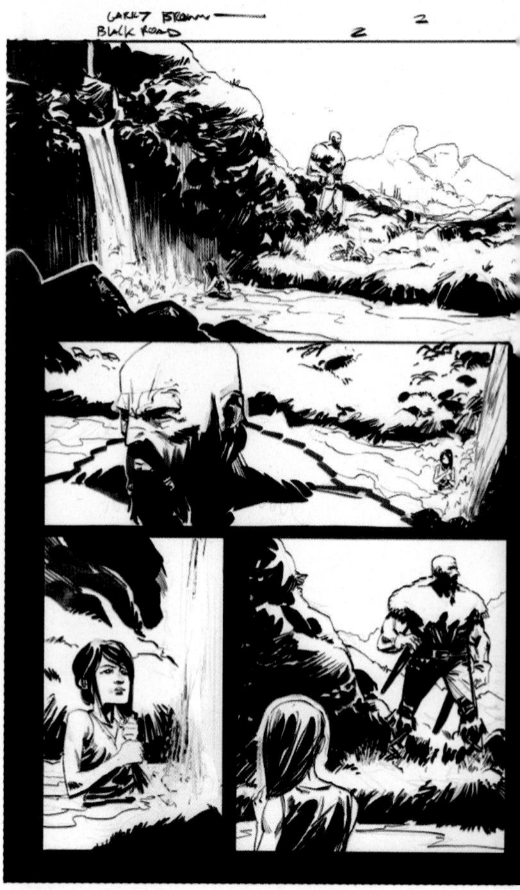
GARRY BROWN
BLACK ROAD

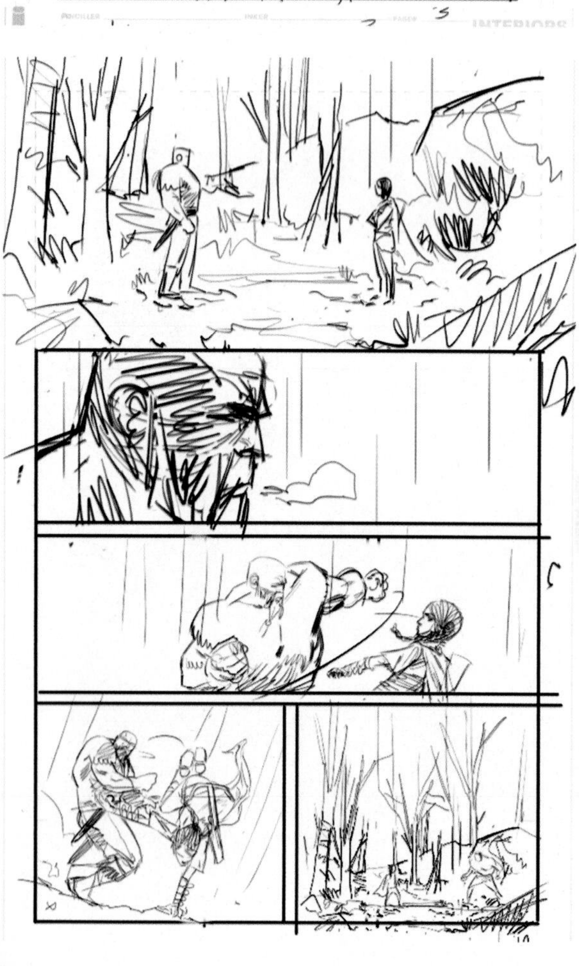

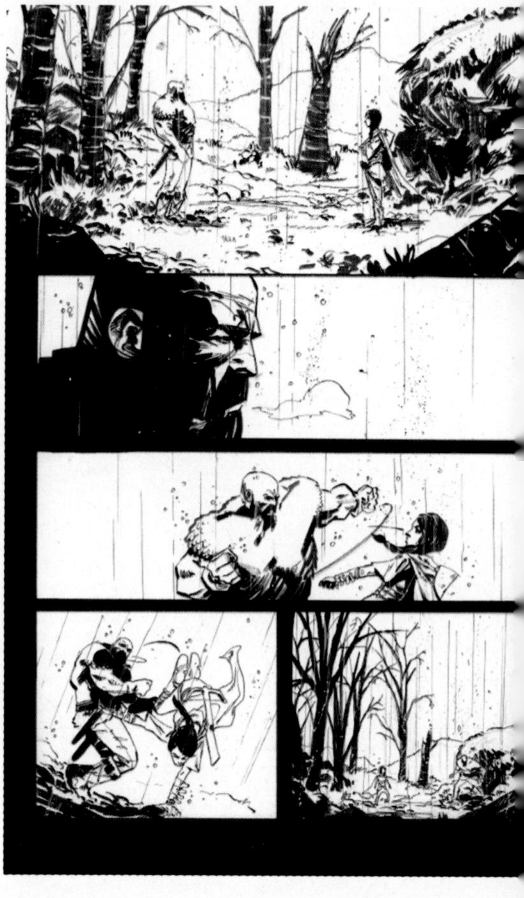

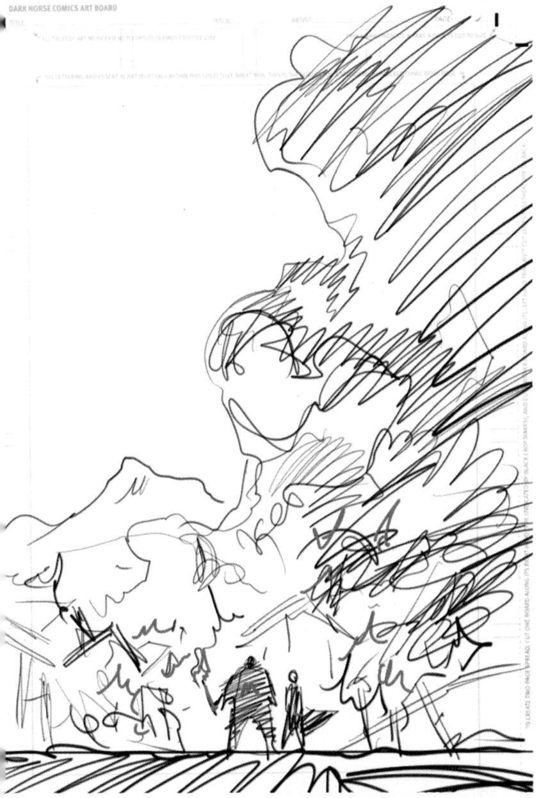
DARK HORSE COMICS ART BOARD

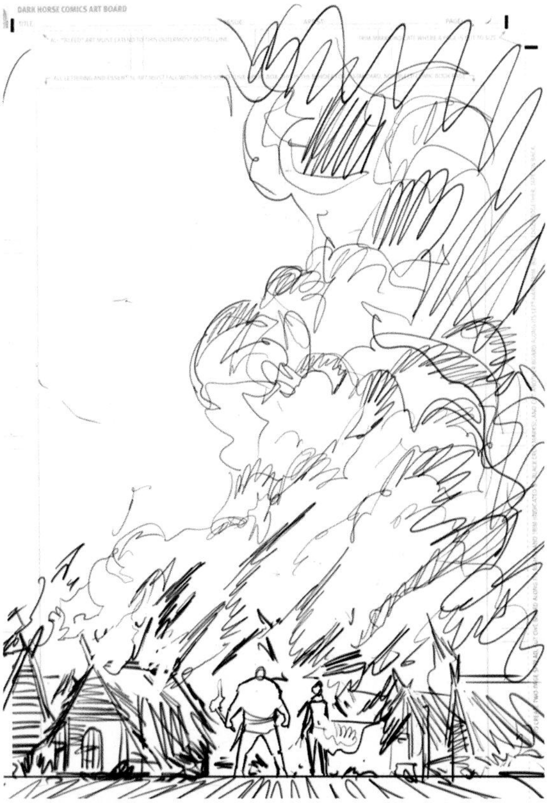
DARK HORSE COMICS ART BOARD

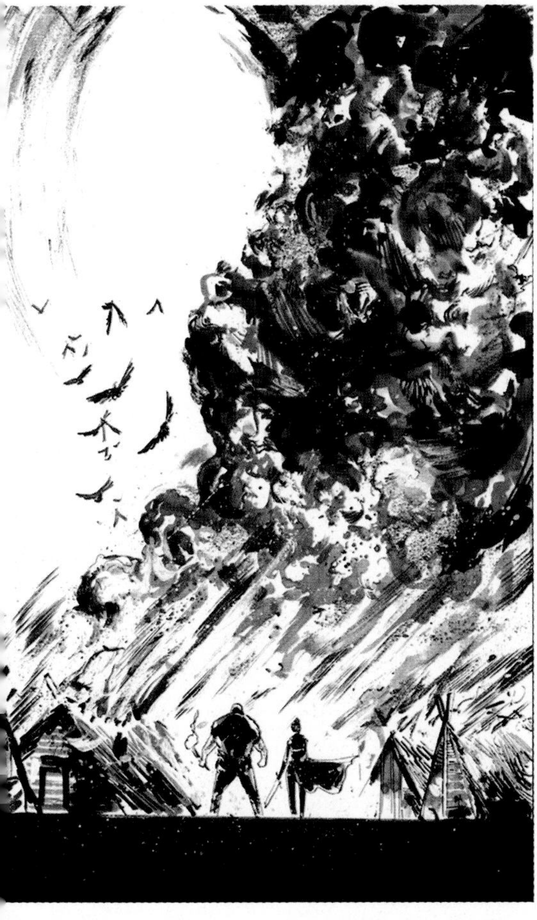

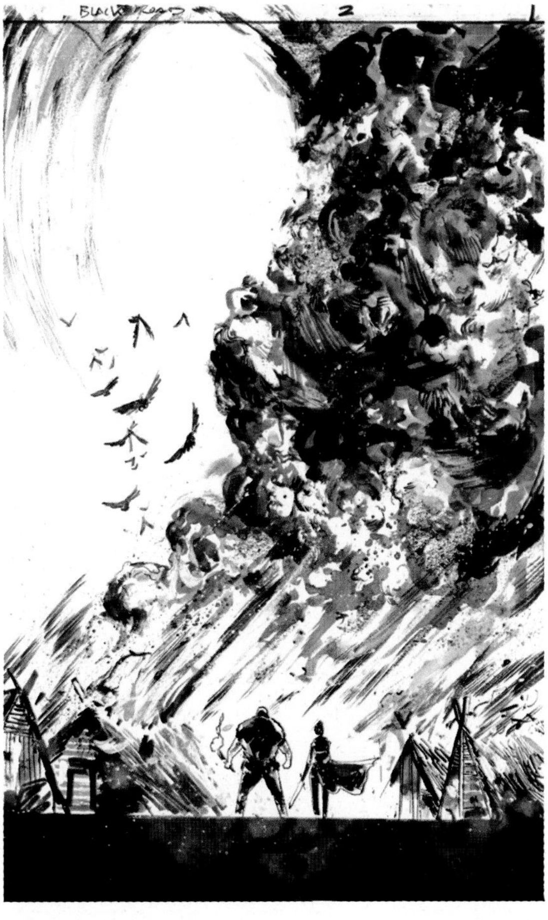
BLACK ROAD
2

#1 SECOND PRINTING COVER ART

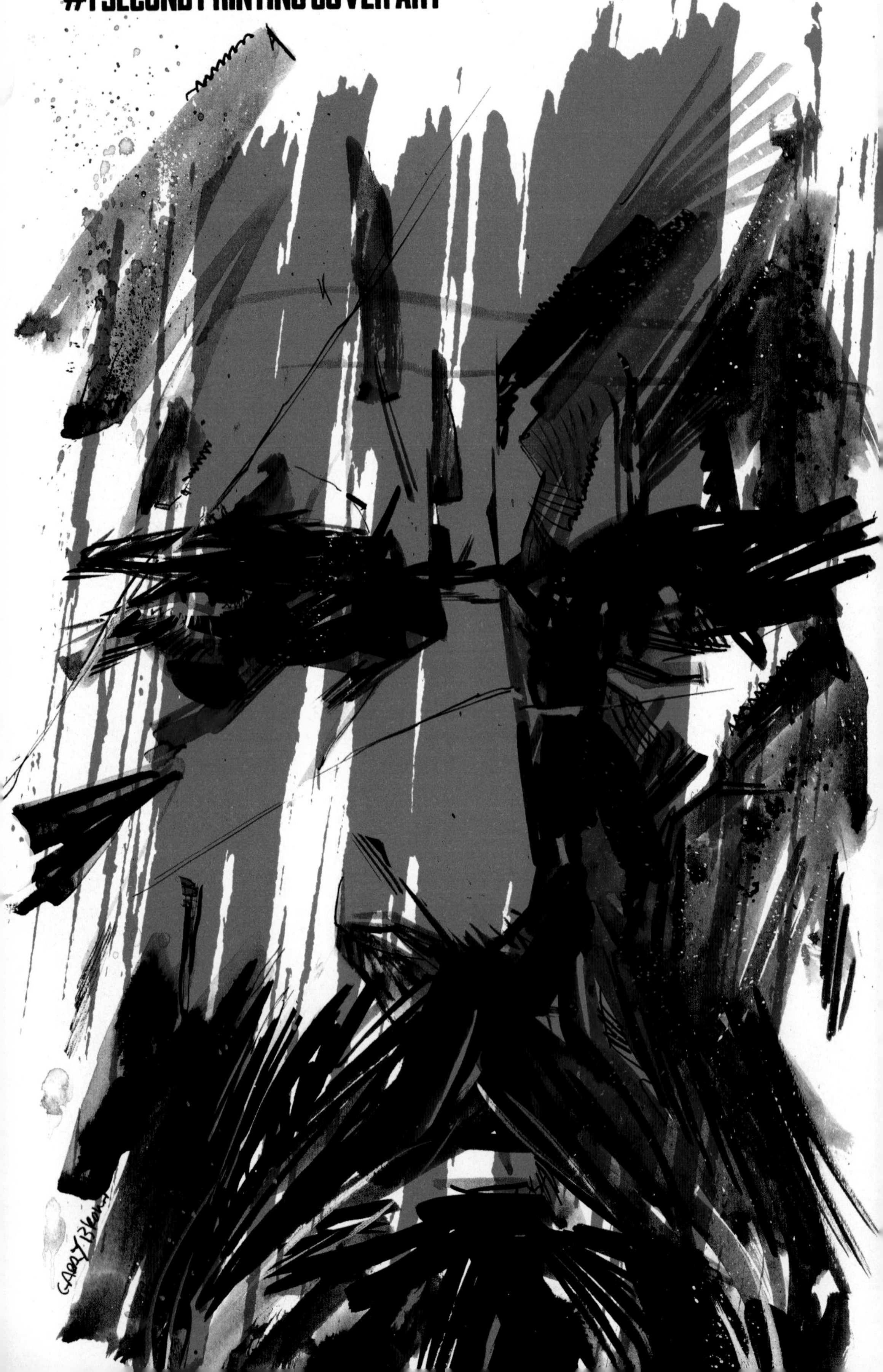

016 IMAGE EXPO VARIANT COVER

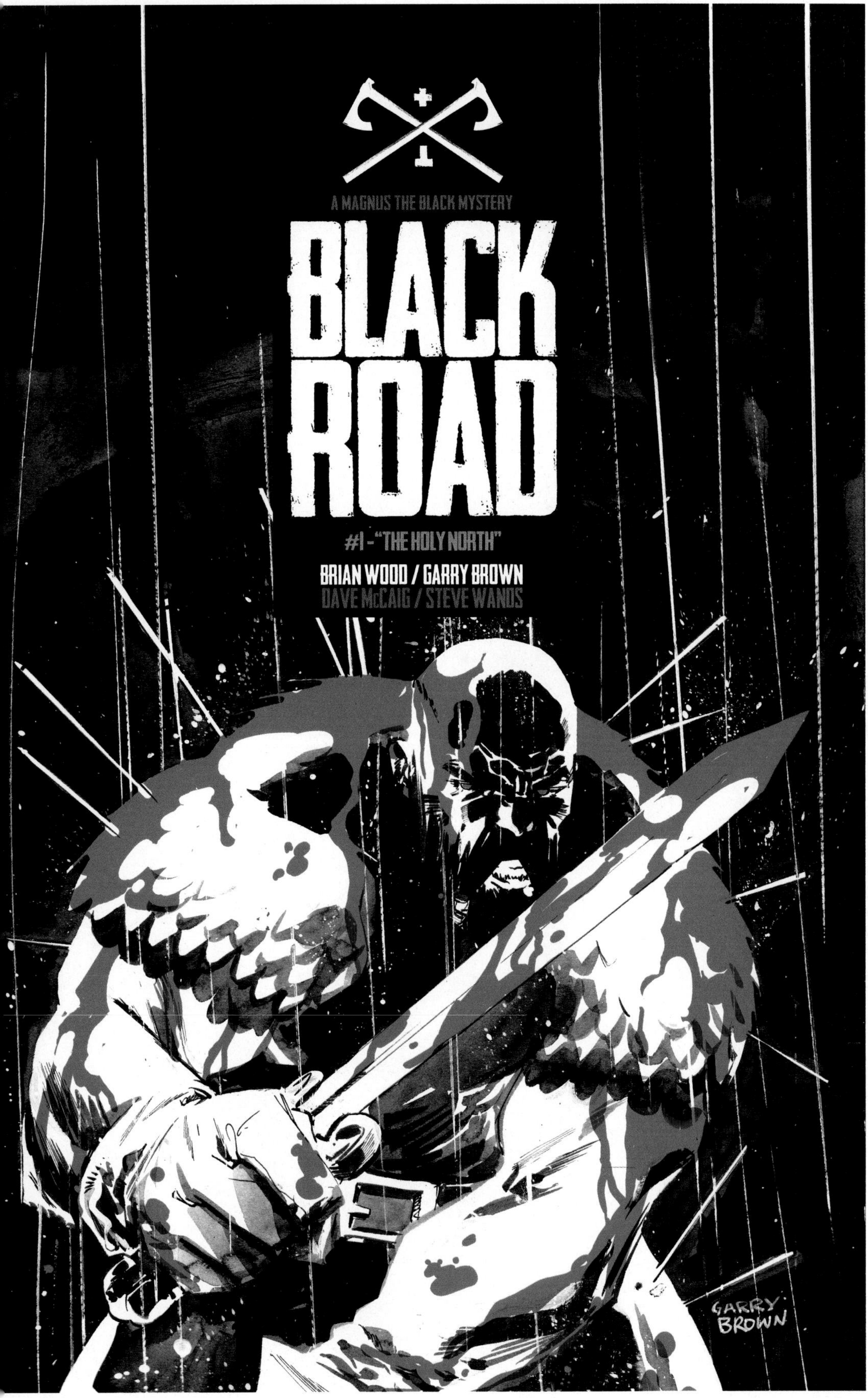
A MAGNUS THE BLACK MYSTERY
BLACK ROAD
#1 - "THE HOLY NORTH"
BRIAN WOOD / GARRY BROWN
DAVE McCAIG / STEVE WANDS
GARRY BROWN

UNUSED COVER ART

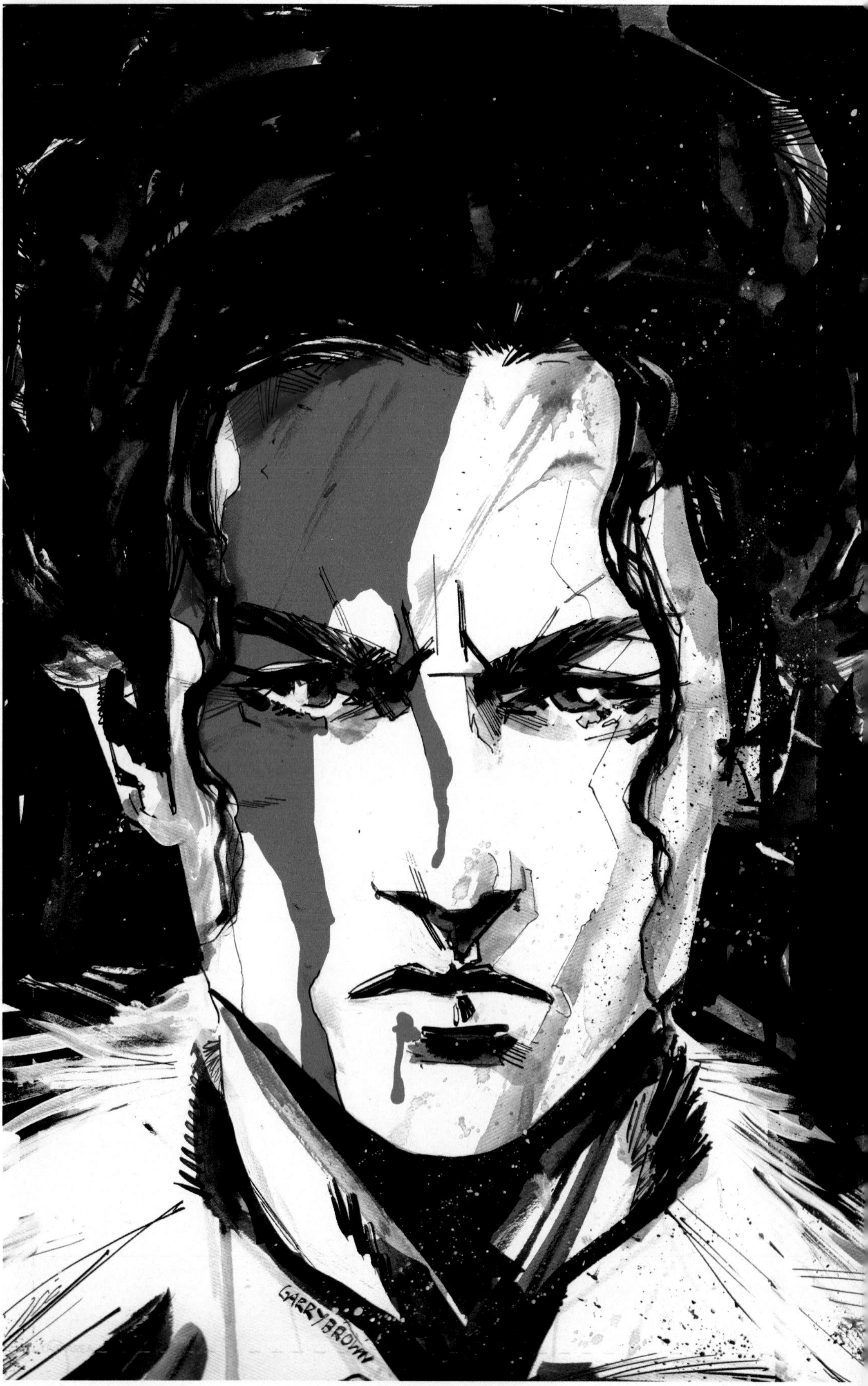
GARRY BROWN